TRICK OF
THE NIGHT

A gripping crime thriller with a huge twist

JOY ELLIS

Matt Ballard Book 5

D0823923

Joffe Books, London
www.joffebooks.com

First published in Great Britain in 2022

ISBN: 978-1-80405-331-7

Dedicated to readers everywhere, plain and simple.

Thank you to everyone who loves books. To everyone who encourages others to read, especially to those who pass their love of books on to children.

And to my own readers, who mean so much, the biggest thank you of all. This one is for you.

CHAPTER ONE

Toby Unsworth was feeling pretty pleased with himself. Another couple of weeks and he would be embarking on the final year of his photography course at university. He had been given a coursework assignment to complete during the holidays. It was voluntary, but he knew that it all counted towards his final mark in the module, so he'd pulled out all the stops. Toby wanted nothing less than to excel. His tutor had indicated that he was heading for the highest grade and he was already building a mega-impressive portfolio — these new low-light photographs were some of the best he'd ever taken. Night photography was his real love, and when he looked at the images he'd recently captured, he knew exactly which direction he wanted to take when he headed out into the real world.

There was just one picture that he needed in order to complete the assignment, and so far, he'd never quite managed to bring together all the factors he needed for that perfect shot. Tonight, however, checking the weather for the tenth time, he was fairly sure he stood a chance of capturing the image he had been dreaming of.

Toby had been to this part of town so many times he thought he probably knew every crack in the pavement, every cobble of this narrow street in the oldest part of Fenfleet. He'd been here four nights in a row now, had taken some great shots, but that elusive "special" one still remained to be captured. He knew the exact spot to set up his tripod, and he even had a couple of chocolate bars in his pocket, prepared to spend hours until the conditions were perfect.

The narrow, cobbled alley widened into a tiny church square which was a veritable time warp. The iron lamps attached to the ancient walls of the buildings and the old-fashioned lamp post in the centre of the square glowed like gas lamps. The church was just visible, nestling in the shadows, and a full moon was slowly making its way across the sky to a point immediately above the church tower. The cobbles gleamed wetly and the few lamps cast pools of glimmering light on the uneven ground. Along with the peeling paintwork on the dark doorways recessed into the crumbling brickwork, and the occasional grimy window, the scene could have come straight out of a novel by Dickens.

Toby spent time taking a series of test shots, checking light and exposure, looking at the scene from different angles. He had it in his mind to make up a kind of collection of the old alley from various aspects, a present-day history of what remained decades after its heyday.

He checked the position of the moon again, returned to his original spot and his tripod and waited. Gradually, tendrils of low mist began to creep through the empty alley from the direction of the river. A wave of excitement began to course through him. Oh, this couldn't be better! As long as no one decided to take a shortcut through the alley and ruin the whole thing, he would get those pictures at last, and then he would ace his assignment for sure.

He took shot after shot — if he took fifty or a hundred from which only two or three really pleased him, he didn't care. This could be the image that changed the course of his life as an emerging artist.

Several times he heard footsteps, once he heard muffled voices, even a car engine close by, but his luck held out.

There were two little side streets that joined the alley and whoever was talking must have been in one of those as, luckily, they never appeared.

Fifteen minutes later he had lost the moonlight, and the mist had dissipated as swiftly as it had come, but Toby was satisfied, sure he had that precious shot he so wanted. He couldn't wait to get back to his room and upload it all onto his computer.

He folded up his tripod and made his way back towards the main part of town and his car. It was a thirty-minute drive to where he lived on the outskirts of Greenborough, in a typical student house, and he had to keep reminding himself not to speed. He knew that Greenborough had some wonderful "old-town" locations of its own, but they had been worked to death by his fellow students and he had wanted something fresh and new. His parents had once lived in Fenfleet and he was brought up there, so he knew the back lanes would provide exactly what he needed.

Toby's room was on the third floor of an old house he shared with four others. It had a sloping ceiling and dormer windows set into the roof. His mother had called it cosy, his father poky. Whatever, he liked it. There was no one stomping around above him, and he picked up the best mobile phone signal in the house. Plus, the only other person on this floor was another photography student called Alex, who was a real swot, and quiet with it. Win-win, as far as Toby was concerned. He liked the occasional party night and went clubbing once or twice a month, but he really was at university to learn, not to piss his grant up the wall, or catch something embarrassing and unpleasant.

Alex was climbing the stairs ahead of him, having just come out of the bathroom. 'Find what you were looking for?' he asked, casting an enquiring smile back over his shoulder. 'Or did the conditions let you down again?'

'I think I got it this time, Al.' He couldn't keep the excitement from his voice. 'I really do.'

'Can I see?'

'Let me sift out the shit first, then I'll show you what's left.' For some reason he wanted to be by himself when he looked at the images. If he'd really got something truly special, he wanted to relish that first sight alone.

'Look, I'm bushed anyway, so I'll come and check them out in the morning.' Alex opened his door. 'Hope they're what you want, bud. Night.'

Toby went into his own room, threw his equipment onto the bed, extracted his photo card from his camera, and went over to his laptop.

It didn't take long to upload the images, but it felt like forever to the anxious student. Soon he had a whole folder of pictures. Painstakingly, he examined every single shot. Some he deleted immediately, simply because the quality wasn't there. Others he left for later, to decide on after he'd considered them all.

Toby stared at the earlier images and was more than pleased. One, taken in a brighter light, threw deep shadows on the scene, and made some of the architecture look sharp and kind of stark. It had lost the creepy Victorian aspect and taken on an edgy and sinister darkness that he really liked.

But this was not what he was looking for right now. Toby pressed on, then stopped, stared, and took a long slow inhalation of breath.

The image on the screen was perfect! It was everything he had prayed he would achieve. The lighting was superb, the composition spot on. The mist had tempered it into a timelessly beautiful photograph. Hell, he couldn't wait to show his tutor.

Toby sat back in his chair and laughed out loud. Then he went to his tiny mini-fridge, a present from his dad, and took out a bottle of Carlsberg. He had earned it.

He saved the folder and dated it. Sipping his lager, he went through some of those earlier photos again. There was one of an old dilapidated three-storey building that had probably stood unused for a decade or more. It seemed to lean precariously into the alley and gave the picture a slightly unreal, almost drunken appearance. There was another of a rusted padlock attached to a rotting doorframe that looked somehow threatening, as if it were daring the person who was looking at it to go in and see what nightmares might lie in the empty building.

Toby took a long slug of the beer. This was awesome! He had done some good work before, but this was in a different league. He stared at the screen, then narrowed his eyes and leaned closer. He was looking at the old disused place again, and at one particular filthy window. Surely what he was looking at had to be a trick of the light?

He placed the beer bottle on his desk and zoomed in on the window.

He was looking at a face. Distorted, indistinct, but definitely a face. 'It's a woman,' he breathed. 'Or is it? But . . . ?'

His euphoria faded, replaced by puzzlement, and then concern. What the hell was he looking at? He thought about that particular building. It had been shut up for as long as he could remember and to his knowledge, squatters had never even tried to get into the old wreck of a place.

He scrolled back to the pictures he had taken over the last weeks. He'd photographed that place numerous times before. Maybe it was just some glitch, dirt on the windowpane that the glow from the wall light beneath had turned into a face. Things like that happened.

He found a dozen other pictures that included that window, but not one had anything resembling a face in it. The more he looked, the more he decided there really had been someone there, in that horrible and probably dangerous place. But was it any of his business?

Now he wished for Alex's company. He was a down-to-earth, no-nonsense kind of a guy. His opinion would be worth listening to.

Toby went and knocked on Alex's door.

'Fuck off! I'm sleeping,' came the reply.

'Alex! I need you to see something.'

'I said tomorrow. Your masterpiece will keep. Some of us lesser mortals need rest, we're not all as brilliant as you.'

'No, really, this is nothing to do with the picture. I've seen something I don't understand. Please. Alex?' Toby waited, then heard grumbling and shuffling.

'This'd better be good.' Alex opened the door. He was wearing shorts and a T-shirt and was yawning loudly.

Two minutes later, Alex stared at the image with him, and finally said, 'It's definitely a face, no question. So, what the fuck is someone doing in that dump?'

'I wish I knew,' groaned Toby. 'But what I want to know is what do I do about it? Ignore it? That'd drive me nuts. Tell the police? They won't give a toss, will they? They'll think it's a student prank.' He threw up his hands.

'We could go and take a look.' Alex was now wide awake.

Toby had already considered that. 'It's a long way to go and then find there's no way in. I remember that the front of that place is shut up tighter than a duck's backside.'

'Mmm, but we could check out a back entrance. If we find out it's squatters or druggies, then that's your answer. If not, well . . .' He shrugged. 'I must say I don't like the feel of this.'

Nor did Toby. That face was giving him the creeps. Possibly he was reading too much into it; it certainly wasn't an imprisoned maiden waiting for a handsome young knight to rescue them, it was far darker than that. 'Okay, grab some clothes, Al. I've got just enough petrol left in the tank to get us there and back, and hopefully see the week out. I'll see you down by the car.'

Grabbing his wallet and phone, he paused and stared at the image on his laptop. 'Who are you?' he whispered.

No one answered. He saved the image, closed the program and shut the laptop down.

It didn't take long to get to Fenfleet. There was no traffic on the roads, nothing parked near the alley.

'Here goes nothing,' said Alex softly. 'Show me this weird building and that window.'

The two young men hunted for a back way into the deserted building, but like the ancient front door, it was locked, bolted and barred, and had obviously been that way for some time. They were just about to give up when Alex, using the torch on his phone, picked up a much smaller door. It was located behind a row of bins belonging to another less dilapidated property, set low in the back wall and down a couple of stone steps. On closer examination they could see that this door had been used, quite recently.

'Look,' whispered Toby. 'There are scratches around the keyhole, as if someone was trying to unlock it in the dark.'

'And the dirt and muck on the floor has been disturbed by the door swinging open,' added Alex. 'I don't think this is a squat, do you?'

Toby agreed. 'No way. They don't have keys. But one thing's for sure, we aren't going to get in through this,' he indicated the door. 'It's well solid.'

Alex turned off his torch. 'So, what now? Do we give up? Or do we back off tonight and try and make some enquiries about this place? See if anyone uses it legitimately. You know, like the owner, because someone must own it, even if it is a dump. Let's go round and watch that window for a bit.'

Unaware that they were now moving silently, they went back out into the alley and took up a position close to where Toby had set up his camera equipment earlier. Nothing. No face, no light, nothing.

'I still don't think I imagined it,' muttered Toby.

'No, I saw that image. The thing is, is that person up there voluntarily, or not? And what the fuck is going on?'

Toby shivered, and it wasn't just the cold night air. 'I think we'll do as you suggested, Al. Let's do a bit of digging. Maybe I'll come back in the daylight tomorrow and ask around about the building and who owns it.'

'Yeah, I'll come with you, and if we hit a blank, how about a stake-out after it gets dark? Watch what kind of people turn up and try and see what they use this place for.' Alex sounded quite fired up, ready for an adventure.

With one last glance up at the dark windowpane, they went back to Toby's car.

All the way back to the house, they hypothesised on possible reasons for seeing a mysterious woman in a deserted building at night, but had come to no conclusion by the time they arrived home.

'See you in the morning. We'll head back over there,' said Alex, unlocking his door, 'and if you're stuck for fuel, I can lend you a tenner till next week.'

'Thanks, Al, appreciated, but let's see how we go. I might be okay.'

Toby took out his door key, but when he slipped it into the lock, he found the door was already open. 'Whoa! I locked that!'

Halfway through his door, Alex stopped and strode back across the landing.

Tentatively, Toby pushed the door open.

The light was on and the curtains were pulled, something he never did, his stereo was playing softly . . . and his laptop was gone.

'Oh, fuck!' hissed Alex.

Toby gasped. 'Jesus! All my course work, all my images! Jesus! Jesus!' Panic swept over him.

'Steady, mate! You back it all up, remember? You told me. You never fail. It's in the Cloud. You've lost nothing, just your device.' Alex sounded so reasonable that Toby calmed down almost immediately. Then another thought struck him.

'My dad is going to kill me. That laptop cost him an arm and a leg.'

'I've got a spare you can borrow so you can retrieve your work,' offered Alex. 'I think we should phone the police, don't you?'

'Better see if anything else has gone,' replied Toby miserably, wandering around the tiny room.

After they'd checked the obvious things, Alex said, 'Looks like the laptop was their only steal. At least there's no damage to the place, so that's a bonus, I suppose. I'll go and ask downstairs if anyone heard anything — that lot never go to bed early, they're probably rat-arsed, but I'll ask anyway.' He stopped at the door for a moment.

'Er, cancel what I just said about the police,' he finally said. 'You'd better read this.' He pointed to a sheet of printer paper stuck to the inside of the door.

Go to the police and it will be the last thing you do!

Toby went cold. This had to be connected somehow with that face at the window. He'd been watched! Someone had followed him home.

'I know what you're thinking,' said Alex quietly. 'It's that damned picture, isn't it?'

Toby nodded. It had to be. 'Well, they've got the uploads, but it's on the Cloud — and they haven't got this.' He removed a memory stick from his pocket. 'And I'm going to guard this with my life.'

'Lock your door, Toby. You and I need to make a plan. This is serious shit, isn't it?' Alex said.

'About as serious as it gets, I'd say.'

Alex sat down. 'Got another beer in that neat little fridge of yours? I could use one.'

Toby got two out and threw one to Alex. 'So, what the hell do I do now?'

CHAPTER TWO

Two weeks later

Matt Ballard, retired detective chief inspector and now private detective, stared at his computer screen. With a flourish, he typed the name *Janie Lowell*, followed by the words *Located* and *Returned Home*. Case number thirty-four. Closed.

Matt smiled. Finding a missing young woman was one of the most satisfying parts of this job. He sat back and took a deep breath, wondering what might come their way next. Not that they were without work. He and his partner, ex-DS Liz Haynes, had been in demand recently, but had become selective in the assignments they chose. A little while back they had agreed not to take on any more adultery cases. Neither enjoyed the covert tracking and photographing of unsuspecting partners. Liz had said she felt like a voyeur and Matt agreed with her, so they'd decided to cherry-pick their new cases from then on.

'So, do you reckon we've earned some time off now?' Liz stood in the doorway to the lounge, looking at him hopefully. 'I'd love to take a run over to the Peak District for a couple of days. Remember that lovely little inn we stayed at close to that lake?'

'Don't I just! Best steak and ale pie I've ever tasted!' Matt hadn't been thinking about taking time off but seeing Liz's eager expression he was soon persuaded. 'You're right, sweetheart. Good idea. We've bounced from one case to another for months with no let-up. We deserve a treat. Ring them and see if we can get a room for three or four days. Sweet-talk them into that luxury suite they have. Let's push the boat out.'

Liz put her arms around him and kissed him lightly. 'Thank you, Mattie. I'll look for their number.' She picked her mobile phone up from the table.

While she was scrolling through her contacts, the house landline rang. Matt listened, screwing his face up to hear the caller. He held up his hand and Liz lowered her mobile. He held the phone out to her. 'It's Gary, darling. He wants to talk to you, and from the crackly line, it sounds like he's some distance away.'

Lt Col Gary Haynes was Liz's ex-husband, and still a dear friend. Presently, he seemed to be stationed in some remote, undisclosed location.

Liz put the phone on loudspeaker, so Matt could hear what Gary had to say. The signal was poor and unreliable, he said, so he'd keep it brief. 'Look, could you ring Alan for me? Young David is really low at the moment — his application to join the police force has been turned down. Alan wondered if you'd have a chat with David. Better still, could you go and see him, or get him to spend a day or two with you?'

This news surprised Liz. 'Why on earth did they turn him down, Gary? He's such a bright lad. I thought he'd walk it.'

'It's his health, he failed the medical assessment. His endurance is impaired, Liz. He was ill as a kid, and even though he's always worked on his fitness, it has let him down badly.'

'Oh, poor David! That was his dream.' Liz sighed. 'Yes, of course we'll talk to him, Gary.' She glanced at Matt, who nodded.

David was Gary's nephew — his brother's boy. Ever since his childhood he had wanted to join the police force. He was a likeable twenty-year-old, full of enthusiasm. Liz had always encouraged him to pursue his ambition but Matt had sometimes worried about his health. He had noticed how easily he tired. He and Liz had treated him to a gym membership to help him build himself up. He went regularly, but clearly it hadn't been enough.

Liz hung up. 'Bugger! Lost the connection. Poor David. He'll be taking it badly, won't he?'

Matt nodded. 'He'll be gutted. And what the hell do we say to him? If it had been me, I'd have been inconsolable.'

'Me too.' Liz sank down into a chair. 'It'll certainly be no good reminding him of all the civilian jobs he could do within the police force because that's not what he's wanting. He had his heart set on the whole package — learning the ropes on the streets in a uniform and working his way up on merit. He won't settle for anything less.'

Matt felt deeply for the lad. He understood, having had a similar feeling of loss when he'd retired. It had affected him badly and only now was he coming to accept it, thanks to DCI Charley Anders, his replacement in the Fenfleet Division of the Fenland Constabulary, who occasionally used their agency as civilian consultants in some of her inquiries. Without that link to active service, Matt was certain he'd have been seriously depressed. Liz had also been retired out, but medically, following a dreadful incident that had left her so badly injured that for a time she hung onto life by a thread. She had found a different way to cope. Cut off, she herself cut all ties to the police, including her former colleagues. It wasn't something Matt could have done but it worked for her. Now she was beginning to rekindle old friendships and had even made a couple of brief visits to the station. It had taken both of them a long time to get where they now were, stable and content with their lot.

His mobile phone rang, startling him out of his reverie. He looked at the display and saw a blast from the past. 'Minty!'

Liz's head jerked up.

'Can I come and see you, guv'nor?' The tone was urgent.

'Maybe I should come to you, mate. We live out in the sticks and you might have trouble finding us. How about the old place at midday?' Matt said.

'I'll be there.' The line went dead.

'Minty!' Liz rolled her eyes. 'I'm surprised he's still alive. What did he want?'

'To see me,' Matt said thoughtfully. 'He sounded frightened.'

Liz stood up abruptly. 'Right, well, after those two calls, I'm shelving my friendly chat with the hotel. I have a distinct feeling our relaxing break just went out of the window. I don't know about pushing the boat out, I think it just sunk! Oh hell. I'm going to make a cup of tea.'

Minty had been Matt's number one snout for more years than he cared to remember — he must be heading for seventy by now. Minty was a character with a chequered past and a sharp ear for trouble. In all the years they had "done business", Minty had never seemed afraid before.

Matt glanced at his watch. It was already ten thirty. By the time he'd had a mug of tea and got himself together, it'd be time to head off to Fenfleet.

All the way to the old cricket pavilion in the Fenfleet recreation ground, Matt wondered what could possibly scare someone like Minty. He was a former criminal, a tough nut with the appearance of a retired prize fighter who had done several stretches in prison before seeing the error of his ways. Matt had always believed him to be fearless.

Matt arrived first. Watching a stony-faced Minty march towards him, he could see this was no friendly catch-up. They wouldn't be reminiscing about old times. Before they had even sat down, Minty pushed an old envelope into Matt's pocket. Matt caught a glimpse of something a utility bill might arrive in. It was folded over several times.

'Look at it when you get home. Not here.'

Matt nodded. 'So, what is it, Minty? Why the secrecy?'

'I wish I knew,' Minty growled, 'but then again, maybe I'm glad I don't.'

They sat down on a wooden slatted bench, in the shelter of the veranda that ran around the closed-up pavilion.

'Okay. From the top,' Matt coaxed.

Minty stared down at his feet. 'Before you have a go at me, I know what you've got in your pocket should be with the police, but no way am I taking it, and if you've got any sense, neither will you — for both our sakes.' Minty's gaze bored into him. 'I came to you, one, because I trust you, and two, because you're a private investigator. Do this your way, DCI Ballard, but for God's sake be careful.'

'I'm not in the police anymore, Minty, so drop the DCI. I'm Matt, okay? Now, just tell me what's going on.' Matt was very much afraid that he was about to inherit a seriously unpleasant situation.

Minty shifted about, looking this way and that, making sure they were alone. 'For a while now I've been noticing that something ain't right in the town — well, in the backstreets, if you get my drift?'

Matt nodded, knowing Minty was referring to the criminal underworld.

'It's nothing anyone can put a name to, but we all know something's going on, and it's nothing to do with any of the old names, you know, the local villains.' He frowned. 'Even the big players are edgy. Eddie Race for starters.'

Race was a villain to be reckoned with in the Fenfleet area. Most of the dirty dealings in and around the town could be traced back to Race's lot or their cronies. If Race was worried, then something really nasty must be brewing in the darker waters of their ostensibly nice little town.

'Anyway, that's just background. This is why I'm here, and why I just passed you a hot potato.' Minty lowered his voice. 'Market day, Wednesday, I was having a word with an old mate of mine, a trader who keeps his ears open for any tasty deals, when there was this sudden ruckus. This young bloke was running through the market stalls like the hounds of hell were after him. He crashed through the stalls, pushing stuff over, looking over his shoulder in, well, pure terror.'

'Was anyone really chasing him? He wasn't a druggie, was he, hallucinating?' asked Matt.

'Oh, he was being chased all right. Two guys, a bit older than the kid.' Minty scratched his head. 'I reckon he only got away because a dustcart was reversing out of a side street and blocked the road. He got through but these other guys had to go round it. I reckon he went in the back entrance to the shopping centre and gave them the slip in there.'

'Well, interesting, but not worth a PI taking it on.' Matt looked at him and raised an eyebrow. 'So, what's the real story?'

'When he ran through the stalls, he sort of bumped into me, and he gave me this look.' Minty frowned, recalling it. 'Kind of, I dunno, wild. Sort of despairing but almost pleading.' He shook his head. 'Then he was gone. Well, anyway, when I got home and got my door key out of my pocket, something fell out.'

'Something that is now in *my* pocket, I suppose.'

'It's one of them photocard jobs. Pictures in a little computer gizmo.'

'An SD card?' Matt said.

'If you say so. Technology left me behind around the time of Betamax. Anyway, a mate of mine has a laptop, so we had a butchers at the pictures.'

Matt could well imagine what kind of pictures they might have seen — porn, child abuse . . . He was wrong.

'Bloody photographs of Fenfleet at night, would you believe. Arty-farty stuff. Nothing raunchy, nothing naughty, just moonlit scenes.'

Matt frowned. Why would pictures like that cause the kid to run for his life, shoving the card at some stranger? The other two must have been after it, but why?

'I know what you're thinking, Matt. I nearly chucked the thing in the bin but something stopped me. I'm glad I kept it now. Unless . . .' He looked anxious. 'Well, next thing that happens, a few days later I sees this headline in the local rag about a tragic accident in Greenborough. Two students died of carbon monoxide poisoning in their rooms in a house in Portland Road.'

Matt thought hard. 'I remember the story. Faulty gas water heater. The ventilator flue had got blocked, or something like that.'

'There was a picture of the two young lads, and one — it hit me like a ton of bricks. It was the kid who knocked into me.'

Pieces of Minty's story dropped into place. 'And you think—?'

'Exactly the same as what you're thinking. Except it don't end there. I've been warned off.' He glared at Matt. 'Me! Warned off by some pathetic little lowlife in my own sodding town!'

'But it must have been a serious warning, Minty, or you wouldn't be sitting here with me,' said Matt.

'Dead right it was. Look, I didn't know this creep but he knew me all right, all too well. Bloke knows a lot about my past, and I mean a lot. Some things you know about, and quite a few you don't.' Minty narrowed his eyes. 'And no offence, but I'd rather it stayed that way. From the stuff he told me, he got his info from someone I was banged up with way back, before I knew you, so I reckon I'm safe talking to you.' Minty was still looking around nervously.

'So, you think that one of the goons chasing that boy must have seen him slip you that card?' Matt said.

'He can't've done,' said Minty quickly. 'Even I never noticed. But he did see the kid bump into me, so if they never found that card, I suppose they took a guess.'

'They must have recognised you, then?' said Matt quietly.

'Well, I certainly didn't recognise either of them. But if they'd checked around the market, everyone there knows me. Wouldn't take much to get my address from one of the stallholders.' He shrugged. 'Anyway, I got an old one of them card things from my mate. I trashed it, stuck it in an old envelope and binned it. When I got up the next morning, the bin had been upturned and the envelope with the trashed card was gone.'

Matt exhaled. 'Whoever this is, they're going to an extraordinary amount of trouble for a series of nice moody photos of Fenfleet by moonlight.'

'I reckon either it's the wrong card, and there's another one out there somewhere with some seriously bad stuff on it, like snuff movies or porn, or my mate and I missed something.' Minty gave Matt a grim smile. 'Now you can have a look, see what you find.' He stood up. 'By the way, I don't want to know anything more about this from now on. I'm sorry that kid was murdered. It'll haunt me, but I'll have to live with it, until one day I'll read the whole story in the newspapers — when you've got the bastards locked up. Bye, DCI Ballard, and good luck.'

Matt sat there for a while, staring across the playing field, watching Minty slowly disappear into the distance. This was a job for the police, not a PI. All the old warning alarms were sounding in his head. He didn't know what they had said to Minty when they'd told him to back off and not go to the cops, but it had certainly had the desired effect.

Despite himself, Matt was excited by Minty's tale. Before he delivered the SD card to Charley Anders, it wouldn't hurt to make a few low-key enquiries, would it? And have a bloody good look at those moody photos. Oh, and maybe check out the deaths of the two students.

Matt got in his car and headed out of town, eager to get home and tell Liz about Minty's strange story. His excitement abated when he saw a car he didn't recognise sitting outside Cannon Farm — a neat and sporty bright red Citroen C3.

Indoors, the Citroen's neat and sporty driver was sitting at the kitchen table drinking coffee with Liz.

Liz smiled at him warmly. 'Glad you're back, Matt. This is Mrs Georgia Hallam. Her teenage son Alex died tragically last week — it was in the papers, carbon monoxide poisoning

— but she believes his death was not the accident it appeared to be. She wondered if we could make some discreet enquiries for her.'

Matt shook Georgia's hand and offered his condolences, wondering, not for the first time, at the mysterious workings of the universe.

* * *

By now, Liz had spent years at Matt Ballard's side, first working and then living with him. She'd thought she knew him inside out, but now he puzzled her. He seemed to know more about what Georgia had told her than her brief outline warranted. He definitely knew something she didn't, and she could only put it down to his talk with his old snout, Minty. But what could this classy woman have in common with the less than polished Minty?

Meanwhile, Georgia was saying, 'There are so many things that don't make sense. I need some answers or I'll never rest. I hope you can understand that?'

She looked devastated. Her desperately sad expression didn't sit well on a fit youngish woman with long straight hair caught back in a sportswoman's blonde ponytail.

'Rest assured, we do,' said Matt gently. 'Can you tell us what you know, and exactly what is bothering you?'

She nodded. 'Of course. It's just . . . some of it sounds so silly, as if I'm just trying to find someone to blame for the loss of my boy.'

'Do you mind if we record this?' added Liz. 'It saves making notes and means we can go over what was said later.'

'Whatever you need to do, just please help me,' Georgia said.

Liz felt desperately sorry for her. 'Tell us about Alex, Mrs Hallam.'

Georgia drew in a breath. 'He was nineteen, my only child, studying at Greenborough University. He wasn't in a hall of residence, he wanted to live off campus.' She sighed.

'I was against it to start with, but he seemed to enjoy being independent. He said he had to start learning to live in the real world, and not be cosseted all his life.' She dabbed at her eyes with a balled-up damp tissue. 'All his life. Nineteen years is hardly a lifetime.'

Liz went and got a box of tissues and placed them on the table. 'What was he studying, Mrs Hallam?'

'His passion — photography. He loved taking pictures, right from when he was a little boy. He was good, too, although maybe not as gifted as his housemate, Toby. Toby was destined for great things, or so Alex told me. He said he specialised in night shots, low-light photography. Even so, Alex had an eye, could find beauty in the strangest of places. Nature photography was his great love. His tutor thought he'd do well because he saw things others didn't. He often had a different take on a subject, saw it from a new angle.' She sniffed. 'Though he struggled with some of the more academic aspects of the course. He was self-taught, you might say. He had a feel for composition without knowing the rules, but he had to work hard on the technical side of it.'

'If it's not too painful for you, could you tell us what happened, Mrs Hallam?' asked Matt.

She frowned. 'This is where it gets fuzzy, Mr Ballard. What they say happened and what I believe don't tally.' She took a sip of coffee and seemed to gather herself. 'Alex rang me the evening before he died. He was excited about something, I could tell by his voice. He wanted to speak to his father, but Terry was playing badminton with a friend, so Alex said he'd call again the next day—'

'Did he say what he wanted to talk to your husband about?' Liz asked.

Georgia responded with an effort. 'He said his dad's work knowledge might be able to help answer a tricky question. That was all.'

'And what does your husband do?' asked Matt.

'He works for the local council town planning department.'

Liz frowned. That was a bit odd. Why would a teen, a photography student, be interested in town planning?

Matt asked, 'So what doesn't add up about your son's death, Mrs Hallam?'

'He was found in a sleeping bag on the floor of his friend Toby's room. His own room was a couple of steps away, Mr Ballard. My boy was a very private person, he had very particular ideas about things. He would never have dossed down in a sleeping bag on someone's floor when his own bed was a few metres away, he just wouldn't.'

'Toby died too, didn't he?' said Matt. 'Where was he found?'

'In his bed. The coroner's report stated that they died in their sleep.' She paused. 'They were both fully dressed. Why? My Alex wore shorts and a T-shirt in bed, winter and summer. Even if he'd stayed with Toby because his friend was ill, why would they both be in their outdoor clothes?'

Liz was trying to weigh up whether this bereaved mother was really on to something, or just chasing shadows.

'The coroner's report also stated that they'd been drinking, which contributed to them not waking up.'

'Students do drink, Mrs Hallam,' said Matt, with an apologetic grin. 'Well, most of the students I've had dealings with, anyway, some of them quite heavily.'

'He was stone cold sober when he spoke to me, Mr Ballard. His speech wasn't slurred and he was wide awake, full of excitement. There was no indication that he was intoxicated, or being poisoned by carbon monoxide, for that matter.' She sat up straighter. 'The report stated that they'd been drinking whisky.'

Liz frowned. Whisky was hardly the tipple of a struggling student.

'My Alex liked a beer,' Georgia said. 'And no more than a pint or two. Not whisky. It made him sick, and he avoided it at all costs.' Tears filled her eyes again. 'Something about this whole thing is terribly wrong. Will you help me? Please?'

'We'll help you,' Matt said, and Liz nodded. 'We'll do all we can to find answers, no matter how painful or difficult they might be to accept. Is that okay with you?'

'Oh yes,' she said. 'That's all I want — the truth.'

Matt smiled at her. 'Just one more thing. Did you tell the police about your fears?'

Her expression became fierce. 'Oh, they were very kind, but I could see they'd written me off as a hysterical mother who couldn't accept that her only son had met with a tragic accident. The moment their death was attributed to carbon monoxide, the case was closed as far as they were concerned.'

Leaving Georgia Hallam to mop up her tears, Liz went and got her investigation notebook. She kept everything on file on her computer, but old habits die hard, and she preferred to record the initial basic facts in her detective's notebook.

'Can you give me your contact details?' she said. 'Then we'll get the ball rolling.'

CHAPTER THREE

'Okay, Matt Ballard! She's gone now, so tell me what's up. When I introduced her your face was a picture — total bewilderment.'

Matt puffed his cheeks and blew out air. 'You are *really* not going to believe this!'

'Then stop faffing about and tell me, for heaven's sake!' exclaimed Liz in exasperation.

Matt took the envelope from his pocket and laid it on the kitchen table.

Liz opened it, took out the tiny photocard, looked at it and up at Matt. 'Photographs?'

'Unless I'm mistaken, this belonged to either Georgia Hallam's son, Alex, or his friend, Toby.'

'But how? Surely not Minty?' She stared at him.

Matt told her what Minty had said, watching the amazement creep into her expression.

'And you came home to find the mother of one of the two dead boys sitting in your kitchen. No wonder you looked so stunned. But if what Minty said is true, it means that Georgia is right about her son's death not being an accident.' Liz picked up the photocard. 'We need to look at this.'

'I've been itching to do that very thing ever since he gave it to me,' Matt said. 'Let's view the pictures on the desktop PC, it's got a bigger screen than your laptop.'

They went through to the old dining room and waited impatiently for the card to upload the dozens of images it contained.

Matt and Liz looked at each other expectantly. 'Let's see what we've got, shall we? Minty said it was all "arty-farty" stuff, nothing that would cause you to run for your life. But Minty's no detective, and since we are, let's do what we do best, and find the clues to this mystery.'

After the first few images Matt knew they were looking at the work of a very talented young photographer. How sad that the boy was dead and would never realise his potential.

'These are amazing,' whispered Liz. 'Not what I expected at all. They're so incredibly beautiful. I know that old Fenfleet back lane well, and the way he's depicted it takes your breath away.' She sighed, voicing Matt's thoughts. 'What a terrible waste! There's no chance Minty got it wrong, I suppose?'

He shook his head. 'No, Liz, he didn't make a mistake. He said the moment he saw the picture of the two students, he went cold. It shocked him to the core.'

She watched the photos roll past her gaze, one after the other. 'Just to get some kind of timeline, what is the date on these images?'

Matt read it off.

'That means they were taken three nights before the students were found dead. It was a Thursday, according to Georgia, so Alex, or possibly Toby, took this last folder of images on the Tuesday night. There's no more on this card after that.' She frowned. 'We can concentrate on just this folder, can't we?'

'This should be where we start, certainly, but there might have been something in the earlier folders. There are only around forty with the Tuesday evening's date. We'll take them one by one and scour them for anything unusual, or something that just doesn't feel right, what d'you think?'

They shuffled their chairs closer to the screen.

'Hell, I wish we knew what we were looking for,' muttered Liz, after the first run-through. 'I keep getting sidetracked by the look of them, the light and the composition. They make me think that I've never really looked at that alley properly before. Look how he's caught the mist and the moon over the church tower. It's absolutely stunning.'

Matt nodded absently, thinking about their task. They could be looking for anything — a person, something about one of the buildings, an object lying in the street. Time to look again.

On their third run-through they both noticed it at the same time.

'Zoom in, Matt!' said Liz. 'It's a woman's face, isn't it?'

He nodded, squinting at the grimy window. 'It's a woman, all right.' He looked closer. 'What is that building?'

'It's on the corner of Bowmaker's Lane, next to what was the Old Poacher's Rest public house, before it closed about five years ago,' said Liz. 'I'm pretty sure it was an old merchant's house, with a store of some kind, probably for something brought into the docks way back. It's been empty for a decade, maybe longer. Georgia is no desperate mother trying to blame someone else for her boy's death, is she? She was right about everything.'

'They were both in the same room, sleeping in their clothes because they were frightened,' said Matt. 'Of course.'

'And Alex wanted to ask his father about that building, didn't he? His dad was a town planner. He'd be in a position to know what it was and who owned it.'

Matt didn't like where this was going one bit. 'I hate to say it, but we should turn this over to Charley Anders straightaway. This could well be a double murder, and we have no idea at all who, or what, is behind it. It could be massive.'

'Then why do I feel so reluctant to do that?' mused Liz, looking at him long and hard.

Matt knew all too well. 'Because we have no actual proof. Just a hazy, distorted face that could turn out to be nothing but a trick of the light. Because Minty was warned off in no uncertain terms, and was more scared than I've ever seen him. Because he insisted I do this my way, and not involve the authorities.' He sighed. 'Or all of the above?'

'Let's do as Minty says, just for a while,' Liz said. 'Let's get some actual evidence. It shouldn't be too difficult to obtain it without being noticed. Georgia wanted the truth. Let's sneak around a bit, do some covert investigating, see what we can discover and if it really looks like murder, *then* we go to Charley.'

Matt remembered Minty's face when he'd said, *"I don't want to know anything more about this."* He had really meant it. 'I'm not sure we should be doing this, but,' he shrugged, 'I agree. I'd rather give the police something concrete than a few fanciful suppositions based on an image that might or might not be there.'

'I'm pretty sure Charley Anders would accept whatever you said, no matter how fanciful,' said Liz with a smile, 'knowing your reputation. But if we can give them a proper case to investigate, she'll thank you for it. I hear they are stretched to the limit at the moment, with some serious cases running and all the cutbacks.'

'I know. I spoke to Jason last week and he sounded even more miserable than usual, if that's possible!'

They both laughed. DI Jason Hammond had been Matt's right-hand man back in the day, but although he was a shrewd and clever detective, he wasn't one to share many smiles, even with the people closest to him.

'Poor Jason! He's at his happiest when he's got something to worry about, isn't he?'

'True.' Matt returned his gaze to the screen. 'So, what are we looking at here? If that *is* a real woman, and not some weird optical illusion.'

'I have no idea,' said Liz. 'But what I *do* know is that two young men are dead because someone doesn't want anyone to see this picture.'

'And we are looking at it right now.' Matt suddenly felt fearful. If he believed in that kind of thing, he'd have said he'd had a premonition. 'If we do take this on, we're going to have to be extremely discreet about it. We cannot afford for anyone, anyone at all, to get even the slightest hint of our interest in that merchant's house.'

'I'll second that,' said Liz gravely. 'I'm also rather concerned about what we do with the photocard.'

'I'm going to rename it on the computer and save it in a secure store. I suggest we lock the card itself in the safe until such time as it's required as evidence, what say you?'

'It's the best we can do,' Liz said. 'There's no chance anyone spotted Minty talking to you, was there?'

'Well, you can never be sure, but he wasn't tailed to the recreation ground, and he said he hadn't been followed since the trashed photocard was stolen from his refuse bin. He's pretty sure they believed that since he was scared enough to destroy the card, that was the end of his involvement.' Matt recalled Minty's face when he'd told him how much these people knew about his past. Even after having gone straight for years, he obviously still had secrets that he wanted kept hidden.

'Did you get the impression that Minty was linking this warning to what's going on with the underworld bosses like Eddie Race?'

'Definitely.' While he spoke, Matt was saving the picture file and ejecting the photocard. They had a home security safe, bolted to floor and wall, located inside a walk-in cupboard in the master bedroom. They used it for important documents, the occasional cash accumulated from their business prior to banking it, and some of the sensitive photos they'd taken during an investigation. The SD card could go in there.

Liz stood up. 'Right, Matt Ballard, Private Investigator, we need to put an action plan together. But before we do that, I have to tell you that while you were out, and before Mrs Hallam turned up out of the blue, I had a call from David.'

Matt looked up. 'Is he okay?'

'Far from it. Even though he tried to sound stoic, he's hurting, Matt.' She paused. 'I said he could come up here for a few days. The open spaces and big Fenland skies might help to give him some perspective — that and a heart-to-heart over a few drinks with two seasoned old coppers who have also needed to find ways to move on from the force.' She pulled a face. 'Although with this on our plates, I'm not so sure now is the best time?'

'Let him come,' said Matt. 'He can see that there are other things to life than writing reports on skanky kids burning out stolen cars and chasing little tea leaves through the shopping arcade to retrieve a pocketful of stolen batteries.'

Liz smiled. 'Thank you, my darling. I hoped you'd say that.' She kissed the back of his neck.

Matt shivered. Liz's touch still had the capacity to send electricity running over his skin. 'Did he say when he was thinking of coming?'

'He'll drive up on Sunday morning, all being well. He should get here around midday,' she replied.

'Perfect, it'll give us time to take a good look at this case and get a better idea of what we're dealing with.' It sounded simple, but neither of them thought it was going to be straightforward. In the past, Matt had been given investigations that had immediately flagged up a sense of foreboding. You knew at once that something out of the ordinary was lurking in the background. This was one of those cases.

'Then let's not waste time. I'll make some tea and we'll draw up a plan. See you in the kitchen!' Liz gave his shoulder a gentle squeeze and was gone.

* * *

Kellie Burton walked dismally back to the kitchen table and flopped into her chair. 'That was the postman, but there was nothing again.'

Kellie's father shook his head in exasperation but said nothing.

'I'm sorry, Dad, but I worry about him. It's a whole week now and not a word. Not a call, not a text. It's not like Simon.' She tried to keep her tone light, aware that her father couldn't handle too much emotion. He didn't do sentiment, didn't do passion, and rarely showed his feelings. Except irritation and impatience. He was good at expressing those.

He set down his knife and a blob of butter flew off it onto the tablecloth. 'I told you yesterday, girl. Simon is fine. He's recovering well and Auntie Jess is very pleased with him. The country air is helping no end, and you know how he loves the Fens. He's probably far too busy out on the edge of the marsh watching the wildlife to text his fretting older sister. Now, please, stop moping around and try to be pleased that he's making such a good recovery.' He took a cloth from the sink to wipe off the butter. 'You need to cut him some slack, lass. He's a nine-year-old boy, he doesn't understand responsibility yet. He'll text you when he remembers.'

And that was the end of the conversation. Kellie knew from experience that it would be futile to pursue it further. She mustered a smile, and gave up.

Upstairs in her room she sat down heavily on the side of her bed and sighed. No one knew Simon like she did. She understood that the death of their mother had damaged him fundamentally, in ways few others would perceive. Only she knew how much his health problems frustrated him. He wanted to be like other kids, do all the things they did. It wasn't fair that asthma prevented an apparently strong and healthy-looking lad from enjoying his childhood.

Before he had been taken off to stay with their Auntie Jess, Kellie had given him a whole pack of postcards, all stamped and addressed to herself. Simon got bored and distracted very easily, so she had done everything possible to make it easy for him to keep in touch. He had a mobile phone that he used only sporadically, preferring books and being outside to technology. What excited him was watching the blue tits nesting in the birdhouse under the apex of the shed roof. More often than not, he forgot to charge his phone, or lost the charger. On more than one occasion he'd lost the phone itself. Hence the postcards. She knew there was a postbox a few hundred yards from Jess's cottage. Soon after he arrived she had received two in quick succession and had high hopes that her plan was going to work. She had another one a week later, and now, nothing.

Kellie wished they weren't so far away, and that their dotty auntie didn't have an aversion to telephones. Since their mother died, Kellie had taken on the role of carer, and now she felt at a loss. She was only fifteen but the responsibility sat heavily on her. She had made a promise to her mum to look out for Simon, and she had no intention of breaking it. She had been heartbroken when it was decided that Simon should stay with Jessie, without her. She had recently started at a new school and the term hadn't finished, plus her father had insisted she sign up for some of the summer activities that the school was offering. He could barely afford it, but having not had the best education himself, he wanted better for his daughter.

Auntie Jessie, her mother's much older sister, was a sweetie but "nutty as a fruitcake," as Simon put it. Kellie was sure she'd be doing a sterling job of nursing her brother, but Aunt Jessie didn't understand all his little ways, all his concerns, his fears. And then there was where she lived. Simon loved the place, but it was very remote, with no public transport, and only one crappy little village store.

Here in town, Simon could be in hospital in no time at all if he should suffer a serious asthma attack, but out there? No wonder she worried! The school holidays had only started a few days ago, and already she was praying they would end so that Simon could be home where he belonged.

She had no idea why, but Kellie Burton was becoming increasingly concerned for her brother's safety.

* * *

Jessie Wright shook her head slowly from side to side. 'I'm really not sure about that boy. Am I doing the right thing?'

29

Her best friend, Anna, gave her a broad smile. 'Here we go again. For heaven's sake, Jess! You worry far too much. Of course you're doing the right thing. You love him to bits and that's what counts.' Gently, she touched her friend's arm. 'He's so much better, which is all down to you. He's a lovely lad, and my heart bleeds for him. He's lost his dear mother so early in his life. You're doing the right thing, for him and for your dear sister, Louise. And that's the end of it. There's no more to be said on the matter.'

'It should have been me, not her. I have no one to miss me, and she had two beautiful children. And she was so much younger. It shouldn't happen that way.' Tears filled Jessie's eyes.

Anna's face wore a patient expression. Her friend had heard this a thousand times before. Jess waited for the usual rebuke, but this time Anna simply agreed. It was true, she said, it should never happen that way.

Jess was forced to smile. Anna never failed to surprise her. Even though she'd been friends with her since their early childhood, the sensible, organising, and sometimes quite calculating Anna would occasionally show a very different side to her usually unsentimental personality.

They sat together in contemplative silence for a while, then Jessie started to get fractious again, this time about how much time Simon spent alone out on the edge of the marsh. It was only a few minutes from the cottage, but it still worried her. You heard of such terrible things these days, of children being taken and, oh, the most awful things being done to them. She couldn't bear to think that anything could possibly happen in this place, her little piece of heaven, but you could never be sure. The world was a far more dangerous place than it had been when she had purchased Marsh View all those years ago.

'He's safe.' As usual, Anna knew exactly what she was thinking, and her tone left no room for argument. 'He's building a hedgehog house at the bottom of the garden, and he's watching out for the black-tailed godwit that he saw last week on the lagoons. He's safe and happy.' She let out an exasperated sigh. 'And if you get too fraught about that boy, we have two options, don't we? You only have to say that having him here is too much for you.'

She was right. Anna was always right. If her nerves got the better of her, she did have options, just being reminded of that made her feel better. One, to send him home, would have upset her terribly, so that was the last resort. But the other — a little adventure she had prepared in advance of Simon's arrival — was all too possible. She loved that boy so much, she would do anything to keep him safe, anything at all. She smiled at her friend. 'Anna, dear, you keep me sane.'

Anna's face broke into a broad smile. 'Sane is not a word I'd use when referring to you, my dearest, mad friend!'

They both laughed, and then Anna said, 'Let's go and bring Simon in for tea, shall we? I bought him some of those little chocolate-covered teacakes that we used to love when we were children. He'll like those, won't he?'

'Oh, he will! I'll go and get him now.' Jessie hurried off into the garden to find her charge, mightily relieved that she had Anna around to help. As she saw him wave happily to her, Jess's heart leaped. What a dear, dear boy! She was so lucky.

CHAPTER FOUR

Fenfleet, like so many small market towns, was a mixture of old and new, but in the main, history prevailed, and Cutler's Alley remained firmly in the past. Even so, it was a tale of two halves, with one end of the narrow and twisty cobbled lane being carefully maintained, with fresh paint and colourful window boxes on the high sills above the shops, while the lower half was shadowy, decaying, the buildings in need of either regeneration or demolition.

Liz had always liked it. There were still a few really interesting old shops in the pretty end, including an antiquarian and second-hand bookshop, and a tiny wool shop that sold all manner of hard-to-find wools, embroidery silks and craft materials. She never knew how they managed to survive in this modern world, but somehow they persisted, although the shopkeepers must have pondered their fate on a daily basis when they saw the rising power of online shopping.

Today, she was heading for a little coffee shop that nestled just off the square and opposite the church. This was the same church that their student had taken his amazing photograph of. Just seeing the place he had depicted brought a lump to Liz's throat, and she felt deeply for the two grieving families, Alex's and Toby's.

She had already identified the window in which Toby had unwittingly shot that strange, hazy portrait of a woman. It was dirty, along with the rest of the old building, but not entirely obscured by grime. If a woman had stood there, looking down the alley, she would have been visible, no question.

Liz entered, to be greeted by an elderly man wearing a black apron emblazoned with a logo of a cat carrying a steaming coffee cup in its paws. Kitty's Café had been there for as long as she could remember, but luckily it had never been a haunt of the local bobbies, so she would not be linked to the "boys and girls in blue".

'What can I get you?' the man asked, his friendly smile folding his face into a thousand creases.

'An Americano, and one of your coffee eclairs, please,' she said, telling herself that this indulgence was absolutely necessary to validate her cover.

'Sit down, duck, I'll bring it over.'

The only other customers were a couple, deep in conversation, sitting at the back of the shop, so Liz took a window seat with an unobstructed view of the church. It looked tranquil, unspoiled and very old-world, a place where little happened and what did was hardly a serious matter. Yet Cutler's Alley held a dangerous secret. Two boys were dead because one of them had taken photographs and his lens had captured more than he'd intended.

'Nice morning,' said the elderly barista, following her gaze out of the window. 'Though there's a nip in the air if you go out early.' He placed her drink and a plate bearing a large and delicious-looking eclair in front of her.

'There certainly is,' she agreed. 'And the leaves are beginning to fall. Although there aren't too many trees in this old part of town.'

'Not too many customers either,' he said a little mournfully. 'We get our regulars, and people like you. I mean, I've seen you in here a few times, lass, over the years, but this end of the town is dying, I'm afraid. But then,' he shrugged resignedly, 'what can you expect when lovely buildings are left to rot?'

33

This was going in exactly the direction Liz had hoped it would. 'I so agree. It's a crying shame. The old pub, for instance. That used to be a real hive of activity, didn't it?'

'Ah, yes, the Old Poacher's Rest.' He gave a little laugh. 'We've seen many an antic at closing time outside that place!'

'You live over the shop?' Liz asked casually.

'Yes, m'dear, nice comfy little flat, two floors and all the old features, you know. Lovely old, tiled fireplaces, it's a little piece of nostalgia. My Kitty loved it, bless her heart.' He sighed. 'Now it's just me and old Walter — that's me cat, duck. Was a right terror in his time, but now he likes his home comforts.'

Time to steer him back to the street. 'I walked down from the far end this morning, haven't been that way for a while. It's really deteriorated, hasn't it? I used to love some of the architecture. I always wondered what those really old places were in their heyday.'

'Well, the old ruin at the far end was originally the Guildhall, believe it or not. And the one on the corner of Bowmaker's Lane was a rich merchant's house, a real period piece so they say. Now look at it.'

'The one that's leaning into the lane?' she asked. 'Looks like something out of Charles Dickens.'

'Aye, that's the one. If ever there was a terrible waste, that's it.'

'If someone said it was haunted, I'd believe them,' Liz said.

The old man laughed. 'I don't think it's haunted, but it does have its fair share of mystery, and we often see strange folk hanging around it.'

'Probably some of the homeless,' suggested Liz. 'It could house an awful lot of squatters if they managed to get inside.'

'Oh, they aren't squatters,' he said. 'Strangely enough, in all the years it's been empty, it's never had squatters in it. But that's probably down to the security company that calls around quite regularly. One of the lads always pops in for a coffee after he's done a check.'

'Oh, they do go in and make sure it's all secure, then?' Liz tried not to sound too interested.

'Not inside. No one ever goes inside that I know of. It's just the doors, the windows, for any sign of damage.'

Money for old rope, thought Liz. Rattle a few windows, check the locks are still holding, then back to the van for a flask of tea and a sarnie. She knew a few retired coppers who had gone that route because it was a cushy job after what they'd been used to, and no one bothered them.

'So, what's the mystery you mentioned, then?' she asked casually.

'It's to do with ownership and some strange clauses about its usage, I believe. In fact, I'm not sure who owns it anymore, seems like no one does.' Two more customers entered the shop. 'Well, can't stand here nattering all morning. Enjoy your eclair, me duck.'

Liz cursed the incoming clients. Still, she'd learned more than she had anticipated. She sipped her coffee and thought about it. So, someone was paying to keep it safe, but who? An agent? And who were the people the old man had seen hanging around it if they weren't prospective squatters? And if no one ever went inside, why had a woman been looking out of an upstairs window?

She sat, apparently peacefully enjoying her pastry, but her mind was far from calm. This wasn't a case that would be easily tackled. They certainly couldn't go down the regular routes — simply questioning the authorities or making general enquiries. Matt had been right about being discreet — Alex and Toby had most likely done no more than any young person would do if they believed they had stumbled on a mystery, and it had cost them their lives. She would have been no different when she was an eager young rookie copper.

She lingered over her coffee, going over possible scenarios. From what Georgia had told them of Alex's work, it seemed as if the owner of that photocard had been Toby Unsworth. Georgia said he was heavily into low-light photography, and according to what Alex had told her, had been going to Cutler's Alley several nights in a row. So, Liz mused, Toby goes out again, takes his precious shots and returns to Greenborough, where he shows them to Alex and they discover the woman's face in the empty building. At that point they must have formulated a plan to check the old place out. There her scenario ended. If and when they carried out their plan was unknown. By the time Minty saw the terrified boy being chased through the marketplace, it would appear that their cards had been marked. They died the following night.

She stood up to go. She'd have liked to talk more to the old man who'd served her, but the place had grown busier. Outside the old café, she stood for a moment, wondering what to do next. She wandered back past the merchant's house, then down Bowmaker's Lane, keeping her eyes open for any back entrances to the dilapidated building. Not wishing to attract attention to herself, she headed for home. She hadn't much to tell Matt, but it was a start.

* * *

Matt had made very little headway going down the Google route. He had rather expected to discover more about the old building — after all, it had been a very prestigious property in its day — but all he came up with was the name of the man who had owned it in the seventeen hundreds. The Latimer family were prominent importers of textiles from Asia, and Latimer himself appeared to have amassed a considerable fortune from these luxury goods — his home was one of the most fashionable properties in the town. But that was it, apart from the fact that it was a listed building with a number of interesting architectural features.

Matt usually felt freer operating as a civilian, but not in this case. As a police officer he'd have been all over this in no time. He would certainly never have surrendered to threats. The force's IT section would have confirmed or denied the veracity of the photograph, and if it confirmed that a woman was inside that locked and derelict building, he'd have had the place searched from roof to cellar. None of the official routes was available to him now.

He paced the floor, wondering if there really was anything going on in that wreck of a property. What if that face in the window had been a trick of the light? In that case, the boys' deaths would have been down to something completely different. But if so, what?

The house phone rang, startling him out of his thoughts.

'David! Hello, lad. I hear we are going to see you on Sunday.'

'That's why I'm phoning, Matt. Would it put you out awfully if I came up today? I really could do with getting away from here, and I'm only kicking my heels until Sunday. Dad's got a job come up and he's heading off to the wilds of Scotland, so I'd be alone.'

It did put them out, but the kid sounded so down that Matt didn't even wait to run it past Liz first. 'Of course you can. We've got a case running, but, hey, maybe you could help out.' He paused, recalling that David had said something about work he'd done on enhancing computer images.

He asked, and David told him it was true. 'I love anything to do with IT, especially playing with images. Why?'

'Then get yourself up to the Fens. I've got a tasty little job for you. I'll tell you about it when you get here.'

Matt ended the call feeling considerably brighter. With David's help, they could confirm once and for all whether the woman was real. Then their investigation could begin.

Liz phoned. She said her morning had not been a complete waste of time but she feared it was going to be a slow old business compared to what they were used to. Matt told her about David's change of plan. 'The guest room is all made up and ready,' she said. 'I'll do some shopping and see you in an hour or so.'

When she arrived and they had unpacked the shopping, they sat over tea to discuss what they had discovered.

'David's early arrival could be a great help to us, him too. I had no intention of letting him mope while he's here, but now I think we could really use him, and it might get him out of himself. I know, as do you, my darling, that not being able to follow the path you had set your heart on, or remain in the one you had dedicated most of your life to, can knock you sideways. But sometimes self-pity blinds you to other exciting possibilities. For David, being kept busy in a totally different environment could be just what he needs.'

'That's what I thought too,' said Matt. 'We know a bit about computers, but you have to be young, or totally dedicated to IT, to keep up with the advances being made these days. Plus, if we have to keep our enquiries secret, we're going to need technology more than usual.' He placed his mug on the table and sat back. 'The moment we get the green light about that photograph, I'm setting up an Incident Room. I reckon David is going to be the linchpin here, what do you think?'

'Oh yes,' Liz said. 'You know what? As that old guy in the café was talking to me, I had that old feeling — you know the one. Those alarm bells in your head that tell you something about a new investigation stinks.'

The Incident Room was their little-used dining room, furnished with a long old refectory table and six chairs, a sideboard, and little else. They had removed the pictures occupying one wall and set up a large magnetic whiteboard in their stead. They had added a PC with two monitors and two printers, some wooden filing cabinets and a tall wooden cupboard to house stationery. The room had been transformed into an office and had the advantage of separating their home life from their working one. None of these fittings were permanent, so if one day they gave up their business, it could return to being a dining room.

Matt experienced a real buzz pulling out the dry wipe markers and the magnets and putting the first names on that empty board. He could hardly wait for David Haynes to arrive!

* * *

In Fenfleet town, two more people were discussing business, their conversation much darker than that of Matt and Liz. Unlike the two investigators, they had no interest in protecting life, but property was a different matter altogether.

'An update, please.' The speaker had his hair dyed black, making him look somehow artificial. He fastened his gaze on his younger companion.

The other stared back, through icy, pale blue eyes. 'At present, our cleaning-up operation appears to have been successful. We have trashed the SD card and the laptop has been destroyed and disposed of. The two sources of irritation have been eliminated, and as we expected, the police are looking no further into their unfortunate accidental deaths.'

'You know this for sure?' said the dark-haired man.

'My contact on the inside confirms it, Mr Palmer. The mother of one of the boys questioned the cause of death, but again, as expected, it was put down to her grief and the natural inability of a mother to accept the death of a son. The law is not interested.'

'All right. That just leaves one possible weak link, doesn't it? One you seem reluctant to do anything about. Unless I'm mistaken.'

The eyes grew perceptibly more glacial. 'You're not local, Mr Palmer, you don't know the man. He was in Parkhurst with my father, a man to be reckoned with in his time. I know things about Minty that he wouldn't dare risk getting out. I reminded him of that fact. That night he put a shattered SD card in his refuse bin, meaning I was right about the kid slipping it into his pocket in the market. Minty's clever, but he doesn't do technology. He probably didn't even know what the card was, and he doesn't own a computer. He denied having the card, but then he would, wouldn't he? So, he trashed it and then dumped it. And he will *not* go to the police. I guarantee it.'

Mr Palmer decided to accept the young man, Jude's, statement, although if it had been down to him, he'd have topped the old lag, simply as a precaution. He might do that anyway. Jude wasn't the only man on his team who was capable of murder, though Jude was the best, and it was unlike him to balk at tying up loose ends. Even more strange was the grudging respect he seemed to have for this aging con. He could only think it had something to do with Jude's father, so he let it drop. 'Just watch him from now on. And I warn you, one mistake, one wrong move, and I pull rank, understood?'

'Understood.'

'And I want no more glowing character references, just a permanent solution to the problem.'

'Also understood,' said Jude flatly.

'Okay, then, moving on, do we have adequate surveillance on our properties?' Palmer frowned. 'Maybe you should consider upping it temporarily?'

'Already have, as of yesterday, just for a week or so until we feel comfortable again. Our business is far too important to risk anything going wrong because of some interfering kids with a camera.'

Now that was something Palmer did agree with him about. '*Nothing* must get in the way. We're doing extremely well, my friend, but we are going to do much, much better. I have new contacts waiting in the wings, and if I can just handle them properly, and you can keep prying eyes away from us, you'll be amazed at how big this business will become.'

Jude didn't answer, but he looked pleased. Jude liked the finer things in life, including expensive women, and you needed money for such women, a lot of it. For his part, Palmer was prepared to pay him enough to support his extravagances. Jude did good work — professional, clean and efficient. Men like him were hard to come by and Palmer wanted to hold onto him. 'Your share will be considerable, and if this deal goes ahead as it should, there is no reason for it to end there. You'll be a rich man, Jude, so I suggest you start considering how to conceal your wealth. You don't want to cause interest in your activities.'

Palmer saw a glimmer in those pale eyes. He knew what it was. The younger man would stick with him until they had wrung every last drop out of their valuable and highly sought-after commodity. He doubted whether Jude was capable of warmth. No, what he had seen in his eyes was greed.

CHAPTER FIVE

'I failed the Bleep Test three times,' said David miserably.

Liz knew what the fitness test involved. The part called the Bleep Test measured stamina — running for around four minutes over a distance of seven hundred metres. He could reapply after six months but, considering the training he'd been doing to get through this time, it was doubtful that more intensive work would improve his fitness. His childhood heart condition had evidently left him with impaired function, and there was nothing he could do to change it.

David's normally thick, dark brown, wavy hair had been cut in a short, rather military style, no doubt for the benefit of the recruitment process. He was good-looking, with a ready smile that had been noticeably absent since his arrival.

'It's hard to reset your mind into thinking of some other future. It just never entered my head that I'd fail.' He gave a bitter laugh. 'I really did have my head in the sand, didn't I? I honestly believed that when it came to it, I'd get the strength from somewhere.' He sighed. 'But it never happened. Those dashes up and down the gymnasium with a stopwatch against you and people yelling nearly killed me. I thought my chest was going to burst.'

Liz recalled that feeling only too well. 'That test is a bugger, even for the fitness freaks,' she said with a pained expression. 'But look, I know you had your heart set on starting as a regular bobby, but the police force contains plenty of other elements, people with different talents. It works as a team, people with different specialisms all having the same aim — to make things better, nail the bad guys. No one group is more important than the others. It could be forensics that comes up trumps in one case, IT in another. If your ultimate aim is to do some good, make a difference, you could still do it, but just by another route than the one you had in your mind.'

Liz had her glass of wine, and Matt flipped the tops off two bottles of beer, handing one to David. Dinner over, they wandered through to the conservatory, a recent addition. Despite the autumn evening chill, it had retained the warmth of the sun that day.

'Liz is dead right, David, but my advice to you,' said Matt, 'is to use the coming week as a complete break. Forget decisions, regrets, plans for the future. Just step away from everything and let the Fens work its magic.'

Liz wholeheartedly agreed. 'You can't stop unwanted thoughts, none of us can, but just try to put everything about what lies ahead on the back burner for a while. We'll do some walks on the sea bank to blow away a few cobwebs. And Matt thinks you could help us with a problem we have — if you're up for it?'

David seemed to brighten. 'If I can help, I'd be happy to.'

They told him about the photograph, leaving out the fact that the boy who took it had possibly been murdered.

'Can I see it now? And what programs do you use for images?'

Already, David sounded interested. Maybe this would help him feel a little easier about the way things had turned out for him.

They took their drinks and went through to the Incident Room. David burst out laughing. 'I thought you were retired! What is this? The Cannon Farm CID room?'

'It works for us,' grinned Matt, 'and it keeps business and home life separate, something we both appreciate.'

Matt sat at the computer, opened the file and began to scroll through the images.

'Whoa!' David exclaimed. 'Those shots are awesome! Who took them? Whoever it is, they're a genius!'

A dead one, sadly, thought Liz. 'We're not actually sure, but we think they were taken by a student as part of a photographic course at the uni.' She glanced at Matt, wondering if they should tell David everything. He gave a little shrug, so she said, 'If it's who we think, we are told he died in a tragic accident.'

'No shit? That's sincerely bad news. These pictures are some of the best low-light shots I've ever seen. And the photographer died? That's such a waste!'

'Indeed,' muttered Matt grimly, scrolling on through the images. He stopped, enlarged the image of the old merchant's house and stood up, offering his seat to David. 'Take a look at this. Tell us if you see anything unusual in it.'

It took David only moments. 'That place is derelict, isn't it? So why is there a woman looking out of the upstairs window?'

Liz looked at Matt and rolled her eyes. 'And we are supposed to be the detectives! It took us three runs through the whole folder to notice that.'

'In fairness,' said David with a smile, 'you'd already said there was something odd about it. Don't beat yourself up, Auntie Liz.'

'Well, next question.' Matt looked at the screen. 'Could it be a trick of the light? Just a shadow on the window?'

David squinted at the photograph. 'Doubtful, but I can do some work on it and clean it up a bit. Thing is, I'll need to work from my own laptop. Not to denigrate your equipment, but mine is very hi-spec and I've got this great app that can produce some pretty stunning images. I'd never be able to get that kind of result with your, er, well, this kind of set-up.'

'No offence taken,' laughed Matt. 'However, these images are hot property at present and we'll have to ask you to delete your work after you're done. Sorry, but it's important, for all kinds of reasons.' He pulled a face. 'We'll fill you in a bit more later, but right now we're kind of feeling our way into knowing whether we have a case or not.'

David grinned. 'I'm intrigued. I can tackle it right now if you like, it's not too late. I'll go and fetch my laptop.'

It was half past nine, but Liz and Matt didn't object. They had to know whether what they feared was true.

'I'll get you another beer,' said Matt. 'It'll help you concentrate.'

In the kitchen, Liz said, 'He looks brighter than when he arrived, but I expect there'll be a few moody days when reality sinks in.'

'Of course, but keeping him busy will help. I mean, look at him now.' He turned to her. 'Liz, how much should we tell him about this case?'

'If he confirms that it's a woman, I'd say everything. We aren't bound by the Official Secrets Act on something like this. It's a private investigation and he's helping out with IT, no more than that.' She lowered her voice. 'And he's a very sensible young man. He passed every other part of that damned selection with gold bloody stars. We've got him here for a week, let's use him. It won't hurt to have a younger person's take on a few aspects. In fact, it might be very useful indeed.' She was thinking that he could talk to students in their own language — Toby and Alex's friends and house-mates, hang out in a bar to pick up gossip from the streets. He could be a real asset to them.

Half an hour later, David called out, 'Here. Good as it gets, but I reckon it's pretty conclusive.' He looked at Matt and Liz, who were standing hesitantly in the doorway. 'The software I use is brilliant at restoring old and damaged photos and correcting blurry images, but this was a bit of a challenge as the glass was so dirty. However . . . Can I use your printer? I'll need to add my device, is that okay?'

Matt nodded, and in moments their printer was whirring into life. David held up a printed image. 'I'd say you have one very worried lady inside that old building, wouldn't you?'

Liz stared at the enhanced photo and gave a low whistle. 'Or a very frightened one.' She looked sharply up at Matt. 'We have an investigation, I believe!'

'We certainly do,' he said. He turned to David. 'How would you like a part-time job, in between your long walks on the sea bank?'

David didn't take his eyes from the photograph. 'Hang the long walks! Maybe it's time to tell me what's going on here, and what exactly happened to that genius of a student photographer.'

Liz and Matt pulled up chairs. It was going to be a late night.

* * *

Kellie couldn't sleep, so she did what she always did when it eluded her, got up and took her mother's memory box from beneath the bed.

When she'd been told her illness was terminal, Louise Burton had made a memory box for each of her children and filled them with mementoes of happy times. Simon rarely opened his. Kellie knew why — it made his mother's death real. All that was left of her were old photos of times he could barely remember, some silly pictures he'd painted for her when he was little more than a baby. None of it had much meaning for him now. The only thing he had taken out and which he kept with him at all times was a little old book called *The Observer's Book of British Birds*. It was his most treasured possession.

Unlike Simon, Kellie loved her box and everything in it. She would get out each item and gently lay a finger on it, knowing that her mother's hand had touched it before she died. Every single thing was precious, it kept her mother alive for her. Perhaps because she was older, and a girl, she understood what her mother had done for her when she made up the box. Kellie had sat next to her mother and listened to her explain the importance of everything that went into it.

'When you were small, my darling, you would love to play on the beach, and you would collect any pebble that had the colour green in it. You especially liked the frosty pale green ones, and when I told you they were actually pieces of glass that had been in the sea a long time so that the water had made their sharp edges smooth, you were fascinated. From then on you always brought me frosty sea glass from whatever beach you went to.'

Kellie gently touched one of the soft green stones. Even though her mother was no longer there, she still looked for them when she walked on a beach. She probably always would.

There were about fifty items in the box, and Kellie knew the story behind each one. She opened a little card and a pressed flower fell out. It was a buttercup which, even after all these years, had retained its glorious yellow colour. Kellie placed it back in its card for safety, and suddenly recalled a conversation she had had with her mum on the day she had picked that particular flower for her.

'Don't trust Anna,' her mother had said, wearing an unusually serious expression. 'I know you will spend time with Auntie Jessie, and that's wonderful, she loves you both to distraction, but don't believe everything she tells you about Anna. I don't think she's good for your aunt.'

Kellie nestled back into her pillows and tried to remember the rest of the conversation, but it was hazy after all this time. Whenever they had been up to the Fens to visit Jessie, or when Jessie came and stayed with them, Anna had never been around. Jessie said her sister didn't approve of Anna, so it was best she stayed away, but it had been clear that Jessie felt very differently about her friend.

This sense of something unspoken worried Kellie. When pushed, her mum merely said she was too young to understand, and that one day she'd be old enough to see for herself.

Soon after that particular conversation, her mother had told her that when Kellie turned eighteen, their solicitor would give her a letter. 'Normally,' she'd said, 'you would get it at twenty-one, but you are old for your age, my darling, and will understand it earlier than that. Don't expect money, it's not about that, it's about our family and its history, and I think you will appreciate it.'

Her mother had given her a long look, full of meaning. 'My precious daughter. I would never choose to leave you, but I have no say in the matter. Sometimes God has other plans for us, and there's nothing we can do about it. You will grow into a strong and intelligent woman, knowing every step of the way that you are sheltered by your mother's love. But that won't be the case for Simon. I fear for him.'

She had been right. Simon had changed when their mother died, and now Kellie feared for him too. Not only was there his asthma to cope with, but he couldn't come to terms with the loss, and Kellie wondered if spending time with sweet, adorable, nutty Auntie Jessie was really what he needed right now. Having seen that buttercup and recalling her mother's words about Anna, she started to worry even more. Her mother had gone, which meant that Anna would be hanging around again, exerting her influence over sweet Aunt Jessie.

Kellie put the box back under her bed and snuggled down under the duvet. She wondered what her mother had meant about Anna not being good for Jessie. If she had been a friend of hers since their childhood, surely she must be a very good friend. Kellie couldn't see herself still being friends with her old playmates when she was as old as they were. Maybe her mother had been wrong. Maybe something had gone on between her and Anna that Kellie didn't know about. As long as it didn't affect her darling little brother, that was fine, but what if it did?

Kellie sat up and left him yet another text message.

* * *

From the shadows at the back of the lounge bar, Eddie Race watched the last of the punters reluctantly take their leave. The sign outside proclaimed it to be the "Las Vegas Lounge", but the regulars, as well as those who avoided it, all knew it as "Race's Place".

Aside from its official role as a bar, it was also the headquarters of a much bigger operation. Eddie Junior had taken over the reins of this business after Eddie Senior died, seven or eight years back, and seen it grow from strength to strength. It had been an empire with two sides to it: one perfectly legitimate, even moderately respected in certain circles to do with merchandising, and a second half, a far from respectable criminal underground network.

Eddie Jr sold off the legitimate business at a considerable profit and invested the proceeds into the far more lucrative side of the Race empire. Some had pronounced it a mistake but it had paid off, and in a relatively short space of time, Eddie Race had become a very rich woman indeed.

Edwina Germaine was not the eldest of the three Race siblings, but it had always been known that she would succeed Eddie Senior. Her brother and sister, Ricky and Paula, had never contested the decision — they possessed neither the drive, nor the foresight, not to mention the business acumen — of their sister. They were content to do their bit, such as it was, and receive a nice little cut of the takings.

Eddie certainly looked the part. Elegant, immaculately dressed, she was a tall, powerful woman with blonde hair and piercing eyes. Beneath the surface, she was calculating, ruthless, and hard as nails.

Eddie sipped her drink and waited for her sister to bring her the total of that night's bar takings. It had been slow for a Friday, but she wasn't much worried. Aside from its official role, the bar served as a meeting house, somewhere to discuss business in comfort and privacy, a place to pick up and pass on useful information and make contacts. The bar was a perfectly legal operation — the only part of the Race world that was. It was properly registered, paid its taxes, and

Eddie was always fully up to date with all the various licenses — alcohol, food-handling and health and safety. The police remained unaware of its real function, knowing it only as a watering hole frequented by shady characters.

There were few ripples in Eddie's pond. She sat in the centre, like an elegant toad, serene in her command of the smaller fish that did her bidding. Tonight, however, she was edgy, and this unaccustomed perturbation made her angry.

Paula, her sister, arrived with the figures, placed them on the table and, seeing Eddie's expression, made a swift exit.

But she didn't make it to the door. 'Paula,' Eddie called. 'You were in the bar tonight. Any more news from the streets?'

Paula turned back, tossing a swathe of long dark hair over her shoulder. 'Unrest out there. More faces no one recognises. Same as all week, Ed, no one has a clue what's going on.'

'Thanks, Sis.' Eddie returned her attention to the cocktail glass. 'By the way, this new cocktail tastes like aircraft fuel. Tell Ivy she should try them herself before she inflicts them on me.'

Paula shrugged. 'I liked it.'

Eddie finished the drink, which was actually very good, and stood up. She had hoped it wouldn't come to it, but this situation couldn't go on. She would be forced, for an exorbitant sum of money, to send Henry to find out just what was going on in Fenfleet town. She hated using Henry. Asking for help didn't come easily to her, but not knowing was far worse.

Eddie pulled her jacket from the back of her chair and left the bar. She knew exactly where Henry would be at this hour of the night. Arlington Lodge, number twenty-three Lansdowne Avenue, was a beautifully kept, detached, older property, dating from the days when richer families had favoured this leafy road on the outskirts of Fenfleet. But it was still a knocking shop, no matter how you dressed it up.

She was admitted at once. The woman who had opened the door knew who Eddie was without asking. She hurried off, extremely reluctant to interrupt Henry, but no one argued with Eddie Race.

'This will cost you, lady! That was the nicest, tastiest fuck I've had in a long time, and you had to come in and spoil it just when I was . . .' Henry strode into the room and flung himself into a chair.

'Shut up and listen.' Eddie hated doing this, and Henry knew it, which made it worse. He was one of the most darkly handsome men she had ever seen, and he knew that too. Prematurely grey, his attraction lay in his compelling, wicked and sexual allure.

'Actually, I've been expecting you,' said Henry languidly. 'Pity your timing was so inappropriate.' He sighed dramatically. 'A little bit of heaven lost forever.'

'Oh, shut up,' growled Eddie. 'Splash enough cash and your particular bit of heaven can be yours any time you want, so stop complaining.'

He sighed again. 'Spoken like a woman with no heart and no soul. But down to business. You want to know what, or who, is moving in on Race territory.'

'In a nutshell, yes.'

Henry's smile faded. 'I put out some feelers when the rumours started, but it's strangely quiet out there. The jungle drums are silent, and mouths that usually open wide at the sight of a twenty-quid note are zipped up tight.' He scowled. 'I don't like it.'

'But you *can* find out, Henry.' This was not a question.

'Of course I can, but it's going to take a while and a lot of patience. Can you wait?'

'Do I have a choice?' She shrugged. 'I have to know why and who. Someone could be threatening our whole set-up, and we can't let that happen — for all our sakes.' He nodded. Life was good in Fenfleet for Henry, and he would want it to stay that way. 'I see we understand each other.'

'The cost will be high. This one could be truly dangerous.' He raised an eyebrow at her.

She met his gaze with a cold smile. 'Your rates are always extortionate but, as always, I'll pay whatever ransom you hold me to — so long as I get results.'

He stared back. 'I get results. I'm renowned for it, dear lady, whatever I do.' The lascivious smile was back.

She stood up. 'That's agreed, then. You can get back to what you were doing before your playmate goes off the boil. Then you can turn your mind to more lucrative matters. And keep it there until you find out what I want to know.'

Eddie turned on her heel and left. The ball was now rolling.

CHAPTER SIX

Even if David had wanted to sink back into his previous despondent mood, Liz and Matt were seeing to it that he didn't get the opportunity. Breakfast had become a campaign meeting — egg, bacon and strategy — and David found himself getting caught up in it.

'I always start the day with a short walk along the sea bank after breakfast,' said Liz brightly, buttering a slice of wholemeal toast. 'I spend far too long on the computer and on office work, and I can't afford to lose what little fitness I have left. Fancy joining me?'

David was beginning to realise that this change of routine was exactly what he needed. At some point he would have to face the central dilemma of his life — what the hell he was going to do from now on — but maybe this break would help him consider it with a clearer mind.

'But before that,' Liz was saying, 'we'll decide on our various assignments. Let's see what the three of us can achieve before we shut up shop tonight.'

'And your shift ends at 5 p.m. sharp, David, because tonight we are going out to dinner at the Pear Tree House,' Matt said, his eyes alight with anticipation.

'Best dining experience in the area,' added Liz. 'Country house setting, the kitchen headed up by a former head chef of a top London hotel and owned by an old acquaintance of Matt's.' She winked at David. 'Of course, there's an ulterior motive besides the excellent grub.'

'The owner and I shared an old friend, who is no longer with us.' Matt stopped abruptly.

Liz leaned across and squeezed his arm gently. She turned to David. 'They keep in touch because Adie, their mutual friend, would have wanted them to. Adie and Bernie were on the opposite side of the fence to Mattie, but,' she shrugged, 'sometimes friendship transcends barriers. Anyway, Matt wouldn't be here if it hadn't been for Adie, so . . .'

Matt coughed. 'Bottom line, Bernie runs a top restaurant, and I love my food. And he's still very much in the know about what is going on in the local underworld.' He raised an eyebrow.

'I get you,' said David. 'I'll look forward to it.'

David's father had mentioned the incident that had left both his aunt and Matt seriously injured. Liz's injuries were so bad she'd had to leave the force and the job she loved. He supposed this was what they were referring to, but he didn't like to pry, since it was clearly an emotive subject. He had a feeling that Liz would tell him about it at some point during his stay, meanwhile he'd have to wait.

'I'm wondering what I can do to help today,' he said. 'I don't want to get in your way, but I've spent half the night going over what you told me. It seems impossible that such a terrible thing could happen to two young students. Hell, they must have been my age, even younger. And all they did was capture some awesome shots of Fenfleet by moonlight.'

'And if what we suspect is true, those photographs got them killed.' Matt looked angry. 'You're right, it's a wicked waste of young lives. But whatever is going on in that building is serious enough to risk going down for double murder.'

54

'I guess we need to get inside somehow,' said David, picturing himself dressed in black and bearing a marked resemblance to Daniel Craig.

'Oh, no!' Liz said. 'Not unless you want to end up like those two students. We have to approach this by means of very subtle enquiries. Imagine how closely that old building is being watched. When they went after the photocard they didn't even know that Toby had captured an incriminating image. The mere fact that they had been taking night-time shots that featured the merchant's house was enough to warrant, at the very least, stealing the card, the camera and the laptop, and checking it out.'

'So,' Matt added, 'common sense dictates that sometime between Toby taking the pictures and Alex ringing to ask his father about something important, the people interested in the merchant's house somehow discovered that there really was something incriminating on that card, and went all out to stop it going any further.'

'It's that part of the timeline that I'd like to see clarified,' said Liz. 'At the moment there is this grey area — what happened during the last few days of those boys' lives.' Her eyes narrowed. 'David, this would be a bit of a risk, but if you're game, we think it's a calculated one.'

He sat up straighter.

'One way we could piece together more of what happened in those final days would be to talk to Toby and Alex's housemates. But we have a problem. Should whoever killed the boys still be watching their house, they would immediately be put on the alert if Matt or I were to go there asking questions. However, what could be more natural than another student dropping by?' She raised her eyebrows.

The penny dropped. 'A college kid like me?'

'Exactly. Like you.'

'Nice one! Yeah, I can do that. Let me go and grill them.' His eyes lit up.

'Your enthusiasm is admirable, but no grilling, please. You have to be subtle about it — no thumbscrews or waterboarding,' said Liz with a laugh.

'And we need come up with a really strong cover story to give the housemates,' Matt said. 'So, to that end Liz is going to go and talk to Georgia Hallam, Alex's mother, and get some basic information from her about her son, facts you can use to get his housemates to open up to you. This is important, David. It's imperative that we find out what Alex and Toby were doing between the time those pictures were taken and when Toby was seen running from someone through Fenfleet market.'

David was suddenly overcome. This was what he might have been doing regularly if he hadn't failed that damn test. All his anger and hurt threatened to well up again. He told himself to calm down, stop thinking of himself. Right now, he had an opportunity to be of real help to another person, Alex's mother. He tried to imagine what his own parents would be going through if he'd been killed, and he shuddered.

'Maybe I could go with Liz to see her,' he said. 'If Mrs Hallam would allow it, one look at Alex's room would tell me what kind of guy he was. It'd be a great help when I speak to his friends.'

Matt and Liz glanced at each other and smiled.

'He'll do,' said Matt. 'Take him with you.'

Liz agreed at once. 'Of course, and while we're there, I'd really like to ask Georgia Hallam if she knows Toby's parents. I'm wondering if they have discussed her suspicions, and if so, whether the Unsworth family feels the same as she does.' Liz turned to David. 'We intend to turn our findings over to the police, but we have to be absolutely certain that our judgement isn't being clouded by Georgia Hallam's reservations about the accidental nature of their deaths. You've really set our enquiry moving by enhancing that woman's face, David, but there's still a chance that there is nothing actually sinister about it.'

'As in she's a squatter or a druggie?' he asked.

'Exactly, or even has some legitimate reason for being in there, only I have no idea what that could be,' Liz added.

'We have to have actual proof for there to be a case to hand over to the police,' said Matt. 'We can't go to them with suppositions.'

'So, what about the lad being chased through the market? As soon as he saw his picture in the paper, your snout swore it was Toby, then he found that photocard in his pocket. Next thing Toby is dead. Surely that's evidence?'

Matt sighed. 'One, Minty would never admit anything at all to the cops, he'd deny all knowledge of it and I'd lose a damned good contact. Two, the kid could have been high, drugged and having a panic attack or a bad trip. And those men following him? Well, they could have been trying to help him, or to apprehend him if he had stolen something. It's all hearsay, son. No evidence at all.'

Liz gathered up the breakfast plates. 'But our gut feeling says that what Minty saw was kosher. We have that all-important photocard, and if we can gather more information, we'll be able to form a picture of what really happened.'

It was starting to make sense. There was a lot of work to be done. David said, 'I see what you mean now, about getting an accurate timeline of exactly what Toby and Alex were doing before they went home that night, shut themselves in Toby's room and never came out again.'

'It's vital,' said Liz. 'And don't forget, there's always the possibility that no matter how scared they were, their deaths really could have been down to a faulty appliance, and it was just a terrible coincidence. Discovering the cause of death is always taken very seriously, and the doctors and forensic examiners are not often wrong.'

'We *believe* something bad is going on, David,' said Matt seriously. 'And we are going to prove it one way or another. Meanwhile, we have to assume the worst — that someone is watching that house in Cutler's Alley and will stop at nothing to keep whatever is going on there a secret.'

'So, we walk on eggshells,' David said softly.

Matt stared at him across his cooling mug of tea. 'Take no risks. Be on your guard the whole time, and only discuss it with Liz or me.'

David felt a shiver of anticipation. When he'd decided to come to the Fens for a break, he had never dreamed he'd be doing something like this. He'd thought it an avenue closed to him forever when he had been rejected for the police. He still couldn't quite believe it. 'Got it, Matt. I'll be careful, I really will.'

'Then I'll ring Georgia and see what time we can visit,' Liz said. 'We'll take a quick walk along the sea bank and discuss what we say to her — is that okay?' Liz pressed the button on the dishwasher. 'And you, Matt? What's your plan for this morning?'

'I'm going to Greenborough. This case calls for some discreet enquiries. I know someone who I think might be able to give us more information on who owns that old merchant's house. I've got another old associate there, too, who has very big ears.' He grinned. 'At times like this I'm glad I kept the details of my contacts from the past — legit and criminal. Matt Ballard is about to call in a few favours.'

* * *

Kellie stared down at the front door mat. Circulars, official-looking brown envelopes addressed to her father, and nothing else. She collected them up despondently and then saw the postcard, stuck between a glossy flyer advertising pizza delivery and a catalogue for cheap winter clothing.

Her heart leaped. She peered at the careful childish writing. His news mostly concerned a hedgehog, and some rare bird she'd never heard of, but at least he had written, and she was thrilled. Until she saw the last line.

Can you come, Kellie? Something's not right.

* * *

Jude kept talking, despite his father's slack, uncomprehending face. He told him about his day, things he'd seen, what people had mentioned, gossip off the streets, childhood days.

'Hey, Dad, remember Minty? I had a few words with him the other day. I gave him your best.'

Though it was impossible, Jude could have sworn he saw a glimmer of recognition in the old man's eyes at the mention of that name. Jude told himself not to be stupid. His father didn't even recognise him, his own son, let alone some old lag he'd shared a cell with in the distant past.

'Had a bit of a dilemma there, Dad. Still, I remembered everything you told me about Minty, and I think I did the right thing by you and the family. He didn't know who I was, and I certainly didn't tell him, but I reckon I saved him a good deal of pain — or worse. My instructions had been to tidy up all loose ends permanently, if you catch my drift.' He moved his chair closer to his father. 'My, er, "senior partner" in the firm is the most ruthless man I know.' He chuckled. 'Sounds good coming from me, don't it? Well, he really would sell his own grandmother if the price was right.' He sniffed and stared at a broken fingernail. 'He wasn't pleased that I hadn't silenced Minty, I'm telling you, but family comes first. I just hope the bastard doesn't get one of the other goons to do the job behind my back. He would and all, Dad, except thanks to you, I have more skills than the others. He won't want to lose me, and boy, business is booming! That's how come you're here, and not in some stinking "God's Waiting Room" run by people who don't give a toss.'

Jude looked around the private room, its opulent décor and expensive drapes. Yeah, family came first.

He glanced at his watch. He'd better go soon, he had work to do, but he'd be back tomorrow. Since his father had been shot, two years ago, he'd never missed a day. Two whole years without his dad saying one comprehensible word to him. Sometimes he wondered why he came, but he knew he'd keep on visiting until the day the old man died.

'Gotta go, Dad. Places to go, people to see.' He planted a kiss on his father's forehead and headed for the door.

'Minty.'

Jude stopped, his hand on the doorknob. He turned and looked back.

But the old man closed his eyes and sighed, sinking back as if the effort of speaking that one word had exhausted him.

Bewildered, Jude left the home. What was so important about Minty Agutter that his name was the only word his father had spoken in two fucking years? Not only that, but there had been what sounded like urgency in that unfamiliar croaky voice.

Jude hated mysteries.

As he drove back into town, he decided that as his father was in no fit state to explain anything to him, he would have to pay another call on Mr Minty Agutter.

Abandoning his plans for the day, he opted for a brief call to three of his operatives. Then, having satisfied himself that nothing required his immediate attention, he drove to Minty's place.

The old house was run-down but not a complete tip, as if Minty had simply given up on maintenance. Jude parked some way from the building, walked down the side and through the back gate.

The back garden was overgrown but not so badly that a day or two with a strimmer and a garden fork couldn't have sorted it. Jude tried the back door, then a patio door. Both were locked. Yet he sensed Minty's presence inside. Shame. He really could do with talking to him.

'I think he's gone away,' a voice piped up from the next-door garden.

'Oh dear,' said Jude calmly. 'And I've driven all the way from up north to see my uncle. We've had a death in the family and I wanted to bring him the news in person, not over the phone.'

'Oh, that's awful,' the neighbour said. 'I'm so sorry.'

'You don't know where he's gone, by any chance, do you?' he asked.

'He never says much about where he's going, but I defi-nitely heard him yesterday morning. I reckon he dropped something or knocked something over, 'cos there was a bit of a crash. Then later I heard his car driving away. He never took it into town, always walked, and as he never came back last night, I guess he must have gone off for a few days. He often does.'

Jude would have loved to see the owner of this reedy, bird-like voice, but the fence was too high. 'Well, thank you so much. I used to have a key, but I couldn't find it before I left. I was in a bit of a state, I suppose, you know, with grief and all that.'

'Can't help you there, I'm afraid. Our Minty's rather private. He's never given me a key, not even when he goes away for weeks on end. Must stink in there when he comes back!' This was followed by a high-pitched laugh. 'Well, you can see, not very houseproud anymore, our Minty.'

'Well, thanks anyway. You might see me back again. I know someone who might have a key. She's an old friend of his, so I'll call round and then pop back, so don't be afraid if you hear me in the house, okay?' Jude was good at this; deception came naturally to him.

Hastily, he made his escape. He'd be back all right, with a skeleton key or glass cutter borrowed from a friendly house-breaker on his payroll.

He didn't believe for a minute that Minty had driven away. He had probably parked up somewhere and walked back under cover of darkness. The only thing that both-ered him was that noise the neighbour had heard. Minty was scared, that much was certain. Jude had frightened him badly, and now Minty was lying low. But they would have that chat, one way or another.

CHAPTER SEVEN

As Liz had hoped, David had fallen under the spell of the sea bank. He marvelled at the big skies, the absence of all trace of a human presence. He wondered at the perspective-destroying high grassy path and how it seemed to lead only into a far horizon. Back at Cannon Farm, it seemed to Liz that the walk had made him less introspective. He was definitely much brighter.

Now they were approaching the home of Georgia Hallam. During their walk, they had decided on what would be the most sensitive way to tackle their questions. Liz had initially wondered how David, who was still only young, would cope with the strong emotion of a grieving parent, but he had sounded so compassionate that she'd decided he'd be fine.

They pulled up in front of a smart detached house with a sweeping drive laid with gravel. 'Very nice.'

'Very expensive,' added David. He sighed. 'But all that wealth makes no difference when you think what they've just lost.'

Liz felt a rush of affection for her nephew-in-law, followed by a stab of sadness. He would have made a good copper. She pushed the thought aside. 'Come on, let's get this over with, shall we?'

On the surface, Georgia Hallam appeared perfectly composed, but Liz wasn't deceived. She was holding it all in, scared to let go in case she never stopped crying. She made them tea, which they drank in the lounge.

'We don't want to upset you, Georgia,' said Liz gently, 'but there's things we need to know about Alex, and Toby too, that will help us in our investigations.'

'Ask away,' said Georgia. 'The mere fact that you're actually listening to me, that you don't think I'm just neurotic, means a lot. If I can help, I will.'

'Have you cleared your son's belongings out of his student accommodation yet?' Liz began.

Georgia nodded, swallowing hard. 'My husband and his best friend did it immediately after the police had checked their rooms — they said it wasn't a crime scene. So he decided to get it over with straightaway. I couldn't . . . couldn't face it at the time.'

'And are his things here now, Georgia?' asked Liz.

She nodded, her chin quivering. 'In his room.'

'Would it be possible to see his room?' asked David. 'We'll understand if you say no, but it will enable us to build up a picture of Alex. Being young myself, if I could see things like his taste in music, his clothes, it would help a lot.'

'Of course, of course.' She managed a weak smile. 'It's all right. I have no intention of making his room into a shrine. He's gone, and that's that. You look around. You can touch anything — open the drawers, his wardrobe, whatever you want. I just need a little more time before I start sorting everything out. But not just yet.'

Liz, thinking with her detective's brain, said, 'Considering your suspicions, Georgia, I would suggest you leave Alex's things as they are until we know more about what occurred. And anyway, you need the answers you were looking for before you start drawing a line under it all.' Liz smiled encouragingly at her. 'Rest assured, we intend to do everything we can to find those answers for you.' She sipped her tea. 'Are you in touch with Toby's parents at all?'

'We have spoken, just to commiserate, really. His mother's in a terrible state. I couldn't talk to her for long, it was just too distressing.' She shook her head. 'She's in bits.'

'Did you mention your fears to her by any chance?' Liz asked.

'Oh no. Lorie could barely string a sentence together. I couldn't have told her how I felt, it would have really sent her over the edge.'

'And her husband?'

'John is the strong, silent type, I think.' Georgia frowned. 'Or maybe it was just shock and he couldn't show his feelings. Whatever, I decided not to say anything to them, although if you should discover something, that would be a different matter.'

Liz made a note of the Unsworths' contact details. Depending on how the investigation went, they could well be needing to talk to them.

'What type of boy was Alex, Georgia? You told us he was a very private young man, very particular. Did that mean he was a bit insular? Did he mix with the other students?'

'No, not exactly. He preferred his own company, or that of a close friend, to being with a group. He did like Toby, I know that. And he admired Toby's work. He thought his friend had real talent — and so did their tutor. He had high hopes for both Alex and Toby, but as I mentioned before, Toby was the star student, destined to make a name for himself as a photographic artist.'

'Can I have the name of the tutor, please?' asked Liz.

'Richard Lake. I think I have his number somewhere. He came to see us, you know. He's a lovely man, and he was completely devastated at what happened. He said everyone on the course was utterly shaken by it.'

Soon afterwards, they went up to Alex's room. Georgia remained standing in the doorway while Liz and David went inside.

'His stuff from his lodgings is in those packing boxes. It wasn't much. He said he wanted his space here to be exactly as it always was when he came home. He needed a safe place, a bolthole, somewhere he knew well and felt comfortable in.' Georgia brushed away a tear. 'Though he wanted to live in the great big world, he still needed to feel he had a home to escape to if things went wrong.'

And things did go wrong, thought Liz grimly.

She and David looked around the room. It was a good size, with a double bed. A single, long unit ran the length of one wall, comprising a desk, bookshelves, and a work surface with cupboards and drawers underneath. Liz didn't think it looked like a teenager's room at all. For one thing, it was spotless and perfectly tidy.

'Has the room been cleaned recently?' she asked.

Georgia gave a snuffle, a kind of stifled laugh. 'I know what you're thinking. That's just the way Alex liked it. Sometimes I wondered if he was borderline OCD, but I think he just liked things orderly.' She pointed to the far wall, which was covered in photographs. They were all arranged in straight lines, as if they'd been organised using a spirit level and a ruler. 'All Alex's work.'

Liz and David went over to take a closer look.

'Wow!' said David. 'What a clever mind.' He scanned the unusual photographs, homing in on one in particular. 'That's amazing! I love that one.'

Georgia seemed to inflate with pride. 'That was one of the images he was going to present in his third-year final project. It was his favourite.'

Liz stared at the photograph, not sure what it represented, until she looked closer. It seemed to be a study in green, every shade and tone of the colour. Alex had photographed a rock covered in a thick carpet of moss. Behind it, slightly out of focus, a backdrop formed of a sea of young bracken fronds and new beech leaves. The detail of the moss against the indistinct background caused it to almost leap out at the viewer. For a moment Liz fancied she could smell the damp of the wood-land. What Alex had done was amazing, taking something so simple and creating such a powerful image from it.

David was now moving about the room, looking at this and that, nodding occasionally as if he was beginning to get to know the dead boy.

Liz was more interested in the packing boxes. 'May I?' she asked Georgia.

'Go ahead, I'll leave you to it. I'll be downstairs when you're through.'

Liz stood watching her go, deeply sorry for her. It was hard to imagine what she was going through, unless you yourself had suffered a similar loss. She dragged herself back to the present. The best she could do for Georgia Hallam was find the truth about her son's death. *So bloody well get on with it, Liz Haynes!*

Half an hour later they were back in the car, on their way home to Cannon Farm.

They were both very quiet. In her previous life, Liz had often been obliged to interview the bereaved. She had never got used to it, nor could she predict how people would react. It was David's first time, and she felt for him.

'You okay, kid?' she asked.

'Uh huh,' he said. 'Just kind of assimilating what I learned about Alex.'

'And that is?'

His voice was slightly dreamy. 'I think we had a lot in common, but chose to move in different directions. He was an only child, he made his own little world as a kid — a room to himself, no siblings to influence him, like me. But he moved further away from people, while I moved towards them.'

'Deep.' Liz glanced at him. 'He did go to uni, though, that meant being with a whole lot of people.'

'A means to an end, that's all. A necessary evil, so he could achieve his aim. The career he chose is a solitary one. Working alone, your own boss. He had to brave uni, but he didn't choose to stay in halls, did he?'

'Very astute, Sherlock. So, what did you pick up more generally?'

David drew in a breath. 'I could be wrong, of course, but I don't get the impression he was a total loner. I reckon he was someone who was content in his own skin but would have made a good solid mate. He certainly had an enquiring mind — you could tell from his work and the books on the shelves — so I totally get why he joined Toby in his search to find the story behind that woman in the window.' He frowned. 'From the photographs on his wall, it wasn't Alex who took those night-time pictures, not in a million years. That was Toby's work. Different style altogether.' He glanced at her. 'Can you get hold of Alex's phone and laptop? I'm willing to bet Alex made notes about it all.'

'I have his phone, it's in my handbag. Georgia said I could borrow it for a while. As to the laptop, her husband still has it. She said she'd ask him if he was happy for us to take it and she'd ring me.'

'That laptop could be vital,' David said urgently.

Liz knew that only too well. 'While you were up in Alex's room, Georgia told me he had a spare laptop, but there was no sign of it in his lodgings. That puzzled her. It was only a backup, in case anything happened to his main one, but he was careful with his things, and it just wasn't there.'

'Mmm, that is odd.' David thought for a moment. 'We need to get inside both their rooms in the student house, don't we? How do we go about that?'

'I need to think about that one,' she said. There were ways, but Liz didn't think the normal route would work this time. The most straightforward way to get inside a house like that would be to ask permission of the landlord, explaining who you were, exactly what you wanted, and why you were there. More often than not people turned out to be perfectly happy to help. On this occasion, however, telling a landlord that two of his tenants might have been murdered, and that someone had used his heater as the murder weapon, was probably not a wise move. She had seen a report on the deaths on an online news site, in which the landlord had sworn that all the heaters and fires were serviced regularly, and she suspected he was telling the truth.

'I've got an idea.' The voice from the passenger seat was thoughtful. David was evidently well committed to this.

'Let's hear it then,' she said.

'Well, why don't I pretend to be looking for lodgings? I can chat to the guys who are living there and ask if the landlord would let me and my mum have a look at one of their rooms at some point? Of course, he may have let the rooms already, but considering what happened, there's a good chance that no one wanted them.'

'So how *are* your acting skills, David?' she asked, smiling.

'No idea! The last play I was in was a Nativity. I was six years old and my role was the donkey, but I'm willing to give it a try.'

'There is another possibility, to save you from launching your new acting career as a solo performer. Georgia said they still had the key to Alex's room — they were going back to clean it. Alex had paid his rent until the end of the month. We could be the cleaners! While I do my bit in the room, you could talk to the housemates. Throw them a line about helping your mum with her cleaning business to earn a bit of money before you started college, when you'd be looking for digs. See if they know how we can get hold of a key to Toby's room.'

'Sounds good to me,' he said.

'I'll ring Georgia when we get home and set it up, hopefully for tomorrow.'

It wasn't perfect, and she'd have to run it past Matt, but one way or another, they needed to get inside those rooms.

As soon as they were back indoors, Liz rang Georgia Hallam and told her what they had in mind.

Georgia agreed at once. 'There won't be much cleaning to do — Alex was pretty fastidious — but there's nothing to see, Liz. It's just a room, all his things are here.'

'I know,' Liz said, 'but we should check, nevertheless, and I want to get an idea of the layout of the place, should this investigation go further. Though it's Toby's room that really interests us.'

'Maybe I can help you there. The landlord lives in the same street as the house. I could ring him, say you're a good friend of mine and that you'll be cleaning the room for me, as I can't face going there. You'll drop off the key with him when you've finished. And could you take a look at Toby's room while you're there, as your son is interested in renting it? It's bigger than Alex's room, so it's a reasonable thing to ask. I happen to know that the Unsworths aren't going to collect Toby's things till next Monday, so the room is still how it was when . . .'

Concealing her delight that the room hadn't been touched, Liz said, 'Thank you, Georgia, that would be perfect. We'll call tomorrow morning at nine to collect the key.'

She ended the call. 'We're in!' she said to David. 'Start working on your new persona, you're going undercover!'

CHAPTER EIGHT

Kellie had no idea what to do about the postcard. Her father was not in the best frame of mind at present, and she knew exactly what he'd say if she showed it to him. He would tell her that her brother was being ridiculous, she should take no notice of him, that if he was building hedgehog houses and studying wild birds he couldn't be very anxious, could he? He would remind her what the summer activities at her new school were costing him, she should be concentrating on her education and her future, not fretting over her little brother, who was probably just missing being spoiled by her. She had heard it so many times before: "Think yourself lucky, my girl. I never had your opportunities, so don't be ungrateful."

Kellie sighed. She *was* grateful, and she never underestimated the value of a "good start in life" — another of her father's sayings. But as far as she was concerned, her brother came first. Kellie tried calling Simon, but the phone was either switched off or the battery was flat. She sent him a text for when he bothered to look at his phone again. She considered writing to him, but decided against it.

Kellie went to the fridge and got herself a cold drink, still mulling it over.

By the time she'd finished it she'd made her decision. This afternoon she was going into town for a three-hour tutorial with her new art mistress, who was holding classes in her studio for some of her more talented pupils. The teacher's home and studio were in a street just off the town centre and, luckily, close to her bank. She had been managing her own money for a while now, and was careful. She knew she had enough money to cover what she was planning but she'd need cash as well. She'd get an earlier bus and visit the bank before attending her class.

That sorted, she found Trainline on her phone and booked her ticket for the following day.

She then sent her brother another text. *Look out for me tomorrow afternoon. I'll be with you then. Hang on, little bro!*

* * *

Albie Grant hadn't changed his routine in the past few years. A late breakfast in the town centre McDonald's, then down to the bookies, just as he'd always done.

Rather than ruin Albie's plans for that big win, Matt waited until he came out.

'Blimey! DCI Ballard! Haven't seen you in a while, guv'nor.'

Matt smiled at him. 'I'm retired, Albie, I'm nobody's guv'nor now, so call me Matt.'

Albie looked horrified. 'Dunno if I can do that. Not with the DCI who put half my family away. Not that I blame you — if the silly buggers were daft enough to get caught, it was their fault, weren't it?'

This was followed by a loud guffaw. 'So, what brings you over to this neck of the woods, sir?'

'If you can spare half an hour for a pint, Albie, I'll tell you,' Matt said.

'Always got time for a quick one, as well you know, squire. How about the Hanged Man? That's my local.'

They strolled along to the pub, where they found a table tucked well out of the way. Matt got the drinks in.

'Well, I gotta say being retired suits you. You look ten years younger now you've left the rozzers be'ind.' Albie grinned broadly. 'Funny, but you always reminded me of that actor that plays Judge John Deed on the telly — dead good-looking for an older bloke. I reckon you're even more like him now!' He gave another guffaw. 'But retired ain't quite the word, is it? You're still out there chasing the bad guys, just not officially like?'

Matt smiled wryly. 'Hard to shake the old job off, Albie, especially when you'd been doing it as long as I had.'

'Bet it galls you, though, not to be able to clap them old bracelets on and shout, "You're nicked, sunshine!"'

'Oh, we have our moments.'

'I bet you do. Yeah, and then you 'and 'em over to the boys in blue to do all the boring paperwork. Nice one!' Suddenly, he became serious. 'So, why've you come lookin' for me then?'

'Because of those amazing ears of yours. The ones that miss nothing from the streets.' He raised an eyebrow. 'There'll be a small remuneration for your troubles, of course.'

'You're a gentleman, DCI Ballard.' He inclined his head. 'So, what 'ave my *amazin'* ears supposed to have heard?'

'Bad feeling in low places in Fenfleet. I've been told that even Race is bricking it.'

'You heard right, and it's not just Fenfleet.' Albie lowered his voice. 'It's here in Greenborough, bad enough to give even the Leonards the willies, and it's in Saltern-le-Fen too.'

Matt let out a low whistle. 'Hellfire, that is bad.'

'What's really bad is that no one knows what the fuck is going on. You wouldn't credit it, would you — people like Eddie Race and Raymond Leonard being in the dark about what's going on in their patches. It's a scary thought.' Albie took a slug of his beer. 'Best I can do is keep you updated, let you know if anything shows its ugly face.' He shrugged. 'Sorry, Matt, I'd help you if I could, but I think you've had a wasted journey.'

'Far from it, Albie. I thought it was a local problem, I didn't realise it was so big. And at least I know that if anything occurs in this neck of the woods, you'll be keeping tabs on it.'

Matt had always liked Albie. He wasn't a crook — okay, he handled a bit of hot merchandise now and then — but he spent most of his time as an old-style market trader. The rest of the family were rogues — one or two of them pretty nasty — but Albie and his old mum had been happy as pigs in shit with their pitch in the marketplace and generally stayed on the right side of the law. There was even a memorial plaque on the cobbles dedicated to Gladys Grant, who'd set up her first stall in the days following the end of the Second World War.

Matt gave Albie one of his new cards and a twenty-pound note. 'Ring me, text me, whatever you like, just keep those ears to the ground, okay?'

Albie lifted his glass in acknowledgement. 'Will do, squire, will do. And it's nice to see your face again.' He pushed the money into his pocket. 'And now you've ditched the warrant card, I can thank you. You were always straight with me, and I appreciate it — especially when Mum accidentally tried to offload those hooky microwaves!'

They laughed at the memory of the old days. Matt had been in uniform then, and the microwave incident wasn't the only time young Sergeant Matt Ballard had saved the old girl's bacon with a swift warning. It had paid off, too; Albie had returned the favour a hundredfold.

Matt got up to leave.

'I don't know if it works this way,' said Albie softly, 'but if you do get to find out what's up before me, would you give me the nod?'

Matt nodded. 'For you, Albie, yes. I'll keep in touch.'

Matt was in luck. After a short walk away from the main street, he discovered that his other contact was at home.

Arthur Skeldyke was the brother of an old detective inspector Matt had worked under for several years. Arthur had provided useful background in a lot of cases, having an encyclopaedic knowledge of the Fenland area, coupled with a passion for architecture. Matt prepared himself to receive a long lecture on Fenfleet's glorious past, but if he could just keep the old guy focused on the merchant's house and the neighbouring buildings, he might walk away with some very useful information.

'Matthew! Dear boy. What a surprise! How fortuitous, I was just making a pot of coffee. Come in, come in!'

Matt held up a paper bag. 'I brought some doughnuts — hope you still like them.'

Arthur flung the door back and smiled like a delighted child. 'Oh, but I do! Let's go inside and catch up on old times.'

Matt followed him in. 'Actually, Arthur, lovely as it is to see you again, I'm here on business. I need your help.'

'Well, sad as I am to hear that, you've undoubtedly come to the right place.' He wagged a finger at Matt. 'But first things first — coffee, doughnuts, and an update on your new life outside the force. And I insist, or I won't help you.' His eyes twinkled, reminding Matt of a mischievous goblin from a kid's storybook.

The diminutive Arthur sported a slightly unkempt beard. He had shaggy grey hair and bright eyes set in a creased and smiley face. He liked to wear antiquated smoking jackets with baggy knee breeches and long, brightly coloured socks. But his eccentric appearance belied a brain sharp as a tack, and a memory that stored more information than the Police National Computer — *if* you could keep it on track.

The coffee was as delicious as ever. Matt sipped appreciatively while rattling off an abridged version of his life from retirement to his present occupation as a PI. 'So now I'm here asking questions again, just like I used to years ago. The case I'm presently investigating is a very serious matter and might involve the deaths of two young students.'

The old man frowned. 'How can I help?'

Matt told him what he knew of the house and the location.

Arthur's face lit up. 'Oh yes. I know that place very well. In fact, some years ago I wrote a paper on the rise and fall of trade and prosperity in that very area. Now, let me think, do I still have my research papers? I do believe I do!' He went over to a bookcase groaning with books and files, and began ferreting around in a box file of loose paperwork. 'Never throw anything away, that's my motto. It's a waste of valuable time sorting out things that might or might not be required again. If they turn out not to be needed, well, when I shuffle off my mortal coil, someone — probably my younger brother — will throw the lot in a skip and do the job for me. Aha! Got it!' He returned to his chair and began rifling through a mess of handwritten sheets of A4 paper.

Matt watched. He had been here before and knew that Arthur would come up trumps. He always did. 'Google said the family who owned it were called Latimer, importers from Asia, but that was it,' he said.

'No, no! That's all wrong! Google hath blundered! The Latimers owned a couple of other places along that street but not the merchant's house.' He held up a sheet covered in scribbles. 'Garnett! That's it, the original owner of that wonderful old building. Benjamin Garnett, a merchant and a trader and a very rich man indeed.' He passed Matt several sheets of paper. 'I remember now. It was the devil's own job to find out anything at all about that building, or those nearby. The Latimer family didn't own it, that was rubbish. Those notes will give you a wealth of information about the days when the house was a coveted treasure of a place where home and business merged. But as to its recent history, well . . . nightmare!'

He set down the box on the floor and drained his coffee cup. 'Take it all, Matt. As I say, the later stuff might not be of too much use, but at least this will point you in the right direction.'

Matt was delighted, albeit not a little daunted at those spidery scribbles. Not a typed sheet or computer printout among them.

Arthur laughed at his expression. 'You'll get used to it quite quickly. You know me. I was always a technophobe, and I shall remain that way, until my thoughts are consigned to that skip I was talking about.' He sat back, his hands in his lap. 'In later years there was a great deal of controversy over the rightful ownership of that old house. It had something to do with a clause in a will, caveats that were contested, I have no idea by whom, but it was part of the reason why it fell into disrepair.'

'You said something about home and business merging?' asked Matt.

'Oh yes. Benjamin Garnett, who was the original merchant, traded in various exotic goods, mainly from the East. His family owned land in India, where they grew the most magnificent pomegranates. Then they realised that these fruits could be grown in southern Europe, and added another string to their bow by introducing this expensive luxury to English tables.' Arthur raised a finger. 'Do you know, it was initially referred to as a "poumgarnet", a play on *pomme*, or apple, I believe, and perhaps a conscious allusion to the fruit's deep red seeds. Garnett. See? Look up their name when you have a moment, and you'll see it means a grower or seller of pomegranates. Isn't that satisfying?'

Matt grinned, picturing himself casually tossing that particular nugget into a dinner conversation. 'I always learn something new when I visit you, Arthur. But you were saying about the house and the business.'

'Apologies. I digress. Yes, the house was originally constructed as a luxurious dwelling, but knowing the value of the various goods he imported, Garnett added a series of massive storerooms on three levels, which could be accessed from both inside and outside the house. He employed a nightwatchman with a vicious dog to patrol the place, thus ensuring the safety of his precious commodities.'

Matt's mind did cartwheels as he imagined the different uses such a derelict property might have — a repository for stolen goods or other illegal commodities, for one. He recalled the security firm that Liz had discovered. What was that all about? It wasn't something a gang of crooks would do. It had to be the owners, whoever they were, or people still contesting that old will Arthur had mentioned. That had to be investigated.

It took him a while to take his leave — Arthur seemed determined to give good value for his doughnuts.

'Come back any time, Matt. And hang onto the notes for as long as you want. Do let me know the outcome of your most interesting case, and if my small contribution was of help. It's always rewarding to know that what may appear to be stuffy old history is actually valuable to the police.'

Matt finally managed to make his escape. Congratulating himself on a very productive morning, he hastened back to tell Liz and David what he'd found out.

* * *

Inside Minty Agutter's house, Jude found signs of a struggle — furniture overturned, things broken. Blood. What he didn't find was Minty. His first thought was that his bastard of a partner had gone over his head and had Minty terminated anyway. On second thoughts, he was too bloody good at his job for Mr Palmer to risk upsetting him that badly.

He looked about him. No, something else had happened here. But what?

He made his exit. He could do no good here. Still haunted by his father's beseeching look, he was desperate to find Minty and the reason behind that single rasped word. He admitted to being hurt. After all, he'd spent two years caring for his father, visiting him every day, only to be repaid with not his own name but that of some old villain his father had once been banged up with.

Jude slipped from the house and returned to his car. He'd need to enlist help in tracing Minty's whereabouts. He had a lot of questions to ask the old lag — if he was in a fit state to talk. Perhaps the blood was someone else's. And as soon as he'd got people out on the streets, he had another man to visit. Mr Sodding Palmer.

Jude was damned good at killing people, but he had another talent, too — spotting a liar. If Palmer had indeed taken matters into his own hands, he would know. And if Palmer had gone behind Jude's back, harmed Minty before he solved the puzzle concerning his dad, he'd live to regret it. Jude had a long memory. He could wait. But when they'd finished with their current lucrative caper, rough justice would be served. He would make Palmer pay.

* * *

Like some distraught wraith from a story by Poe, Jessie paced the floor, wringing her hands.

'For heaven's sake, woman. Relax, can't you?' Anna was rapidly losing patience.

'But I saw him talking to those men, Anna! How do we know they're not planning to snatch him? Oh dear, oh dear!'

'How many times do I have to tell you? They were twitchers! Bird enthusiasts. You've seen them, Jessie. At certain times of the year they turn up in their droves in this part of the marsh to tot up sightings of rare birds.'

'Well, yes, but it's the perfect disguise, isn't it? A pair of binoculars and you have an excuse to talk to kiddies, to get close to them, to . . . oh dear, this is terrible.'

Anna shook her head and gave a long sigh. 'You aren't going to let this rest, are you, Jessie? It's making you ill, you know.'

'Probably,' Jessie twittered. 'I'd just die if something happened to that dear, dear boy while he's in my care. And sweet Kellie, what would I tell her? That I'd lost her darling little brother? I can't face it. I just can't.'

'Then you know what you have to decide, don't you? Send him home, or take him away for a few days, like you planned.' Anna stared hard at her. 'What's it to be?'

'I can't send him home. He's getting so much better and, well, I don't want him to leave me just yet, I really don't.'

'I'll get the cases down from the top of the wardrobe, shall I?' Anna stood up. 'It's for the best. And when you feel stronger, we'll come back and start again, like we said.'

'Is this the right thing to do, Anna dear?' She could hear the plaintive wail in her voice and despised it, but she needed her friend to be strong for both of them.

'Oh yes. It's not just the right thing to do, it's the only thing.' Anna looked at her sorrowfully. 'You need to get away from here, from the marsh. You can't afford to allow all these worries and fears to build up again, like they did before, can you? Take a break, along with your boy, and get better. I'll help you all I can, I promise.'

'You always do, dear Anna. So, yes, get the cases down, please.'

* * *

After lunch, the private investigators, along with their new recruit, held a briefing in the Incident Room. The white-board now had a central picture, the enhanced photograph taken by Toby Unsworth. It was an odd image to see on an investigation whiteboard, strange and almost nightmarish, real and uncanny at the same time. That ghostly face staring out through a filthy pane of glass looked totally out of place. Matt decided he preferred the good old police ID mugshot. You knew where you were with one of those.

Now that he knew something of the history of the house, he was even more concerned about that woman, and her reason for being in that old building.

After they had shared their morning's findings, they broke for a few minutes while Liz made them all coffee. It gave them a chance to mull everything over before they decided what to do next. By the time Liz came back with the mugs, Matt said, 'I think we all agree that we need to see what you and David can come up with at the students' house before we go any further.'

'Makes sense,' said Liz. 'Hopefully, one or more of Alex and Toby's old housemates will help us fill in some of the gaps in our boys' timeline. We've already added a couple of new questions to the growing puzzle, one of which is Alex's missing spare laptop.'

'There's a chance he lent it to one of the other students,' suggested David. 'I'll do my best to find out when I talk to them. If it's all right with you, I'll spend a bit of time this afternoon perfecting my cover story. For instance, if I'm telling them I'm getting a place at their uni, I need to pick a course the uni holds.'

'Absolutely, and make it something you really are interested in, not a subject that sounds impressive but that you know nothing about,' said Matt. 'And try to keep it simple. Don't invent too much or you'll forget what you've said to whom.'

'Yeah, good advice,' said David. 'I was thinking about what Mrs Hallam is going to say to the landlord, and I thought I'd tell them my "mum" knows Alex's family well — that's why she's helping them by cleaning the room — but that I'd only met Alex once or twice. I'm not sure I'd chat openly about a dead mate to a complete stranger.'

'Good idea,' said Matt, 'but keep it vague, and tread warily. You don't have to prove anything to Liz or me, and don't be disappointed if you come up with nothing — that's par for the course in this game.' He looked at Liz. 'I guess you and I'd better start sifting through Arthur Skeldyke's handwritten notes.' He pulled a face. 'Can't say I'm looking forward to it, but it has to be done.'

'Before I join you, I'm going to ring Richard Lake, Alex's tutor, and ask if we can talk to him. I think I'll be pretty safe in saying it's a private investigation on behalf of the Hallam family and asking for complete discretion. I think I should suggest that it's to help put Mrs Hallam's mind at rest, rather than that we believe there has been a serious crime. We have to take a few people into our confidence, or we won't get anywhere.'

'So long as it's no one connected to that merchant's house, I agree,' Matt said, 'but just be really careful who you open up to.' Matt would have preferred to say nothing to anyone, but how could they find answers without asking questions of people? 'One last thing. Are we all in agreement that we continue as we are, working for Mrs Hallam at her request, and that we don't approach the police yet?'

They all looked up at the whiteboard and its single, mysterious piece of the puzzle.

'I think we need more before we go to Charley Anders,' Liz said.

David seemed somewhat taken aback and not a little pleased to be included in this decision. 'I think, as private individuals, we have a better chance of getting answers from people. We don't represent a threat, we're not authority figures, just members of the public.'

'I'm good with that. So, to work.' Matt looked at the box of papers and heaved a sigh. 'Why do I think I've picked the short straw here?'

CHAPTER NINE

By late afternoon, Jude was growing angry. He had mobilised a small army in the search for Minty, and they had come up with a big fat zero. He had kept away from Mr Palmer, having given him the benefit of the doubt, but now he was on his way to see him.

Beneath his calm exterior, Jude was boiling. Again and again he heard his father's rasping voice. *Minty.* Why?

Palmer looked up when he entered. 'Trouble?'

Jude shrugged. 'Not as such. Just a bit of a puzzle, Mr Palmer. You see, I went to our Minty's place and when I got there, he'd disappeared. I just wondered if you'd, er, made an executive decision to . . . You know.'

Palmer frowned. He looked perplexed.

'What, offed him myself? You must be joking.' Palmer pulled a face. 'I have no idea where the old bastard is, and I've certainly not taken out a contract on him. You should know by now that I leave that kind of thing to you. I expect your warning has sent him scurrying away into some hole somewhere, until he thinks it's safe to crawl home again.'

Jude had to admit that Palmer's surprise looked genuine, but he was still suspicious. Jude didn't trust Palmer — he didn't trust anyone in this game. He decided to back off and instead gave Palmer an update from the streets, assuring him that no more unwanted interest had been shown in any of their places of business. He liked that term. "Places of business". It gave an air of respectability to an activity that was anything but. 'Are we scheduled for the next delivery as arranged, Mr Palmer?'

Palmer nodded. 'All on track so far. It'll be finally confirmed at seven this evening. I'll ring you the minute I hear from the courier. Is everything in place to receive our, er, "commodity"?'

'All arranged, and our people are aware that extra stealth is essential, after our recent minor irritation.' A disruption ending in two deaths was far from being a "minor irritation" but Jude merely continued, 'I've increased personnel, everyone's going to be doubly cautious. I've put a few diversions in place and changed the routes again. I'll be frank, Mr Palmer, it would have been better if we'd let a bit more time pass before we took a new delivery, but it wouldn't do to let our supplier know there's a problem, so I've covered all bases and tried to pre-empt any possible glitches.'

'Good, good.' Palmer nodded. 'It's a big one this time, so I'm pleased you've upped security.' He gave Jude what he obviously believed to be an enigmatic smile. 'Even you'll be pleasantly surprised by the returns on this particular shipment, as I've negotiated a deal with a new buyer, who is very interested indeed in what we have to offer and is prepared to pay top dollar for quality.'

In Jude's opinion a man with hair dyed that badly ought not to even try looking enigmatic. It just didn't work. Though he had to admit that even if Palmer was a total failure in terms of his personal appearance, he was a brilliant negotiator. This was why they worked so well together, despite having no real liking for each other. 'Music to my ears, Mr Palmer.'

'So, Jude, concentrate on seeing this cargo through to safety, and don't fret over that old lag, Minty. He'll turn up when he thinks the heat's off, and if you are as certain that he won't talk as you say you are, that's fine by me. I trust you.'

Like hell you do. Jude ignored the part about Minty and simply said, 'The consignment will come in like clockwork, never fear.'

Meeting over, Jude left. He would do the job, and do it well, because he wanted the money. But his father's hoarse voice still rang in his ears. No way was he going to forget Minty Agutter.

* * *

Henry was back in work mode. He amazed even himself by the ease with which, like throwing a switch, he moved from one world to another. Yesterday he had been a man steeped in carnal pleasure. Today, he threw all his energy into the task Eddie Race had given him.

He had known it would come down to him in the end. As the whispers and speculation mounted, with no conclusions being reached, he had known that sooner or later Eddie Race, or one of the others, would come to him.

Now, he was becoming a little intrigued on his own account. He had already put out feelers and reaped no return, which was odd. Henry had the reputation of paying very well for reliable information, which meant that none of his contacts had anything to tell him. He would have to take a different route to get to the truth.

Henry had more than one persona. His current one required him to dress in a tailored Hugo Boss suit, hand-made Italian shoes and a crisp Oxford shirt. He checked his elegant Swiss wristwatch and listened out for his taxi. He had thirty minutes to get to Greenborough, attend a swift business meeting and proceed to the best hotel in the area for a meal. This should give him an idea of where to start with Eddie's assignment.

The meeting, little more than a brief report and discussion, was over in half an hour. The real business was always conducted during the more relaxed dinner afterwards. The members of this group were an eclectic mix of those involved in running commerce and trade in the four main towns in this part of the Fens.

Tonight, Henry engineered things so that he was seated next to Niamh Conran, the editor of the local paper, the *Fenlander*. Niamh, a splendid-looking woman with red hair and piercing green eyes, was a rich source of information from all sorts of places. Henry had often fantasised about burying his face between Niamh's ample breasts, but she was happily attached to a nymph-like young woman some ten years her junior. Tonight, however, Henry wasn't thinking of her bosom. He wanted her brain and her local knowledge.

They ate and chatted amicably for a while, then Henry casually said, 'I was in Fenfleet yesterday, and I wondered what was going on. I'm very susceptible to atmosphere, you know.'

She put her fork down and took a sip of wine. 'Whatever it is, it's escalating. People are worried. I'm worried. I love my town, and I don't want to see bad things happening there.' She turned her startling green eyes to him and whispered, 'Go carefully. I know you, but if you get involved this time, it could backfire. I believe someone is moving in and stealing territory that doesn't belong to them. The grapevine says it's not just here, either. It's like a spider's web, encompassing Greenborough, Fenchester and even Saltern-le-Fen.'

'Who do I talk to, Niamh? Someone must know something.'

'I'll give you a name, but it didn't come from me, okay? It might be a blind alley, but you could try a woman called Ava. She works as a physio at the sports and fitness centre on the Fenfleet Road. You should have no difficulty chatting her up, she likes fit bodies. What you need to find out about are some new clients of hers that arrived a couple of months ago, and are single-minded about maintaining an extremely high level of fitness.' She paused. 'Like as if their lives depended on it.'

Henry raised an eyebrow. 'Very interesting. Thank you, Niamh, I appreciate that.'

'You can show that appreciation by keeping me in the loop. I won't publish what you find, it's purely for my own peace of mind.'

He nodded. 'Of course, one good turn and all that.'

Henry returned to his steak. It was time he joined a gym. That aching back of his could do with a good pummelling. He might just ask Ava.

* * *

Bernie Wetherby, the owner of the Pear Tree House, welcomed Matt, Liz and David like long-lost friends. Matt knew that their closeness was due to their shared grief over the loss of Adie but he still liked seeing Bernie. In a funny kind of way, their friendship kept Adie alive.

They had secured a table that looked out onto the gardens of the picturesque old restaurant. It was twilight and the solar lights were coming on, lending the place a magical air. David expressed his surprise that the Fens had so many good restaurants and inns. Laughing, Liz said that there was little else to do in this vast rural area but eat.

David was even more impressed when the first course arrived. Matt found his enthusiasm quite gratifying. Unlike most people, who called the Lincolnshire Fens flat and uninteresting, David praised the huge skies, the endless space. Matt knew they had much to contend with — the slow-moving tractors and other farm vehicles, the bitterly cold winds blowing in from the North Sea. The mud. But he still loved it, and he wouldn't live anywhere else.

'So, did you learn anything exciting from those handwritten notes?' asked Liz. 'If you could decipher them, that is.'

'A whole lot of history, that's for sure. I get the impression that the place is disused because it still belongs to the Garnett family, though it's been almost impossible to verify it.' He pulled a face. 'I've hardly scratched the surface yet, but I can't afford not to plough through the lot.' He accepted a dessert menu from the waiter. 'You sounded well impressed with Richard Lake, the boys' tutor.'

'I certainly was. He seems like a lovely man, so cut up about his two students. I have a feeling that what happened to them is going to stay with that man for the rest of his life. He's struggling to come to terms with it, I could see. Anyway, he's offered to talk to us about the two boys, so tomorrow, after I've done my cleaning, we'll call at the uni and see him.' She glanced across at David. 'It's great having you with us for this particular investigation because your presence makes everything seem so natural. We're nothing but an older woman and a young man calling in to see a tutor.'

David looked up from his menu and grinned. 'Frankly, I don't think my real mum minds losing me to you at all.'

Liz opened her mouth to respond but just then, Matt felt a hand on his shoulder. He turned to see Bernie smiling down at him. 'Want to come to the back office after your dessert? Oh, and I recommend the chocolate lava cake. Our chef makes the best I've ever tasted.' And then he was gone.

Matt wondered if the Fenland grapevine had already sent messages about the underworld unrest in Bernie's direction. After all, he hadn't mentioned anything when he booked.

After dessert, which was indeed superb, he left Liz and David chatting over coffee and made his way to Bernie's office.

Bernie shut the door behind him. 'Delicious as it might be, I'm guessing you're not here just to sample my lava cake?'

Matt returned the smile. 'You're right, of course. I seem to have inherited something that might be too big for me to handle.'

'No such thing.'

'Don't be so sure. I might well have to resort to DCI Charley Anders before long.'

Bernie sat forward, elbows on the desk. 'I'm assuming it's about this rumour of an imminent takeover. That's certainly big. It covers the whole area, so I've heard.'

'Even that's not for certain, Bernie. So far, we have two "accidental" deaths, if you see what I mean.'

'In other words, murder.' Bernie drew his eyebrows together. 'That is nasty.'

'Two young men, university students who appear to have seen something they shouldn't.' At the mention of the two dead boys, Matt felt a weight descend on his shoulders. 'The police have accepted the coroner's report on cause of death and dismissed one of the boys' mothers as a hysteric, so I'm gathering some actual proof before I try to tell them they're wrong.'

'You're sure they *are* wrong, I suppose?' asked Bernie. 'Forensics plus a coroner's report is pretty definitive.'

'If Professor Rory Wilkinson had conducted the tests, I'd probably have accepted their word,' said Matt, 'but I'm told he's taking a holiday in warmer climes, and we have a temporary Home Office pathologist at the moment. Plus, things are coming to light that point in a more sinister direction.'

Bernie exhaled. 'One of my girls is at uni, and I worry about her all the time.'

'Only one?' Matt asked, knowing Bernie had twins.

He laughed. 'Yes, Tanya's the academic. She's taking psychology and says I'm the perfect subject for a case study, cheeky mare! Lyndis has gone the apprentice route. Wants to be an engineer, would you believe?'

'Handy!' said Matt. He recalled that the twins, despite being very close, had always had different interests.

'I must say, I'd rather have an engineer in the family than a psychologist.' Bernie chuckled briefly. 'So, how can I help? I assumed you were here to ask about the takeover, not two students' deaths.'

'The reason for their murder, if indeed that's what it is, relates to one particular place in Fenfleet, but we can't be seen making enquiries about it. Do you think you could find out if anyone has shown an interest in the place recently?' Though they were alone, Matt lowered his voice. 'And I can't stipulate strongly enough that this has to be extremely low-key. We have no idea who we're dealing with, but we know they're dangerous.'

'Give me the address.'

'It's an old merchant's house on the corner of Cutler's Alley and—'

'Bowmaker's Lane. I know it.' Bernie thought for a moment. 'An old, er, associate of mine heard that there was a storeroom attached and thought he could use it unofficially, but it was a big no-no. A security firm paid regular calls, and it was shut up tighter than Strangeways.'

'That's the place all right,' said Matt. 'And we suspect someone else *is* using it unofficially.'

Bernie gave a surprised little grunt. 'Hats off to them, then, because my mate said he wouldn't touch it with a bargepole! Anyway, Matt, I'll have a little dig around for you. Don't worry, I'll keep it close and only use trusted contacts.'

'Ring me if you find anything, won't you?'

'Of course,' Bernie said, 'and if anything else occurs, let me know.' He paused. 'What do you reckon they're using that storeroom for then? Any ideas?'

Matt wasn't sure. He thought about that woman's face at the window. 'It could well be people trafficking — women to be sold into the sex trade. Or maybe cocaine? The storage area is apparently very big, so it could even house a counterfeit money press. Who knows?'

'So we really do need to find out,' mused Bernie, and lapsed into silence.

As always, their conversation drifted to Adie, until Matt went back to Liz and David.

'Mission completed?' asked Liz.

He nodded. 'If nothing else, it's another channel opened. Let's just pray this one results in something we can actually work with.'

* * *

As Fenfleet grew darker and colder, a number of people were out on the streets, their business shady as the night.

Jude was verifying that the way was clear for the new consignment. The drop was to take place the following night. The delay suited him, giving him more time to check for possible complications. A dark shadow, he followed the route, from delivery to final secure hideaway, checking and double-checking any possible cause for concern. There being none, he went home, satisfied that as long as no one cocked up, all would be well. Human error was the one thing you could never quite plan for, but they paid the highest rates, so the people they used were the best.

* * *

Unbeknown to him, Jude had been followed. Every step he took was dogged by a figure even more phantom-like than him.

He watched and waited, his eyes glittering, taking pleasure in the trail. It was satisfying to know he was better than them.

Finally, seeing that Jude had finished his careful checks, he melted away into the fine mist that came seeping up from the river, as if he had never been there.

* * *

Jessie lay in the darkness. All was ready for tomorrow and the start of what was, for her, a great adventure. She would have a few wonderful days alone with her beautiful boy, far away from any threat from those men on the marsh edge. She wouldn't have coped but for Anna, who had organised the whole thing down to the last detail. She had even drilled Jessie in exactly what she should say to Simon when she woke him at an unusually early hour.

She closed her eyes and tried to sleep, but her excitement made sleep impossible. The main thing was that darling Simon would be safe. They could spend some quality time together with no evil men stalking their every move. She loved the marsh, but not when her precious charge was staying with her. Then it was far too dangerous. The place they were going to was safe.

With the word "safe" on her lips, Jessie finally succumbed to sleep.

CHAPTER TEN

He didn't like to admit it, but David was nervous. It felt like his first interview for the police force, except he'd had a carefully rehearsed script for that. This was new territory, and despite Matt's repeated assurances that even if he messed up or got nothing, he wouldn't be letting them down, he didn't feel that way. He wanted to do well, to be worth something. His failure to make it through the Bleep Test had knocked his self-confidence badly. He had to get this right.

A solemn, grey-faced landlord, who called himself Lucas, had unlocked Toby's room for them, apologising for its state. He assured them it would be completely redecorated before it was let again. Then he had left them to their cleaning.

For over half an hour, they furiously scrubbed and polished, even though the room was far from dirty in the first place. Finally, Liz said she wanted to go through Toby's room undisturbed, so David headed downstairs to have a casual chat with the other occupants.

He found two of them in the living room, which was a tip. He dreaded to think what state the kitchen must be in. He pictured empty pizza boxes, unwashed plates. He decided not to accept tea if it was offered.

He took a deep breath and smiled, a little nervously. 'Hi, guys. I'm David. I'm helping my mum clean upstairs.' He paused. 'Er, I'm really sorry about what happened to your mates. You must miss them.'

This elicited no response, so he went on. 'I knew Alex. Not that well, but his mum and mine are friends. That's how come she offered to do this, save Mrs Hallam the distress of having to do it herself.'

The two students seemed to relax.

'Oh, right. That's kind of her.' A thin, rather scruffy boy of perhaps nineteen spoke up. 'I'm Cole, and this,' he pointed to his friend, who was sprawled on a tatty settee, 'is Brandon. Yeah, it's sincerely weird without Alex and Toby. I can't believe they're really dead. It doesn't seem possible, your mates just dying like that.'

Sadly, it is, thought David, *when someone sees fit to kill them*. He sighed. 'Yeah, they were both really talented too. Alex showed me some of the shots he took and I was like, wow. He reckoned Toby's work was awesome, but I never got to see any of that. Were you on the same course?'

Brandon's voice was deeper than Cole's, more middle-class. 'No, we're studying Applied Computer Science, and Liam, who's out today, is doing Law.'

David leaned against the door frame. 'I'm coming here myself soon. I'm going to be taking Biomedical Science.'

'Nice one. Here, wanna sit down?' Cole pointed to the sofa.

'Ah, better not. I might make myself too comfortable, then I'll have my mum after me.' He laughed. 'But listen, can I ask you guys something? I saw Alex a few days before he died, and he seemed really bothered by something, but he didn't want to talk about it. When we heard what happened, my mum wondered if that carbon monoxide had been affecting him for a while. Did he seem a bit, well, different to you?'

Had he gone too far? Did he sound natural? Then he saw the two students glance at each other.

'Actually, we thought they were up to something,' said Cole flatly. 'Or more likely in trouble. In and out all hours of the day and night, and both of them looking like shit.' He sniffed. 'Alex was a clean freak, wasn't he? Well, he even stopped yelling at us for not cleaning the kitchen and the bathroom, and that wasn't like him.'

'We were going to corner them and get them to tell us what was up,' added Brandon, not unkindly. 'We were pretty worried about them, but they looked so wound up when they came home that night — you know, when they died — that we didn't have the heart to do it. So I guess we'll never know what it was now.'

Cole flopped down next to Brandon. 'We did wonder if it was something to do with the rotten shite who got into Toby's room and stole his laptop.'

'Got in?' David feigned surprise. 'These places have fire-lock doors, don't they? Had he forgotten to lock it?'

'He swore he locked it,' said Cole. 'And he was usually real hot on that. They had expensive cameras, and they'd often check out specialist equipment from the college store when they needed it.'

'But no one could get through a fire-locked door,' Brandon added. 'I think he just forgot to lock it.'

'Didn't the police find out?' said David.

'We don't know if Toby ever reported it,' said Brandon. 'The police never came round, not until the accident.'

'So was it just Toby's laptop that was nicked?' David asked in as casual manner as he could muster. He was wondering about Alex's spare one.

'Seemed that way, they didn't mention anything else.' Brandon sighed. 'But Toby was doing his nut because of his coursework being stored on it.'

David wanted to ask more, but thought they might get suspicious. 'I'd better get back upstairs, I suppose. Might see you again, when I get to uni, or even before. My mum's asking your landlord about a room for me here.'

'Here?' said Cole, wide-eyed. 'Wouldn't it bother you that someone had died in it?'

David shrugged, thinking he'd rather sleep on the streets than lodge in this place. 'No, not really. It was an accident, after all. Nothing sinister.'

Cole still looked shocked. 'I don't even like being down here, let alone up there.' He jerked a thumb at the ceiling. 'We're thinking of finding somewhere else for our final year.'

'Oh well, might never happen. Anyway, better go. Take care, guys. Nice meeting you.'

David hurried back upstairs and found Liz making a meticulous check of Toby's room. 'Anything?' he whispered.

'Nothing of interest,' she murmured. 'Other than this.' She held up a piece of paper. He noticed the nitrile gloves. 'I found it screwed up in the bottom of the wastepaper bin.'

Written on it was a stark warning.

Go to the police and it will be the last thing you do!

David looked at Liz. 'The guys downstairs said they wondered if Toby ever reported the theft of his precious lap-top, since no one came to talk to them. I guess that's why.'

'Undoubtedly. We may be in luck. There's a small piece of sticky tape on it, that stuff is brilliant for forensics. If we ever do hand this case over to the police, it could be vital for trace evidence.' She looked around. 'Other than that, I've found nothing of any help.'

'No spare laptop? Alex's one that's missing?'

'No, and I've done a pretty careful sweep.' Liz looked puzzled. 'This is nothing like the way student accommodation usually looks, you know. It's far too tidy and clean. We know that Alex was obsessively tidy, but Toby as well? I'm wondering if someone has been over this room before us.'

'You should see downstairs, Liz! It's a total pigsty! Pizza boxes, a traffic cone in the corner of the sitting room with a pair of scanty knickers hanging on it, rows of empty bottles along the shelves, and everywhere grubby.'

'That's how I'd expect student accommodation to look, David. Not like this.'

'But don't villains make a mess when they do over a house? I thought they always trashed the place,' said David, puzzled.

Liz laughed. 'If they're looking for valuables and money, you're right, they'd rip the place apart. So it looks like whoever came in didn't want anyone to know they'd been here.' She gazed around. 'Think about it. The parents haven't been in yet, and the only other people would be whoever discovered them, the police, the doctor and the undertakers. Then, a bit later, whoever checked the appliances and declared the water heater faulty. Oh, and the landlord, who would check the place over and lock it up.'

And none of them would carry out a spring clean, David thought. He looked at the room again. The bed was in disarray after Toby's body had been removed. The sleeping bag Alex had been using remained screwed up and cast aside. Some of the furniture was disturbed, probably to facilitate the removal of the bodies, and there were muddy footprints on the carpet. But Toby's desk and workstation, the shelves and windowsills — all clean. Too clean. No trace of dust, the surfaces shiny. 'You're right,' he whispered. 'Someone has been through all Toby's stuff, then wiped the place clean.'

'And what do you make of that?' Liz indicated a small handbasin in the corner, probably left from when the house had been a family home and this simply a bedroom.

David looked. Sure enough, the water heater above it had "Condemned" tape across it, and a large red and yellow sticker with "Danger" written along the top, and "Safety Warning, Do Not Use" emblazoned across it. But instead of the old appliance he had expected to see, this one appeared to be relatively new. He saw Liz smiling at him.

'It can happen, even with newer ones. A fault, a clogged flue or ventilation outlet. We had a death from one of these not long before I left the force. Pet hair and dust had collected in the air intakes, and the fuel wasn't combusting properly. The gas man told me that weather conditions can play a part in keeping gas inside the property instead of being expelled. Very sad.'

'Surely there's a CO alarm here? Aren't they a legal requirement nowadays?' David asked.

'They are,' Liz said. 'Private landlords are required to have a carbon monoxide alarm on every storey of the property, along with a smoke detector. There's one here, but I'm not sure how often he checked the batteries, because the students had disabled it.'

'Oh shit! So, indirectly, they assisted in bringing about their own deaths.'

'Well, let's say *someone* had disabled it. The batteries were gone,' Liz said. 'And I know it's a favourite trick of students, especially if they are smoking weed, to take them out, then put them back in case of inspection, but I'm thinking that someone else might have done it.'

'Oh, I get it,' David said. 'You mean the killer.'

'That would be my guess. Anyway, I don't think there's more to be gathered here, so let's check Alex's room one last time and take Toby's key back to the landlord.'

Alex's room had looked fine before. Now it was pristine. David absent-mindedly took a last look around and noticed a tiny white scrap of paper sticking up from behind the empty workstation. He leaned over to brush it away, then realised that it was the corner of a larger piece, stuck to the back of the desk between it and the wall.

Calling over to Liz, he lifted out a large A4-size photograph. Attached to it was a note inscribed with a date, time, and what to David looked like a coded message until he realised it was the readings from a photographic light meter, the shutter speeds and f-stop aperture size that the photographer had used.

He let out a soft whistle. 'That is beautiful!'

Liz came and looked over his shoulder. 'It has to be one of Toby's, surely? It's a night-time shot.'

David shook his head. 'No, I think it's Alex's. For all his praise of Toby's work, I think Alex had the edge. And the note is definitely Alex's neat writing. I saw plenty of it in his room at home, remember?'

The composition was simple but perfect, consisting of a tall standard lamp post situated in a grassy, tree-lined area scattered with old gravestones at the confluence of two paths.

He couldn't be certain, most likely it was just a shadow, or a bush, but David thought he could make out a figure disappearing into the darkness. He peered more closely, feeling oddly light-headed. The more he looked, the more convinced he became. This picture was as important as the first — the face in the window. It had certainly been important to Alex. He had hidden it, and it had almost been missed completely.

'I know that place,' breathed Liz. 'It's a tiny hamlet about eight miles out of Fenfleet, nothing but a disused twelfth-century church and a cluster of houses. I recall that actual spot because of Lamplight Larry.'

David blinked. 'Who?'

'Every night he would walk the four miles from a neighbouring village, patrol those paths for an hour and trudge home again. He was searching for his daughter who went missing while taking a shortcut through the old churchyard. He returned again and again, hoping to find some sign of what happened to her.'

'Does he still do it?' David asked.

'No, he died last year. He never found out where she went, or what happened to her, bless him. People say they still see him sometimes. There used to be a seat under that lamp, until the council removed it because druggies started to meet there, but lots of the old locals reckon they've seen him, sitting on the seat and waiting.' She took the picture from him. 'Let's bag it and get it home, and well done, super sleuth, I didn't notice it at all.'

For once, David felt genuinely pleased with himself. He had made a contribution, found something that could be really important. It felt good, bloody good.

'We need to get that key back to Mr Lucas, and then you can tell me about the other students.' Liz tugged on his arm. 'Let's go, kiddo.'

* * *

Jessie and Simon sat next to each other on the edge of a large old bed with a carved wooden headboard. She had her arm around his shoulders.

All in all, it had gone very well indeed. The boy had listened carefully. He had been anxious at first and had needed his inhaler, but she had soon calmed him down. The journey had been no problem at all, and now they were here.

'It won't be for long, will it, Auntie?' he asked uncertainly.

'Oh no, darling. Just a few days, that's all, then it will be time to get you home to Daddy and Kellie.'

'Oh, Auntie! What about Kellie? She'll be worried.'

'It's all right. I phoned them and told them we'll be away for a couple of days. I didn't mention the bad men, I just said I thought a little break would be fun. They want us to enjoy our adventure, and look forward to seeing you soon. Kellie sent her love, and your daddy told you to be good and look after your old auntie.' She gave a twittering laugh. 'Cheeky Daddy. Old indeed!'

He seemed to accept what she'd said. 'Are we really safe here, Auntie?'

'Oh yes, perfectly safe. It belongs to a dear friend of mine, who told me we can stay as long as we want, and no one will come here to frighten you. All right, Simon?'

'I really liked those men, Auntie. They told me a lot about the birds. I had no idea they were dangerous, they seemed so nice and friendly.'

'They would, darling. They were pretending. They think your parents are really, really rich, and will pay a big ransom to get you back. But they've got you mixed up with another boy who looks just like you, whose name is also Simon. So, if we hadn't run away, they would have kidnapped you.'

She had already told him this but went over it again, just to make sure he understood. She gave him a broad smile. 'We're on the run, Simon! Just like in the movies. Isn't it exciting?'

'Will it be in the papers when we get back home?' The hint of a smile was beginning to touch the corners of his darling little lips.

'Oh yes, certainly! You'll be a hero. It'll be on the front page. The brave boy who outwitted the gang who tried to kidnap him!'

'Really?' He almost inflated at the thought. 'That would be so cool!'

She could almost see him telling his school friends about his amazing adventure, and how he'd outwitted a gang of villains. But the thought of him leaving her, being back at home, was hard to bear. She pulled herself together. 'Right. Now you know what we have to do, don't you? We can't cook hot food because we don't want to attract attention. No one must know we are here. But we've got loads of nice goodies and snacks, so we'll survive for two days, won't we?'

'Phew! So we don't have to eat witchetty grubs and forage for weeds and stuff, do we?' Simon had seen a TV programme about survival and thought that eating grubs was totally gross.

'We have some lovely treats, don't you worry, not a grub in sight.' She stood up. 'I'd better get our beds sorted out ready for tonight, then we'll explore the house. I brought lots of games, and books and puzzles, so we won't be bored. I know you won't miss the TV much, and as I said, it's just a couple of days and then we'll be safe again.'

'But how do you know, Auntie?' he asked suddenly. 'I mean, if we're in hiding, you won't know where those men are, or if it's safe to go back out, will you?'

She gave him a reassuring smile. 'Because if it's not safe, my friend who's let us stay here will let me know. She's being very brave and watching them for me. And anyway, it shouldn't take them too long to figure out that they are hunting for the wrong boy.'

She unpacked the two top-quality sleeping bags she'd bought and unfolded a camp bed for Simon. She would use the old bed that was already there. Other than that, the room was already set up. She had done some of it earlier in the week, and Anna had done the rest. Anna had provided a camping stove so they could boil water. She hated the thought of not showering or washing her hair, but needs must. They had gone underground, so to speak, so she'd just have to rough it. She doubted Simon would mind going unwashed for a few days!

'Hey! This is really neat, Auntie! Is it for me?'

Simon had found the colouring book she'd got for him. It was an anti-anxiety book intended for adults to colour as therapy. It was full of beautifully drawn birds, and would be perfect for Simon. 'Yes, it's yours, darling.'

Jessie had often dreamed of this, spending days alone with just her boy. Now it was really happening, and the world could go hang!

CHAPTER ELEVEN

Matt rubbed his sore eyes. He needed fresh air. He had been trawling through Arthur Skeldyke's handwritten notes so long it had given him a thundering headache. With some relief, he remembered that he needed to check the mower for fuel before the gardener arrived the next day. He stood up and stretched.

It was a bright day but autumn was already taking hold. The trees were beginning to lose their leaves and the days were getting shorter. Matt had liked the idea of gardening but when it actually came down to it, he'd realised he wasn't that keen after all, and he actively disliked grass cutting — so a local man came every week in the summer and kept things from getting out of hand. It was a good-sized garden, and rather "au naturel," as Matt liked to term the overgrown wilderness of shrubs and trees. He and Liz had made a start on redesigning some of it, and now they had garden paths, flower beds and an arched pergola at the bottom of the lawn, covered with a climbing rose and a honeysuckle. They had been considering building a pond, as Liz had always loved watching the koi carp in a friend's pool, but a large grey heron and his regular visits had made them think again. They liked the heron, but to breed koi just for his lunch was rather extravagant.

Matt filled up the ride-on mower with fuel and checked the spare cans. They would do for another week but he made a mental note to get them topped up soon. Then he locked the garage and went down to the garden shed where the self-propelled petrol mower was kept for use on the smaller areas of grass.

The shed was big, having been used in his youth as a store for over-wintering racks of seed potatoes, other root vegetables, dahlia tubers and the like. Matt didn't like going there much, it reminded him of his father. When he got to it, he noticed that the padlock was open. His gardener habitually forgot to fasten it so he wasn't particularly surprised, but he certainly hadn't expected to see a miserable-looking figure lying on the floor wrapped in old car rugs.

'What the f—? Minty! Is that you?'

The figure disentangled himself from his coverings. ''Ello, Mr Ballard. Wondered when you'd turn up.'

'For heaven's sake, man, what are you doing here? Never mind for now, get up and come into the house. You can tell me after I get a hot drink inside you.'

In the kitchen, Minty sat with his hands around a mug of tea, slurping thirstily. Matt sat down opposite him and looked across the table at his dishevelled unexpected guest. 'Come on, Minty, let's have it.'

Minty sighed. He shook his head. 'Ever since that guy turned up at my house and warned me off, I've been frettin'. How come he knew so much about me and my past? Like I said, it had to be from my stretch inside, so I've been racking my brains tryin' to think who I was close to.' He drank more tea. 'Before I could work it out, I realised I was still being watched, and that bothered me. A lot.'

Matt tensed. 'Do you think it was because you met me?'

'No. I doubt that very much. It was my house they were watching, especially at night. Never saw anyone to be certain, but I just knew it. When you've been enough years in my old game, you do, don't you?'

Matt knew what he meant. Coppers, too, developed a sense for something not being right.

'Anyway, it really bugged me. How did that slimeball know so much? Then I saw him again. The man who warned me off. He was just standing outside my house, staring up at it like, then he was gone. That's when I thought the house weren't safe anymore, but I didn't rightly know what to do or where to go.'

'And you decided on my garden shed?' said Matt incredulously.

'No! Of course not! I've got a mate who lives in Norfolk. Lonely little place but the fishing's good, so I decided to pack a few bits and go missing for a week or so. I got all ready to take off yesterday morning when I had a funny turn, went all dizzy and fell over. I smashed a photo frame as I went down and cut me arm on the broken glass.' He rolled up his sleeve to reveal a large bloodstained dressing. 'Blood all over me carpet. Looked like one of your crime scenes.' He drained his mug. 'It was dead funny, really. There I am, sitting on the deck wondering what happened, and it came to me in a flash. I knew exactly where the guy who threatened me got his info from, and it scared the shit out of me!'

Matt looked at him expectantly. 'So who was it?'

'I spent quite a bit of time with a man who most people thought was a nasty piece of work, but there was something about him I liked. I'd say we even finished up friends.' He pulled a face. 'Until he got himself shot a couple of years back. Name of Sherriff. Paddy Sherriff.'

A whole string of offences unfurled in Matt's head, all connected to Paddy Sherriff. 'Bloody hell, Minty, he was a serious shitbag! Armed robbery, the lot. And he was your mate?'

'I saw the family man in him, Matt. The older guy who missed his wife and son. Don't think he was looking for pity, not him. Tough as old boots, he was. He knew the risks, knew that if he got caught — which he did — he'd have to pay. But that didn't stop him longing for his family. I got the best part of him, and we shared some secrets when we were locked up.'

'Okay, well, that's answered one question,' said Matt. 'But I don't get it. If you and Sherriff were friends and he's now dead, what made you so frightened?'

'*He* wouldn't hurt me, and anyway, he's not dead. Although he'd be better off if he was, in my opinion.' Minty pushed his mug towards Matt. 'Couldn't have another of those, could I?'

While Matt made more tea, Minty went on, 'He's in a swanky nursing home in one of the Fenfleet villages. I've visited a couple of times, but he's well away with the fairies, and I reckon he ain't coming back. Pitiful to see, when you remember what a big strong man he was.'

'Hmm. A big strong man who wasn't afraid to threaten people with a shotgun, as I recall,' Matt said.

'You're right of course, but that's as may be. Some might say it's a kind of poetic justice, but I still thought it was sad, so I sat with him and gassed on about the old days, then I left. I never hung about too long. Didn't want people to see me there, and the nurses told me his son visited every day, regular as clockwork, never missed.'

'Ah, I'm beginning to see where this is going,' said Matt.

'Yep. I guess you are. Now, I happened to mention to an old mate of mine about Paddy's son being so good and seeing him every day, and my mate swore like a trooper. He said the son was worse than his dad, much worse. Really good-looking, dead smart, and a psycho. Someone you definitely didn't want to mix with.'

'And was your visitor, the one who warned you off, good-looking and dead smart?' asked Matt, already knowing the answer.

'Oh yes. And I'm pretty sure that's how he knew so much about me. His dad told him. And, thinking about it, that may be why he just warned me off and didn't top me, like he did those kids. Because Paddy liked me.'

Matt passed him his second mug of tea. 'All that makes perfect sense, but I'm still not quite understanding how come you finish up in a shed on Tanners Fen and not by a peaceful river in Norfolk.'

'Fear, Mr B, pure and simple.' Minty stared into his cup like a gypsy into a crystal ball. 'I didn't want another call from this psycho, so, not being totally brain-dead, I hatched a plan. Sitting there happily bleeding into my favourite shag pile rug, it came to me. I'd get myself abducted. Well, make it look like that. The blood was real, and I'd broken a photo frame, so I tipped some furniture over so it looked like a right struggle had gone on. I left my bags packed, exactly where they were in the hall, and scarpered. If Paddy's psycho son came back, and I was sure he would, he'd think someone either killed me and took the body, or abducted me.'

Matt nodded in approval. 'Nice thinking. So you gave up on Norfolk?'

'Had to. It was too obvious. I went there a lot. He could have asked anyone and they'd've told him. So then I got a bit scared. I drove my car to a lock-up that I used to share with another bloke who's currently on remand and I left it there. Then I hitched a ride with a delivery driver to a mile or so from here and footed the rest of the way. I reckoned the last place he'd think to look would be a copper's garden shed.'

'Very true. You even shocked the copper! But you can't stay there, man! For a start, my gardener comes tomorrow, and I think he'd be a bit shocked to find you curled up with his precious mower.'

But Minty's customary humour and bravado had deserted him. He looked frightened and vulnerable. 'Can you help me, Matt? I don't know where to go or what to do. That psycho let me go once, but I'm sure he won't do it again.'

'You didn't take anything with you? What, nothing at all?' Matt asked.

'Money, a credit card and my spare car keys. That's it. I wanted it to look genuine, Matt. I just knew he'd be calling, and I had to get out, fast.'

'Right, well, a shower and a change of clothes might help you feel human again. I'm a fair bit bigger than you, but I'm sure I've got something that will do. Then, when Liz gets back, we'll decide what to do with you, especially as you're missing presumed dead! Come on, bring that tea with you, and let's get you sorted.' Matt sniffed. 'By the way, were they old dog blankets you were wrapped up in? Because you stink to high heaven.'

'I had noticed,' said Minty huffily. 'I found them in the lock-up, and yes, my friend used to have a guard dog. Been dead two years at least.'

'If that's the case, I'll bin them, shall I? If you need a blanket, I'll provide something that's been washed a bit more recently.' Matt opened the bathroom door. 'Get yourself in there, Swampy. There's clean towels on the rack, you'll find some plasters and dressings in the cupboard for that cut. Meanwhile, I'll find you some clothes.'

* * *

When she and David arrived home, Liz was surprised to see Minty sitting at the kitchen table. And weren't those some of Matt's old clothes he was wearing? Odd, she hadn't seen his car parked outside. She looked at Matt and he burst into laughter. 'Don't ask! You'd never believe it anyway.'

'Try me.'

Matt endeavoured to keep a straight face. 'I found him in the garden shed.'

She shook her head. 'You were right, I don't believe you.'

'Okay, okay, that's enough of the laughs,' grumbled Minty. 'Just fill them in, and do it quick, so we can decide what the hell I'm going to do.'

Liz stopped grinning. Minty sounded truly desperate. 'Okay. We're listening.'

Matt gave the two of them a brief account of Minty's plight.

'So who is this psycho son?' Liz asked, frowning. 'I remember Paddy — what copper doesn't — but who's the son?'

'My mate said he's called Jude,' said Minty. 'Which got me confused, cos when I knew Paddy, the only son he ever mentioned was a Fion or Finn. He never talked about no Jude.'

'But the description fits the man who warned you off,' added Matt. 'So he's either changed his name or Paddy had two boys, one of whom he never spoke of.'

In the ensuing silence, Liz wondered if the latter might be true. If one of Paddy's sons was really a psychopath, maybe he had done something that even his father, hardened criminal that he was, couldn't handle. But if that was the case, why would this very son pay daily visits to his father now he was in a nursing home? Whatever the case, whoever this man was, he'd scared the life out of Minty Agutter. 'Do you have anyone you trust completely, who would put you up for a while, Minty?' she asked.

Minty shook his head. 'I've got no family left that I know of, and they all wrote me off years ago anyway. My handful of mates are all local, other than the one in Norfolk, and I'd not wish a call from this guy on any of them.'

'Then you must stay here, for tonight at least. I'll make up the bed in the spare room. Meanwhile, we'll try to think of somewhere safe you can go, preferably out of the area. That's the best I can come up with. What say you, Matt?'

'Fine by me, if that suits you, Minty?'

Minty smiled. 'More than I hoped for. You're good people — for coppers.'

'Coppers *are* good people on the whole, you old rogue,' said Matt. 'Now, we'd better put our minds to sussing out a safe house for this ne'er-do-well — preferably not my garden shed.'

Liz had just finished making up the spare bed for their unexpected guest when she heard the doorbell ring. She looked out of the window and saw a 4x4 parked outside. Wondering who it was, she went downstairs.

A tall, smartly dressed man was standing in the hall. He looked haggard.

'This is Mr Hallam,' said Matt. 'My partner, Liz Haynes.'

The man held out his hand. 'Terry, please. I'm pleased to meet you, and I'm very grateful for the compassion you have shown towards my wife. As you can imagine, she is devastated and barely holding it together.'

Looking at him, Liz thought that Georgia wasn't the only one on the verge of breaking down. She led him to the lounge, pointed to an armchair and offered him a drink.

'Thank you, but I can't stay. I just came to give you this.' Almost reverently, he laid a laptop on the coffee table. 'When Georgia told me about it, my initial reaction was to say no, it's far too precious to let out of our keeping. Then I changed my mind when I thought about your reasons for needing it.'

'We appreciate that,' said Matt. 'And please don't worry. You'll have it back as soon as we've examined it for any clues as to what happened.'

Terry nodded and, evidently changing his mind about staying, sat down. 'Originally, I was against my wife's decision to hire you.' He rubbed hard on his chin. 'Not that I didn't think there was something not right about Alex's death, I did, but I wasn't certain. I thought we might be in denial, or feeling guilty at having let him down in some way. Now I have absolutely no doubt that Georgia was right to call you in, and you can be assured of my fullest cooperation.'

They thanked him and said they would do all they could to get to the truth.

'This might help you with the laptop.' Terry handed Liz a small spiral-bound notebook. 'Like most of us, Alex could never remember his different passwords. They're all in here.'

Liz breathed a sigh of relief. At least they wouldn't have that to deal with!

'Something you might find interesting, although I haven't had the courage to read it yet, is his reflective journal. You probably know that students keep a personal record of their learning experiences. They use it to explore and analyse ways of thinking and observe their responses to situations. It might help, it might not, but if nothing else it will give you an insight into my son's character and way of thinking.' Terry swallowed hard, and stood up abruptly. 'I need to go.'

'One more thing, Terry,' said Matt gently. 'Can we ask you something before you leave? It's important.'

'Yes, yes, of course.'

Matt looked sombre. 'Your wife mentioned that Alex wanted to talk to you about something related to your work. We now think we know what it was. We'd like to ask you the same question and, please, would you keep it just between us?'

Terry sat back down. 'That's been tearing me apart. The one time my son needed me and I wasn't there. Who knows, maybe if I'd spoken to him . . . ?'

'It would have made no difference, Terry,' said Liz quickly. 'If what we believe is true, it wouldn't have prevented what happened.'

'And the question?' Terry said.

'Well,' said Matt, 'we think he was going to ask you to make enquiries about a certain property in Fenfleet — who owned it and the like.'

'In Fenfleet?' Terry said. 'He rarely even went to Fenfleet. Why on earth would he be interested in a property there?'

Liz wondered how much Matt was prepared to tell this man at such an early stage in the enquiry. Then again, who better than a town planner to unearth such details?

'You see, Alex's friend Toby took a photo of an old property at night, and when he looked at it again, he saw something odd in it and told Alex. It obviously worried them and they may have tried to find out what was going on in there. So we assume Alex thought you might be able to tell him who owned the place.'

'Oh my God! Then whatever they were worried about got them killed?' Terry Hallam sat up straight. 'No offence, but surely we should go straight to the police?'

'Because we have absolutely no proof, and there are a number of other possibilities to be ruled out first,' Matt said.

'Please, Terry, we assure you that the moment we feel there's a case here, it will go directly to the DCI at Fenfleet police station,' added Liz, hurriedly. 'But as you know, they told your wife that they're satisfied that it was an accidental death. The forensics all point that way too, so they'll need a lot of convincing to change their minds.'

'What we are doing,' continued Matt, 'is building up a true picture of what happened, piece by piece, and we're having to tread very carefully as we do it, in case we're right. We cannot afford for anyone else to get hurt.'

'I suppose you're right,' Terry said rather dubiously.

'The thing is, if we tell you which place they were interested in, are you able to make discreet enquiries?' asked Matt. 'We don't want to place you or your wife in danger. I'd rather use other means if that was the case.'

Terry drew in a long breath. 'I've worked in this area for twenty years now. I'm head of my department, and a lot of my research is done discreetly anyway. Initially, when offers are made, some companies like to keep it quiet. I do confidentiality very well.'

Liz glanced at Matt and gave him a slight nod. They could risk it.

'It's the old merchant's house in Cutler's Alley,' Matt began.

Terry interrupted with a sardonic laugh. 'What! That old chestnut! For heaven's sake, I can tell you about that without even moving from my chair!'

Liz's eyes widened. Were they finally in luck?

'I can't tell you how many people have wanted to get hold of that place and convert it for any number of uses. I've had to say the same to everyone: that building is at the centre of a massive dispute over its ownership. It's going nowhere in the near future.' He shrugged. 'But I can give you the name of the solicitor who's dealing with it.'

Now this was something. Liz went and got her notebook.

'It's Boon and Mallinson, an old established Fenfleet company in Lower Fen Lane. You'll need to speak to the old man himself, Edward Boon. He's been dealing with that property since the dawn of time, or so it seems.'

'I know Edward Boon,' said Matt, excitedly. 'Not well, but many years ago my family lodged their wills with his company, and I met him when my mother passed away. I'm astounded he's still working.'

'You're not the only one,' Terry said. 'Most people are astounded he's still alive. He's well into his eighties, possibly his early nineties, he won't say exactly. But he's still razor-sharp. He swears he'll remain at his desk until the Garnett case is finally sewn up.'

'So there are still Garnetts living in the Fens?' asked Liz. 'I've never come across them.'

'Talk to old man Boon,' said Terry. 'It's his favourite subject. Been batted around various courtrooms for eons. Oh, and by the way, not many people know it but the property's called Satara House. Boon told me it was named after a city in India where the family owned a business, way back in time.'

'Have you ever been inside?' asked Matt.

'I haven't, but Edward Boon has.' He looked at them. 'What do you think is going on in there?'

'We have no idea,' said Matt. 'Maybe nothing whatsoever, and the boys simply mistook what they saw. There might be no connection to that house at all, but we have to check it out. We can rely on you to say nothing about it to anyone?'

'Of course. Except for Georgia. I assume I can do that?'

'Keep it low-key, Terry,' said Matt. 'Make her promise to keep it to herself. We don't yet know what we're dealing with, and we can't afford any casualties. And as Liz said, the minute we have proof of any wrongdoing, it goes directly to the police.'

Terry stood up. 'If there's anything else I can do to help, please ask.' He turned his gaze to his dead son's laptop and sighed. 'Please, find out why our boy died, no matter what it takes.' There were tears in his eyes.

Liz's own eyes welled up. What must this man be going through?

'We'll do everything we can,' said Matt. 'And we'll get that laptop back to you as soon as we've gone through what's there.'

When Terry had closed the door behind him, Liz gave a long, heartfelt sigh. 'It's draining, isn't it? Trying to find the right words at a time like this. That poor man.'

'It certainly strengthens your resolve to get answers,' Matt said. 'I'm going to ring that solicitor and find some pretext to get inside that place. I'll do it now. After that, I want to run a few ideas past you for where to hide Minty.'

'And Terry's surprise visit has made us late for lunch. I'd better get something together, especially for Minty, he must be starving,' Liz said.

'And then with David's help, I suggest we look at Alex's laptop. It could be key.'

Liz looked at him thoughtfully. 'I've been wondering why the killer didn't take it. It's just occurred to me that that could be the reason why we can't find the spare one.'

'Ah! You think the killer took the wrong one! Maybe his father only found it when he was clearing the room. Good thinking, Liz.'

'And if that was the case, there might be something worth finding on this one.' Liz headed for the kitchen. 'I'm going to get lunch out of the way. I can't wait to fire it up.'

CHAPTER TWELVE

Having rung the doorbell twice and got no answer, Kellie's excitement faded. She was tired and hungry after her journey and couldn't understand why they weren't there to greet her. Surely her brother would know she'd be coming, so why go out? She knew Simon. Even if their aunt had planned some outing, he would have dug his heels in and stayed put.

Kellie wandered around to the back of the house and into the garden. She sat on a seat that looked out over the marsh and wondered what had happened to them. Maybe they were walking the marsh path, looking for one of her brother's rare birds, and would be back soon. That was quite likely, knowing his obsession with birdwatching. Auntie Jessie was nervous of travelling any distance from her home, so Kellie couldn't imagine her taking Simon to the seaside or anything like that. Likewise, motorways terrified her, and she panicked at the thought of driving into a city like Lincoln or Peterborough.

Had she overreacted to her brother's message? What if there had been some misunderstanding? He might have sent her a second card to explain, and she'd left before the post was delivered. Had she done something that would cause an argument with her father and get him all upset over nothing? Kellie began to feel thoroughly wretched. Then the taxi from the station had cost more than she'd thought it would, and there were no buses into this remote little village, so she had no idea how she was going to get back. What if her aunt really had taken Simon away for a couple of days? What if something really was wrong? Half of her wanted to cry, and the other half was angry. Angry at her aunt, her brother, and most of all at herself.

The full immensity of the situation hit her, and she was suddenly frightened. She went to the front door and banged on it with her fists in frustration.

'That might wake the dead, dear, but it won't make Jessie Wright open the door. She and her nephew have gone away.'

She turned to look at the speaker, a tall woman smiling down at her.

'I'm guessing you're Kellie,' the woman said.

Kellie stared at her. How did this stranger know her name? 'Who are you?'

She hadn't meant to sound rude, it had just come out that way.

The woman didn't seem offended at all. 'Sorry, I should have said. I'm an old friend of Jessie's. I used to live just up the road but I moved to the other side of the village a while ago. I saw her yesterday and she said they were off early this morning, and knowing how forgetful your aunt can be, I just popped round to make sure she locked up properly.'

So they had gone away. Now what should she do?

'Call me Belle, dear.' The woman eyed her with mingled amusement and concern. 'Now, you'd better tell me what you're doing here. Jessie obviously either had no idea you were coming or completely forgot, which, knowing Jessie, wouldn't be unheard of.'

Kellie wondered what to say, and decided on the truth — well, part of it. She had no intention of mentioning Simon's postcard. 'I look after my brother, you see, and I was worried about his asthma and him being so far from a hospital here. I just got on a train and came to see for myself that he was all right.' She paused, staring at the ground. 'I never even told my father where I was going, I just went, and now I realise it was a really stupid thing to do.'

'Wasn't it just!' Belle said. 'So, what are we to do with you now, I wonder? Look, I'd better just check this place and make sure Jessie hasn't left any doors or windows open — after all, that's why I came today. Then we'll see what's the best thing to do.'

She marched off. The cottage was small, so she was soon back. She checked the front door and looked up at the first-floor windows. 'Wonders will never cease! She actually remembered to lock everything.'

Kellie was forced to smile. This Belle seemed to know her aunt very well.

'Now, young Kellie, as you obviously can't stay here, I think we should phone your dad, don't you?'

Kellie's heart sank. 'I know, but I can't till four o'clock. He has to switch his phone off and leave it in his locker while he's working.'

'And there isn't anyone else you could contact?' Belle asked.

Kellie shook her head. 'No. No one.' Her loneliness and pain at the loss of her mother almost overwhelmed her. The three of them were the only inhabitants on a small island, separated from the rest of the world. One of them was who knew where, leaving two. Now, thanks to her impulsive decision, she had alienated the only other person left.

'Okay. Well, at least we know what we have to do,' Belle said. 'You come home with me and I'll see what I can find you to eat and drink because you are probably starving, then at four, we ring your father. As soon as he knows you're safe, I'll get you to the station and pop you on a train back home. How does that sound?'

Kellie smiled, grateful. 'If it's not too much trouble, thank you very much.'

It wasn't until she was in Belle's car and driving away from Marsh View that several thoughts hit her all at once.

Where had Jessie taken Simon? Why had she forgotten one of her father's cardinal rules: never get in a car with a stranger? The name Belle reminded her of a school friend whose name was Annabelle. They'd always called her Anna.

Kellie shivered. Was she sitting next to Anna? The woman her mother didn't trust? Who was not good for Auntie Jessie?

Where were Jessie and her beloved brother, Simon?

* * *

Jude drove away from his father's nursing home in a state of utter frustration. A single word, after years of silence, and now even his best men had failed to find a single trace of Minty. If only his father would explain. Why him? Why Minty Agutter? And then there was tonight's shipment — he couldn't afford to take his eyes off the ball there, but he couldn't seem to push these unwanted thoughts away. How could an old lag like Minty get one over on his boys? They were hardly amateurs at this game. Hardened criminals, every one of them, if they wanted someone found, they found them. But not Minty, it seemed. His anger and resentment smouldered. He had a good mind to dispose of blasted Minty — once he'd discovered why his father had called out Minty's name instead of his. Dad would never know.

That decided, he turned his thoughts to the coming shipment. It should proceed without a hitch, and in the unlikely case of some unforeseen problem arising, they had a plan. By the end of the day — assuming Palmer had been straight with him — he could be in possession of a consignment worth millions.

Jude stared at the road ahead, his thoughts on Palmer. No matter what he said, Palmer would be creaming off the lion's share, while it was Jude who did most of the work. Palmer sat in a comfortable office with a laptop and a phone. He networked, made the connections, arranged the onward movement of the goods, all without shifting his scrawny arse from his chair. It was Jude who exposed himself to danger ensuring it all went smoothly. And when a problem arose, Jude was the fixer, the man Palmer turned to.

From Palmer's point of view, there would be no consignment at all without his connections, so he awarded himself a generous bonus, far larger than that allotted to Jude. In his words, '*Without me, boy, you'd just be a thug. With me, you'll be rich. Just never forget who made that happen.*'

Jude hated Palmer, hated everything about him, except for his ability to find markets for their particular commodity. In that, he excelled.

Jude was almost "home," though he didn't consider it such. He was biding his time until his bank balance allowed him to move on — as far as he could from Palmer — and pay for the house of his dreams. With the assistance of one of his father's former associates, he had invested wisely, and could look forward to a bright future.

Jude parked the BMW in his numbered space outside the luxury block of apartments where he resided. He checked his watch, a purely reflexive action, since he always knew what the time was. His father had had the same inner clock. Right now, he had precisely three hours and fifteen minutes before the consignment was due to arrive. He would visit Ava and receive a relaxing massage, followed by a more stimulating activity. It had become a ritual with him, serving to clear his mind for the job ahead.

Jude smiled. If anyone could rid him of his anger and frustration, it was Ava and her supple fingers.

* * *

Henry rolled off the smiling woman and lay on his side facing her. He chuckled softly. 'You *are* full of surprises, aren't you? I'm rather glad I found you.'

Ava gave him a look that said much the same. He looked at her with interest. Had he seduced her, or she him? It had certainly happened fast. A mere ten minutes after he'd entered her massage room, they had been engaged in an exercise the health club brochure hadn't advertised.

This was new to him. Henry was always the seducer, and he was slightly bewildered. However, he had work to do. This remarkable woman would have to be his reward for when it was done.

Meanwhile, Ava was kneeling above him, her nipples just brushing his lips. Henry smiled. He had a lot to thank Niamh Conran for.

Ava's phone rang. She took the call, disentangled herself and swung her legs over the edge of the bed. 'Sorry, have to go. Business.'

'Forget business. Stay with me,' he whispered. 'I'll pay you more than them.'

She gave him a strange look. 'I don't want your money. But I really have to go. And so should you. I must shower.'

Through narrowed eyes, he watched her hurry to the en-suite bathroom. He heard the sound of running water. She was scared. He had seen it on her face when she'd looked at the caller's name. He recalled her expression when he'd asked about the clients at the fitness centre — distaste, or possibly fear. He'd seen the same expression just now. Henry slipped from the bed and pulled on his clothes.

He'd made a new discovery. This woman was going to give him answers to a number of the questions he and Eddie Race were asking. He would follow her, and find out exactly who was frightening her so badly.

* * *

Matt sat opposite old man Boon, the solicitor, who had fitted him in before the office closed for the day.

'I remember you and your mother. Your father, too, when he was alive. He died when you were quite young, if I'm not mistaken.' With his bent back, wrinkled, time-worn face and sparse, wispy, white hair, Edward Boon appeared to be in his dotage. Matt had begun to think he was wasting his time until he caught the old man's piercing gaze. His eyes were clear, bright, and Matt guessed they'd miss nothing.

'That's right, sir.' Looking at the old man, Matt suddenly felt like a schoolboy.

'And if my memory serves me well, there was little love lost between you and your late lamented mother. Or is that still a sore point?' Did Matt detect a hint of mockery in those sharp eyes?

Matt shifted in his seat, impatiently. He hadn't come to discuss his relationship with his mother, for heaven's sake. Then he recalled his behaviour at the time and lowered his gaze.

Edward Boon tilted his head. 'We'll say no more, dear boy. Now, how can I help?'

Matt rattled off the story he'd prepared, involving Alex Hallam but leaving out the photograph. It sounded unconvincing even to him.

Edward Boon leaned back in his chair. 'Now, son, how about you tell me what you really want to know? And why.'

Again, Matt blushed like a kid caught out in a lie. But he still wasn't prepared to tell Boon the whole story. 'In a nutshell, sir, the parents of Alex Hallam, along with my partner and I, suspect that there was foul play involved in the deaths of Alex and his friend, Toby. They were out one night in Cutler's Alley and saw something. It appears they tried to investigate it, and a few days later they both died.'

'And what did the inquest conclude?'

'Accidental death by inhalation of carbon monoxide.'

Boon pulled a face. 'Hard to prove one way or the other, I'm sure. But what do you think they suspected was happening in Satara House? And what did they see?'

The man must have been brilliant in court. Matt could see no way round it but to tell him the truth. 'Toby was taking night photographs for his university course, and he thought he'd accidentally captured the face of a woman looking from the window of the sealed-up building. They tried to make enquiries and were warned off — we found a note screwed up in a wastepaper basket. Also, a laptop was stolen from them, presumably because it contained the images Toby had uploaded. One of our guesses is people trafficking, possibly women for the sex trade. That, or drugs, most likely cocaine.'

Boon pursed his thin lips. 'Sorry to disappoint you, Mr Ballard, but Satara House is most definitely empty. I can assure you of that. One of my staff — my son, actually — carries out a discreet security check of the interior, approximately once every six weeks. The last visit was the week before last, and I can assure you, there are no nefarious activities going on in there.' He looked at Matt and gave a shrug. 'I think they must have been mistaken.'

'I suppose—'

'No, I'm afraid not. You want to see inside for yourself. Understand that my company has sole responsibility for that house until the last surviving member of the Garnett family has been located. I am sorry, but it's in our agreement: no one other than myself or one other designated member of my staff may enter.'

Matt knew not to push it further. 'What is it like inside, sir? A dangerous ruin? A decrepit old wreck of a place?'

The old man looked into the distance. 'The last time I visited in person must have been six or seven years back, and I expect little will have changed since then. No, Mr Ballard, it's not a ruin. It was carefully sealed up and all the utilities shut off. Oh, there is some damp and natural deterioration, of course, but it was once a very elegant house, and remains so. I am still hopeful of tracing its legal owner.'

Then you need to get a wriggle on, thought Matt darkly. *Unless you expect to live for ever.*

'But we are almost there,' Boon added, reading his thoughts. 'Another few months could see the dispute finally brought to a close, after thirty-six years.'

'It's been standing empty for almost four decades?' asked Matt.

'Oh no. It was only finally closed up twelve years ago after the last known member of the Garnett family passed away. A bachelor, he approached us to draw up his will, and at the same time set us the task of tracing three missing relatives that he had lost touch with over the years. They proved extremely elusive until, finally, we found they were all deceased. However, they had produced four children between them — one had died in a boating accident, one in a hospice, and the last two, well, they've been a thorn in my side ever since.' Boon looked up. 'But at last, we believe we have a viable lead.' He gave Matt an odd, almost painful smile. 'We've persevered for so long because the will of that last surviving family member is rather complicated. He was adamant that the house go to no one but a true Garnett. He was a rich man, and he paid us a lot of money in order that his wishes be followed to the letter. It has been contested a number of times over the years, especially by the Latimer family, who produced an old document which stated that Satara House had been signed over to them as payment of a massive gambling debt. But we have staved them off, Mr Ballard, though it took over ten years to lay to rest.'

'Talk about an albatross around your neck!' exclaimed Matt.

'Like the Canadian Mounties, we always get our man — or woman.' Boon gave a rattly laugh. 'And my family has run this business for four generations, so I rather understand the feeling behind it. Diligence is our motto, although some see it simply as my being a stubborn old bastard!'

Matt laughed. 'Then you can see no way that someone besides yourselves could have been inside that house?'

'None whatsoever,' said Boon emphatically. 'But if it makes you feel easier, I can ask my son to conduct another check early next week. He could even take some pictures to give you an idea of the condition of the place. I will contact you with his findings.'

Matt thanked the old gentleman and took his leave, pausing at the door. 'I know it goes against the terms of your agreement, but may I suggest that your son does not go alone, just in case there is something amiss since his last visit.'

The old man smiled patiently. 'Thank you for your concern. Duly noted.'

Matt drove home feeling somewhat deflated. Thank heavens they hadn't handed this case straight over to Charley Anders. She'd have gone storming in with a warrant and found an empty house. For the first time, he doubted what they'd seen in that photograph. Young David had done a good job at enhancing it, but he was no professional. He wondered if he dared take it — unofficially — to Sarah "Spooky" Dukes at Greenborough, or even the IT wizard, Orac, at Saltern-le-Fen? But no. The last thing he wanted was to get anyone into trouble. Maybe they were seeing crimes where there were none.

Matt drove on towards Tanner's Fen in a low mood. He had set out with high hopes of either seeing inside that merchant's house, or at least receiving some information that could lead him forward. All he had come away with was an old man's assurance that absolutely nothing illegal was going on in there.

Grey clouds gathered and blocked out the sun, then a few big splashes of rain hit the windscreen. 'Oh great,' muttered Matt. 'This day gets better and better by the moment!'

The sound of his phone made him start.

'DCI Ballard? It's Albie Grant. I can't talk much but I've got a little titbit for you.'

From the tinny noise and voices, his old friend with big ears was phoning from inside the betting shop. 'Go ahead, Albie.'

'The vine tells me Henry's on the prowl, and he's looking at a certain area in Fenfleet that could be of interest to you.'

'Cutler's Alley?' Matt perked up.

'Well, that vicinity, yes, guv'nor, and some others close by. Nothing concrete but he's been sighted, which speaks volumes in my book. I'll keep you posted.'

Matt put his foot down.

CHAPTER THIRTEEN

Jessie and Simon were at the table sharing their evening meal which, since she couldn't cook, consisted of his favourite biscuits, chocolate bars and crisps.

Simon was busy unwrapping a chocolate roll. 'You know, Auntie, it's funny about my phone. Do you think the bad men stole it that day I talked to them on the marsh? I know I had it in my pocket cos I needed to charge it up, but when I went to check the battery, it was gone. Dad'll be really angry. He knows how careless I am with it, and he'll think I just lost it.'

'No, he won't, my darling. If it was stolen — and I'm quite sure you're right about the bad men — Daddy won't be cross with you. I'll explain, so don't worry, and as soon as we get you back home, I'll buy you a new one. Maybe we can get one with a better camera for taking pictures of birds.'

He jumped up and down in his chair. 'Really? I'd never thought about photographing the birds before. Gosh, that would be so cool! Thank you, Auntie!'

Oh, how she hated to lie to him! But she couldn't afford for him to contact his sister — or his father for that matter — and give away the secret of their adventure. His phone would remain where she'd locked it away, and the blame could stay with the bad men.

Jessie gazed across at Simon and saw her beloved little sister. Louise lived on in this little boy, and it gladdened Jessie that she hadn't lost her completely.

They finished eating and cleared away. Jessie was thankful that her nephew's life wasn't ruled by the television or computer games, it made keeping him here a great deal easier. Simon asked if he could colour in some of the birds in his book, and they settled down for the evening. Jessie wondered anxiously how soon it would be before he grew bored. What would she do then? She couldn't afford for him to start running about attracting unwelcome attention.

She pretended to read her book, watching him covertly. Her next worry was the cold. What would she do then? She couldn't light a fire because people would see smoke coming from the chimney. Luckily, it was a warm autumn and not cold at all yet.

Jessie settled back in her chair, at peace at last. This was how it should be. Just the two of them, her and her darling boy.

* * *

Ava had gone, leaving Jude feeling somehow cheated. As always, she had delivered, but she seemed absent. The whole thing had been too businesslike, all technique and no real warmth, which wasn't like Ava.

Maybe he was feeling extra sensitive because of the issue with his father and Minty. He'd wanted comfort, but Ava could hardly be expected to provide that. She didn't belong to him and he wasn't in love with her. He paid well and expected good service, which Ava provided in bucketloads. Why, then, was he upset because she had done the job she was paid to do?

He should just admit that he was strung out, and would remain that way until Minty had been run to ground. It was a dangerous state of mind to be in, however. There was a lot at stake tonight.

He took a quick shower and dried himself vigorously. *Enough of this bollocks, Jude. Just get tonight sorted and you can go and look for the little creep yourself!*

* * *

As soon as they'd finished their evening meal, Minty went to bed. The hours spent hiding in Matt's shed, along with the realisation that he was now a hunted man, had taken their toll. Matt sent him off to bed with a glass of Scotch, while he, Liz and David went over the day's events. Liz had not been as excited as Matt to hear that Henry had been seen around Fenfleet.

'It's not so much him being seen as *where*,' said Matt. 'Cutler's Alley. Right in the middle of our target area.' He took a sip of his drink. 'And just when old man Boon had me convinced that we were barking up the wrong tree.'

'Come on, Matt!' Liz said. 'Just because some old dodderer hasn't noticed anything doesn't mean nothing's going on in there. People could be using it to store drugs and have hidden them well out of sight. The people from the solicitors will only be checking for signs of vandalism or a break-in. I expect they've done it so many times by now that they're pretty perfunctory about it too.'

She was probably right. Matt started to wonder why he'd been so convinced of Edward Boon's sincerity.

'Who is Henry?' asked David.

Liz laughed. 'An enigma. A throwback, really — a kind of modern-day Raffles but dangerous.'

'Raffles?' David said. 'I've heard that name somewhere, but . . .'

'Probably a bit before your time, lad,' Matt said. 'Raffles was a fictional gentleman master thief created by someone called Hornung. He was a cricketing star by day and a cracksman by night. Our Henry is a similar sort of character, fond of Savile Row suits and Ferragamo shoes, beneath which lurks a ruthless criminal.'

'He's a kind of troubleshooter for the underworld,' added Liz. 'The expert they call in if they find themselves in shit street and can't get out. And they pay a fortune for his services.'

David chuckled. 'Sounds a bit far-fetched to me. Like Robin Hood meets *American Psycho*.'

Liz raised an eyebrow. 'Henry is far from being a latter-day Robin Hood. His ill-gotten gains are all spent on himself and his luxurious lifestyle.'

'The police have never able to pin anything on him. Henry's innocent as a newborn babe, so far as the records are concerned,' said Matt. 'And he has an unbelievable number of contacts in high places.'

'You seem to know an awful lot about him, Matt,' said David.

'Oh, we've always kept an eye on him. We must know just about everything his underworld pals do, except how to nail him!' Matt said.

'So, who would have sent him to investigate, do you think?' asked David.

Matt shrugged. 'At a guess, Eddie Race. He's been on her payroll for years, though she rarely uses him. Her network is pretty tight, but he'd be her go-to man if she needed to bring out the big guns.'

'Whatever is going on around here is really worrying our criminal fraternity, that's for sure,' said Liz, 'so it has to be something big.'

They sipped thoughtfully at their drinks, until Matt asked if they'd got anything interesting from Alex's computer.

'Not as yet,' Liz said, 'but David's still trying. We're beginning to think that Alex got twitchy about leaving that laptop in his flat and hid his reflective journal somewhere among his files.'

'And he had so many!' David looked pained. 'I've resorted to trawling through them, hoping and praying he didn't delete it.'

'His parents said he was an inveterate note-taker, constantly adding new thoughts to his journal.' Liz smiled encouragingly at David. 'It'll be there. I reckon the best way to hide it would be to leave it in your documents under a different filename.'

'I tried checking dates,' said David. 'I thought it would have to be one of the latest entries, but there are folders within folders and all are recent. I think he deliberately opened lots of different files, causing them to be reset to the day they were accessed. It'll be a case of hunting through them all until I find it. And then, if I do find it, I'll need to check he hasn't made any of it invisible.'

'Invisible?' Matt queried.

'Yeah, it's easy to hide pieces of text. I can show you if you like.'

'Well, I'm sorry it's turned out to be so difficult, lad. From the way his father spoke I thought it would be simple — just open the file and read it.'

'Our Alex must have been far more frightened than his mum and dad realised,' said Liz sadly. 'And maybe it's best they didn't. You'd hate to think that your son's last days had been spent in fear.'

David stood up. 'Well, the night is still young. I'd better get back to that laptop.'

Matt and Liz were left alone. 'So what are we going to do about Minty?' asked Liz.

Matt said he wasn't sure. 'I had some great ideas earlier but on reflection, none of them seem workable, or safe enough. I wondered about packing him off to a guest house in some busy seaside town but he might be there for ages.'

'The way he got out of his house was really clever,' Liz said, 'but if he goes anywhere local, someone is sure to recognise him, he's so well-known. He's not that well off either, so money could be an issue for him. I did think of asking Bernie if he could help hide him, but again, Minty's face is probably well-known among Bernie's lot.'

Matt shrugged. 'Then he'd better stay here for a bit longer, until we come up with something more satisfactory. You okay with that, Liz?'

She nodded. 'I couldn't think of anything else either. But he'll need to realise that even out here in the back of beyond, he must keep a low profile. There's the postman, delivery people, and various other folk call, and he must not be seen. Our postie mentions seeing Minty Agutter's ugly mug at that retired policeman's house and he could be back in some other garden shed.'

'Or hanging from the rafters,' said Matt darkly. 'The last thing I want is to bring danger to our neck of the woods. If he stays, it will just have to be until we work out something better. Agreed?'

'Agreed,' said Liz. 'But we'd better get our thinking caps on. I'd never live with myself if I sent him anywhere less than safe.'

The doorbell rang, making them both jump.

'Not expecting anyone, are you?' Liz asked.

'Nope,' said Matt, daring a look out of the window. 'Especially not Bryn Owen!' He hurried to the door and opened it. 'Bryn! This is a surprise! Come on in.'

'Couldn't resist calling by, sir,' said Bryn brightly. 'I had to do an interview down at Fenmoor Lodge and I thought, since I'm only ten minutes away . . .'

Bryn, a likeable fellow, had been their DC back when they'd been in CID, and had recently been made detective sergeant. He followed them into the lounge.

'Rumour has it that Charley Anders and you lot are run off your feet at present,' said Matt with a grin.

With a groan, Bryn flopped into an armchair. 'I'll say! It's non-stop. I suppose you two wouldn't like to pop back and give us a hand?'

'We've done our bit for queen and country, thank you,' said Liz firmly. 'I'm afraid you'll have to manage without us.'

'I bet you're working as hard as us, though, aren't you?' Bryn smiled. 'You guys haven't stopped since you took your so-called retirement.'

'You can say that again.' Matt laughed. 'In fact, the other day we were talking about going away for a few days' well-earned break, but then—'

'Another job came in,' said Bryn. 'Tell me about it. Every time I plan anything special for my leave days, some major crime occurs and the whole thing goes tits-up.'

Liz made Bryn a coffee, and while they chatted, Bryn said, 'I don't know if your work has brought you into town recently, but there's a peculiar undercurrent. Thing is, no one can point a finger at what or who is the cause. I suppose you haven't heard anything or got any theories?'

Matt had wondered if the situation had reached the ears of CID. 'It's been mentioned, Bryn, but like you, we're completely in the dark. If we hear anything, we'll pass it on.'

'We're worried it's something big. And if it is, we're going to be in deep shit. When I said the work was non-stop, I meant it, we're really struggling to keep our heads above water. If anything else serious hits, well . . .' Bryn shrugged.

Liz threw Matt a warning glance. Maybe now wasn't the time to tell Bryn they were working on a case that could well be heading in CID's direction in the fairly near future.

Bryn brightened. 'Happens, doesn't it? One month we're inundated, the next we're scratching around for something to do.'

Ah, the rollercoaster! Matt felt a pang of nostalgia, having ridden that particular fairground attraction on a daily basis.

'So, what are you working on at present?' Bryn said.

'Oh, this and that,' said Liz offhandedly. 'My nephew's staying for a while, which is very nice, so we're showing him the Fens.'

Matt thought of their other guest and hoped he wouldn't decide to get up and wander downstairs. Bryn would recognise him immediately.

As if sensing their reticence, Bryn politely looked at his watch and stood up. 'Better get home. Early start tomorrow. If you hear anything about what's going on, you've got my number, haven't you?'

'Likewise,' said Matt. 'We like to keep apace of what's going on, especially in the shadowy corners of Fenfleet.'

Bryn nodded and saluted. 'You got it, boss! Anything breaks, I'll keep you posted.'

After he had gone, Liz raised her eyebrows. 'All the time he was here I was shitting myself. I was sure Minty was going to wander in wearing your old pyjamas!'

Matt chuckled. 'You and me both!'

'Has your visitor gone?' David stood in the doorway, beaming.

'He certainly has, and guessing from the expression on your face, am I right in thinking you've found a certain journal?' Liz said.

'Oh yes! My mum's always saying that patience is a virtue, and in this case, she was right. It's in a file within a folder, labelled *Overexposed*. I hope you don't mind but I used your printer and printed out the last couple of pages of entries.' His face darkened. 'It fills in all the gaps in what we know happened to those two kids. It's not pleasant reading.' David heaved in a long breath. 'In fact, I'm not sure I could do what you do. Reading that journal has made me believe that all these years I've been looking at policing through rose-tinted spectacles.'

Matt knew exactly how the young man felt. What David had said brought back memories of his own early years on the force. 'It's because it's real, David. It hits home, and feeling someone else's pain isn't pleasant.'

'That, and the injustice of it.' David stared down at the pages in his hand. 'Those two lads were just ordinary students, working hard and wanting to make something of their lives. They didn't deserve what happened to them. How can people be so wicked?'

Liz went to him and gave him a hug. 'That's exactly *why* we do what we do, Davey-boy, to stop those wicked people from doing the same thing to some other innocent victim. Now, can we see those?' She pointed to the printouts.

He handed them to her, still looking dejected.

'Want another beer?' asked Matt.

'No thanks, but I'd love a coffee. I can make it myself, if that's all right?'

'You know where everything is, lad. Help yourself.' He gave David an encouraging smile. 'And don't beat yourself up. We all feel that way at some point, and if we have any compassion, we always will. But in the end, we will continue to fight the evil that exists out there, simply because we can't allow it to win. Oh, and you don't have to be a copper to do it. There's a lot of different avenues you could take. Liz and I have chosen one that suits us, but crime fighting comes in various forms. When the time is right, you'll find your niche, never fear.'

This seemed to placate David a little. 'And in the meantime, we do all we can to get justice for Alex and Toby, right?'

'Right! That's exactly what we do.'

It was after nine by the time Matt and Liz had read Alex's journal. Both fully appreciated why David had been so upset.

First excitement, then anxiety, followed by fear. The two boys' emotions as they went deeper poured from the narrative. Alex told how they had decided to carry out their own covert observation of the house in Cutler's Alley after dark, but though they saw nothing, they both sensed they were being watched. They returned the following day and believed they saw men watching them from the shadows.

At that point Alex had made some notes about what they had observed, but none of it seemed particularly suspicious to Matt or Liz.

Alex had then searched the internet to try and find out more about the old house. When he came up empty, he wondered if he should ask his father if he knew anything about the place. He held back because he hadn't wanted to involve his dad, or anyone for that matter. They were still pretty shaken by the warning that had been tacked onto the back of Toby's door.

Then, the day before they died, Toby went into Fenfleet on his own, believing he'd be quite safe in broad daylight. Alex stayed behind, still searching for information about the merchant's house on the internet. Toby returned home terrified. He described to Alex being grabbed by two men as he emerged from the back street car park where he'd left his vehicle. They had ripped his wallet from his pocket and searched through it, clearly looking for something in particular, but he managed to slip out of their clutches and run for his life. As he hurtled through the open-air market, he remembered the SD card in his pocket. Certain that this was what they were looking for, in desperation, he picked on an older man, who he described as looking as if he had taken a few hard knocks himself, slipped the card into his pocket and ran.

He was too scared to eat or sleep alone that night, so Alex offered to stay in his room with him. In his last entry, he wrote that Toby believed someone had been in his room again while he was out. The two boys searched the room from top to bottom but found nothing amiss. Still, Toby was sure there had been an intruder. The last paragraph read: *'We are both scared now, so I have told Toby that enough is enough. Tomorrow morning early, we go to the police and make them understand that this is not a student prank. I've decided to hide this journal, in fact I'll probably hide the laptop too, but in my own room, as Toby's seems to be particularly vulnerable. Then we'll batten down the hatches, lock ourselves in and wait for morning.'*

But morning never came for the two young men. 'Toby was right about an intruder, wasn't he?' said Matt.

'Someone got in and tampered with that water heater.' Liz frowned. 'It's only a hypothesis, but I'm guessing that their killer returned to see if his handiwork had been a success, and decided to add a little whisky to the equation, making it look like the boys had been drinking prior to crashing out.'

Matt agreed. 'So, is this the proof that sends us straight to Charley Anders, or do we try to get something more?'

Liz shrugged. 'If they were less stretched, I'd say call it in. But as it is, I think we should press on. Let's see if we can provide a bit more hard evidence.'

Matt narrowed his eyes. 'Do I detect a hint of professional pride in that voice, Liz Haynes? Does a large part of you not want to hand it over until we have an irrefutable case for Charley to follow up?'

'Dead right,' muttered Liz. 'We have a client desperate for answers, and I want to be the one to give them to her. And I hate to give up halfway through something.'

'Spoken like a true zealot.' Matt laughed. 'But I completely agree, adding only that we jump ship should things get dangerous for any of us, okay?'

'Certainly, but right now we're in a perfect position to keep quietly digging away. I'm sure we can achieve more than a load of uniforms stalking the streets of Fenfleet.' Liz frowned again. 'As long as no one discovers Minty. He's the biggest threat to our anonymity, isn't he?'

'My thoughts exactly. Maybe we should think a bit harder about where we can safely move him.'

David, who had been listening to their discussion, said, 'I might know somewhere, if he doesn't mind travelling.'

They both looked at him. 'Go on,' said Matt.

'Well, I have this friend in Thetford whose father is a vicar. He has a big old vicarage in the grounds of his church and provides rooms in it for people in need. It's only on a short-term basis, mind you, ten days maximum. If you want Minty to go somewhere right out of the area where no one will know him, I'm pretty sure Peter would take him in.'

Matt looked at Liz. 'Well, I've got nothing better in mind, have you?'

'Not at all, and it sounds perfect. He'd understand that we need to keep Minty's whereabouts totally secret?' she asked David.

David chuckled. 'He's taken in some right cases, believe me. He won't ask questions or judge anyone. Shall I ring him?'

Matt looked at his watch. 'If you don't think it's too late, that would be great. Then if the answer's yes, we can put it to Minty tomorrow.'

David made the call. 'Peter says he can take him, but not till after ten tomorrow. I've told him we'll go ahead provided Minty agrees. Is that okay?'

'Excellent! I should think he'd like nothing better than a nice trip to Thetford. It would get him well away from the Fens and put some forest air into his lungs.' Matt grimaced. 'And it gives us ten days to find that proof we need.'

'I'll take him if you like,' said David. 'Then I'll be able to make sure Peter understands the importance of keeping shtum about his new guest.'

'Are you sure?' asked Liz.

'No problem. I can do it easily in under two hours. I might even call in at home and collect a few extra bits and pieces.' He gave them a determined look. 'It's something practical I can do to help.'

Matt said it certainly was. Their young assistant was proving very useful indeed.

CHAPTER FOURTEEN

Kellie sat nursing a hot drink. She was feeling desperately frightened for her brother, and guilty at having rushed off to the Fens without a word to her father. She was also pretty sorry for herself, having spent a chunk of her savings only to cause herself problems.

At four o'clock they called her dad and Kellie told him what she'd done and where she was. She had expected a torrent of angry abuse but after a moment's silence Donald Burton said he was sorry. This was totally unexpected. He told her he should have understood how concerned she had been, should have taken more notice of her. He asked if she knew where Jessie had taken Simon, but she had no idea. She asked Belle who said she didn't know either. All Jessie had told her was that they'd be away for a few days, having a "wonderful adventure," but she hadn't said where. Her father asked to speak to Belle, and the two adults conferred for several minutes.

Belle told Kellie her father was checking the train times and would ring back shortly. Which he duly did, and was most concerned. There was some disruption on the line and the train from Peterborough, which was the last one of the day, had been cancelled. Kellie was marooned. Belle offered to put her up for the night, but Kellie's father said he couldn't possibly ask that of her. He would drive up to the Fens and collect his daughter.

And that's where she was now. Waiting.

Later that evening Belle had to go out for a while. She left Kellie with a sandwich and a hot drink, promising to be no longer than an hour. Kellie should watch TV while she was gone, and try to relax.

Kellie felt bad about having believed this woman to be the sinister Anna, the woman her mother had so mistrusted. Belle had taken her to her cottage, which was on the other side of the village, exactly where she'd said it would be, and fed her scrambled eggs on toast. She was obviously no threat; instead she'd been kind to her, concerned about her plight. Kellie was starting to think she should take a serious look at herself — she trusted no one these days, seeing dark motives behind what were probably simple and quite normal actions. Right now, Kellie Burton didn't like herself very much. However, the biggest thing on her mind was Auntie Jessie, and where she had taken her little brother. She didn't like the sound of this "wonderful adventure," not if it had been dreamed up by batty Auntie Jessie.

Kellie stared unseeing at the TV screen, relieved her father was on his way. He was always so down to earth, maybe he could make some sense of it.

Twenty minutes later Belle returned, and a little after that they heard a car draw up outside. Kellie ran to her father and hugged him, a torrent of apologies flooding from her lips. She had expected him to have returned to his old self by the time he arrived but he was still not angry, or even disappointed at her foolishness. He hugged her back, saying she had nothing to apologise for. On the contrary, he had let her down and she must forgive him.

Belle took them inside and made more tea. 'So, are you driving straight back?'

'No,' he said. 'I spotted a Travelodge about five miles back on the main road, so I called in and booked us a room.

I've been working twelve-hour shifts, and I'd not be safe to drive all that way home again.'

Belle said it was a sensible decision.

'And I need to find out where the hell Jessie has taken my son,' he added. 'I can't believe she'd go off and not tell me where she was going, it's so unlike her.' He looked apologetically at Belle. 'You know her, so you'll agree that she's mad as a box of frogs, but this I don't understand. She rang me a couple of days ago and said Simon was fine, but she never mentioned any expedition. The boy has asthma — all sorts of things can trigger an attack. Sure, she knows what to do if that should happen, and he has his inhalers, but even so, she should have said. I'm his father, for heaven's sake. I should have been allowed to decide if I thought it was a suitable trip for him.'

Belle said she agreed. It was strange. 'She gave me the impression she was doing it with your blessing, and she didn't tell me where they were off to either.'

Listening to this, Kellie became even more worried.

Donald thanked Belle profusely, and gave her his mobile number should the "adventurers" return early. As her father started the car, Kellie turned to wave at Belle, echoing her father's thanks. 'I suppose you don't know where Anna lives, do you? Auntie Jessie's old friend?'

An odd look passed across Belle's face. 'Anna? I'm sorry, Kellie, I can't help you there.'

By the time they set off for the Travelodge, Kellie was shivering, though the evening was quite warm.

Her father had thought to bring her what she would need for the night, plus clothes for the next day. Freshly showered, Kellie sank onto the bed, exhausted. 'Um, Dad. I ought to have shown you this, but I thought you'd say it was Simon being silly.' She handed him the postcard.

Her father read it through in silence. 'So that's why you took off like that.'

She nodded. 'And now I'm really frightened for him.'

137

She expected her father to tell her she was being over-dramatic. She felt even more anxious when he said, 'So am I, sweetheart. So am I.'

* * *

Jessie heard a soft knock on the door. With a quick glance at the sleeping boy, she went to the door and let her friend in. 'It's all right, he's fast asleep,' she whispered.

'There's been a development, Jessie, and I really don't want the boy to hear.'

'Oh, he won't wake. He was a bit restless earlier, so I put a few drops of that mixture you gave me into his hot chocolate.'

'You might need to keep him here a little longer, my dear,' said Anna. 'I have one or two things to attend to, and I won't be able to look out for you if you go home tomorrow or even the day after that.'

'Oh, that's wonderful,' cooed Jessie. 'I wouldn't mind keeping him here for ever. He is so like my darling Louise was as a child that I feel as if I've got her back again. Take as long as you have to. We have food for a few more days, and if necessary, I'll slip out to the shop while he's asleep. We've had the most wonderful day. I'm so grateful to you for letting us stay here.'

After Anna left, Jessie locked the door and lay awake in her makeshift bed. They could stay! Oh, how wonderful. She'd be able to hold onto him a little longer.

* * *

It was going well. In fact, it was flawless. With nothing on his mind but the job, Jude watched the consignment move smoothly from point to point. It was all in the planning. Like constructing a house, good groundwork and strong foundations formed the basis for success. It had taken the best part of a year to set up the infrastructure, bring in the right personnel and find the best locations, and tonight was a testament to his organisational skills.

As the final leg of the operation fell into place, and the doors closed and locked, Jude relaxed. Palmer would be pleased, very. Phase Two was far less hazardous and rarely presented any problems at all. Naturally, he would still keep a close eye on everything, but he could more or less delegate this part to his second in command. But Jude didn't trust anyone, not even Deezer, who was extremely competent and very dangerous. Deezer felt no fear. On the one hand, this was a bonus, on the other it was a failing. Jude suspected Deezer of a lack of imagination. You needed to have experienced fear yourself if you were to instil it in others.

Job completed, he strode away from Cutler's Alley. With the adrenaline slowly leaving his body, the thought of Minty Agutter rose again in his mind, and his satisfaction was replaced with anger.

His next job was personal. He had to track down fucking Minty and then — what? Discover what lay behind his father's words and take it from there.

* * *

Henry melted back into the shadows, watching Jude pass by. He was exceedingly pleased with his night's work. It had been pretty gruelling, moving unseen from place to place as he followed the shipment, but now he knew exactly what was going on in Fenfleet.

It was all down to a woman called Ava. Without her, he would never have found Jude's home, thus saving himself a lot of time and legwork trying to pin him down in the streets. So, what had he found?

One, it had been a very professional affair. They weren't dealing with a few low-level crooks here but a criminal ring of serious proportions.

Two, it had been in the making for a long time. What he had observed had been choreographed to perfection. It had a cast of thousands, old hands to a man. This was no one-off hit. These people planned on staying.

Three, and best of the lot as far as he was concerned, was that this information was worth a great deal more than he'd initially thought. What was it worth to Eddie Race? How high dare he go? Would Archie Leonard's son, Raymond, pay more? Because there was no doubt about it, this gang would threaten his empire too.

He thought of a fourth point. He had an idea he'd seen something this Jude had missed. It was a small thing, but Henry knew that it only took a tiny glitch to scupper an entire job. He would need to come back and check it out.

For the time being, he dismissed the thought. With or without that small detail, Henry was perfectly positioned to make himself a killing.

* * *

Matt looked at his alarm clock. One in the morning. Was he ever going to fall asleep? He'd just nodded off when a thought occurred to him and it wouldn't go away. He'd been wondering if having Minty hide out here had put Liz and David in danger. This led him to ask himself if there was more to the threats on Minty's life than he knew about. Minty had said they'd retrieved the wrecked SD card from his rubbish, so why continue to harass and threaten him? They'd know who he was — no innocent bystander but a one-time crook himself. So, what did they want? And who was this hitherto unknown son of Paddy Sherriff?

Matt sat up, pummelled his pillow and lay back again. Tomorrow, before he left for Suffolk, he would have a quiet word with Minty. The more he thought about it, the less he liked the thought of the young and naive David sailing off into the sunset with an old ex-con with a mystery hanging over him. If necessary, Matt would take him himself.

With every hour that passed it felt like this case was becoming more and more dangerous, yet they still had no positive proof that anything sinister was going on. That thought put paid to sleep for another two hours.

* * *

Palmer was still awake and working hard. His part of the job started now, with phone calls to men who also did their serious business in the small hours of the morning and made the most of darkness. He had had his customary visit and update from Jude, and although he had expected no less of his junior partner, he was relieved to know there'd been no hitches and their shipment was safely stashed away.

After Jude had gone, Palmer stared at the closed door. Something was going on in that young man's messed-up head, and he was sure it was still to do with that idiot Minty. Once again, he considered drawing a permanent line under that old man before he caused any real trouble, but he had a sneaking suspicion that Jude might have changed his mind on that score, and was about to save him the bother. Well, it hardly mattered: in either case, when the deals had been made and their precious commodity relocated, Palmer was going to make sure this itch was well and truly scratched.

CHAPTER FIFTEEN

Matt felt like shit. He had never functioned well on two hours' sleep, even when they were working a major crime and he had no choice.

As soon as Liz was up and around, he told her about the concerns that had robbed him of a night's sleep.

'Well, I'm about to cook us all a proper breakfast,' she said. 'I was going to ask if you'd sort out a few more cast-offs and some toiletries for Minty to take with him to Thetford, so why not have a word with him now, before David comes down? I don't want to put the frighteners on the lad.'

Matt went back upstairs and knocked on the guest room door.

'Come in,' Minty called.

Matt went in and sat down by the window.

'Nothing wrong, is there?' Minty asked.

'No, mate. In fact, we have somewhere sorted for you.' Matt told him about the temporary refuge David had found.

Minty's face lit up. 'Oh, yeah! That sounds perfect.'

Matt eyed him steadily. 'But there's something I have to know before we move you out of here.'

Minty flopped down on the bed. 'I don't think I'm going to like this, but ask away.'

'I don't believe you're being threatened just because of that incident in the marketplace. There's another issue here, and I think someone, namely this Jude Sherriff, is gunning for you because of something else. Now, come on, what do you know? What did Paddy Sherriff tell you when you were cellmates that his son considers worth topping you for?'

Minty looked pained. 'Still as shrewd as ever. Look, Mr Ballard. Matt. I do know things. Stuff Paddy told me, stuff his kid definitely won't know about . . . You've been really good to me, and I owe you, so I'll tell you some of it, but I really can't say too much. And, please, don't share what I tell you. It won't do no one no good, so just forget it afterwards.'

'I'm not a policeman anymore, Minty, so for starters I can't make you tell me anything. And if it won't do anyone any good, I'm hardly likely to try to use it, am I?' Matt said.

Minty stared down at the carpet. 'I was due to get out long before Paddy, and as it happened, I got out in six months. He'd asked me to do him a big favour, and like I told you before, we had become good friends, so I said yes, I'd do it.' He folded his arms across his chest, as if he was cold, and rocked slowly backwards and forwards. 'Remember the Scarlet Jewel Case robbery?'

Matt remembered it well. 'Three masked men, all armed, held up a swanky jeweller's shop in Lincoln, and got away with a fortune in precious gems and jewellery. Only a very small part of it was picked up when they tried to move it on; most is still missing, I believe.'

Minty nodded. 'That's the one.'

'Don't tell me that was Paddy Sherriff?' asked Matt. 'I thought he was abroad at the time?'

'It wasn't his job, Matt, and you're right, he *was* abroad, but Paddy had marked that jeweller's shop a long time before, and he knew exactly when the specialist valuer was expecting a delivery of some very valuable items from this stinking rich county family who wanted a valuation done for insurance purposes. He was going to fly in and hit it on the Wednesday, then fly straight back out again, but someone else got there first, on the Tuesday. Someone stole his thunder, and his megabucks haul.'

'Oh, shit! He must have been doing his nut,' breathed Matt.

'Believe me, that was one heist Paddy was not going to put down to experience. He told me he used every trick in the book and every contact he'd ever made to find out who had pulled off that job — and he did. The reason the stuff never turned up and no one was ever arrested was that Paddy got there first!' Minty pulled a face. 'The ringleader mysteriously disappeared shortly afterwards, and his gang were given a going-over that made them forget all about a life of crime in this area, and Paddy retrieved a considerable amount of the stolen goods before they could be fenced.'

Matt sat forward, wondering what Minty had been asked to do that was so important.

'However, by hanging around to carry out his vendetta, Paddy gave the authorities time to finger him for another crime committed several months before, and just as he was about to do a disappearing act out of the country again, he was caught and arrested.'

'And later on, you found yourself cellmates?'

'Yes, that's right.'

Matt frowned. 'And? What was this favour he asked of you, Minty?'

Minty seemed to sink lower into the bed. He said quietly, 'There was one really special diamond necklace that Paddy had held back from fencing.'

His voice was so low and muffled that Matt struggled to hear him. 'Minty, it's just you and me, okay? No one's listening.'

Minty swallowed. 'Paddy knew he could get a much better deal for the necklace abroad, so he hid it. He was arrested before he had a chance to move it on.'

'Ah, and you were sent to find it. I see.' He paused. 'And did you?'

Minty nodded miserably. 'I did. I followed his directions and took it to a certain person and I left it with them. As far as I know, it's still there, waiting for Paddy to collect it, but of course, he never will. He was shot two days after he was released from prison, and now he's little more than a vegetable.'

'So that necklace has long since been hocked and someone is considerably richer because of it. There's not too much honour among thieves, Minty. You should know that better than anyone.'

'Normally I'd agree with you, Mr Ballard,' Minty said, 'but not this time. This person is loyal to Paddy, and the necklace will stay safe until either Paddy makes a miraculous recovery or his obituary appears in the papers.'

Somehow Matt couldn't imagine *The Times* or the *Telegraph* featuring Paddy Sheriff, notorious armed robber, in their death announcements. But he could see why Minty was a person of interest. 'And you alone know where that necklace is. Other than its keeper, of course.'

'For my sins, yes, and it weighs heavy, Mr Ballard, believe me. I always thought Paddy would be out one day and I could forget all about that bloody necklace, but it hasn't worked out like that.' He sniffed. 'Last time I visited, I tried to get some sign from him, something that would tell me what to do, but he just got agitated and I had to disappear pronto, before the nurses threw me out!'

Matt now knew that young David would not be driving Minty anywhere. When he went to Norfolk, Matt Ballard would be the chauffeur. He stood up. 'Then we need to get you a long way from here. I'll find you some stuff that you can take with you — clothes and toiletries and the like. And we should sort you out some money, unless you have enough for ten days' food and extras.'

'I've got enough, Matt, you don't have to worry about that, but I'd appreciate some more underwear — and maybe a few clothes? A toothbrush?'

While they packed, Matt asked, 'If what you've told me is the reason for this Jude bloke coming after you, how on earth do you think he found out about you and what his father asked you to do?'

Minty scratched his head. 'That's what I don't understand. No one knows about it, no one, just Paddy. Maybe he did speak, I dunno. He never has, but how else would his son know?'

'What if Jude or someone saw you at that nursing home and discovered you were his old mate Minty from prison days? Perhaps he doesn't know the whole story, but wonders why his dad liked you so much. Maybe he's looking for you to find out.'

'Possible, I suppose, but right now I really don't care. I just want to put some distance between him and me. I've been around the block a few times, as well you know, but that young man scared the shit out of me.'

'Then get some breakfast in you, mate, and we'll hit the road. One thing's for sure, I doubt even your clever psycho will think of looking for you in a Norfolk vicarage.'

Minty gave a faint smile. 'I hope not. But thanks for not asking any more, Mr Ballard. It's harmful knowledge, so best it's only me that's in the firing line.'

Matt said no more about it, but in his detective's heart, he longed to know who could be *that* loyal to a ruthless criminal, and who was quietly sitting on a fortune in diamonds.

* * *

Kellie woke to the sound of her father speaking softly on the phone. She looked at the bedside alarm — seven thirty. She sat up and whispered, 'Dad! Work! You'll be late.'

He held a finger up to his lips and continued to speak. When he'd finished the call, he said, 'Don't worry, that was my boss. She's let me have a couple of days off. Her child had asthma too, and she's pretty fair with single parents. I told a white lie, said Simon needed me, which is true in fact, so it's not really a lie.' He came over and sat on the edge of her bed. 'I've been awake most of the night wondering where that idiotic woman has taken Simon. What was she thinking of, going off like that?'

146

Knowing Auntie Jessie, it could be anything. 'She's not on the same wavelength as most people, Dad,' she said. 'She probably had some great idea, something she decided Simon would love, and just took off. The only thing that really scares me is that postcard.'

'I know, Kellie. That's what worries me too. But right now, we have to decide what to do, how to find out where they went.' He stood up. 'Get a shower and get dressed, girl. We'll get some breakfast inside us and have a think, okay?'

Kellie hadn't thought she was hungry, but when they got down to the restaurant, she wolfed her food. Her father seemed a bit distant. All this not knowing was obviously upsetting him.

They returned to the room and her father took her hand in his. The gesture was practically unheard of, and she almost jumped at his touch.

'Before we do anything, Kellie, I need to tell you a few things.' He looked in her direction, but avoided meeting her gaze. 'You must sometimes wonder why I seem so cold, so, well, unaffectionate, and I want you to know that it doesn't mean I don't love you or Simon. It's just . . .' He hesitated.

'That you miss Mum,' said Kellie simply.

He sighed and hung his head. 'Out of the mouths of babes. Yes, I miss your mum. I miss her so much it's like a light went out, like she stole something from inside of me and took it with her, and she's keeping it until we meet again. All that's left is a shadow. You kids deserve so much more than that, but until now, it's all I've had to offer.'

Kellie was completely taken by surprise. She'd never heard him speak like this. It was almost poetic. Deep. She didn't quite know how to respond.

'The thing is, this . . . event, or whatever you like to call it, has been a wake-up call for me. When I heard that you'd travelled a hundred and fifty miles because your brother needed you and you couldn't even tell me why, well, it shook me rigid and I knew things had to change.' Now he looked her in the eyes. 'We'll get your brother back, lass, and we'll

147

become a family again. Oh, and no more staying with dotty Auntie Jessie. It's me coming too, or Jessie visits us at our home. I can't have something like this happening again. Big adventure! Bloody hell, Kellie, the woman's a fruitcake!'

Kellie laughed. 'You're right there, Dad, but how do we find out where she went?'

'Well, she took her car, which means she hasn't gone far — she hates driving on motorways or through big towns — so it's probably somewhere pretty close by. Or she's driven to the station, left the car in the car park, and they've taken a train.'

'Do we start with the station, then?'

'We do.'

'Dad, can I ask you a question?' He nodded. 'It's something Mum once told me, and it's really bothering me.'

'And what was that?'

'Dad, what do you know about Anna, Auntie Jessie's best friend?'

He knitted his brow. 'Anna? Well, not much really. For some reason your mum never wanted to talk about her. I got the feeling she didn't like her, though Jessie thought she could do no wrong. I think they were childhood friends or something like that.'

'Mmm, they were. You see, Mum told me not to trust Anna. She said she wasn't good for Auntie J. She never told me why, she just said I was too young to understand. She said she'd left a letter for me with your solicitor, and I'd get it when I turned eighteen. She said it would explain everything.'

Finally, her father looked her in the eye. 'She didn't tell me anything about this!'

'So, you've never actually met Anna.'

He shook his head. 'It was odd. She was never there when we visited, even though Jessie was always going on about how wonderful she was.' The frown deepened. 'What? Do you think she has something to do with your aunt taking off like this?'

'Yes, Dad, I do. I'm sure of it. I could be wrong, but yesterday I asked Belle if she knew where Anna lived, and she gave me this really strange look, then said no, she didn't. Well, before you came to collect me, she went out for a while. After she'd gone, I noticed some unopened post on the table, addressed to Miss A. Rackham. I suppose Belle might be short for Annabelle, or Anna . . .'

'Mmm.' Her father said nothing for a while, then, 'After we've tried the station, we'll go back to the marsh and have another word with your kindly rescuer. I've decided to give your aunt one day to either contact me or bring my son back before I go to the police.'

'I was hoping you'd say that, Dad.'

* * *

Her boy woke up listless, looking miserable for the first time since they'd embarked on their adventure. He refused to eat his cereal, saying he wanted toast and Marmite, but she couldn't make toast with the power switched off, it was cold food or things that could be boiled on the camping stove. After a while she cajoled him into eating a strawberry jam sandwich. He drank tea, which was at least warm. He cheered up a bit after a while, but he had lost his sparkle. Jessie wondered if she'd given him too much of Anna's sleeping medicine.

'Can we go home soon, please, Auntie? My chest feels tight. It's being inside all the time.'

He had indeed developed a bit of a wheeze, and the place did feel stuffy with all the windows shut.

'It's still not safe.'

'Why can't we just go to the police and tell them about the bad men?' he said. 'They'll protect me, they've got guns! They'll catch the bad men and lock them up forever.'

Jessie sat down next to him. 'Listen, Simon. Last night while you were asleep my friend came round. She had the same thought as you, so she went to the police station and told them everything.'

Simon brightened immediately.

'Now, the policeman in charge told my friend they knew about those awful men and he was laying a trap for them.'

'Oh, cool!' exclaimed Simon.

'He told her that if she didn't mind us being in her house a bit longer, we would be safer here than anywhere. He said we must stay in hiding just a bit longer. Then they could concentrate on catching the gang, and not have to worry about you.' She took his hand and squeezed it. 'He said to ask you if you could be a really brave boy and help them get this gang arrested by keeping your head down and staying put until we hear from them. Can you do that, Simon? Can you be brave for just a day or so more, to help the police?'

'Oh, sure. I'll be brave, if that's what the police want.'

How she loved him! 'My brave, brave lamb,' she crooned. 'I'm so proud of you. And it's not so bad really, is it? We have lots of games to play, and you can colour your birds. That woodpecker was really good.' She beamed at him. 'And guess what? As a reward for being such a good boy, your auntie might just go and get you a McDonald's for your tea. I'll have to lock you in, of course, when I go out, but no one knows we're here so you'll be perfectly safe. What do you think?'

His beaming smile said it all.

'Good lad! I'll buy you your favourite. Which one do you like best?'

'A quarter-pounder with cheese!' he said at once. 'And lots of chips!'

'Of course,' she said faintly. She hated fast food. But if it would lift the boy's sprits and get them through another day, she was prepared to indulge him.

* * *

After Matt had left for Norfolk, Liz wondered what they should do next.

'Can we have a bit of a catch-up, Liz?' said David. 'There's a few things I'm having trouble getting my head around.'

'Let's go into the Incident Room and run through what we know,' she said.

Going back to the very beginning, they followed the events as they'd occurred, starting from the night Toby ventured out in search of the perfect atmospheric photograph. When they'd finished, they sat in silence for a while. For her part, Liz was frustrated at how little they knew. What had caused the whole incident in the first place? Why did they still know so little about the old house at the centre of this whole affair?

'What really bugs me is this,' David said. He held up a copy of the photograph he had discovered down the back of Alex's desk. 'This path through the old graveyard has to be connected to what happened to the boys, but it doesn't seem to fit in anywhere. It's not even Fenfleet. What was the village called where this was taken?'

'Amblekirk,' Liz said. 'It's tiny, just a few cottages, a farm and the old church. If it wasn't for Lamplight Larry and his missing daughter, I don't think anyone other than a few locals would ever have even heard of it.'

'Could we drive there and take a look at it for ourselves?' David was still staring at the picture.

'Sure, it's not far, maybe ten miles from here, and tell you what, we'll come back via a nice little coffee shop I know in Cutler's Alley. How does that sound?'

'Sounds good to me.'

When they got to Amblekirk, Liz drew up close to the church on an overgrown stretch of land that had served as the car park for the church when it was in use.

'It feels lonely,' said David quietly. 'Makes you feel sorry for all the old souls buried here.'

'The last burial was held a long time ago, so I suppose there aren't many people left now to tend to the graves. Most have just the headstones.' She too thought how sad and lonely it felt.

They walked to the place Alex had photographed. Two paths converged, illuminated by a solitary lamp standard.

Scattered around were headstones leaning drunkenly, some so worn that the names were illegible. The autumn leaves were collecting in little heaps around them.

'This is where the old seat used to be,' said Liz, pointing to four squares of cement just visible through the encroaching grass. 'It was one of those wrought-iron frames with scrollwork on the legs and arms, and heavy wooden slats to sit on. I don't know why they removed it. Just taking their seat away wouldn't deter kids from coming here to have an illicit smoke. They'd just sit on the ground or a tombstone.' She indicated the lamp standard. 'And that was a beauty, a real old Victorian lamp post converted for electricity. Why they swapped it for this thing I'll never know. It's probably got pride of place in some councillor's back garden by now.'

But David seemed lost in thought.

'Earth calling David Haynes! Come in, David.' Liz grinned at him.

He returned her gaze, unsmiling. 'Where does this path lead?'

'The one we're standing on comes from the church, the left-hand path goes into Amblekirk, and that one winds out over the Fen lanes to Ferndyke Village.'

'Is there anything along that lane?' he asked.

She thought about it. 'Just a farm and some derelict outbuildings, then it's fields all the way to Ferndyke.'

David was staring at the picture in his hands. 'It's impossible to tell from this, and I couldn't enhance it any further, but there's this kind of shadowy form that could be a person. I saw it immediately when we first found the picture, but I still can't quite make it out.'

Liz took it from him and stared at it. It could be a hunched figure, but just as likely it could be nothing but a shadow. 'I wouldn't like to say either. Sorry, but the jury's out on that one.'

David sighed. 'Probably just a trick of the night.'

'Don't you mean light?'

'Not in this case,' he murmured. 'It's definitely the night that's playing tricks on us. Anyway, I was just thinking that if it was a person, he or she would have been heading down this path to the next village, and I wondered if there was anything on the way.'

'Barngate Farm was up for sale the last time I came out here. Maybe it's sold by now,' said Liz.

'After a fashion.' The deep voice came from behind them, and they both jumped.

'Sorry!' The man grinned apologetically. 'I did call out, but you were so busy talking you can't have heard me. I don't normally creep up on people in graveyards.' He looked quizzically at Liz. 'Don't I know you?'

His face was vaguely familiar, but that was as far as Liz's memory took her.

'Oh well, it'll come to me,' he said.

The man, casually dressed and wearing walking boots, appeared to be about fifty-five, possibly older.

'I wondered if you were looking for a particular grave. I live in the house next to the church and I generally try to help visitors locate old family graves. Had a few Americans recently, a couple of Aussies too, trying to trace their ancestors.'

Now Liz remembered him, although the name still eluded her. 'I was telling my nephew here about Lamplight Larry, and as we were on our way back to Fenfleet, I thought we'd stop for a few moments to see where he used to sit.'

'Of course, that's it! You were one of the police officers who came out here when the lass — Lamplight's daughter — first went missing! You never found her, did you?'

'You've got a good memory, sir,' she said, and the name surfaced. 'Mr Woodhall, isn't it?'

He let out a guffaw. 'I'm not the only one with a good memory!'

She didn't tell him that Woodhall was the name of her favourite teacher at school who happened to bear a remarkable resemblance to him. 'Actually, it was never even proven

153

that she was missing. Her friends were nearly all of the mind that she ran away with a man her father would have disapproved of.'

'Rubbish! Sorry, that was rude, but that kid was abducted. She was seen heading for the village, and then she vanished. Someone took her, we all know that.'

'The police work on proven facts, sir, not conjecture. People only assumed she was taken, no one actually saw it happen.' She shrugged. 'If something bad had happened to her that night, a body would most likely have been found by now. And we did look, believe me.'

He let it drop. 'You were talking about Barngate Farm?'

'Oh yes. Did it ever sell?' Liz said, relieved to get away from Lamplight's daughter.

'It did, but we're beginning to wonder if anyone will ever actually live there. The new owners — not farming people, you understand — have done that many alterations and "improvements" I doubt much of the old place is left.'

'What about the land? It had a really big parcel of arable land belonging to it, didn't it?'

'All sold off, but not for building, thank God. A couple of farmers gobbled it up to extend their acreage. Now there's just a good-sized garden.'

'What are the new people called?' asked Liz.

'No idea. They're not exactly friendly. I guess they're incomers, but I've not even passed the time of day with them yet, and they've been there almost six months.'

Liz thanked him for telling them about the farm, and Woodhall took his leave.

'Maybe we'll drive home via the lane to Ferndyke, take a look on our way past,' suggested Liz.

David nodded. 'Sure, but can we take a look at the church before we go?'

'I think it's locked up, what's left of it. It's a shame. It was small but beautiful and very old indeed. Now it's been left to fall into ruin. Oh, and I'm told it's dangerous. Someone told me that signs had gone up urging people not to try to enter because of falling masonry and cracks in the foundations.'

'Then maybe just a peek inside?'

They walked back along the path towards the old church.

There were signs, several of them, warning of danger. The front door, its great iron hinges now rusted with age and disuse, had not been opened for some considerable time. But Liz thought the exterior didn't look too bad. She remembered coming here one Christmas for a candlelit service, followed by mulled wine and mince pies. The church wardens had placed lamps like old-fashioned storm lanterns all along the path to the front door. With the arched windows alight from within, it had looked peaceful and festive. A lovely image of a traditional country Christmas on the Fens.

A far cry from now, she thought sadly, watching the dark shapes of rooks fly from the tower at their approach. How things changed. How beauty could degenerate, turn to ruin. How the job you loved and had dedicated your life to could disappear in the space of a night. She sighed.

'You look sad, Auntie Liz.'

David rarely called her auntie these days, and she was rather touched. 'Sorry, Davey, it's just . . .' Then she remembered that he too had had the career he had long prepared for snatched away before he was even out of the starting block. 'I guess I'm beginning to pick up on that loneliness you mentioned earlier.'

'Then let's get out of here,' he said. 'I had some fanciful idea that someone might have been using the crypt to stash drugs or something, and that the boys had followed them and taken photographs.' He gave a sheepish laugh. 'But if the foundations are shifting, that wouldn't be too smart, would it?'

'And anyway, it doesn't have a crypt,' added Liz with a smile. 'This part of the Fen is very silty, and back when the church was built, it was surrounded by marshes. The ground is all drained now but, sorry, no underground chapel to stash crystal meth in.'

'That clinches it, then. Let's go.'

Liz drove out of the parking area and into the single-track lane that led between deep ditches to Ferndyke Village. 'There's the farm.' She pointed to a rambling building set a couple of hundred metres back from the lane. 'I see what Woodhall meant.'

It was a large solid old stone farmhouse. It probably had five bedrooms or more, but even so, it looked like the new owners were already extending it. Scaffolding had been erected at one end, and what once had been the farmyard was full of builders' materials and assorted machinery. She slowed right down to look closer. There were cement mixers, a dumper truck, a mini-JCB and several tradesmen's vehicles. One was a plumber's van, and another bore a logo showing a ladder and a paintbrush.

'Major project in progress,' said David.

'Probably not much wrong with it in the first place,' added Liz. 'I came here when we were searching for Lamplight's missing girl. It was a really lovely classic farmhouse. I know you shouldn't disparage people's taste, but I get the feeling someone is tearing the heart out of a nice piece of rural Fenland history.'

'And adding a home cinema, a spa and a games room, no doubt,' said David dryly. 'Just what a traditional farmhouse needs.'

Liz took a last look at the place, recalling the inglenook fireplace and the Belfast sinks, and accelerated away. 'Real shame, that. Now I need that coffee I promised us.'

* * *

Henry was enjoying a late breakfast — fresh croissants, along with a pot of his favourite coffee, which he had sent over to him from a Spanish supplier who produced a superb blend of three kinds of the finest Arabica beans.

He had spent most of the morning on the phone, and by the time he sat down to his croissants he had satisfied himself that he had made a shrewd decision as to the way forward. Meanwhile, knowing the foolhardiness of acting too hastily, he decided to wait a while before committing himself.

Meal over, he made one last call, to his financial advisor. 'Neil? Henry here. I'm hoping you can earn some of the extortionate sum I pay you by making yourself available in the next hour or so. We have a little windfall coming in, and I need it dealt with particularly carefully, if you get my meaning.'

Call over, Henry sighed contentedly. Just one tiny loose end to sort out, and a call to the lucky recipient of his newly discovered knowledge, and he could think of taking a break. The south of France came to mind. He wondered if Ava liked luxury yachts.

CHAPTER SIXTEEN

Liz told herself firmly that two coffee eclairs in one week was excessive, but gave in when she saw them beckon from the display cabinet of Kitty's Café. David opted for an oversized raspberry jam doughnut and, after ordering, they went to the table Liz had sat at before. This time they were the only customers and, aware that that could change at any moment, Liz decided she'd better waste no time in engaging the elderly waiter in conversation.

As soon as he brought their drinks across, she said, 'See, I'm back again! It's those coffee eclairs.'

'And here was me thinking it was my sparkling personality,' the old man said, and chuckled.

'Oh, that goes without saying, of course,' added Liz, smiling broadly at him. 'I've been telling my nephew here about your excellent coffee.' She paused. 'I also told him about some of the old buildings down here and I promised to show him the old Guildhall and the merchant's house.'

The old man pursed his lips. 'There seemed to be something going on down there last night. Apart from those night owls I told you about before, there were quite a few vehicles further down the alley in the early hours. I wondered if there'd been some kind of emergency.'

Three customers walked in. Liz swore to herself, glanced up at the last one and froze. She leaned forward and whispered to David, 'Start chatting away as if you were talking to your mother! Nothing to do with why we're here.'

Looking puzzled but not missing a beat, David said, 'Shame Dad missed my last goal at the match. It was awesome. Even I couldn't believe I'd netted it. And do you know, not one of my mates managed to get it on video. Best goal of my life and no chance of YouTube fame, what a bummer!'

Mumbling a reply, Liz had her head turned to the window, apparently looking out. In fact, she was watching the reflection of the man at the counter. She breathed a sigh when she heard him order a coffee to go.

David rambled on, now extolling the virtues of soccer over rugby.

'Oh, it's all so confusing to me,' she said and simpered. 'I've never understood all those silly rules they have.'

David looked a little startled, since it was Liz who'd taught him the offside rule when he was a little kid.

After what felt like forever, the man left, carrying his beaker of coffee.

David stared at her. 'What was that all about?'

'A real blast from the past.' She lowered her voice. 'Around five years back I was seconded to help the Met with a big investigation that involved one of our local villains. That man's face was on their whiteboard, and bang in the centre too. He's a London-based career criminal, David, a logistics man specialising in organising transport — you know, obtaining vehicles and managing collections and deliveries.'

'So why is he buying coffee in a back street in Fenfleet?'

'One thing is for sure, Davey, whatever we've stumbled on here, it's big. It would take a whole heap of cash to prise that man away from the Smoke. Matt needs to hear about this.'

'Oh wow. What's his name? Did you ever actually meet him?'

'Yes, to both questions, that's why I was so eager for him not to recognise me. His name is Andre Dassault, but

don't be fooled by that, he's a Londoner, born and bred —
Cockney mother and a French father.'

'I heard him speak to the barista. He obviously wasn't
local,' David said.

'I sat in on an interview with him once, just observing.
My God, I've come across some cool crooks in my time but
he was something else. He was totally unfazed throughout
— and they were tough questions. He had an answer for
everything, gave nothing away. And you couldn't tell a thing
from his body language, which is quite rare. No way were we
able to hold him, and he knew it.'

David wiped sugar from his lips. 'How come you know
so much about what he does, then?'

She pulled a face. 'Knowing something and proving it
are two quite different things. He never does a job without
having a watertight alibi in place before he even sets foot
outside the door. He's a pro, no doubt about it.'

And now he's here in Fenfleet, she added to herself.

David sipped his coffee and gazed out of the window.
'And he's on this particular street just after we've been told
there was a lot of unusual activity here last night. That's
"hinky" in my book.'

'About as hinky as it comes, Davey. And I can't wait to
tell Matt about it.'

* * *

Matt had not hung around on the drive to Norfolk, and had
kept an eye open for anyone following. There was no reason
there should have been, but he knew from experience not to
assume anything.

He was delighted with David's choice of hideaway, he
couldn't have done better himself. The rambling old vicarage
was tucked away in the grounds of a lovely old church in a
quiet corner of a village on the edge of a forest. Matt took
an instant liking to Peter, who had given his new lost sheep
a warm welcome. While Minty settled into his room, Matt

made it clear to the vicar that absolutely no one should know Minty was here. From his reaction, Matt soon realised that Peter was used to such situations. He asked no questions. He had seen and heard it all before.

Leaving Peter his phone numbers, Matt drove home. They had less than ten days in which to make Fenfleet safe again, otherwise, they'd be shunting poor old Minty from one safe house to another.

Twenty miles out of Fenfleet, his phone rang.

'Don't drive into a ditch now, but what would you say if I told you I'd just seen Andre Dassault?'

Matt uttered a loud expletive.

'Thought you might. He walked right past us while we were sitting in Kitty's Café. Don't worry, he didn't notice me, and I chatted away to David like a Stepford wife. He was quite amused.'

'Thank heavens for that. You wouldn't want Dassault to know you're nosing about in Cutler's Alley. But, hey, Liz, this speaks volumes, doesn't it? Dassault's an elite member of the London-based criminal fraternity. For him to slum it in the Fens, whatever he's up to must be big.'

'That's what we thought,' said Liz. 'What's your ETA? We need to talk as soon as you get home.'

'About half an hour, I reckon. See you soon.'

Unconsciously, Matt sped up, his mind churning out different scenarios, none of which were comforting. Just the thought that whatever was going on could attract a villain like Dassault gave him the shivers. That man had detectives throwing in the towel the moment his name was mentioned. Dassault never failed to come up with a rock-solid alibi, and always used the very best solicitors. He had been operating now for fifteen years, and had never yet been caught.

Soon, Matt was back at Cannon Farm, sitting at the kitchen table with Liz and David.

'The whole thing just moved up a gear, didn't it?' said Matt. 'We can't keep this to ourselves. If we have men like Dassault in town, Charley Anders has to know.'

'The thing is, what? And how much?' Liz said. 'There's the presence of big-time crooks like Dassault and Henry, plus suspicious goings-on in Cutler's Alley connected to the death of those boys.'

Matt grimaced. They needed to weigh everything up. 'I suggest the bare minimum. I'll do it now.' But his call went to voicemail. He tried her DI, and heard the familiar miserable tones of Jason Hammond. 'It's Matt. Now listen, no time for pleasantries. I tried Charley but she's not picking up, so can you get this message to her, please? It's important.'

'Go ahead, Matt.'

'Andre Dassault has been sighted in a café in Fenfleet town. Charley needs to know about it straightaway.'

He heard a sharp intake of breath at the mention of the name. 'That's bad news. The DCI is in a meeting but I'll get this message to her immediately, and she'll phone you as soon as she's free.'

Matt thanked him and ended the call.

'Well, that certainly was the bare minimum.' Liz smiled. 'But at least you've given her the important bit, and we haven't sat on it for days either.'

They sat in silence, all wondering what to do next. Finally, David said, 'So, is that it? Are we giving up on the case?'

Matt and Liz stared at him.

David grinned ruefully. 'Silly question. So, what now?'

'We are not ones to give up, lad,' said Matt. 'But the reality is that we might have to hand it over. Dassault's expertise is organising the collection and dispatch of illegal merchandise. Now, if that merchandise consists of people, as in slave labour or the sex trade, lives are at stake if action isn't taken quickly. If it's drugs, thousands of lives could be at risk. Not to mention all that money flowing into the hands of unscrupulous drug dealers.' Spoken aloud like this, he could see there was no way round it.

'If we doggedly press on,' said Liz, 'it will be for the wrong reasons.'

Matt's phone rang. Charley Anders wasted no time. 'Matt, I've got five minutes. I'm in a meeting with the commissioners. Are you sure it's Dassault?'

'Liz eyeballed him, Charley. She knows Dassault, she's met him, even participated in an interview with him. It's him all right.'

'This couldn't have come at a worse time! Half the squad are knee-deep in this horrendously complex money-laundering caper, and the other half are either working with a cyber-fraud unit or tracking down a possible paedo ring. It's hell on earth here right now!'

'I could be wrong, but I don't think Dassault would be involved with any of that, other than perhaps the movement of children,' said Matt.

'It's not that kind of paedo ring, Matt — thank God! It's all online images.' She paused. 'Please don't tell me something else big is about to hit? We simply do not have the resources.'

Matt knew that they could call in outside help but it wasn't something any officer wanted to do.

'Tell me, Matt, and be quick, do you know anything else? Something I'm not aware of. Be honest, now.'

'Nothing we have hard evidence of, Charley. We do have something, yes, but it's all suspicions and possibilities. We're working on a case that could be much bigger than we initially thought. Something serious, and if it is, it's the kind of thing that might interest Dassault.'

'Shit! Shit! Shit! Okay, come on then, what are we looking at? What exactly is the basis for this "something serious"?' Charley said wearily.

Matt closed his eyes. 'Unusual activity in an area of mainly derelict old buildings. Possible but unconfirmed sighting of a woman inside a sealed-up house. Possibility that the accidental death of two young men who were in the same area after dark is actually suspicious. Henry sighted in the same area, now Dassault. Finally, a suspicion on the streets that some kind of new racket is being set in place by persons unknown to even the local criminal gangs.'

Charley was silent for a while. 'Is there any of these things you've mentioned that doesn't have a question mark hanging over it? Other than the presence of Dassault and bloody Henry?'

'Not yet,' Matt said. 'Every indication points to a major crime taking place right under our noses, but further investigation seems to prove otherwise. To our mind, one thing would probably give us definitive answers, and it's something we don't have the power to do — but you do.'

'And that is?'

'Get a warrant and search the old merchant's house on the corner of Cutler's Alley and Bowmaker's Lane.' Matt crossed his fingers.

She muttered something. 'Matt, I have to get back into this meeting, then I'm tied up for hours, but we can't do this over the phone. Get down to the station this afternoon, say four-ish?'

'I'll be there, Charley, but listen, we think something went down last night. Action needs to be taken fast, or whatever goods were brought in could be gone by tonight. You know how quickly they work.'

'Four o'clock, Matt.' She ended the call.

'Do you think she'll do it?' Liz asked.

'I do,' said David quietly. 'She can't afford not to when the info comes from Matt Ballard.'

Matt wasn't so sure about that, but he could only hope.

* * *

The day was not going particularly well for Kellie and her father, Donald. There was no sign of Jessie's car in the railway station car park, so Kellie and her father went to Belle's house. They had no luck there either. Belle was absent, the garage door open and the car gone. They drove to Marsh View in the faint hope that Jessie had returned home with Simon.

The house was still locked, the garage empty.

Kellie's father was trying doors and windows. 'I hope she forgives me if we're wrong about her, but I'm about to take up breaking and entering. This window has a faulty catch, and with a little bit of . . . ah! Got it.'

A small downstairs window swung open.

'Kellie, can you climb in here and go and open the front door? I think I'm a tad porky.'

In a couple of minutes she opened the front door, and her father stepped inside. She felt a bit naughty getting in like this, but what else could they do? She hoped they wouldn't be arrested.

Inside, the cottage smelled of lavender polish. Nothing seemed out of place. There was no washing up in the sink and the rubbish bin had been emptied. Kellie climbed the stairs to the little bedroom they always used whenever they stayed with Auntie. She looked through Simon's things. Only a few items were gone. 'I don't think she was planning to be away long,' she called to her father. 'Most of Simon's clothes are still here, although his rucksack has gone and a lot of his underwear.'

Kellie knew exactly what was missing down to the last pair of socks, as she'd packed Simon's case and rucksack for him. She touched his clothes, wishing he'd never come here in the first place.

She flopped down on his bed, suddenly angry — partly with her father, for not letting her go with Simon, but mainly with her aunt for taking him away and not telling them. She was supposed to be an adult, for heaven's sake, but this was such a stupid and irresponsible thing to do. What about Simon's asthma? Didn't she think of that? Even the stress caused by rushing off somewhere new could bring on an attack, and what if there were animals there? Their hair, especially cat fur, could set it off. Didn't Auntie know that?

Kellie felt tears well up. She didn't want Simon to have an attack somewhere strange, with only their aunt to help. He'd be so frightened. She, Kellie, should be with him. She knew exactly what to do, and when to be concerned enough to seek professional help. She knew how to calm him when he panicked. She sank her head back on her brother's pillow, determined that she would never let anything like this happen again.

'Kellie? You okay, girl?'

She had no right to be angry with her father. He was doing his best. She understood now that losing Mum had hit him harder than she'd realised, and he was struggling to bring up his two children on his own. 'I'm in the bedroom, Dad. I'll be straight down.'

She fluffed up the pillow and her hand touched something hard. She pulled it out. It was one of the postcards she'd given her brother.

Dear Kellie. Auntie says the bad men are looking for me and we have to hide! I have to be brave and it'll be an adventure and my school friends will think I'm a hero. I can't tell Auntie but I am a bit afraid. She says I can come home when the bad men have gone. Her friend will let us know. Love Simon xx PS Miss you.

Kellie gasped. Had he forgotten to post it, or hidden it here for her to find? 'Dad! I've found something!'

She ran down the stairs and thrust the postcard into her father's hand. He read it and groaned. 'What has the stupid cow told the boy? Sorry, Kellie, I know you love her, but . . .'

'Oh, Dad! But why'd she say such a thing?'

'I'm starting to think she's really lost the plot this time. And where on earth has she taken him? *Hide*? What is she thinking of?'

Her father was pacing up and down.

'Did you read the bit about Auntie's friend letting them know when it's safe? That's got to be Anna, hasn't it? So, they're in it together. Dad, do you think this is Anna's fault? Mum didn't trust her, and Mum was always right.'

'Slow down, kid. There can't be some sinister plot. That's crazy.'

'Yes, but what if it's true, Dad? I bet Anna's behind it all. Auntie is so trusting she'd believe anything, especially if Anna told her.'

'But why, honey? What for? If Anna wanted to kidnap Simon, she could just have walked off with him. No, there's something else going on here. I think it's time to go to the police.'

Relieved, Kellie took her father's hand. The police would know what to do. 'Come on, Dad, let's get out of here.'

CHAPTER SEVENTEEN

It took them an hour to lock up again, drive into Fenfleet and find the police station. Kellie's heart sank when she saw the queue of people waiting ahead of them at the front desk. When it was finally their turn, her despondency almost turned to panic. The woman behind the desk didn't seem to understand what her father was trying to tell her.

A uniformed woman police officer came in and stood behind the civilian receptionist. Kellie stared at her, silently imploring her to help. The officer looked over the receptionist's shoulder at what she was writing, and said, 'Want me to have a word, Pat?'

Kellie almost punched the air when the woman said, 'Oh, would you, Debs? I don't know what to make of it.'

'Hello, I'm PC Debbie Hume. Let's take this somewhere quieter, shall we?' She led the way into a small square room with a single table and four plastic chairs. She winked at Kellie. 'Sorry about the décor. Now, please sit down and tell me what's wrong.'

It didn't take long. When Donald had finished, Debbie Hume said, 'What you are telling me is that we have a missing, vulnerable, nine-year-old boy with asthma who, to all intents and purposes, has been abducted by an older woman who is possibly mentally unstable. Have I got that right?'

'It sounds harsh, Officer,' said Donald, 'but that's the crux of the matter. She didn't have my permission to take him anywhere. As far as I was concerned, my son was being looked after by a loving, if a little scatty, aunt, in order to give him a holiday in the fresh air and help him recover from an illness.' He pointed to the postcard that lay on the table. 'And now there's this.'

Debbie stared at the card. 'I neither like nor understand what Simon means by "bad men" but it is a cause for concern. I don't wish to worry you further, but if this Auntie Jessie is rather, well, fragile, do you think she could possibly have seen anyone that really did frighten her enough to run away with Simon? Maybe it wasn't all her imagination. Perhaps some chance meeting frightened her and she overreacted.'

'It's possible, I suppose,' said Donald. 'She is very sensitive.'

Debbie frowned. 'Even so, it's not the most sensible course of action. He's a vulnerable child. I'd have thought the first thing she would think of would be to get him straight home to you.'

Kellie said, 'I think her friend influenced her.'

Debbie pointed to the card. 'The one mentioned here?'

She nodded. 'Anna. She's an old friend of Auntie Jessie's. Auntie always says how clever and strong Anna is and that she doesn't know what she'd do without her.'

'Then she should be our first port of call. Can I have her full name and address, please?' asked Debbie.

Her father sighed, while Kellie pulled a face.

'We don't know them,' said Donald miserably.

'But I think we know someone who does,' added Kellie grimly. 'She might even *be* Anna, for all we know.' She told the police officer about Belle Rackham and gave her the woman's address.

'Do you, by any chance, have a recent picture of Simon?'

To Kellie's surprise, because she hadn't known he carried their pictures with him, her father pulled out his wallet and extracted three photos — one of her mother, one of her and one of Simon. He passed Simon's picture across the table and asked Debbie to be sure to get it back to him as soon as possible.

Debbie asked him for his contact details and stood up. 'I'll run all this past my sergeant. I do have to tell you that we are unusually busy at present with major cases, but I'll do what I can.' She gave them a case number and said she'd be in touch.

Back in their car, Kellie turned to her dad. 'Thank heavens that officer walked into the front office when she did.' She had a strong feeling that Debbie Hume was going to find her little brother.

* * *

'Sorry, Skipper, I don't think you're going to like this. It's about something I just heard, and I have a very bad feeling about it.'

The sergeant stared at Debbie and tightened his lips. Debbie Hume was a good officer whose intuition almost always turned out to be right. 'Okay, what is it?'

Debbie gave him the gist of what Donald had told her. 'Knowing that CID are dealing with a paedo ring right now, I can't help but worry. At a time like this I don't think we can ignore a report of a boy of that age going missing.'

Though her sergeant agreed, he was aware that CID were stretched to breaking point. 'Okay. I suggest that you and Swifty start by getting out there and trying to find out if this Burton fellow is overreacting. We'll see what you come up with before I contact CID.'

'Thank you, Skipper. I'll go and get Jack immediately.'

He watched her go, picturing a little boy hiding in some remote location from the "bad men". It made him go cold. He had boys, three of them, and imagining them in such a situation tore at his heart. Still, he mustn't get ahead of himself. It could all be completely innocent — a case of a youngster misunderstanding something, an older lady acting on impulse. They could already be on their way home, completely unaware of the consternation their actions had aroused. Back to work — if the father in him would just let up.

* * *

Jude was a Fenlander, local to the area, and made sure not to work there, keeping the crimes he committed well away from his home territory. He worked only with people who had no connections to the Fens, especially those belonging to the local criminal groups, like Race's people, or the Leonard family. Anyone seeing him in Fenfleet or any of the other Fen towns must view him as nothing more than a businessman. He had even constructed a bogus identity as the managing director of an IT company. He owned no property in the area, preferring to rent luxury apartments which he changed frequently. He had no friends, just acquaintances who might be of advantage to him.

Jude had no intention of remaining in this backwater a moment longer than necessary. He had set himself a financial target, and it looked like Palmer's new contacts, who were apparently all clamouring for their merchandise, might deliver that figure in months rather than years.

The only thing that might stand in his way was greed. If there was a fortune to be made by continuing with their enterprise, would he know when to call a halt? He'd have to face that problem when he came to it. After all, they'd barely got started with this new scheme.

It had been his idea to set the venture up here, but now he was on home ground he discovered he had mixed feelings about it. Knowing the location was a massive bonus. In fact, without his knowledge, they would not have been able to set up their "places of business" nearly as fast as they had. He knew the best routes to take in order to move the merchandise swiftly and safely. He knew the possible pitfalls, and the ways around them. He had been invaluable to the operation.

However, he had no contacts in the place. He had never dared cultivate even the slightest connection with anyone in the local underworld, for fear of being identified by someone working for Eddie Race or the Leonards. He had no one at ground level, no ears to the ground, no grapevine to keep him in the know. His own operatives, being from out of the area, were all in the dark as to the word on the streets. It was like working in a bubble, and Jude didn't like it.

Maybe he'd feel better when he had sorted out the nagging problem of Minty and his father. Now that the second part of the operation was well underway and out of his hands, his plan was to go and visit his father, then concentrate entirely on Minty Agutter. The next consignment was due to arrive in four days, considerably sooner than usual, but Palmer had declared that supply and demand needed to be met, and Jude wasn't about to object if the payout was anything like what Palmer had suggested. That gave him the rest of today, plus two full days, possibly more if there were no glitches prior to delivery. If he couldn't find Minty in that time, he didn't deserve to find him at all.

* * *

Matt arrived at the police station a little early and went directly to the CID room. He had hoped to corner Bryn, but was instead met by a grim-looking Jason Hammond. Though was that the hint of a smile when he walked through the door? It was gone in an instant, but it was gratifying to know he was still able to cause the ice on that wintry countenance to crack.

'I have an idea why you're here, boss,' said Jason gloomily. 'And if it has anything to do with Andre Dassault, I'd really rather not know.'

'Don't get too desperate, old friend,' said Matt. 'It may be nothing. I'm here to ask a favour of the DCI, and if she acquiesces, we'll know whether to start panicking or not.'

'Well, good luck with that. She's almost running on empty given what she's having to deal with at the moment.

I'm not sure she has much left for granting favours.' Again the hint of a smile. 'Not even for Matt Ballard.'

'Don't be too sure about that.'

'Then it has to be serious!' His face took on an even gloomier expression. 'I have to tell you, your timing is shit.'

'Sorry, Jason, but crime still doesn't keep to time. Feast or famine, just like it's always been.'

The office manager, a new face to Matt, called his name.

He looked up and nodded.

'The DCI has just rung down and said would you go up to her office, please. Do you know the way, sir?'

He nodded again and heard a stifled snigger from Jason's direction. 'Rather too well, miss. It was my office too, in another life.'

Charley Anders rarely showed her emotions, so it was something of a surprise to see her so agitated. He knew only too well what she was feeling: *"How long can I keep juggling all the balls in the air without dropping one?"* There was another thing too, that spoke of something just about to come together. One of her high-profile cases, he presumed. He suddenly felt extremely grateful that he no longer had to shoulder all that responsibility.

'I'm truly sorry to have to land something else at your feet,' he said. 'But I'd have felt bad if I kept this one to myself.'

Charley smiled. 'And I'd never have forgiven you if you had, Matt. Now, all the meetings are over for the day, and barring any emergencies, I'm all yours, so tell me about this suspicion of yours, in detail.'

He gave her all of it, everything they suspected along with what they actually knew.

Charley listened. 'So, you think Greenborough might actually have missed some crucial aspect of those two students' deaths?'

'I'm not blaming them. Far from it. There was absolutely no reason to doubt the forensic reports. Don't forget, Charley, they didn't have the information I have. They knew nothing about the photographs, the robbery at the boys' student house, nor about Minty's involvement. They were presented with a tragedy with a perfectly explicable cause. Even the mother's concerns were those of any bereaved parent who is unable to come to terms with such a terrible loss. It's only human to find someone to blame at a time like that.'

Charley stared down at her desk. 'I can see the reason for your concern, especially about that merchant's house, but I'm not sure we have enough corroborated evidence to treat this as a priority case, especially not with all we have on at present. I can put a few uniforms in the streets around that area, maybe a couple of plain clothes, to see how the land lies, but that's about it.'

'I'm not sure that would be advisable, Charley,' said Matt. 'One whiff of police presence and they'll melt away like the morning mist, only to start up again elsewhere.' He looked at her gravely. 'Go with me on this. I *know* something serious is going on, and that house is at the centre of it. Old man Boon is sending his son in next week, but that's too late. We need it checked out now, or whatever is there will be long gone. Look, I'm willing to state that I was passing that old place and heard cries, then you would have just cause to ask for a warrant, especially as with my background, I'm a reliable source who suspects a life is in danger. In fact, you could go in without a warrant if a life was under threat.' He left it there. He had no more cards to play.

'If I didn't know you better, I'd say you were trying to blackmail me, Matt Ballard!' Charley grinned.

Yup, he thought. *You got it.*

Charley shook her head. 'Okay. But this is all I'm going to do, so listen up. And you owe me one for this! I will get a warrant and we'll go and see that ancient solicitor, but — and this is non-negotiable — you have to wait until tomorrow to get into that house. We have a dawn raid here in town in connection with the big money-laundering case we have on. This is likely to be the biggest arrest in the whole investigation and I'm not messing that up for anything or anyone — including you, my friend.'

Ah, so that was the reason for her look of suppressed excitement. 'Understood,' he said. 'I appreciate it.'

'You better! Anyway, I'll get it underway immediately, and a team will go in at around ten in the morning. And before you say anything else, I'm assuming you want to go with them?'

'I do, Charley, very much.'

'Then be here at nine forty-five. By then we should have the keys from old man Boon and be ready to go. We'll keep it low-key — enough officers to cope but not half the station. And no charging in with big boots and enforcers, just a quick and thorough search. Then, depending on what we find, if anything, we'll take it from there.'

'Can't ask for more than that,' said Matt, sorry it couldn't happen that day but relieved it was actually going to happen at all. He stood up. 'Thanks, Charley. I'll be here tomorrow.' He paused at the door. 'And, yes, I do owe you one.'

* * *

By late afternoon, Donald Burton had really begun to panic. He tried to hide it from his daughter, who was already pale and looking far more stressed than any kid her age ought to be. This was all his fault. He couldn't forgive himself for letting his own grief come first, before the safety and well-being of his children. But what was done was done. He couldn't undo the past, but he vowed that the future would be different. Donald Burton was going to make his two children feel like the most important and well-loved kids in the world. He just needed to get Simon back home.

'You look like you're a million miles away.'

'No, sweetheart, I was just wondering where my brain was when I let our lad go off to stay with your aunt. I mean, she's always been a bit of a birdbrain, hasn't she? I should have thought first, and I should have listened to your worries too, not just shouted you down.' He meant it. Kellie was

175

old beyond her years and he should never have assumed that because she was only fifteen, she wasn't capable of working things out.

'Auntie does love Simon, Dad, and me too. She'd never deliberately hurt him. I just wonder how much influence her friend has over her. Maybe Anna asks too much of Auntie Jessie, tells her to do things Auntie is just not up to.'

'It's possible,' he said. 'Who knows? Maybe she's finally had enough, and actually run away from Anna.'

'Or run away *with* Anna,' said his daughter. 'The more I think about it, the more I wonder how our sweet, dotty aunt could have managed to get them away all on her own.'

She was right. If Jessie was in one of her sensitive moods, just getting to the supermarket would cause her a major panic. A sick feeling overcame him. When he had bundled Simon off for a break on the Fens, Donald had been thinking only of his beloved wife's older sister, the happy, loving woman who adored the children, could cook beautifully, recite whole verses of poetry, play the piano, and quote from a hundred works of literature. He had completely overlooked her other side.

His phone rang and he met his daughter's gaze. Could this be good news?

'PC Debbie Hume, sir. I just wanted to update you, and I forgot to ask, do you have a key to your sister-in-law's house?'

He admitted he didn't. He confessed to PC Hume that earlier that day they had climbed in through a downstairs window with a broken catch.

'Then I wonder if you would be so kind as to meet us at her cottage in half an hour? My partner and I would like to have a look around ourselves, but we'd appreciate you being there. If the catch is broken, we'll go in the same way.' He detected a hint of amusement in her voice. 'We've been around the area to see if anyone noticed them leave, which is where we are now. There's still no sign of Mrs Belle Rackham at her address, but we'll persevere with that. We'll make our way to the cottage now.'

They were there in fifteen minutes and had only just parked when Debbie and an older police officer arrived, whom she introduced as PC Jack Fleet but called "Swifty" when they spoke together.

The police constable was a rather fatherly-looking man with a warm smile who looked as if he'd been doing this job forever. 'Something bothers me,' said Jack, as his slimmer partner slipped through the open window. 'Hasn't your boy got a mobile phone? I mean, it's odd that he hasn't contacted you himself, isn't it?'

Donald sighed. 'He's not your average kid, PC Fleet. He isn't interested in technology. He has got a phone, but half the time he forgets to charge it, or even carry it with him. His schoolwork suffers because he hates computers.'

Jack Fleet nodded. 'I see, but I'd have thought he might have used it if they were in trouble.'

'I would have hoped so,' said Donald rather miserably. He explained that Jessie hated telephones and often refused to answer. 'I've had two calls from her in all the time Simon has been staying with her, both lasting less than three minutes.'

'And up to now you've never had any serious qualms about the lady's, er, well, mental health?' Jack asked.

'No,' said Kellie. 'She's quirky all right. My mum used to call her the original scatterbrain. But she's kind, and artistic, and she loves us very much, she just lives in her own little world and doesn't always see things as others do.'

'Jessie is certainly eccentric, in fact she's quite unique, but it's just the way she is,' added Donald.

'Well, that's told me!' laughed Jack. He looked at her, his expression serious. 'But you really are worried about what she's done now, aren't you, young lady?'

Kellie nodded dismally. 'Yes, sir. I'm very worried indeed, especially about my brother's asthma.'

'That's the reason we're taking this so seriously too, miss. We can't afford to have anything bad happen to him, can we?' He patted her shoulder gently. 'Now, let's take a look around, shall we? You can be the leader.'

CHAPTER EIGHTEEN

Jessie realised that their great adventure, a time she would treasure in her heart forever, was soon going to have to end.

Simon had been good all day, playing games and painting his birds, but now he was beginning to fret again and had even needed to use his inhaler. It was time to go home.

Now she needed to go and get them that dreadful supper she had promised him. Luckily it wasn't far — unless there was a queue she could be there and back in under half an hour. When she got back, she'd tell him she had met her friend who'd told her they were safe to go home the next day. Jessie didn't want to go, but for Simon's sake she had no choice.

So that he didn't panic while she was out, she'd slipped a few drops of Anna's mixture into his hot drink, and already he was looking more relaxed.

'Now, my darling, you put the bolt across the door when I leave, and don't open it for anyone but me. I'll knock like this . . .' She rapped three times on the tabletop. 'And I'll call your name, all right? Then you undo the bolt and let me in. I promise not to be long, and I won't forget the fries.' She smiled warmly at him. 'All ready, sweetheart?'

He nodded. 'Hurry back, Auntie.'

She pulled on her jacket and checked that she had money in her handbag. 'One double cheeseburger and fries coming up, sir!'

Outside the door, she heard the bolt slide into place and looked around furtively. She had to be very careful not to be seen, even at this late stage in the game. She took a deep breath, terrified of this trip into the unknown. She let it out again, slowly, and reminded herself that for Simon she would walk through the gates of the fiery furnace of hell itself.

She scurried away, wanting nothing more than to get this task over with. Head down, she failed to notice the cold, hard eyes following her along the street.

* * *

It would be an understatement to say that the occupants of Cannon Farm were on edge. The thought of what was happening in Cutler's Alley, probably right now, coupled with having to wait until the following morning to do anything about it, was becoming intolerable. Liz was trying to prepare supper, but her mind kept wandering.

'If it's drugs, that place will be clear after this evening, won't it? They're hardly going to sit on their stash, it'll be moved on as fast as they can shift it.'

'It's bloody frustrating,' Matt said, 'but we can't scupper what is probably years of painstaking work on Charley's money-laundering investigation. You know how important the dawn raid always is.'

She did, of course, but that didn't stop it being galling.

'And if it's people trafficking, would they do the same?' asked David. 'Move them in and then straight out again?'

'That would depend,' said Matt. 'If they thought it was a really safe location, they might keep them there for a while, and filter them quietly out to wherever they were being sent. It would depend on how many people were involved.'

'If Andre Dassault is the logistics man,' said Liz, 'I'd stake money on a big haul. If it's women for the sex trade,

I would guess he's organised a swift passage out. The merchant's house could just be the terminus. From there they head out to different destinations. The place could have been emptied by as early as this morning.'

'It is frustrating, my love, but we have to hold on to the fact that at least that damned house will be searched properly tomorrow,' Matt said. 'No matter who's been in there, or what they've been doing, they will have left traces. They might even have left enough evidence behind, in the form of fingerprints or DNA, to point to whoever is behind it. And if the fates were really on our side, we could find a whole consignment awaiting distribution.'

'And pigs might fly!' exclaimed Liz, sounding uncharacteristically downbeat. Matt was talking like a police officer again, not a private detective. If that house threw up anything suspicious, the whole thing would be turned over to Charley Anders, and their private investigation would come to an abrupt end.

'It's happened before,' he said. 'Remember the Smith brothers? They shipped in a haul of heroin with a two-million-pound street value, and sat on it to get a better price.'

She smiled. 'But we got there first, and they paid the price instead of getting it — in the form of a long stretch in prison.' But that certainly wasn't the norm. Illicit goods changed hands fast, and for a reason. Big money was to be made, but the risks were high, so the less time spent in possession of such commodities the better.

There was nothing they could do now but wait.

'Mind if I take a run through all those amazing photographs again?' asked David. 'The night ones that Toby took.'

'Sure, go for it,' Matt said. 'Looking for anything in particular?'

'Not really, I'm just interested in getting an idea of what Toby felt that night.' He looked from Matt to Liz. 'I must confess, the deaths of those students has really got to me. They were my age, so maybe that's why. You kind of think you have your whole life ahead of you, then something like this happens . . .'

Liz had been there herself. She told him about a close friend of hers who had been killed in a car crash at the age of twenty-one. 'It stays with you, Davey, but it also makes life, and what you do with it, all the more precious.'

'It certainly does,' he said softly, and left the room.

They heard the sound of the computer starting up. 'We've rather thrown that kid in at the deep end, haven't we?' said Matt softly. 'There he was thinking he was coming for a few days of walks in the fresh air with his loving aunt and he finds himself helping with a case involving double murder!'

'It sounds a funny thing to say, but I think it will have helped David enormously,' said Liz. 'He's had very little time to dwell on his own problem, and being faced with something as serious as this, seeing the suffering of the bereaved parents, makes a glitch in his career plans seem a bit trivial.'

'Well, yes, I see what you mean, but I still think the whole thing must be a bit of a shock.' Matt looked pensive. 'He hasn't mentioned his mother's reaction to him failing to pass his entrance exam, has he?'

'No,' Liz said. 'He doesn't talk about her too much. He loves her, but I think he wishes he saw more of her. Maybe he feels rejected. Even at twenty, it can still hurt. It wasn't a messy divorce or anything like that. In fact, other than my own split with Gary, it was probably one of the most frictionless divorces you could hope for.'

'Parting amicably from your spouse must run in the Haynes family,' said Matt, grinning.

She laughed. 'Probably. But David does miss her, especially after her promotion. Her work takes her all over the country, so he sees even less of her than before, poor kid.' She bent down and, amid a clatter of saucepans, said, 'Dinner at six? Is that okay?'

'Fine, then it's a case of trying to fill in the time between tonight and tomorrow's house search.' Matt sighed.

'Hell, I wish I knew what was going on. I mean, what is important enough for them to snuff out two young lives?'

'Me too,' Matt said. 'Hopefully, tomorrow will bring the answers.'

Liz wondered if it would. She had a bad feeling about the coming day, totally irrational, she knew. Nevertheless, it nagged away at her.

* * *

'How many inhalers does your brother have, Kellie?' Debbie wasn't sure why, but it seemed more appropriate to ask the girl than her father.

Kellie counted them on her fingers. 'He has a preventer inhaler, he uses that daily to cut down the chance of triggers. Then there's a blue reliever inhaler from the doctor. Our pharmacy let me have an emergency inhaler for him since he was going to be away for a while, just in case he ran out. Oh, and he has a spacer too — it gets the medicine down into his lungs better than just the inhaler.'

Debbie stared down into the open kitchen drawer, seeing the spacer, a brown preventer inhaler, and one blue reliever. That meant the kid only had one inhaler. How many doses did it have left in it? Her concern increased.

'Oh no!' Kellie was beside Debbie, her mouth slightly open, her eyes on the inhalers in the drawer. 'He's supposed to have all of these!' She called out, 'Dad! Auntie never took Simon's preventer or his spare inhaler!'

'Then she probably wasn't planning on being away for too long,' said Jack Fleet's soothing voice from the doorway. 'Let's not get into a panic. And he does have his main inhaler, that's the important thing.'

They continued to search for any indication of where Jessie Wright had taken young Simon. Debbie was fully aware that this was not exactly good police practice but she told herself that the house had been left unsecured and they were simply checking that nothing untoward had occurred to a vulnerable minor.

Leaving the others, she went into the aunt's bedroom. It was a mass of ornaments, collectibles, photos — mainly of Kellie and Simon, but also of another woman, who Debbie guessed must be their mother, Jessie's deceased sister. She glanced at them, hoping to spot an image of Jessie's best friend, Anna, but there weren't any that she could see. Jessie herself wasn't featured at all.

She slid open the drawers, wondering if she might find a diary, or a brochure telling them where they might have gone. She tried a drawer in the bedside cabinet but it was locked and she couldn't see the key.

Debbie's eyes narrowed. Why lock a bedside drawer? Medication she didn't want Simon finding? Debbie went to the dressing table and looked at the clutter of bottles and sprays, little trays and boxes. She found the single key in a china pot with a painting of a kitten on it. Some people could be very predictable.

She opened the drawer and groaned. Inside was a charger and a mobile phone in a bright blue case bearing a picture of an eagle. A small Dymo label had been carefully stuck onto it — *SIMON*. Debbie didn't think for a moment that it had been placed there to keep it safe. It was there, locked away, because it was being hidden from the boy. But why?

All at once, Kellie was at her side. She took the blue phone from her hand and stared at it. She then lifted the charger from the drawer and plugged it in. One missed message flashed up: *Look out for me tomorrow afternoon. I'll be with you then. Hang on, little bro!* Her brother had never received her message.

'PC Hume . . .' Her voice trembled. 'You *really* need to find my brother.'

* * *

Half an hour later, having sent Kellie and her father back to their hotel, Debbie and Jack Fleet were sitting in their car.

Their shift had ended, but they were both loath to walk away from this problem.

'How the hell are we going to cope with all this, Jack?' she asked. 'There's the raid tomorrow, plus the other major cases that CID are trying to hold down, and now Cindy's told me she's been sent to get a warrant for some house search in Fenfleet tomorrow — heaven knows what that's all about. We're struggling, mate, no word of a lie!'

'I imagine they'll probably draft in some extra bodies from other divisions, Debs. Both Saltern and Greenborough are pretty good like that when we need backup,' said Jack. 'One thing is for sure, we can't possibly ignore this one. There's a twisted mind at work here — it has all the hall-marks. Tack that onto the missing child having a medical condition and, well, it doesn't bear thinking about.'

Debbie started the car and they drove back to Fenfleet police station, both trying to work out why an apparently loving aunt would suddenly take off with her nephew, without telling his father, and concealing the kid's mobile phone prior to leaving. One thing they could agree on — it made no sense whatsoever.

As they went in, they heard the laughing voices of another crew returning from their shift. They caught up with them at the door.

'What's occurring?' asked Jack.

PC Angus West shook his head. 'Some nutter, mate. About an hour ago we got called to assist the ambulance guys with a drunk, but when we got there, it was this dotty old bird who was yelling the place down.' A broad smile spread across his face. 'Dingo here took a hefty swipe from her handbag when he tried to calm her down. Wish I'd got it on my camera, it was priceless!'

'Where was this?' asked Jack, hurrying in after him.

'Outside McDonald's,' grumbled PC Ken "Dingo" Wolfe. 'Mad cow. That handbag bloody stung. Caught me right round the earhole!'

She had no idea why, but Debbie wasn't laughing. 'Did you find out what upset her so badly?'

'Ambulance woman said it was a panic attack,' said Angus. 'They've taken her down to A&E to get her looked at, especially as they found an inhaler in her pocket. She wasn't drunk, so you can't be too careful.'

Debbie swung round to face Jack, her eyes wide.

'Come on.' He grabbed her arm, and with the other two officers watching in amazement, they raced back out of the station. 'We have to get to the hospital before they throw her out!'

The newly opened hospital was situated along the coast road on the outskirts of town. Debbie drove as fast as she dared, screeched to a halt close to the ambulance bay and they ran into the A&E department.

Jack stopped at reception and asked about a woman who had been brought in suffering from a panic attack. A few minutes later, a security door swung open and they were directed inside the busy unit.

'Third bay on the left,' called out the receptionist. 'They'll be glad to see you two. She's caused a right rumpus, I can tell you. You can hear her from here!'

On entering the bay, they were met by two har-assed-looking nurses and a young man Debbie assumed to be a doctor.

'I didn't know we'd called you guys out,' he said over the cries of the woman lying on the stretcher. 'She is calming down, believe it or not.'

Debbie explained that they were looking for a missing person, possibly this very woman.

The young man looked relieved. 'It would help a lot if we knew her name, poor thing. She's had a serious episode. We've given her a sedative but she's fighting it.'

'A panic attack?' asked Jack.

'Kind of. Maybe she has a history of mental illness.' He gave them a weary smile. 'I'm Dr Rod McLeod, by the way.

I've asked for a psych to come and take a look at her but they're all tied up at the moment, so we're just doing our best to keep her safe.'

Debbie stared at the woman on the trolley. Her age and appearance fitted Donald Burton's description of his sister-in-law. However, if this was Jessie, she was nothing like the timid little twittering soul they had spoken of. Her eyes positively blazed at them, like those of a cornered animal. Initially, Debbie had thought she was angry, but now she decided it was fear.

'Jessie? Jessie Wright?'

Momentarily the woman stopped struggling, and glanced helplessly at Debbie. Then she began twisting and turning again, but with slightly less intensity.

Debbie spoke softly. 'Jessie, we're here to help you. You are Jessie, aren't you?'

Everything in the cubicle became still. The figures around the bed stood motionless. 'Jessie, where is Simon?'

The silence was shattered by a wail, a keening. Jessie cried out, 'She never came! She never came!'

'Who never came, Jessie?' Debbie said.

'She always comes when I need her, but she didn't!' The woman's sobs seemed to rack her whole body.

There was little doubt in Debbie's mind that this was Jessie Wright, but what had happened to her?

'I'm going to ring this in,' Jack whispered in her ear. 'Will you keep on asking about Simon?'

She nodded. 'Of course. And I want to know who "she" is as well.'

Debbie asked the doctor if she could sit next to his patient and try to talk to her.

'Be my guest,' he said, pulling up a chair for her. 'You're doing better than us. And now one of the nurses can go and check for any record of a Jessica Wright.'

Gently, Debbie took the woman's hand in hers and sat with her, letting her cry. When the painful sobs eased, becoming gulps and sniffles, Debbie decided to try again.

'Jessie, I know you're terribly upset, but we are really worried about little Simon. Do you know where he is?'

'She never came,' she croaked. 'I wanted to get back to him, but she never came.'

'Back where, Jessie? Where did you leave Simon?'

'Safe. Very safe.'

The voice had taken on a sing-song quality that Debbie found a bit unnerving. 'I'm glad he's safe, that's very good, but where is he? Can you tell me?'

All at once, Jessie was behaving like some twittery little old lady. 'Sorry, dear, do I know you?'

Debbie swallowed. She wasn't exactly trained for this. 'Hello, Jessie. No, you don't know me, but I'm Debbie. I'm a police officer. You haven't been very well.'

'Oh dear, haven't I?' She looked around as if she'd just woken from sleep. 'Am I in hospital?'

'Yes. They're looking after you, so don't worry.' She patted her hand. 'But we think you might have left your nephew Simon somewhere, and we are a bit worried about him. Can you tell me where he is, Jessie, so we can go and fetch him and bring him here to you?'

'Simon?' She looked blankly at Debbie. 'Oh, Simon! My lovely boy!' A look of terrible distress flooded her expression. 'Where is he?' Her cries grew louder. 'Simon! Where are you?'

'Hush,' said Debbie, trying not to panic herself. 'You said he's safe. Try to remember where that safe place is, and I'll go and get him for you.'

An ear-splitting scream tore from Jessie's throat. 'I can't remember!'

CHAPTER NINETEEN

The hours that followed were some of the most difficult of Debbie's life. Jessica veered between bouts of hysteria and apparent catalepsy as Debbie tried to guide her through the events of the past evening, and find out why she had gone out and left Simon alone.

By the time Jack arrived back from trying to organise a search of the area around McDonald's, Debbie was sitting outside the cubicle, exhausted and close to tears.

'This is useless!' she exclaimed. 'We've been going round in circles. I'm no closer to finding Simon than when I started. All I can think of is that little boy, alone and frightened.'

He handed her a styrofoam cup of coffee. 'Have you managed to glean anything at all from her?'

She accepted the coffee gratefully. 'She said she had promised him a double cheeseburger — she recalled that bit clearly — and kept saying, "With fries! With fries!" over and over again.' Debbie shivered. 'That bit was quite freaky, actually. She said she heard the bolt click across, so she knew he was safe, but where the hell they were, God only knows!' She sat back on the plastic chair and exhaled. 'Look, this is just a guess, but I think the woman she was yelling about when she kept saying "She never came!" was the one Kellie is so anxious about, this Anna. I wanted to ask her, but she got so agitated I didn't dare.'

Jack went and found another chair and sat beside her. 'Anything else?'

'Well, it was all so confused, but she did say they were staying in a friend's place. So then I wondered if she meant it belonged to Anna. Oh, I don't know.' She sighed. 'And even if it was Anna's, it's no help to us because we don't know Anna's surname or where she lives.'

'Unless it's Rackham, Annabelle Rackham, and she's still not at home. I checked.'

They sat in silence for a while, sipping their coffee.

'I do have one idea, but be honest, if you think it's unwise, just tell me. I'm not sure if I'm capable of rational thought after all these hours with Jessie Wright.'

Jack smiled at her. 'You're doing a brilliant job, lass. There's not many people who'd have stuck at it like you did. Go on, tell me. What's this idea?'

'Well, I was just thinking of all the photos Jessie has of Simon and Kellie. Jessie is obviously very fond of both of them, not just Simon. Suppose we brought the girl in to talk to her auntie?'

'I'd say that's a bloody good idea, Debs. If anyone can get anything out of that daft old bat, it'll be Kellie. We'd need Skipper's consent, of course, and her father's, but I think she could do it. She's sensible enough.' He stood up. 'You stay here and I'll phone the sergeant.'

Debbie rubbed her tired eyes. She needed to sleep. She'd been on the go now for thirteen hours, and there'd be no time to lie in tomorrow and catch up. But she couldn't leave now, she'd just have to hang on.

Jack didn't take long. 'A car is going to the hotel to collect Kellie and her dad.' He stared at her. 'And you are going home, lass. You've done your bit.'

'No, Jack, I could no more go home now than I could fly. I'll sit in with Kellie. I think we have a bit of a bond, and

189

she might need a bit of prompting. Let's see what happens, and then I'll be off.'

'Is it worth me arguing the point?'

'Nope. Let's give it this one last shot, shall we?'

* * *

It would have been an understatement to say that the news travelled fast, and this was true of both the guardians of the law and the crooks.

Matt and Liz turned in at around eleven o'clock, but immediately their light went out, Matt's phone rang.

'Sorry to ring so late, Mr Ballard, sir, it's Albie Grant. Stop me if you've heard this already, but Fenfleet town is crawling with uniforms.'

Matt sat up abruptly. 'What? Why?'

'Ah, I gather you haven't heard then,' Albie cackled. 'But don't panic, guv'nor. It's not what you were asking about. They reckon it's a missing kid. Even so, I wouldn't want to be up to anything naughty on the streets tonight, it's alive with coppers.'

Matt grunted in frustration. 'Do you know which area they're concentrating on? Or is it across the whole town?'

'As far as I can make out, it seems to be around the High Street and Market Square, and a bit beyond, but I can't be more specific than that, I'm afraid.'

Thanking Albie for putting him in the picture, Matt told Liz what he'd said.

She groaned. 'This case is fated. I'm sorry it's a missing child, but the timing couldn't be worse, could it?'

'Well, if there ever was anything in that old house, it'll have gone by tomorrow, you can bank on that,' Matt muttered. 'If only . . .'

'Don't go there, Matt.' Liz sat up. 'And if *we* think it's bad, then consider how Charley will be feeling. Their dawn raid may be aborted, after all that work, and now, on top of all the other serious cases, they might have a missing child as well. That really stinks.'

He knew all that, and he understood. But he also understood that their own case would now be low on the list of priorities, and it did smart that they'd been halted in their tracks. Still, a child must come first, and he wished he was back in the force and helping with the hunt. He recalled Charley saying they were working a case that involved a paedo ring, and he prayed this missing child had nothing to do with that. With luck, it was just a kiddie who had wandered off and got lost, and was probably already safe at home, tucked up in bed with hot chocolate and biscuits.

They lay down again, and Liz snuggled into him. 'I get the feeling neither of us are going to sleep too well tonight, Mattie. You know, one thing that does get to me about not doing our old job is that we're out of the loop. I hate not being able to just pick up a phone and within seconds have the whole situation in front of me.'

'I know what you mean,' he said, stroking her hair. 'But we're better informed than a lot of private detectives. I'm just thankful I kept in touch with many of my old, er, associates. Our big-eared friend seemed to know all about the goings-on in Fenfleet tonight, even though he's based in Greenborough. That was hot off the press info, breaking news. In real time.'

Liz laughed softly. 'Oh, darling. I'm not knocking your very capable networking friends, it's just the basic knowledge, the facts that I miss.' She sighed, her breath brushing his chest. 'This missing child, for instance — that's all we know. I would dearly love to know the facts — age, gender, description, how long missing, in what circumstances, who reported it, is the child particularly vulnerable in any way, like learning difficulties, impaired hearing, the exact time he or she was last seen, and—'

'Whoa! I get the picture. And I do agree. It *is* frustrating but, as you're always telling me, we've moved on now — different life, and all that. That missing child is not our problem. It's the Fenland Constabulary's concern, nothing to do with us. And they'll pull out all the stops, you know that.' Matt was mildly surprised to hear Liz telling him of the things she missed about the police force when it was usually the other way round. In fact, it was always the other way around. Thinking about it, he would be hard put to recall her *ever* saying that she missed anything from her old life, but this time she'd sounded quite vexed by it.

'I wonder if the search will go ahead?' Liz whispered. 'It's in the lap of the gods, isn't it?'

'It will all depend on the results of tonight's search for the child, and the raid, if it goes ahead. At least it's in a different part of Fenfleet, or so I gathered from what Charley said.' Matt closed his eyes. 'Let's just try and get some sleep and hope for the best, shall we?'

Liz didn't answer, and from her regular breathing, he realised that she was already asleep. 'So much for having a sleepless night, lady,' he whispered, and kissed her hair. If only he could sleep too.

* * *

The moment the news reached Jude, he sprang into action. He had a programme set up for just such an eventuality, and his men had it underway immediately. This was an emergency situation that required not only clearing anything incriminating from their facility, but in a way that wouldn't draw any unwelcome attention to it. It was far too good a location to lose and Jude wanted to ensure they could continue to use the place. Hopefully, it wouldn't even be searched, but he was taking no chances.

At least the merchandise itself had already been dispatched. It had been their fastest turnaround so far, which, with another consignment arriving in four days' time, was all for the best. Something like a search for a missing child was the sort of thing you could never plan for, but even so, you had to be prepared for any eventuality.

He double-checked the back entrance. It was clear. His men had texted him to say they'd vacated the site and there had been no hitches. Now it was his turn. Trusting no one, Jude would check it alone. If there'd been the slightest oversight, he would see it. He always did.

With one last glance around, Jude entered the old building.

* * *

Henry's personal bush telegraph was the fastest and most efficient in Fenfleet. As soon as he got the first call, he donned his usual dark clothing and went to take a second look at what had bothered him in Cutler's Alley. While he was at it, he thought he'd find out how this new gang were dealing with tonight's sudden police presence in the neighbourhood.

He wasn't surprised to find the gang had done exactly as he would have had he been in charge. They were professionals all right, but they'd have to be. There was an awful lot of money at stake, given the merchandise they were handling.

Hidden from view, he watched the clean-up operation for a while. There were two faces he could put names to. It surprised him to see these big-league, London-based hard men here in Fenfleet. For them to bother with the Fens meant this must be even bigger than he'd thought.

Henry waited until they moved out. If things went as he believed they would, there would be one more visitor before the usual silence reigned in Cutler's Alley.

There he was. Right on time — the man he had followed two nights ago. Henry watched the man let himself in, then he crossed the road and went around to the back, and his alternative way in. He knew just what this man was up to — ensuring the place had been cleared completely. He wouldn't be long, unless he came across the anomaly Henry had noticed. Then Henry could make his own investigation and, hopefully, work out how to make use of this valuable piece of information.

* * *

Late as it was, Niamh Conran felt impelled to look at the message on her phone. She reached across her sleeping partner and picked it up.

Henry.

Her interest piqued, she lay back and read: *Wanted to thank you, you gorgeous woman! That introduction to Ava was an inspired move, in more ways than one!* Niamh smiled into the darkness. Henry was so predictable — always a randy git. *In return, I can tell you I believe a crime extraordinaire is being committed, right here in town. Here's the name of the man I suspect to be in charge of this monster. Keep it to yourself for now, I have no proof, but I've seen something like this before and then it was the brainchild of a man called Palmer. You won't be seeing me around for a while, I have a rather fortuitous windfall coming my way and I plan on taking a long holiday. With a companion. You might just have been instrumental in changing my life, so thank you again, your friend, Henry.*

Niamh deleted the message. Palmer? It meant nothing to her, but it might be worth investigating. She'd never known Henry to be wrong. It would be the first thing she did next morning. She wished Henry well but admitted to herself that she'd miss him. He was a one-off, and his sexual charisma rolled off him in waves. If she had been attracted to men, Henry would be her first choice of bedmate.

She snuggled back against her partner and sighed. Lucky Ava.

* * *

Debbie Hume didn't get home until after one in the morning. Her idea of getting young Kellie to talk to her aunt had worked in part, but not quite as she had hoped. On seeing Kellie, Jessie had initially been distraught, showering the girl with heartfelt apologies, so that at one point Debbie had feared Kellie might succumb to impatience and lose her temper. However, Kellie managed to contain herself.

The medics had given Jessie a sedative which reduced her agitation but didn't send her to sleep. She continued to fluctuate between forgetting why or where she was and dwelling on events from the past.

194

But Kellie couldn't remain awake all night, so, despite her protestations, it was decided that both she and her aunt should get some sleep. A police officer took her place at the bedside and would continue to listen and press for answers should the old lady wake and become lucid.

Debbie, too, was forced to throw in the towel, but not before snatching a few moments with the obviously exhausted psychiatrist who had been sent for to assess Jessie Wright.

The doctor — a woman of around fifty — confessed to being puzzled. Jessie, she explained, was suffering from a sort of dissociative amnesia, usually brought about by a trauma. She couldn't understand why they had no record of her in the hospital files — most unusual in a patient of her age who had spent so many years in the local area. She exhibited other nervous traits that the doctor felt should have been treated with medication. Debbie asked how long an episode like this could be expected to last, and was told sometimes hours, sometimes days, possibly longer, depending on the cause. As Debbie was about to leave, the psychiatrist suggested they might try a rather unusual course of action — hypnosis. They would wait till she had had some sleep, in the hope that that would restore her, but if there was no change, this might be the avenue to follow, bearing in mind the need to find a young, vulnerable child.

Debbie lay in bed, desperate to sleep. It seemed impossible to calm her racing thoughts. Her colleagues were out on the streets around McDonald's, combing the area, looking in parked cars and knocking on doors. Just how much time did that little boy have? And where on earth had his loving aunt hidden him?

As she finally slipped into a troubled sleep, she recalled Jessie's words, *"I heard the bolt click across, so I knew he was safe."* If Simon had secured the bolt himself, he could have got out, but what had Jessie told him before she left? "Don't open the door to anyone?" Suppose the room itself was in a securely locked house.

Debbie drifted off to images of locks and barricades. And a frightened little boy not daring to even try to escape the prison his auntie had confined him in.

CHAPTER TWENTY

Having heard nothing to the contrary from Charley Anders, Matt went to the station as planned and got there at nine forty-five exactly, fully prepared to be sent away again. As he walked from the car park, he seemed to sense excitement in the air — or was it tension? On entering the foyer, he realised it was both.

To his relief, Bryn came hurrying towards him. 'This way, sir. Come upstairs away from the furore, and I'll fill you in on what's occurring.'

Bryn proudly ushered him into his office in the corner of the CID room, which was miniscule, and partitioned off with glass. 'Tiny, but perfectly formed,' he commented, noticing Matt's gaze. 'Squeeze into a chair and I'll bring you up to speed.'

'Am I still on?' Matt said.

'Looks that way, boss. I've heard nothing to the contrary. And I'm to come with you. We have four uniformed officers in case we find anything we can't handle, but that's it, and we have to be as quick as we can.' He smiled apologetically at Matt. 'Briefly, the dawn raid went ahead as planned, and it was a blinding success. If the money-laundering gang knew about what was happening in the streets, they obviously saw it as a lucky diversion and our team were able to round up all the main suspects along with a vanload of evidence.'

'That must be a relief. One less thing for your boss to have nightmares about,' said Matt, now realising where the excitement he'd felt came from.

'She's swapped it for another one, Matt. A missing nine-year-old boy with asthma.'

Matt closed his eyes for a moment. His own case suddenly seemed less important. 'Look, if that's the case, maybe all hands should be on deck, not on loan to a retired detective with a bee in his bonnet.'

Bryn shook his head. 'DCI Anders says that because Dassault's been sighted in that area — and we know he had nothing to do with our money-laundering case — this needs a "swift and thorough investigation". Her words.'

'You've got help in looking for the boy? I saw a whole lot of extra vehicles in the yard,' Matt said.

'From all over, and they're still coming in. It's the kid's medical history has speeded everything up.' Bryn grimaced. 'If we aren't already too late. It's complicated, but we don't think he has an inhaler with him, and a serious attack could be fatal if he doesn't get help.'

Matt would have liked to know the circumstances, but he merely said, 'Then let's get our search out of the way, so you and the officers with us can get on with the important thing.'

Bryn checked the time. 'Right, I'll go and get the warrant from the boss. We already have the keys and the plans of the old building from the solicitor. We'll have a look at that and get straight round there.'

While Bryn went down to see Charley Anders, Matt called Liz. 'We're on, sweetheart! Moving out shortly.'

She replied that for once the fates must be with them. She'd just had a call from Alex's father asking if there were any developments. At least, Matt thought, this would stop them wondering about that face at the window and whether it was real.

Bryn returned, carrying the warrant and a large envelope that must contain the plans. Matt felt a thrill of excitement.

This was just like the old days! Reminding himself that he was no longer DCI, he said, 'Okay, Bryn, how do we play this?'

Bryn laid out one of the drawings on his desk. 'We have keys for this door here. The solicitor said that all the interior doors are unlocked, except for the one leading to the adjoining storerooms. It covers three floors, and according to his son's last report, it is still sound, in good structural order. There's no unsafe stairs or anything.' Bryn looked up at Matt. 'Boon admitted that they don't always check the storage areas — they're massive, apparently, and quite empty of anything except old shelving units and tables. The most they ever do in that section is shine a torch around. There's nowhere for anyone to hide, and a quick scan is sufficient to show whether it's been disturbed. Oh, and apart from very large external doors where the merchant's goods were all brought in from the docks, and which are securely sealed, there is no other way into the store.'

'Good. Then what are we waiting for? Let's get it done.'

* * *

Liz and David were unsettled, restless. It was tough being the ones left at home with nothing to do but wait for news. DS Liz Haynes as was would have been at Matt's side, and she couldn't help feeling bitter about the way life had treated her. This resentment was quite new to her. Until this particular case, she had been determined to move forward, consigning the incident that had almost taken her life to the past. And now? These new emotions were painful, but perhaps they would give her a bit more understanding of how Matt felt about being retired out of the job he had given his whole life to.

David had been watching her. He said, 'Is it the waiting? Or something else, Auntie Liz?'

Caught on the hop, she said, 'Both, I guess. We desperately need to know if it was that photo with the face at the window that got those two boys killed. Plus, I hate just sitting on my backside doing nothing. And, well, this case is making me feel so inadequate, if you know what I mean. Helpless.'

'Yeah, I kind of get that. I guess when it comes down to it private investigators shouldn't really be handling a case like this, should they? To get the answers you need, you should have all the powers you used to have as serving police officers. If it was me, I'd be climbing the walls by now!'

Liz stared at him. 'You just answered the main question there, our Davey. That's it! This case is different to all the others we've tackled so far. It is a police investigation, but due to all sorts of weird circumstances, it has temporarily landed in our laps. Apart from not being able to handle it as we would when we had warrant cards, we know that when we reach a critical point, we'll have to hand it over to the officials, so we'll probably never see it through to the end.' Personal pride came into it too. They had wanted to hand Charley Anders a fait accompli. But from the moment her eyes fell on Andre Dassault, it had stepped up a league.

The house phone rang. They both jumped, then glanced at each other. Surely Matt would call her mobile?

She answered. 'No, I'm sorry, Matt's out this morning. Can I help? I'm his partner, Liz Haynes.'

It was the Reverend Peter from Thetford. 'I'm rather worried, to be honest. Your friend Minty seems to have disappeared.'

Liz went cold. 'When?'

'After breakfast, Mrs Haynes. He seemed to be in really good form, quite relaxed, happy to be away from the Fens and whoever was looking for him. He even offered to help me tidy the church, ready for the weekend service. He went into the village, came back, and an hour later his room was empty, and no one had seen him leaving. I thought he might have changed his mind about helping and gone for a walk, but as time is getting on, I'm getting anxious about him and I thought I should let you know.'

Liz thanked him, told him to keep in touch using her mobile number if the house phone wasn't answered, and hung up. How the hell . . ? Her mind raced. Matt had sworn he hadn't been followed, and he'd have known. You didn't lose that kind of instinct just because you'd retired.

199

Hopefully, Minty had just sloped off for a woodland stroll and gone further than intended, or even got lost. Fenlanders weren't used to acres of forest. But her copper's instinct told her it was more than that.

'What's happened?' asked David anxiously.

'It's Minty. The vicar said he's gone missing.'

'But . . . but no one knows he's there. Even the locals around that vicarage don't know what Peter does for people in trouble. I don't get it.'

'Well, we mustn't panic,' Liz said, 'but even so . . .'

'Maybe someone did know, and that same someone has caught up with him.' David's voice was grave. 'So, what do we do now, Liz?'

Liz wasn't sure, and until they heard from Matt there was nothing they could do. 'We wait. Tough as it is, we can only decide when Matt's through with the search.'

* * *

This was it, finally. Matt's heart beat faster. Bryn slipped the key into the lock, which was scratched, he noticed, and Matt mentioned it to Bryn.

'It's not what you think, boss.' There was a hint of amusement in his voice. 'When old man Boon talks about his son, you forget said son is far from being a youngster himself. Terence Boon has a mild form of Parkinson's. His hand shakes.'

'Ah, the downside of being a policeman. You see dark deeds in everything.'

The door swung open and, taking a deep breath, they stepped inside.

Matt's immediate reaction was surprise. Yes, there was a musty smell, that still, airless quality of a place long closed up, but it was a long way from the stink of dampness and decay that he'd expected.

Reading from the plan, Bryn led the way. 'The DCI wants every room checked, okay? So, down here we have a reception area for receipt of deliveries, the below-stairs kitchen and a scullery — whatever that is. Walk-in larders, stores for cleaning materials and a boot room. There's also a couple of big rooms where the servants would eat and pass their off-duty moments. We'll get these sorted first, then tackle the first floor.'

It was like stepping back in time. Nothing had been altered except the kitchen but even that was still antiquated. The modern age was represented by a fridge, an electric oven and little else. Matt wondered if the other floors would be any different.

'All clear,' said one of the constables, closing the door to the last room. 'No sign that this area has been used, and nothing has been tampered with.'

'Agreed,' said Bryn, 'and none of the old windows showed signs of having been forced. Let's take the next floor, shall we?'

They used the back stairs, up which countless servants had trodden in days gone by, carrying trays of food back and forth.

So this was why old man Boon had been so confident that no one had broken in or was using the place for illegal purposes. With a sigh, Matt trudged up the stairs. Maybe this whole thing was one big mistake, and the merchant's house had nothing to do with what had happened in Cutler's Alley. Meanwhile, a kiddie was missing and he was taking officers off the search for nothing.

They emerged into the main entrance hall. Matt thought it would provide a great setting for one of those sumptuous historical dramas the streaming services were so fond of. He imagined himself to be a servant, opening up the house after the family had been away. Or a long-lost relative, just returned from war to find the house empty. He told himself to look at the place as it really was. Even now, after years of sitting unoccupied, the place was full of atmosphere.

Bryn was saying, 'We'll split up into three pairs. I can't see us finding anything, but check thoroughly for any indication that someone's been in here. Okay, let's go.'

Despite the peeling wallpaper, and the damp that lingered in the corners, basically, the building was sound, just as old man Boon had said.

The rooms were still grand. It was hard not to get distracted by the architecture and the objects left behind from a bygone era. Paintings still hung on the walls, their gilded frames dark with age. The velvet drapes, caught back with golden tassels and plaited braid laced with cobwebs, framed windows now coated in grime. Matt wondered that it hadn't been burgled or vandalised, or both.

It took twenty minutes to thoroughly check the first floor. Finding nothing, they mounted the grand old staircase to the top floor.

'Six bedrooms, three bathrooms and there's an attic at the top of a narrow staircase, but Boon told me it is sealed. Locked, bolted and barred from the outside, and it's never been accessed. If we don't find anything here, I suggest we take his word for it.'

Matt disagreed but kept silent. He'd known many a villain to hide out in the loft, having found another way in. He recalled the evil murderer, Levi Bellfield, who'd been discovered, naked, hiding beneath the loft lagging in an attic. But this was down to Bryn, and if the rest of the place hadn't been touched, maybe he was right to call off the search.

'Sir, we never checked the big storerooms off the basement,' said one of the police constables. 'I saw that the doors were locked, but I think we have the keys.'

'I was leaving those until we'd checked the house itself, but as it seems the solicitor was right . . .' Bryn handed the two constables a key. 'You two go down and take a look, the four of us will finish up here.'

Matt tried to visualise which room the woman would have been looking out from, but couldn't work it out. The corridor they were now in was wide, still carpeted, and lined with framed pictures. The first room he tried was small, but still contained furniture, now covered with dust sheets. It had clearly seen no more activity than the brief occasional visit from the solicitor's son.

Matt could hear the voices of the others calling out "no sign of life," and gave up. Now just wanting the whole thing over, he tried the last door on the corridor and found it jammed. He pushed hard and went inside.

He stopped.

Bryn came up and looked over his shoulder. 'What the fu—?'

The room was spotless. They saw a table laid for a meal. Clothes and towels lay neatly folded in little piles next to a sink with a plastic bowl in it. There were flagons of fresh water, a cool box, and several battery-powered lanterns on the freshly wiped surfaces.

As in a trance, Matt stepped into the room and stood over a camp bed with a sleeping bag and a soft fleece blanket thrown over it. On top of it, a child's hoodie. He turned and saw an aged carved bed on which lay another sleeping bag and a woman's anorak. Two people — one adult, one child. Was this the woman at the window?

Bryn was holding up a book. 'A colouring book! A child's colouring book! Matt! It's the missing boy. He was here!'

Matt had already arrived at the same conclusion. But where was the boy now?

Bryn rang the station, but before he'd finished the call, a shout went up. 'Sir! You need to see this!'

The voice came from an old bathroom. Matt and Bryn ran across and stopped in the doorway. On the floor lay a body that, from the clothes, size, and physique, Matt assumed to be male. Seeing the blood pooled around him, Matt also assumed him to be dead.

'Shit!' exclaimed Bryn, and told whoever he'd been speaking to what they'd found.

This didn't make sense. From what Bryn had told him, the missing boy had bolted himself in, and his aunt had told him not to open the door to anyone but her. Then the old lady had apparently suffered some kind of panic attack or seizure and had forgotten where she'd left the child. Well, this was undoubtably where she'd left him, but why had he unbolted the door to someone else? And why had they taken him? More to the point, *where* had they taken him?

And what the hell did all this have to do with a dead man in the bathroom?

Glad this wasn't his enquiry, Matt was just about to ring Liz when another mystery revealed itself.

'The storerooms, sir! They seem to be empty and unused, until you actually get in there with a torch. They've been used all right, and recently.'

'And what's more,' added his companion, 'we've discovered another door. It's hidden in a recess behind some shelving units that the solicitor would have missed, and we think it connects to the old, deserted pub next door — the Old Poacher's Rest!'

Matt began making connections. It wasn't the merchant's house itself, it was the storage areas and the old pub that Dassault and Henry were focused on. He still had no idea how the woman and the boy fitted in, maybe it was coincidence and the gang didn't know she was there, nor she them. But in that case, why kill those students for taking a photo of the face at the window?

Matt called home. Briefly, he told Liz what they'd found, then asked to speak to David. Handing this directly to Bryn would take time, while David had those pictures at his fingertips.

'I want you to go through those photos again, David. We missed something, I swear. I don't think it was the face that got those boys killed at all. It was something else that appeared in the pictures. You have to find it!'

Matt hung up and tried to order his thoughts. They had inadvertently found where the woman had been keeping the boy, but someone else had got to him first. As far as he could make out, other than the old woman and the child, those entering this old place did so as either part of a drug smuggling ring, or maybe a people trafficking racket. And the body in the bathroom showed that they were perfectly capable of murder.

This was bad. Worse than they had ever contemplated. And the irony of it was that discovering who was behind it could come down to a twenty-year-old lad who had been rejected for the police force.

CHAPTER TWENTY-ONE

Kellie insisted on being allowed to go back and sit with her aunt. For once, no one argued with her, one doctor even admitting that if she could get her aunt to remember more, it might help both Jessie and the police.

Kellie entered her aunt's small private room determined to get some answers from her. She wasn't surprised when PC Debbie Hume joined her, dark shadows beneath her eyes.

'Try to find out more about her friend, Anna,' whispered Debbie. 'I'm sure she holds the key to this mystery.'

Kellie was beginning to hate Anna. She wanted to be angry with Jessie too, but seeing her distress, she could only feel pity for her. What else could she try in order to get her to remember where she'd left Simon?

For the umpteenth time that morning she pushed her anxiety about her brother's asthma to the back of her mind. She sat beside the bed waiting for her auntie to rouse herself from yet another doze, and couldn't help envying other teenagers, who spent their lives agonising over pop idols and their hair. She knew why her life was so different, of course. Simon. Her darling mother had died, passing on his care to her. And now she'd been handed sole responsibility for saving his life.

Her aunt shifted in her bed and Kellie leaned forward, smiling.

Fifteen minutes later, having got nowhere, she saw a grim-faced PC Jack Fleet beckoning to Debbie. Her heart sank.

Kellie stared at the door for what seemed an age. Finally, Debbie opened it and beckoned to her. In the corridor outside, Jack was in solemn conversation with her dad.

She swallowed, and took a deep shaky breath. Debbie put her arm around her shoulder and led her to a seat.

'Kellie, we think we've found the place where your Auntie Jessie took your brother. The thing is, it's empty.'

Kellie took a while to comprehend her words.

'Your father has confirmed that a hoodie we found there belonged to your brother. We also found a colouring book — birds.'

'He loves birds.' A thought hit her. 'Did you find another small book? It's called *The Observer's Book of British Birds.*'

Debbie turned to Jack, who shrugged. It hadn't been mentioned, but he'd ring the officer who was still at the scene.

'Tell him to look under my brother's pillow.'

Kellie waited, her throat dry.

Jack turned to her. 'Definitely not there.'

She breathed a sigh of relief. 'In that case he'll have taken it with him. Which means he had time to think before he left that place.'

It wasn't much to hold onto, but it was a small comfort.

* * *

Palmer could never have dreamed that things could go so wrong so quickly. From the sweet satisfaction of pulling off the perfect operation — with money rolling in like an unstoppable tide — to the bitter aftertaste of utter disaster, and in a matter of hours!

His mobile phone lay silent in front of him on the desk. He stared at it and cursed. Where was fucking Jude, and why wasn't he picking up? Palmer knew the bare bones of it, but he needed to know what exit strategy Jude had implemented.

The phone rang. He snatched it up. 'Deezer. Where the hell is Jude? He hasn't reported in.'

'Jude? No idea, sir, but he did the final sweep of the site, I saw him myself. The minute we'd cleared away, he went in, like he always does. Then, oh, about five minutes later he rang me and asked me to do a recce of our other places of business. He said I should report directly to you instead of him.' Deezer sounded puzzled. 'And that's what I'm doing. I can report that the other sites are all still stable and viable. There's no issues with any of them, it's only Cutler's Alley that needed vacating.'

Palmer was relieved to hear that their other premises were okay, but even more confused as to Jude's whereabouts. Why tell Deezer to report straight to him? He ended the call.

Palmer frowned. He and Jude stuck to a strict protocol. It suited them both. Jude in particular liked routine. He was what Palmer thought of as a tidy worker — no loose ends, and everything sewn up tight as a duck's backside. The frown deepened. Ever since that ridiculous run-in with Minty Agutter, Jude had been acting out of character.

That was it! Jude had executed his duties last night as per usual, but had something to do immediately afterwards, and that something concerned that bloody nuisance Minty. Jude had instructed Deezer to report directly to Palmer because he didn't want to wait while his second in command did the rounds of the other sites.

No longer puzzled, Palmer became angry. He could foresee that there would come a point when Jude's personal connection to this washed-up old crook would cause an irreconcilable rift between them. Jude was the best he'd ever come across, a ruthless killer and efficient organiser. But . . . And it was a big "but". Palmer demanded total dedication to their operation. If Jude wasn't able to commit, then, despite all his attributes, he was history and Palmer would look for another partner. Andre Dassault was a distinct possibility; Deezer, too, was another contender. There was little doubt that offered the right financial incentive, both could be tempted to up their game. Palmer would regret losing Jude and his ability to quietly remove any obstacles that might arise. Jude's brand of "death from natural causes," which kept unwelcome attention from them, was quite an art form. Dassault and Deezer would be far more mainstream in their methods — most likely a knifing. That might be effective, but it drew the police's attention.

Palmer sent Jude a final warning text. Jude should know that a fortune was at stake: money that had yet to go into his account was hanging in the balance. Now it was up to Jude.

* * *

Jessie was adrift, detached from reality and wavering between different worlds, none of which felt safe. On some level, she knew what lay behind her derangement — Anna. For the first time since she had known her, Anna hadn't come to her aid, and without Anna, Jessie was powerless, gripped by panic. She was experiencing a rare moment of lucidity. She knew she was in a hospital room and that at some point her darling Kellie had been there. She knew too that if she tried to recall the events that had brought her here, terror would overcome her, and she would sink once again into incoherence.

She tried to fix her thoughts on ordinary things — objects in the room, the window, the colour of the paintwork, the cup on her locker. It worked for a while, but soon the questions began to creep into her head. In moments they were clamouring for her attention.

Why hadn't Anna come? She knew where Jessie was going and had promised to help her, accompany her to McDonald's and see her safely back again. But Jessie had found herself alone on the streets amid the noise and confusion, and panic had robbed her of all coherent thought.

In the quiet of the hospital room, the panic returned.

Jessie tried to keep it at bay. Desperate now, she sought something concrete to hold on to. The door of her locker was ajar, so she tried to recall what she had been wearing when she'd been brought here. 'Flat shoes . . . Navy ones from that nice shop in the town, the one next to the baker's.'

Reciting this inventory brought a little more sanity, so she pictured the stretch slacks, the blue ones you couldn't tumble dry because they would shrink.

Jessie gasped. Simon was alone and no one knew where he was.

She needed to tell someone! At that moment, she knew exactly where she'd left him. She tried to get out of bed but it was already too late. As the clouds once more engulfed her mind, she had one last clear thought. There was one person who did know where the boy was — Anna. It was all right, Anna would save him. She didn't know what had prevented her friend from meeting her, but nothing would stop Anna from going to Simon in his hour of need.

As always, Anna would help. Jessie gave a sigh of relief.

* * *

A nurse and a cleaner, who had been idly chatting in the corridor outside Jessie Wright's room, stopped in their tracks. A blood-chilling cry filled the air. They rushed into the room and found the patient half in, half out of bed. Her face bore a look of such torment that for a moment they were barely able to move.

'Get the doctor!' yelled the nurse, shaking herself into action. 'She's had a serious episode. Hurry! I need help here.'

This was way beyond general nursing. This woman should be in a psychiatric facility, and the sooner the better in her opinion.

* * *

Charley Anders beckoned to Matt and Bryn, and they followed her outside. The old property was now a double crime scene, site of a murder and an abduction. It was heaving with police officers and SOCOs, all in coveralls and masks, all silent, all busy with their respective tasks.

Out on the street, Charley exhaled as if she'd been holding her breath for hours. 'Matt Ballard. I really should listen to you more closely. That instinct of yours never fails, does it?'

'Believe me, Charley, by the time we'd gone over most of that place and found sweet FA, I doubted myself. And who the hell is the dead man?'

'We've got Rory Wilkinson and his team arriving in five minutes or so. Until then the SOCOs are photographing and protecting the area. After Rory checks out the body and moves it, hopefully we'll know more. With any luck he'll have some ID on him.'

Charley didn't look too convinced of that, and Matt wasn't either.

'I have something to say to you, Matt. Normally I'd be telling a private investigator — including you in different circumstances — to pull out, hand over everything you have and let us take it from here. However.' She paused. 'However, you are an integral part of this whole bloody thing. We don't know what's actually going on here, but it's big, and it's complicated. I don't know what I can arrange, probably some kind of consultancy, but I'm asking you to keep your diary clear of other cases for the duration. Once we have the preliminary forensic report back, I need to debrief you. You must give me every damned thing you know or suspect. Then I'll ask you to work with me on aspects you and Liz might be useful on. Is that acceptable?'

Matt nodded. It was more than he could have hoped for, and it would have the added advantage of giving him access to the police sources he'd so much missed having available to him. They wouldn't have carte blanche, of course, but they wouldn't be so hamstrung as they had been. 'We'll give you all the help we can, Charley.'

She smiled. 'So, what does your gut tell you that big storeroom was being used for?'

'Drugs. From the speed they were brought in, moved out again and the place decontaminated, I don't think it was people trafficking.'

Charley agreed. 'My thoughts precisely. Well, forensics should find something to prove or disprove that. It's almost impossible to thoroughly clean up a place that old and disused. You can get rid of the obvious, but trace evidence will still be there, and if anyone can find it, it'll be the man I see walking towards us right now.' A tall figure carrying two large metal cases had unwound himself from an old lime green Citroen Dolly, and was striding in their direction.

'What a lovely surprise!' exclaimed Professor Rory Wilkinson. 'Now that really has made my day! The inimitable Matthew Ballard himself. I am beside myself with delight.'

Matt tried to suppress a smile and failed. 'Good to see you too, Rory.'

'The delectable Sergeant Liz not with you?' remarked Rory, looking around. 'She's well, I trust?'

'Very well. Busy pursuing another line of enquiry at present.'

'Slave driver! Here you are, both retired but up to your necks in crime as usual.' He shook his head. 'I guess if it's in the blood, crocheting blankets and growing marrows doesn't have the same appeal.' He transferred his beaming smile to Charley Anders. 'Now, dear lady, what delights do you have for me today?'

Matt watched as he became all business. Despite his awful quips, Rory was undoubtedly the best pathologist Matt had ever worked with. As Charley had said, if there was anything here, Rory would find it.

Until now Bryn had remained silent, but with Charley and Rory deep in conversation, he looked at Matt with a slightly amused expression. 'Just like the old days, boss, eh?'

'Not quite,' said Matt. 'You're the boss and I'm the hired help, but that's good with me.' And it was, up to a point. Matt was beginning to wonder if he would ever really be able to walk away from all he had left behind.

A sudden memory came out of the blue and hit him with considerable force. It was the day he had left the station for the last time. His last case had affected him badly. Well, to be more accurate, one of the people involved in it had affected him. He should have been driving away reflecting on the achievements of a long and successful career. He should have enjoyed a massive leaving party with his colleagues and friends — one they'd not forget in a hurry. As it was, he had handed over his warrant card, cleared his office, and slipped out through the back door. He had wanted nothing more to do with the police force, ever. So why now the longing to be part of it all again?

'That's a deep look, boss. You okay?'

Matt smiled at Bryn. 'I'm fine. Sorry, just trying to get my head around a few things.'

'You and me both,' Bryn said.

Then Rory was moving away and into the old house, and Charley was back in organising mode.

'Okay, Matt. I suggest you get away and start gathering up everything you have for us. We'll be a while here yet, sorting this shambles and trying to separate out the murder, kidnapping and whatever criminal activity has been taking place in the storerooms. I'll ring you as soon as I have some idea of what we're looking at, then you and Liz can come in for the debriefing.'

'Right. If anything major strikes us that you really need to know, I'll ring Bryn, okay?'

'Perfect.'

She turned and hurried after the pathologist.

'Keep in touch, boss,' said Bryn, getting ready to follow them.

'And you, son, especially if anything really interesting shows up?' He raised an eyebrow.

'You got it, boss.' Bryn winked.

Matt was left alone with a head full of conflicting thoughts, and one or two questions about his own direction in life. He grunted. Now was not the time for this. Still, if nothing else, his life had one firm anchor. Liz.

Hurrying back towards his car, he rang and told her he was coming home.

CHAPTER TWENTY-TWO

Eddie Race stared out of her office window on the floor above the club. She felt as if she'd run the gamut of every possible emotion during the previous night and the earlier part of the day. Now, she was on the verge of desperation.

The door had just closed on her financial advisor, Harrington, a man now as worried as Eddie herself. He was to return at seven that evening, by which time he would have made certain discreet enquiries, the answers to which would hopefully indicate which direction they should take. Until then, Eddie was left with the possibility that her previously flourishing empire was on the verge of collapse.

Since Henry's first phone call, which had left her gasping at the figure he demanded, Eddie had made several calls of her own regarding the situation in Fenfleet. It was these, not the exorbitant ransom Henry was demanding, that had made her realise the extent of the trouble her business was in.

She contacted Raymond Leonard in Greenborough, who didn't seem surprised to hear from her. Talking to him, she realised it could just as easily have been the other way around — him ringing her. He spared her a further call by telling her that in his game to find the highest bidder, the devious, money-grabbing Henry had also been in touch with their counterpart in Saltern-le-Fen. Their offers all still on the table, she decided to go for broke. She would pay up and look big. It was impossible to operate while not knowing what the fuck was going on right under her nose.

So, early the previous evening, she had rung Henry and told him that if he stopped hawking his wares around the local criminal fraternity, she would agree to his demands.

With his usual nonchalance, he had said he was glad to hear it. He had, of course, intended to give it to her all along, and had merely been seeking offers, so as to gauge the value of his information. What a load of bollocks. She told him so, and Henry laughed. She set the financial transaction in motion, after which he divulged what he had discovered.

Eddie flopped into her comfortable leather chair and sighed. Everything was now clear, and she was caught in the worst dilemma of her life. Even Harrington offered no reassurance. Talk about the devil and the deep blue sea.

What it boiled down to was that a London-based organisation had chosen her patch as a reception and distribution centre for their illicit imports. Henry suspected they had multiple sites, whose location he would pass on to her in due course, but their main depository was accessed through an old disused pub in Cutler's Alley.

This was bad enough. No one could function with an operation like that on their doorstep. But here was the stinger. The most lucrative side of her business — into which she had invested practically everything — came from the distribution and sales of one particular commodity. There was only one person supplying this item, and who was he? The very man who had set up shop in her own backyard! If she took him down, she would destroy her own business. If she left him alone, it would only be a matter of time before the police came sniffing around, and if they caught him, they would have her too, since she was one of his main buyers. He wouldn't hesitate to shop her to the authorities immediately.

The options churned around in Eddie's brain. Was it worth attempting some kind of compromise? Would he consider a working relationship, perhaps? What if she promised to up her already mammoth order if he would close down the Fenfleet site? She needed him badly. There was no one else who could supply her demands, and she had a constantly growing market. But she certainly didn't need him here in Fenfleet, within walking distance of Race's Place. If he had other places around the county, as Henry believed, then closing one place of business wouldn't hurt him at all. And if she upped her order, it could be beneficial to both parties.

She groaned. Oh sure, it sounded feasible, but she had a feeling this unnamed man, someone she dealt with several times a week, wasn't about to play ball with anyone.

Eddie poured herself a generous glass of malt whisky, needing the alcohol to deaden the pain of seeing her life's work flushed down the pan.

It did its work. Like hell she was going to let everything she and her father had worked for end in nothing. She, Eddie Race, wasn't going to let some clever fucking smartarse from the City ride roughshod over her business. If Harrington couldn't come up with anything, she had one final card to play.

Eddie's eyes narrowed. It meant interrupting the supply chain, which was unfortunate, but if properly executed it would keep her from going down with Mister Big and ending up in a cell. One of her acquaintances was a professional hitman who, if paid enough, would do the job and disappear like the morning mist. She exhaled. It was a last-ditch manoeuvre. She would have got on the phone at once, but two things stood in the way. One was Harrington. And the other was that she had no idea who Mister Big actually was. That was Henry's next job — to get her a name.

* * *

Matt paced the kitchen. 'Minty! Gone? But how? Why? He was perfectly happy with Peter's retreat. And we weren't tailed, I bloody well know we weren't!'

'I feel awful,' said David glumly. 'It was my idea for him to go there.'

'Listen, you two,' said Liz. 'Stop beating yourselves up. We have no idea why he's disappeared, and now I've had time to think it all through, I've come to the conclusion that we should put it on the back burner for now, and concentrate on what's going on here. I know that sounds harsh, but we have enough to contend with, and one of us chasing across the country on what could be a wild goose-chase won't help the investigation, will it? Peter has promised to let us know if he hears anything. Anyway, we don't know that Minty's disappearance has anything to do with Jude Sherriff.'

Looking unconvinced, Matt flopped into a chair and nibbled at his bottom lip. 'I suppose you're right. I just feel kind of responsible for the silly old sod.'

'Just because he pitched up as a rent-free lodger in your garden shed, Matt Ballard, doesn't make you his registered keeper. Come on. That man has been round the block more times than anyone I know. He's been in Parkhurst, for heaven's sake! I know it shook him but he's no fool, Matt. I'm thinking he's seen or heard something that's spooked him and he's gone to ground. Maybe he's had an accident of some kind — Peter has a group of local ramblers keeping a lookout in the forest. Really, there's little more we can do.'

Matt nodded somewhat grudgingly. 'You're right, Liz. It just rankles that we go to all that bother to get him there as surreptitiously as possible, and he disappears! With all this serious shit going on I can't help wondering if someone very clever managed to find out where we took him. That information he has — you know, about the diamond necklace that Paddy Sherriff stole — is pretty hot stuff. For once in his life, Minty Agutter is a valuable commodity.'

'Especially to Jude Sherriff,' Liz added. 'But it's all guesswork, isn't it? It could boil down to Minty getting involved with Toby and that photocard, and whatever Jude is mixed up in. Meanwhile I suggest we get on with what Charley Anders asked you to do — collate what we have and get it ready to hand over to her at our debriefing.' She suddenly remembered the note that had been stuck on the back of the door in Toby's room. 'I'll add that warning note with its piece of sticky tape attached. It could well have forensic evidence on it.'

'Can't argue with that. I suppose Minty is big and ugly enough to fend for himself.' Matt glanced at David. 'Keep in regular touch with your vicar, David. Tell him that any news he gets, he should pass it on, no matter how trivial it sounds.'

'Will do,' said David. 'Meanwhile, I'll crack on with those photographs. I've been right through them several times, but I still can't help thinking there's something I've missed.'

'Good lad. Sometimes that's the only way. Keep at it, and hopefully something will show up,' said Matt.

Liz and Matt got down to photocopying their files and pages of notes. They still worked as they had done when they were serving police officers, which Liz thought was lucky. She made notes of names, times, dates of meetings and conversations and so on, then typed up her findings in a report and attached photographs or any other relevant material. It would make life easier for Charley when she came to go through them.

'We have accrued a whole lot of info when you look at it like this,' she remarked, gazing at the piles of paperwork and photos stacked on the big dining table. 'It has to save someone an awful lot of legwork.'

Matt was busy slipping some papers into a clear plastic file. 'Normally, it would hurt to be handing all this over mid-case; it would feel like failure, but at least this time we're still going to be working it — with the added bonus of getting our hands on the reports of some of Charley's experts, like forensics, or things they've thrown at the Police National Computer.'

Liz laughed. 'Better not get too used to it. Next case we'll be back to using Google and our own two eyes.' She stopped laughing. 'And I hope our next case is a damned sight less harrowing than this one. If it turns out to be as serious as it appears, we may have bitten off more than we can chew here, Matt. Without all the official information sources, we've been batting way out of our league from the word go.'

'But we had no proof until today,' Matt reminded her. 'We always said that if we found evidence we'd turn it over, and we have. We might still be helping out, but it's firmly in Charley's lap now.'

This case, more than any other that they'd taken on as private detectives, had frustrated her because it made her feel so amateurish. It had even dragged her into feeling bitter about having been injured and retired out of the job she had loved so much. She'd never felt that way before. From the start, she had realised that the extent of her injuries meant there would be no going back and accepted her fate. Knowing she could not change her situation, she had dealt with it by distancing herself from anything to do with the force, including old friends. But this case had undone all that. She might as well face up to it, she was angry. All their suspicions were proving to be correct, all their intuitive feelings had been accurate. There *was* a case to answer, but it wasn't going to be theirs, because they were not the police.

'You've gone very quiet.' Matt was looking at her, head on one side. 'Is it because you really didn't want to hand this over to Charley?'

'Oh, take no notice of me, Matt. I've got in a temper and thrown my teddy out of the pram simply because it's not ours to draw a line beneath. Really I'm delighted it's going to Charley because hopefully, with all the might of the Fenland Constabulary behind it, Georgia and Terry, and Toby's family too, will have answers to the mystery of their lovely sons' deaths — and some evil bastard will pay for it.' She forced a grin. 'Right. I'm going to put the kettle on, I need strong tea!'

* * *

Debbie and Jack sat in the police car and stared at the open garage door next to Belle Rackham's bungalow.

'Would you go away overnight and leave your garage door up?' asked Debbie.

'My garage is full of all manner of stuff, so absolutely not. Hers is pretty well empty, but I'd still not leave it open to the elements,' said Jack. 'Time to talk to the neighbours, I think.'

Debbie went one way, Jack the other. No one knew where Belle might have gone. One man told Debbie that Belle didn't usually leave her garage open unless she was popping across to see her friend on the other side of the village and even then, she often closed it.

Debbie started to wonder about Belle Rackham. Was she missing too? Or had she left in such a hurry that she'd had no time to close the garage door? After all, she'd been gone since yesterday evening. A shiver trickled down Debbie's spine. She didn't like the feel of this at all.

She and Jack moved around the bungalow, looking in the windows. Nothing was out of place that they could see, nothing left in the kitchen to indicate a sudden exit — no cup of tea or half-eaten meal. It was all locked up with the exception of that garage.

Jack checked the garden and the shed, while Debbie kept peering in windows, hunting for some small clue to indicate where Belle Rackham might have gone.

Debbie returned to the car and ran a check on the name Mrs Belle Rackham. It threw up nothing. Then she recalled that Kellie had said she'd seen an envelope addressed to Mrs A Rackham and had suggested that Belle could be the mysterious Anna, so she searched for Anna and Annabelle Rackham as well. Again, there was nothing.

'Got something.' Jack was leaning in the door. 'Not much, but it might help.' He eased himself into the car. 'I saw her neighbour working in his garden and I asked him about her car. He said it was a five-year-old silver Kia Picanto. He couldn't remember the full licence number, but the letters were ARR, which are her initials.'

Debbie perked up. A partial was better than nothing, and it could be traced.

'Hold up,' said Jack. 'There's more. He also said she bought it at Crayford Motors, it's on that little trading estate just off the main road into Saltfleet. Fancy a detour on the way back to the station? Their records will tell us everything we need to know.'

'Then buckle up, Swifty. What are we waiting for?'

Half an hour later they were looking at a document giving the registered owner as Mrs Arabella Rosa Rackham, plus her vehicle registration number, and even a mobile phone number. Debbie called it straightaway. It went to voicemail, so she left a message asking Belle to call her as a matter of urgency. Even as she did, she knew there'd be no return call.

She sat in the car for a few minutes, calculating that little Simon had been missing from the merchant's house almost exactly as long as Belle had been gone from her home. Belle knew Jessie Wright, that was definite, she knew Jessie had her nephew staying with her. Now both woman and child were missing.

'We need to get that reg number to our guys,' said Jack, evidently having come to the same conclusion as her. 'Maybe the traffic cameras could pick it up.'

'Yes, but I think we need to get them to put out an "attention drawn". There could be a vulnerable child in that silver Picanto, being ferried off God knows where.'

She called their skipper and told him what they feared. That morning's discovery had made her more anxious than ever.

* * *

The call came at four o'clock in the afternoon. A harassed-sounding Charley Anders asked Matt if he and Liz could get to the station as soon as possible.

Liz hesitated as they approached the main door. Matt put his hand on her arm and felt how tense she was. He immediately forgot about his own earlier angst and felt a rush of concern for her. Having established a way to help herself cope with what had happened to her, this case was undoing her carefully constructed strategy, forcing her to move back into the territory that she had been so careful to avoid. Until now, her only visits to the station had been a brief hello to a few friends, and then she'd leave. He and Liz had no option but to assist Charley — but at what cost to Liz? Matt determined that the moment this horrible case was finally closed, he would whisk his beloved Liz away to a luxury hotel and pamper the life out of her.

Charley and Bryn were waiting for them in her office. On the desk, which was already overloaded with papers, stood four steaming mugs.

Matt handed over a bulky folder. 'It's pretty well all we have so far, Charley. You'll see there's a sheet of observations on top. It's a kind of suggestion box, listing aspects of the case that might be more easily followed up using police channels.'

Charley smiled. 'I get the message, Matt. My very capable predecessor is reminding me of what I might miss.'

He returned the smile. 'I prefer to call it friendly advice from one who's in no position to do it himself.'

She glanced at the sheet. 'I see your number one priority is a certain Jude Sherriff. That name — Sherriff — causes my hair to stand on end. I'm assuming he's related to our old friend Paddy?'

'We believe he's what you might call a prodigal son, and his reputation is just about as bad as Daddy's.' Liz frowned. 'We've been told he never operates in this area, since the Fens is his old stomping ground. From what I've found out, his only local connections are to a legitimate IT business and a few others just as clean. So why is he apparently breaking the habit of a lifetime?'

'And his connection to the present case?' Charley asked. 'I'll read it all later, obviously, but a brief summary of events would help me get the overall picture.'

Matt told her what Minty had said about Jude, but omitted any mention of Paddy Sherriff's diamond necklace. That was Minty's secret, and irrelevant to the case. He said they were sure Jude was the kingpin in the criminal operation that had been using the deserted pub and the storerooms at the merchant's house.

'Along with Andre Dassault, that makes a scarily well-organised set-up,' added Liz. 'The arrival of a crack London-based logistics man like Dassault, plus a ruthless killer who has previously avoided this area like the plague, means an operation that has to be making a fortune. Otherwise, neither of those two would bother with a place like Fenfleet.'

'But you have no idea who is behind the operation?' asked Bryn.

'None at all. All we do know is that our usual suspects — people like Eddie Race and Raymond Leonard — are also in the dark. That's why Henry has been sent on the prowl. Apart from appraising what's going down, he's hunting out the head honcho for them.' Matt grimaced. 'No doubt at huge financial gain to himself.'

'Definitely,' said Charley. 'And initial reports from forensics — only verbal ones at this early stage, of course — indicate that large quantities of drugs have been moved in and out of the storeroom, and that the clean-up was one of the most efficient Rory Wilkinson has ever seen. He doubts it's heroin, and it is definitely not cannabis. He found a minute speck of something that has yet to be identified. That, too, had been cleared up but some residue remained. He'll be able to tell us what it is by close of play — or so he hopes.'

'We thought as much, although we did think people trafficking could be a possibility, given the size of those storerooms.' Matt felt relieved, in a way. Drugs were bad enough, but the thought of someone moving innocent people into another country, enslaving them or sending them into the sex trade made him utterly sick. The people who did that were inhuman.

Bryn passed round mugs of tea and coffee. Matt felt quite moved that the young detective had remembered how he and Liz liked their drinks.

Skimming through the folder, Charley stopped at the photographs. 'I can see why you got so intrigued by this.'

She held up the enhancement of the face in the window. 'But now we can assume that this is a picture of Jessie Wright, who hid her nephew in that room because of what she told him were "bad men".'

'The timing would be right,' said Matt. 'It would have taken a considerable amount of time and repeated visits to get that room clean enough for a boy with asthma. But how the dickens did she gain access? Old man Boon keeps that place shut up tighter than a gnat's chuff!'

Charley shrugged. 'Well, I sent an officer over to the hospital and he found a key in her handbag. It fitted one of the back doors to the merchant's house. Sadly, the woman is well away with the fairies and can't tell us anything. Her niece told us her auntie had said it was her friend's place, and that's all she could get out of her.'

Bryn added, 'This friend, a woman called Anna, keeps cropping up. We're now considering that Anna might have the boy, although we have nothing to substantiate that assumption.'

Charley added that the family had no idea where Anna lived, or even what her surname was.

'Bit weird,' Matt said. 'What kind of people are these Burtons?'

'The father is a down-to-earth, hard-working bloke, trying to make enough to hold his shattered family together after the death of his wife. They're all grieving, but we are told the boy is affected particularly badly; apparently, he refuses to even talk about his mother.' Charley sighed. 'Poor little kid has asthma and is prone to other ailments as well. The sister, a fifteen-year-old called Kellie, is a different animal altogether. She stepped up to be a surrogate mother to little Simon and, boy, she's an old head on young shoulders. Debbie and Swifty have built up a real rapport with the kid. Debbie says she's a bit of a force to be reckoned with.'

'And dotty Auntie Jessie?' asked Liz.

Bryn puffed out his cheeks. Charley rolled her eyes.

Matt grinned. 'That bad?'

Charley told him as much as they knew.

'So you believe she had a panic attack simply because her best buddy didn't turn up to help her buy the kid a Big Mac?' Matt said incredulously.

'A quarter-pounder with cheese, actually,' said Bryn. 'With fries.'

'And it escalated into some kind of manic episode?' The simplest thing, Matt supposed, could be the catalyst that sent a damaged mind into freefall.

They all sat sipping their drinks, contemplating what had been said. Liz cleared her throat. 'Okay, the scenario seems to be that Jessie goes out, telling Simon not to unbolt the door for anyone. He's left alone. Auntie freaks out, has a kind of dissociative fugue and forgets where she left the boy. Then there's a gap in our knowledge, but we do know that the villains were spooked into moving all their stash out at around that time, and either one of them, or someone unknown to us, possibly Jessie's friend Anna, made away with the boy. The next morning the police and Matt here search the house and find the room he'd been kept in. Have I got that right?'

Charley nodded. 'Not forgetting that someone got themselves topped in that same time period.'

The desk phone rang, making them all jump.

'DCI Anders. How can I help?' Her face relaxed. 'Rory. What have you got for me?'

Her eyes widened in surprise.

'Really? Well, I'd never have expected that!' The muffled voice continued speaking until, thanking him, she said she'd be in her office until late should he have anything else for her. She replaced the receiver, shaking her head. 'Well, that answers one question.'

They all stared at her.

'The dead man in the bathroom. Let's just say our local criminal fraternity won't be getting any more of Henry's costly information. The body has been identified as that of Theodore Henry Arbuthnot, late of Fenfleet.'

'Henry!' exclaimed Matt and Liz in unison.

'That's a turn-up for the books!' added Bryn, surprise making his Welsh accent stronger than ever.

'And there's more,' Charley said solemnly. 'The substance the gang are dealing in is a new designer drug that Rory says has been showing up recently — in dead kids. He said it's proving hard to analyse, mainly because it was such a tiny sample but also because no one has managed to get their hands on any of the raw product yet. He believes it goes by the street name of "Roolet", spelled R-O-O-L-E-T.'

'Never heard of it,' said Matt. 'But then, we're pretty out of touch with that sort of thing.'

'We've only recently been alerted to it ourselves,' said Charley. 'We've heard it called by a couple of names. Roolet is one, Bullet Six is another. Both names refer to the risk involved in taking it.'

Liz pulled a face. 'If it's that dangerous, why take it at all?'

'Because of its staggering effects. Apparently, kids think it's worth it. It's an NPS, a "new psychoactive substance,"' said Bryn. 'And it really is new. We've never come across it before. Someone, somewhere, has produced something really unusual with Roolet.' He pulled a face. 'Prof Wilkinson gave me a lecture on it. He said there are very few genuinely new designer drugs, they all fall into one of four categories — synthetic cannabinoids that mimic cannabis, stimulants that mimic cocaine, ecstasy or amphetamines, downers that mimic tranquillisers, or hallucinogens that mimic LSD and methoxetamine. This new one is a kind of hybrid that contains a compound the others don't. It's mainly hallucinogenic, enhanced to produce six to seven hours of "energised euphoria".' He shrugged at this last expression.

'And the danger? Apart from what we already know with other drugs,' asked Liz.

'One in approximately sixty people suffer potentially life-threatening toxic reactions. Seizures, psychosis, and death is said to be "common".' Charley smiled faintly. 'Rory gave me the same lecture. He said it's the nastiest drug he's met to date, and because it's so scarce, it's mega expensive.'

'And a whole shipment of that stuff passed through the merchant's house last night.' Matt sighed.

'One of many. Worth millions, I expect,' added Charley. 'It's little wonder Eddie Race was prepared to pay Henry's rates.'

'But someone stopped our modern-day Raffles in his tracks,' said Liz.

Despite his unlawful activities, Henry would be missed in a number of circles. He was a true man-about-town, a latter-day James Bond. Likeable, handsome, rich, sophisticated, he had had so much charisma that even people like Matt had to admit to a certain grudging respect for him. 'Why do I feel angry about it?' he mused.

'Because he was ours,' said Charley at once. 'He was part of the "rich tapestry" of Fenfleet life. How dare some incomer drug dealer come here and snuff him out. I feel the same as you.'

For a moment, she really did look angry.

'Anyway, right now, Matt and Liz, I'm going to throw a few things your way. I'd be grateful for whatever you can find out. Matt, you seem to get on okay with old man Boon the solicitor, so, with our backing, can you see what you can find out about Jessie Wright having a key to that house? Find out all you can about the missing relatives of the Garnett family. Jessie was dead certain it belonged to her friend and, as she had access, we have to wonder if she was possibly right. The key must have come from this mysterious Anna. Perhaps Boon can help with that.'

He nodded. 'Sure, we'll get straight on it.'

'And then there's this.' Charley held up the photo of the graveyard at Amblekirk Village. 'You've written that this was taped to the back of a desk in Alex Hallam's room. If they needed to conceal it, the image must have meant something to the two students. Can you try to find out why?'

'We've been out there already,' said Liz, 'and found nothing, but we'll go again, first thing tomorrow. We agree, it has to have some significance.'

They left Charley head down, reading their reports, and drove back to Cannon Farm. 'Back in the saddle?' murmured Liz.

'Sort of,' said Matt. 'But not for too long. That hotel by the lake is starting to look very good to me.'

'I'm struggling to see further ahead than tomorrow at present, let alone dreaming of peaceful walks and hot tubs.'

Liz sounded unusually downbeat. Matt glanced at her but decided not to pursue the topic. He'd bring it up again when they were nearer a conclusion. Whenever that might be.

CHAPTER TWENTY-THREE

From what he knew of Reverend Peter, David guessed he'd be feeling responsible for Minty having gone missing while in his care. Peter did amazing work with the homeless and others who had fallen on difficult times, and David was feeling pretty shitty about having dumped yet another problem on his doorstep.

He decided to call him.

Peter sounded anxious. 'No news, David, and not a soul has seen hide nor hair of the man. I just can't understand it.'

'Look, I'm really sorry about this,' apologised David. 'I feel awful having suggested he come to you at all. He just seemed so frightened, so alone, and you were the only person I could think of who might help him.'

Peter chuckled. 'Oh, David, don't feel bad. You did exactly the right thing. And it's not a new occurrence, believe me. It happens all the time. People can't cope, so they run away rather than face their problems head on. I am more concerned about your friend Minty than I would normally be, because of his particular circumstances. Mr Ballard was certain he hadn't been followed, but maybe he had a real pro on his tail, then Mr Ballard wouldn't have known, would he? I hope that's not the case. I liked Minty, fundamentally he's a good man. I mean, I know he took to a life of crime and paid for it by a stint in prison, but I get the feeling he sees good in people where others don't.'

He was right. Minty had seen the family man in his gangster cellmate, not the thug. Not only that, he had troubled to visit him after he'd been shot.

'I'll keep you updated, it's all I can do,' said Peter. 'I can hardly get the police involved, can I?'

'Best not,' said David, still idly scrolling through the photographs on his screen. 'But I'll contact you if that changes at any point.'

Peter thanked him. As he rang off, another of Toby's pictures came up on his screen. Suddenly rigid, David stared at the image. He had gone through these photos any number of times, but had never noticed this particular detail.

In a flash he knew that this was what Jude had been looking for. This was the reason the two boys had died. It had nothing whatsoever to do with the face in the window. He printed it off, went back and edited and cropped the picture. The printer whirred. 'Yes!' he hissed. 'Gotcha!'

It was a different window, filthy, plate glass, looking out from an old shop front. Reflected in it, you could just make out the shape of a vehicle. You could also make out the licence plate. That vehicle could be traced.

He heard Matt and Liz come in and scrambled to his feet, waving the printout. 'I've got it! You were right, Matt, it was something we missed.'

Matt and Liz hurried in, pulling off their jackets.

'Look!' David held out the enlarged image. 'What do you think?'

Matt clapped him on the shoulder. 'You've done it! I do believe that's it. Not that I know why it should be so important. The vehicles they use would be replaced after each job, or the number plates changed. But for some reason, I just know that this is what the whole thing pivots on.'

'What if on the night that picture was taken a delivery wasn't due. Maybe someone else was there, not one of the gang, someone who wants to keep his involvement secret.' Liz squinted. 'I can't make out what kind of vehicle it is, can you?'

'It could be an Audi,' murmured David. 'It's definitely a saloon, not a van or a truck. The window's so dirty it's hard to make anything out.'

'This is where working alongside the police comes in handy,' Matt said. 'They'll have no problem tracing that number. I'm ringing Bryn. We'll send him that picture and they can let their IT guys loose on it.'

Liz ruffled David's hair. 'Well done, our Davey! Keep this up and we'll be taking you on permanently.'

David felt quite overcome. He was full of gratitude towards Matt and Liz for picking him up when he had been so down. Now he was actually doing something constructive, making a difference. He hadn't been in Tanners Fen any time at all, but his outlook on life was already changing. He didn't feel nearly so bitter, and he was coming to realise that joining the police wasn't the only option for him. There were a whole lot of other jobs that might be just as fulfilling.

Matt lowered his phone. 'Can you send that as an attachment to Bryn's email address, David?'

'Thanks to you, Davey, that's another question answered, another box ticked,' said Liz softly. 'Feels good, doesn't it?'

'I dunno, Liz,' he said. 'I'm a bit scared to count my chickens. It could be another red herring. I mean, when I saw that woman's face in the original pictures, I was so certain she was an illegal immigrant or some girl being held there against her will, maybe I'm wrong about this too.'

'You aren't. I just know it.' Liz tapped the side of her nose. 'Intuition, Davey-boy. Someone definitely didn't want that vehicle to be seen. And that very someone considered it worth terminating the boy who took the photographs — and his friend too — to ensure it stayed that way.' She smiled at him. 'I'll lay good money on it. Fancy a bet?'

David grinned. 'I'll take your word for it. So, what next?'

'Well, we have a small errand to run for the DCI, but first, Matt and I want to know a couple of things ourselves.

As it happens, we've nothing for tonight's dinner, so as soon as he's off the phone, I'm going to suggest we all drive over to Pear Tree House and grab a meal. Then we can have a private word with Bernie Wetherby about one of the men involved in this caper.'

David's face lit up. 'I'm not turning down a meal in that place! Who're we trying to find out about, Liz?'

'Jude Sherriff. All we really have is what Minty told us about him, which isn't much. I want that man's whole story, chapter and verse, and Bernie is the person to ask. He has friends in very low places, believe me.' Liz suddenly looked pensive. 'And although it will do no actual good, because he won't be able to talk to us, I'd like to go and take a look at Paddy Sherriff for myself.'

'Maybe the nursing home staff might know something about Jude,' David said. 'You know, small things like what he talks about to his father, or what car he drives.'

'First thing tomorrow, while Matt is speaking to the solicitor again, we'll go hospital visiting. Okay, Detective?'

'Yes, Sergeant!' He saluted and Liz cuffed him affectionately around the ear.

* * *

The Pear Tree was fairly quiet for once, but then they had arrived early for an evening meal. Matt disappeared into the back office, while Liz and David checked out the menu. When time passed and he still hadn't returned, Liz ordered for him.

He returned just as the food arrived, his face creased into a frown.

Once the waiter had left, Matt lowered his voice. 'Well, that was informative! I found out more than I expected.'

'About this Jude Sherriff? What are we dealing with, then?' Liz asked.

'As nasty a thing as we'll ever meet this side of the gates of hell, according to Bernie.' Matt raised an eyebrow. 'He knows someone who worked with Jude up Durham way a while back. His description of him was not exactly warm and fluffy. In short, he's a psycho. Clever, very well organised and totally ruthless.' Matt looked around to make sure they couldn't be heard. 'Bernie's mate told him Jude Sherriff was the arranger for a diamond robbery, from which they got away with a fortune in uncut stones. Not only that, these were blood diamonds. Having fewer scruples than a sewer rat, this didn't bother him one bit, and for a while he continued on that course.'

'Blood diamonds are the ones mined in African war zones, aren't they, Matt?' David said.

'That's right, and the profits go back to fuel the conflict, although it's complicated. Read up on it sometime, Davey, start with an article in *Time*. It's not as simple as it seems. Without those mines, in which even school-age children work, whole families would starve to death.'

Matt had read up about conflict diamonds following a case he'd been on that involved a consignment of them, and felt strongly about it. Fearing a lecture, Liz steered the conversation back to Jude. 'And now? He's turned to drugs instead of precious stones?'

'Seems that way. Bernie said he's known as someone you don't mess with. According to his friend, he's meticulous. If you're good at your job and concentrate on getting it right, you'll be okay. Screw up, and you could be history. You don't mess up on one of Jude's jobs, certainly not more than once.'

'Doesn't quite gel with the loving son who visits his cabbage of a dad every single day, does it?' said David, cutting himself a portion of fillet steak.

'Does Bernie's friend know anything about that side of him? His family?' asked Liz.

Matt laid down his knife and fork. 'Bernie's working on that right now. He thinks he might have a contact who can help us. And if he doesn't, he knows a woman who is rather well acquainted with some of Fenfleet's shadier characters. Ah, and before I forget, Jude Sherriff is known in the

232

underworld as the "Natural Causes Killer". So far, no one has ever proved any of the deaths he engineered were anything other than an accident, misadventure, or natural causes.'

'Like Toby and Alex,' muttered David.

'Like Toby and Alex. There's just one difference this time. The previous deaths didn't have Professor Rory Wilkinson looking into them. If there's the slightest hint of anything hinky about them, Rory will nail it.'

For a while they ate in silence, relishing the good food. Then Liz said, 'I'm still reeling from the news about Henry. I can't believe he got topped. He was larger than life, and I can't imagine Fenfleet without him. I wonder how the hell he came to get himself murdered?'

'Well, it wasn't anything even vaguely resembling natural causes, so that lets Jude out.' Matt looked disappointed.

Liz nodded. From what Matt had told her, the scene in the bathroom had not been pretty. The copious quantities of blood involved pointed to something very unnatural indeed. 'From what you heard about him, it's not Jude's MO, but he was very likely in that house when they cleaned it out and moved the merchandise, maybe he got someone else to do the deed.'

Matt shook his head. 'Doubtful. That wouldn't be very meticulous, would it? Jude wouldn't have wanted anything that pointed to them. They practically sanitised the place! I suggest Henry was killed by someone else altogether, although I cannot begin to guess who.'

'Something to do with the kidnapped boy, I should think,' said David. 'Maybe Henry discovered him.'

Liz nodded slowly. 'Quite possible, I would say.'

Before they could discuss it further, Bernie came hurrying over, carrying a sheet of paper.

'This lady is expecting you in an hour's time. Meet her at the address I've written here. It's not far, so you have plenty of time for pudding and coffee.' He smiled benignly, every inch the charming restaurateur, then whispered, 'It'll be worth your while. She knows a lot more about that certain person than I'd realised.' And then he was gone.

Matt pushed the paper over to Liz. 'I know that house, it's on the outskirts of this village. It used to be the Golden Thorn pub before the brewery pulled out and it was sold off.'

Liz looked at the name — Isla McGowan. It rang no bells.

She glanced at her watch. Things were beginning to happen, and for the first time since they'd begun this investigation, she appreciated their odd position. Neither official, nor unofficial, they occupied the fringes, yet were still an integral part of it all. Well, she'd cope with that.

Having chosen plain ice cream for dessert, she wondered about their latest source. Isla McGowan at the old Golden Thorn. It had a quirky ring to it, and she tried to imagine what this Isla might look like. It wasn't until they were half-way there that she realised she was actually enjoying herself again.

* * *

Matt recognised the old inn immediately. It certainly looked a great deal nicer as a residential property than it had as a public house. It had been a bit of a dive back in the day, and its mossy tiled roof had sheltered a fair few dodgy deals. Now it was clean and neat, while retaining its original character. A large sign hung over the door, reading *Golden Thorn House*, and beside it an ornate brass bell on a chain. Matt was just about to give it a tug when the door swung open.

Without a word of introduction, Isla McGowan hustled them inside and closed the door. 'Come straight through to the garden room. We can talk there away from the others.'

Matt wondered who these "others" were but didn't ask.

He recalled that the garden room had once been a kind of conservatory used as a dining area. Since they only ever served plain pub grub, they had never bothered with a proper restaurant section. In its days as a pub, the place had always been a bit tatty, but now it looked comfortable and inviting, with two big low sofas, a long coffee table, a number of different-sized bookcases and dozens of houseplants.

Isla pointed to the sofas. 'Sit, please. I hear you want to know about that freak, Jude Sherriff.'

Matt reckoned she must be well into her sixties. She had a wild mane of copper hair streaked with grey, and was somewhat unconventionally dressed. The effect was as if she had rummaged her way through a charity shop, chosen whatever appealed to her and worn them all at the same time. Certainly nothing matched, and it all seemed to come from different eras. Different sizes, too: her present outfit was topped by a baggy knitted men's cardigan, the sleeves of which covered her hands.

Tearing his eyes away from her unfortunate dress sense, Matt said, 'It's his early history we need to know about, Ms McGowan. His childhood, his family if possible.'

Isla sat back, pulled up her sleeves and laced her fingers together. 'He should have been drowned at birth. If ever there was a spawn of the devil, it was Jude Sherriff.'

'That sounds pretty harsh,' Liz said softly. 'I gather from that you actually knew Jude as a child.'

'Regrettably, yes, Ms Haynes. I was his father's lover for many years. I was a very bad girl back then, and Paddy Sherriff was a very bad boy. But, oh, what charisma he had. He loved his wife and his child — young Fion that is, not Jude. I was a pleasant distraction, something different, you might say.'

Matt could imagine that Isla might have been quite exciting back in the day. Beautiful, wanton, rather wild.

'But that's irrelevant. I merely told you so you would appreciate that I did know the family, intimately. Often when his wife was out, Paddy invited me to the house, where I met the boys.'

'Jude,' Matt prompted.

'Jude.' She said nothing further.

Matt, slightly impatient, said, 'Help us here, Ms McGowan. If Jude is so awful, why does he visit his disabled father every single day, and has done so since Paddy was shot?'

'Guilt.' Isla stared at each of them. 'And determination. Paddy was the only person Jude had never been able to exert his will over. He wanted to break him.' Isla gazed into the distance. 'You see, Jude was utterly controlling. Almost from birth, he had a need to dominate others. It started with his toys. If they didn't work, didn't do what he wanted, he destroyed them. And this extended to people. His father saw it from the start, but his mother, a gentle, sweet person, always went to his defence. Paddy started to hate her constant "Be patient, darling, it's just a phase. He'll grow out of it." When Fion came along, a little angel, Jude's behaviour seemed to change. Brenda believed it would be the making of Jude. Paddy was afraid the opposite would happen.' Isla closed her eyes for a moment. 'Paddy was right.'

Matt sensed what was coming.

'Of course, nothing was ever proven, but when Fion, playing in the woods with his brother, fell from a tree and broke his back, Paddy knew exactly what had happened.'

'Oh my God!' exclaimed Liz. 'Did the boy die?'

'No, but he was confined to a wheelchair, paralysed from the waist down. There were apparently other injuries as well, including possible brain damage. Whatever the case, he never spoke again.' Isla smiled sadly. 'I spent a little time with him, and he was the most beautiful child. I always believed he could speak, he simply chose not to.'

'Jude pushed him from that tree?' Liz said.

'I believe so. You could say it was the first of his "natural cause" incidents. Jude swore the branch broke, said he did all he could to help his brother, ran to get assistance, but when Paddy thought about it, the timing didn't fit. Of course, nothing could be proved one way or the other.'

'Did Fion live at home after the accident?' asked David.

'Until their mother died. By then, Paddy was well into his prison sentence, and there was no one to care for Fion, so he went into a home.'

'How did the mother die?' Matt asked, guessing the answer to this too.

Isla raised an eyebrow. 'Oh, an accident, of course.'

Matt shook his head.

'Swerving to avoid some animal, her car skidded off the road into a tree. She wasn't wearing her seat belt, and she broke her neck.'

'Who was driving?' asked Liz, almost reluctantly.

'Who do you think?' Isla said.

Someone swallowed.

Isla stood up. 'We need tea, or would you prefer coffee?'

Matt would have liked a large brandy at this point, but he said tea, as did the others.

Isla went off to the kitchen.

Finally, David broke the silence. 'Matt. Ask her about when Paddy was shot.'

Matt had considered it but seemed to recall that it had come about when Paddy confronted an old rival. 'Yes, I will, although I don't think we can credit Jude with that one, not if you go by the newspaper reports.'

Isla came in with a tray on which four assorted mugs rattled. These ranged from a delicate bone china cup covered in flowers to a massive beaker emblazoned with a football club motif.

'Help yourself, they're all the same. Sugar's in the bowl.' This turned out to be a porcelain ginger cat with a removeable head.

The tea was very welcome after what they'd just been told. Tea dispensed, Matt posed David's question.

'Not Jude for once,' Isla said, 'though it was rather interesting that the suspected gunman happened to die shortly afterwards — in an accident involving a faulty shotgun.' Isla smiled enigmatically at them.

'Yet Jude goes every day to visit his father, even though Paddy can't speak.' *Why?* Matt wondered. It could hardly be out of love — Jude was clearly a psychopath.

'Who says he can't?'

Matt stared at Isla. 'But . . . but the nursing staff, and an old friend who visits occasionally. They all say he's never uttered a word since he was shot.'

She gave a little laugh. 'He's never spoken to *Jude*, that's true, but that doesn't mean he can't.'

'But the nursing staff?' asked Liz. 'Do they know?'

'Their patient comes first. Of course they know, they're just taking care of his well-being.'

'You've visited him, haven't you?' said Liz.

'Once a fortnight without fail. More if he asks me, but he tires easily.' Her expression took on a faraway look. 'When I was young, I slept with a lot of bad men, but none attracted me like Paddy. That sort of feeling usually fades fairly quickly, but not this time. I still feel for him as deeply as ever. You couldn't really call it love, it's more a kind of kinship. I think he's what people call a soulmate.' She shrugged. 'I'm not sure there's much more I can tell you.'

'One last thing,' said Matt. 'Do you know a man called Minty?'

She smiled. 'Ah, the "keeper of the secret"! The honest villain, Minty Agutter. Yes, I know him.'

Matt suddenly realised he was probably sitting opposite the trusted friend, the person safeguarding the diamond necklace.

'Leave it there, Mr Ballard. Minty's the one keeping that secret, not me.'

'But Minty is missing,' said David.

Isla's face clouded over. 'Then one of two things has happened. He will have met with an "accident", or his capacity to sniff out danger has sent him deep undercover. Expect the worst and hope for the best. There's nothing you can do for Minty.'

* * *

Palmer had to decide who should fill the gap left by the treacherous Jude, but neither of the candidates filled him with much delight. Jude was going to be a hard act to follow.

He was pouring himself a large malt whisky when his mobile rang. He put the bottle down and snatched it up. Jude, the bastard.

'Mr Palmer, before you start tearing into me, just shut up a minute and listen.'

'This had better be good.'

'It's all you're getting,' Jude said, 'and it's the truth, so hear me out.'

Palmer hated being put on the back foot in this way. 'Well, spit it out then.'

'First, other than the one now defunct location, the others are both working properly. I know Deezer's already told you that, but I've checked myself and can guarantee that we have no worries about them. Luckily, they're both big enough to take the additional shipments that will be diverted from Cutler's Alley. I've made a couple of adjustments and everything will be in place for the next delivery, so our suppliers needn't be alarmed. It's business as usual, Mr Palmer.'

Palmer felt a kind of buzzing inside his head. This was not what he had been expecting to hear. Before Jude called, Palmer had been thinking in terms of damage limitation, how to withdraw from the area without losing too many of his valuable contacts.

'Now, this you don't know,' Jude said. 'While I was doing my final recce of the merchant's house, I encountered two obstacles that needed very careful handling. I'll explain more fully when I see you, but for now, just be thankful it was me who discovered them, because I know how to deal with them without comeback. I'm not sure what anyone else would have done, but it would most likely have proved disastrous for us.'

Us. Jude was making it clear that he was still a partner and intended it to stay that way. Palmer made no comment for the time being. He sipped his whisky. 'Go on.'

'Number one. The police will, or most likely already have, found a body in that house. There was no way to either remove or disguise it fast enough, so it stayed where it was. The cops can fumble around trying to fathom that one out. It has no direct connection to any of us, and it'll distract them.'

Palmer wondered who the dead man was, but decided to wait until Jude had finished his story.

'The other one, Mr Palmer, is a bit complicated, and will take a few days to sort out. Now . . .'

Jude sounded almost patronising, talking down to him as if he was a kid. It took all Palmer's self-control to hold his tongue.

'I will sort it efficiently and permanently, so long as you give me the time I need to do it in. If you do, then all will be well, and we won't suffer financially, or in any other way. If you don't, like the bard said, you'll be right royally stuffed.'

Palmer heard that word "you". What happened to the "us" he'd been talking about a couple of minutes previously? But before he could retaliate, Jude was talking again.

'This is a critical point in our business, Mr Palmer. It could destroy us, or simply go away. Luckily for you, I can achieve the latter option, but it's worth a lot more than I'm getting from you at present.'

Palmer felt a pulse in his temple start to pound. He gritted his teeth.

'I won't press the point right now. However, what I do know is that my normal cut isn't yet with my financial advisor, and it should be. Put it through, Mr Palmer, immediately. When I get a text to say it's been received, I'll proceed, and all will be well in the world. Cut me out and that wonderful world won't look half so beautiful, or so lucrative.' Jude softened his voice. 'Trust me, Mr Palmer. I've got this, so don't ask me any questions right now. You'll see soon enough that I'm still on your side and I always was. We need each other, at least for a bit longer. Don't we?'

After a stony silence, Palmer reluctantly agreed. 'The dead man? Not one of ours, you said.'

'Absolutely not. He was just an irrelevance, a handy little distraction for the police to play with. But right now, Mr Palmer, if you would be kind enough to get my payment sorted, I'll attend to the more pressing situation and get us back on track. Do we have an accord?'

An image rose in Palmer's mind of Jude as a pirate, complete with three-cornered hat and cutlass. *Do we have an accord indeed!* 'I'll sanction your money. You seem to have earned it.'

'Oh, I have, Mr Palmer. I'm sorry I didn't contact you earlier, but it wasn't possible, and you must forgive me if it stays that way until I've concluded what I have to do. You'll just have to trust me, okay?'

'One last thing. Does this have anything to do with Minty Agutter?' Palmer said.

'Nothing whatsoever. Now, I'll wait for that text, and then I'll put everything to rights again.' The line went dead.

Palmer stared at his phone. He took a long gulp of the whisky and felt it burn its way down. He was both deeply relieved and horribly uncomfortable. For the first time in their strange partnership, Palmer was on the back foot. He had no idea what the fuck was going on. His junior partner had just demanded payment, and there was nothing he could do but comply. If not, the empire he'd so carefully built up could come crashing down around his ears. He drained his glass and picked up his business phone.

CHAPTER TWENTY-FOUR

Kellie Burton never cried. Only after her mother's death had she given way to tears and then only in secret. But now, as night fell and darkness enveloped the hotel, her eyes filled and a feeling of desolation swept over her.

Outside in the car park, reporters and cameramen murmured and shifted, waiting to catch a glimpse of the teenager who was hunting for her missing brother, the distraught widowed father who had put out an impassioned plea to whoever had taken his son to please bring him back.

Unheeding of the waiting crowd, Kellie lay on her bed and stared up at the ceiling. Things had gone from bad to worse. Poor Aunt Jessie had been taken to a psychiatric hospital in a nearby town called Greenborough and was being allowed no visitors until they had stabilised her and decided on her treatment. The police were no further forward with finding her little brother. Simon was in far more danger now than when Auntie Jessie had been hiding him. At least she had meant him no harm, but now . . . Who had taken him, and what did they want from him?

Kellie had heard the police whispering. She knew what a paedophile was, and prayed Simon hadn't been taken by one of those. Still worse, she felt responsible. She had promised her mother that she would look after Simon, and she had failed. More than anything, Kellie wanted to *do* something. Doing nothing allowed your imagination to run wild.

Debbie had called in earlier to check on them and make sure the reporters weren't harassing them. Seeing the number of people camped out in the car park, she had reported it to her sergeant, resulting in Kellie and her dad being moved to an undisclosed location. Right now, her father was gathering their few bits together in preparation for their evacuation.

Already packed, Kellie wondered where they were to be taken. She was beginning to feel a bit like a prisoner.

There was a knock on the door, and she was relieved to see Debbie and Jack. These two were her one safe haven in this terrible storm. Solid and dependable, they seemed to really care about Simon.

'Your carriage awaits, madam,' said Jack, whom she now called "Swifty". He gave a little bow. 'And let me tell you, where you're going has the edge over this place. We'll sneak you out of a side door so you won't have to face the press. Just lie on the back seat till we're out of here and are sure no one's followed us.'

Kellie noticed that instead of their usual uniforms they were wearing normal clothes. They were taking no chances, sparing no effort. This made her want to cry all over again.

'I suppose you haven't found that woman who looked after me, have you?' she asked. 'Belle, who I think might really be Anna?'

Debbie shook her head. 'Sorry, honey. We haven't found her yet, but we have found out her full name. It's Arabella Rosa Rackham, and she's always been called Belle. Her neighbours all say they've never heard anyone call her Anna.' She smiled gently at Kellie. 'But we've not given up. Swifty and me never give up.'

Kellie was sure they didn't. Still, doubt remained. 'Suppose it was just a pet name that Auntie Jessie had for her from when they were kids. When I was small my best friend called me Kellie-Welly and it turned into just Welly.

She always called me that even when we got older, but it was just between us.'

Debbie nodded. 'Could be, but we need to find her first, then we'll ask. To be honest, we're getting a bit worried about her. She usually tells the neighbours if she's going to be away, and they keep an eye on her bungalow for her, but this time she just went off, suddenly.'

But Kellie remained dubious. If she ran off with Simon, then she wouldn't say anything, would she? Kellie wasn't sure which frightened her more, the sinister woman that her mother never trusted, or a stranger who'd taken Simon with heaven knew what on her mind.

Soon they were on their way to their new location. Kellie felt as though everything was out of her control. She was being swept along with the tide, and she hated it. 'Debbie, is there anything I can do? I mean, when I was talking to Auntie Jessie I felt as if I was doing something useful, but waiting around like this is awful.'

'I'm sorry, sweetheart, but waiting is all you can do right now. Just remember, half the Fenland police force is out looking for Simon. We have a special TV appeal going out and officers are being drafted in from other areas too. We'll find him, Kellie.'

'Come on, love.' Her father put his arm around her and pulled her towards him. 'We have to be strong for Simon.'

Snuggling into his side, she realised she hadn't sat with him like this since she was little. It felt warm and reassuring, but she sensed how empty he felt. Dad was just as terrified as her.

* * *

Matt, Liz and David were too hyped up to think of going to bed. They sat in the Incident Room going over everything they had learned from Bernie and Isla.

'Do you think Isla has that diamond necklace?' asked David. 'I do.'

244

'I'm not so sure,' Matt said. 'Maybe, maybe not. She certainly didn't want to talk about the "Big Secret," did she?'

'And that sneaky old sod Minty never mentioned that Paddy could talk if he wanted to.' Liz smiled. 'I'm looking forward to going to that home tomorrow. Knowing what we know now, it could be quite a different visit to the one I expected.'

'Golden Thorn House was a funny kind of place, wasn't it?' David looked puzzled. 'I noticed several other women as we were leaving, all about the same age and all quite, well, quirky.'

Matt had seen them too and reckoned they shared the house; possibly it was a kind of commune. He had wanted to ask at the time but had decided it might be better to make some discreet enquiries. It wasn't connected to the case, he was just curious. 'From what Bernie intimated, I believe that Isla was what they used to call a "good time girl". She almost said as much herself. Not quite a prostitute, but—'

'I think she was,' said Liz. 'I could be wrong, but I think she has assisted us before, a long time ago. It was a case concerning a convicted conman who came out of jail and put his wife in Intensive Care. It wasn't my case, but her name rang bells, and I'm sure she helped the detectives with the suspect's background, which she knew about because he'd been a client of hers.'

'One sure thing is that she thinks a lot of our Paddy Sherriff,' Matt said.

David nodded. 'I'll say. And she hates Jude's guts!'

They fell silent for a moment or two.

'I hope our old colleagues find that lunatic pretty smartish,' said Liz with feeling. 'Just the thought of a man like that on the loose in Fenfleet gives me the heebie-jeebies.'

'Me too.' Matt stood up. 'I think we should clear the whiteboard and start again, writing up our new targets and new info as it comes in, what do you think?'

The board wiped clean, it felt like a new investigation. Matt picked up a marker pen. 'Charley Anders wants us to try to find the rightful inheritors of the merchant's house, and figure out how Jessie Wright came to have a key for the place.' Pen squeaking, he wrote, *The Merchant's House*, and *Key?* followed by *Visit Boon A.M.* 'She also wants us to look into Amblekirk, and why Alex photographed the graveyard there.' He stuck up the photo showing the lamp post and the path, and wrote, *Why Amblekirk?*

'And we are going to do a little undercover sleuthing into Jude and his father,' added Liz. 'I don't think I'll be able to sleep well until that man either does a runner because it's too hot for him here, or Lincolnshire's finest throws him into the slammer and turns the key.'

'I know it's not really our concern, but . . .' David hesitated. 'Who do you think took that little boy from the merchant's house?'

Neither Liz nor Matt answered immediately, then Matt said, 'As I see it, it can be only one of two people — Anna or Jude.'

'That's what I thought,' said Liz. She turned to Matt. 'And if you believe that Jude didn't kill Henry, then I suggest that Anna did, which places her fair and square in the crosshairs for having abducted Simon Burton.'

David stared unseeing at the board. 'So, no matter who has him, that vulnerable little boy is in the hands of someone very dangerous.'

Matt shivered. 'Seems that way.' He put down the marker. 'I think I've had enough of all this for one night. Shall we turn in?'

No one objected.

* * *

Simon snuggled down under the duvet, warm and safe. He had his *Observer's Book of Birds* beneath his pillow and two inhalers on the bedside table. He even had a night light ready, in case he got frightened in the dark. Thank heavens that detective had found him and brought him to this safe house.

No one would hurt him here, that was for sure. He'd even had a McDonald's for his supper! He wasn't sure what had happened to Auntie Jessie, but given how flaky she was, and getting worse all the time, who knew what had gone on in her mind? She even talked to herself. He was mighty relieved to be in the care of the police. Just a little longer and he would be home with Kellie and Dad.

Simon closed his eyes. The detective had assured him that they were very close to making an arrest, so the worst was over and he was safe. As he drifted off to sleep, he hoped Auntie Jessie was safe too.

CHAPTER TWENTY-FIVE

News of Henry's murder spread like a virus through the underworld grapevine. By early morning there weren't many people who didn't know. Different rumours circulated like flames in a forest, each new supposition catching hold and flaring before burning itself out, only for another to rise up in its place.

Eddie Race, for one, had spent the night working her contacts, intent on getting to the truth. By the time the sun rose, she had the whole story.

What did it mean that he was doing a job for her at the time? This enraged her. Henry was unique, irreplaceable. She knew no one else with the contacts Henry had. His loss forced her to turn to Raymond Leonard and his like, and Eddie was not a team player. She always worked alone, and the thought of having to cooperate with people she considered beneath her sent her into paroxysms of fury.

For the umpteenth time, she went over what Henry had said during his last visit. He had given her a lot, but it hadn't been quite enough. Eddie needed the name of the man in charge. Meanwhile, Harrington had come up with a contingency plan, and had blocked the funds she had agreed to pay Henry. All well and good, she wasn't out of pocket, but she had to know how to proceed. Her empire depended upon it.

Eddie paced her office like a caged animal. Either she continued to deal with the man without a name and risked going down with him if the police discovered what was going on, or she cut her ties with him, thereby kissing goodbye to the biggest profit she'd ever made. Bullet Six was the hottest designer drug to ever hit the streets, and she, Eddie, held the franchise for the entire Fenland area. Eddie herself had never taken anything stronger than two paracetamol and a glass of malt, but she'd been told that this drug produced a hit like nothing on earth. The punters certainly seemed willing to pay the enormous amount it was going for.

Considering the money to be made, there wasn't much contest when it came down to it. She'd wait until her supplier contacted her later that morning, and, depending on what he told her, take it from there. Meanwhile, she'd have Harrington ring-fence her assets as far as he was able. He'd do his best, obviously, because if he didn't, he'd stand to lose a great deal of money himself, and Harrington liked to live well. Her father had once said that if you paid greedy people top money for their services, you would retain their loyalty. No one wanted to kill the golden goose, did they?

It didn't occur to her that she was included among the greedy. Bullet Six was the golden egg, and Eddie Race couldn't bring herself to kill the goose that laid it.

* * *

Edward Boon agreed to see Matt as soon as the office opened in the morning. After all, this was police business, even though Matt Ballard had no official role.

The old man admitted to being utterly at a loss as to how the drug dealers had gained access to those storerooms.

'We only ever gave a cursory glance to those rooms, but they were empty, and we never saw the slightest hint of anything having been disturbed. Our priority was the house itself.' He looked quite contrite. 'I am saddened to think that we were guilty of a dereliction of duty, Mr Ballard, especially having made such a show of knowing better than you in the matter of intruders.'

Sorely tempted to say *I told you so*, Matt said instead, 'They did an exceptional job of clearing up after each shipment, Mr Boon. Without a very detailed examination of those rooms, it's unlikely anyone would have noticed anything untoward.' He levelled his gaze at Boon. 'However, our priority right now is not the drug dealers, it's the woman, Jessie Wright, who commandeered one of the upstairs rooms as a hideaway for her young nephew.'

Boon spread his hands. 'This I simply cannot understand.'

'She had a key, Mr Boon. Can you tell me how on earth she could have obtained it?'

'I can't! Ever since I heard what happened, I have been over every conceivable possibility any number of times, and I'm sorry to tell you, I've arrived at no conclusion at all.' He stared helplessly at Matt. 'It's beyond me.'

Matt tried a different tack. Maybe the old man would have an answer for this one. 'Okay, we'll come back to that. Last time we spoke, you told me you were close to finding one of the missing heirs to the merchant's house. Can you tell me who it is? And also, whether you have made any more progress in the last few days.'

Edward Boon took a file from his top drawer. 'It all got a bit exciting a month or so ago when we learned of the missing Garnett heirs. Then, to our chagrin, the son of the last documented Garnett on our client's list, a man called Carson Garnett, took his own life. It seems he had mental health problems and had made several attempts in the past. All terribly sad, of course. It meant we were left with one last heir — heiress, actually — to find.'

Matt was suddenly reminded of something PC Debbie Hume had told him. At some point in her ramblings, Jessie Wright had sworn that the place they were staying in belonged to her friend, Anna.

'What is the woman's name?' he asked, with a shiver of anticipation.

Boon looked down at his records. 'Anna Davina Garnett.'

Matt took a sharp breath. So Mad Jessie had been telling the truth. No. That couldn't be right, could it? The will hadn't been finalised at the time. He tried to sort out his tangled thoughts. 'And did you find her? Have you met her, this Anna Garnett?'

'I thought I had, but now, well . . .' Boon looked down.

Matt wanted to shake the old man.

'Sorry, I know that sounds ridiculous. Let me explain,' Boon said.

He looked so apologetic that Matt almost pitied him. The poor old man was in a difficult situation through no fault of his own.

'We had a letter from Anna Garnett, as we believed her to be. It was in answer to one of our many notices in *The Times* newspaper. She wanted to come to the office and she also wanted to see Satara House for herself. As you can imagine, we were in a state of high excitement and welcomed her with open arms. I mean, we had been searching for so long, it seemed like a miracle.' His expression showed intense disappointment. 'She produced a copious amount of documentation — including her birth certificate and so on — and she knew details about the history of the Garnetts that only a Garnett would know. At my suggestion, my son took her to see the house. We didn't want her to think she was inheriting some mansion that she could move into after a lick of paint had freshened it up.'

'What was she like, this Anna?' asked Matt.

'Oh dear, rather scary! A bit of a tartar actually. Very forthright. Spoke to us as if she was a headmistress addressing unruly children. Needless to say, she was singularly unimpressed by Satara House. Some of her comments were pretty damned rude as a matter of fact. She said she didn't know that she actually wanted to inherit such a dilapidated old pile, and would come back to us after she'd decided what best to do with it.'

'Do you have the documentation she left with you, Mr Boon? We're extremely anxious to speak to this Anna, and her address would make a great start.'

'I have it, but it won't do you any good, Mr Ballard.' Boon sighed. 'We verified the records she'd left with us and made a startling discovery — Anna Garnett died over fifty years ago. We have no idea who came here, but it wasn't our missing heiress.'

* * *

Liz and David didn't get much of a welcome at the Linden House nursing home. Even after Liz showed them her ID card and explained that they were working in conjunction with the police, the administrator was still reluctant to leave them alone with Mr Sherriff. Only when she mentioned Isla McGowan did the woman's attitude soften. 'All right, Ms Haynes, but only ten minutes. Paddy tires quickly. I'll take you to his room, but please don't overexcite him. He is a very sick man, you know.'

Liz said she wouldn't. 'Has his son visited today?'

The administrator shook her head. 'No, and I'm wondering if he will. He didn't come yesterday. It's the first time he's missed a visit in two years.'

She didn't sound much concerned. In fact, at the mention of Jude, her face assumed an expression of distaste.

'We know Jude's father never speaks in his presence,' Liz said, 'and we believe we know why, but we have absolutely no intention of upsetting Mr Sherriff.'

'Can I ask the reason for your visit?' This time her voice was much gentler. 'Only to be frank, we don't think Paddy will be with us much longer, and we're doing our best to make his last days tranquil and pleasant.'

This made Liz want to laugh. The man had been a career criminal, a dangerous thief who had been responsible for a number of major heists, and here he was being treated like royalty in a private nursing home, and by people who genuinely cared for him. Oh well, she thought, at least he never actually killed or maimed anyone. Unlike his son.

'We need to find Jude. He's suspected of involvement in a number of serious crimes in Fenfleet. We wondered if there was anything Paddy could tell us about where he might be, or anything else that might help us, like what car he drives.' Liz looked hopefully at the administrator.

'Call in at the office before you leave. I have those details, including his application for long-term parking here if it comes to that. I have quite a few other details too, as he pays his father's bills. Don't bother Paddy with all that, just keep it to a few personal questions if you really must. I'll give you more concrete information myself. Right, here we are.' She opened a door and called out brightly, 'Visitors, Paddy. Friends of Isla's.'

Liz had never met Paddy Sherriff, only knowing him from mugshots, and old ones at that. The man she saw now was a far cry from the rather dashing hoodlum who had robbed several high-class jewellers.

Liz knew from Minty that Paddy must be approaching seventy, but he looked much older than that. His face was pale and haggard, his features on one side had collapsed. His hair was thin and wispy, and he was so skinny his pyjamas hung loosely. Yet his eyes had a steely glint. According to the administrator, Paddy was drawing near the celestial pearly gates, but he clearly had no intention of checking in with St Peter just yet.

'You're coppers,' he growled, then grinned. 'Well, *you* are.' He pointed to Liz with a bony finger. 'Not sure about the schoolboy, but you know what they say about policemen and doctors getting younger.'

Liz returned the grin. 'Nice to meet you, Paddy. I'm Liz and this is David. And we do know Isla, and we really are friends of Minty. In fact, we've had to magic him away — see, we think he's in danger.'

'And I know who from. My fucking psycho son.'

'Jude's in a lot of trouble, Paddy. We need to find him. We think he may have abducted a child, a vulnerable little boy who suffers from asthma.'

Paddy's wrinkled features creased up even further. 'Asthma? A little boy, you say. That's not good at all.'

'The police will be watching this place, Paddy. If he does come and visit, he'll be picked up. I'm sorry, he's your son after all, but—'

Paddy gave a stiff wave. 'Forget the apologies! Believe me, if I could get him to come, I would. Then you could catch him. But he won't come near the place if he suspects you're watching him.'

'There's a chance he might not suspect. He has never worked this area before, and we only learned his name from someone undercover. He could believe he's untouchable and simply go about his usual routine. You see, he's been involved in bringing in and distributing drugs, and we're pretty sure the operation is still ongoing, even though we've busted one cell. They're cool as cucumbers, this gang of his.'

Paddy nodded. 'He told me his boss is even more ruthless than him. But we all know that's not possible.'

'He didn't mention a name, I suppose?' asked David.

''Fraid not. But they hate each other, I picked that much up.' Paddy started to cough. 'Sorry, time's up. You better go now before they chuck you out.'

Liz and David stood up. 'We'll see you again, Paddy.'

'Then don't leave it too long,' he wheezed. 'Clock's ticking.'

Downstairs they found the office of the administrator, whose name was Carole Courtney. She handed Liz a sheet of paper. 'Not much, but it might help. Jude Sherriff doesn't give much away and if, as you say, he's mixed up in criminal activities, I see why now.'

Liz glanced at the page in her hand and saw that Jude drove a BMW. The licence number was there, along with the details of the bank account from which Paddy's medical bills were paid. To crown it all, Carole had written down a mobile phone number.

'It's not as useful as you might think, I'm afraid,' Carole said, evidently having noticed her smile. 'He emphasised that we were only to use that number in the event of his father becoming seriously ill. He also stipulated that we have to call from this number here,' she pointed to her own phone, 'or he won't answer, so there's no point you trying it. Otherwise, he said, he'd be visiting on a daily basis, so any new treatment or medication could be discussed then. And true to his word, he came every single day, until yesterday.'

'You have no idea where he lives, I suppose?' Liz asked.

Carole Courtney frowned. 'Not officially, but . . . I could be wrong, but I suspect it's that posh gated community by the river just outside town. It's called Ravenswood.'

Liz knew it, and it certainly was posh.

'I had to deliver some rather sad news to one of the residents there whose mother had taken a turn for the worse. I couldn't get them on the phone so I drove over to tell them. Jude's BMW was parked in a resident's parking bay. It struck me then that he must be very well off if he could afford to live in that place.'

'He probably rents.' Liz was thinking out loud. 'Most of the apartments there are leased to big companies or high-flyers in the business world.'

In Fenfleet, Jude Sherriff was known only as a young hotshot who ran a successful IT company. The address would fit this guise perfectly. She decided to check out his company's registered address as soon as she got home. 'Thank you for all this, we do appreciate it. I'm sure we don't have to tell you to let us know immediately if Jude shows his face here.' She handed Carole her number and also that of DS Bryn Owen. 'Ring the detective sergeant first. There'll be officers close by that he can call on.'

'Don't worry, Ms Haynes, if I even catch a glimpse of him, I'll ring. He's a very unsettling young man to have around. For some reason he makes us all a bit frightened.'

And they were right to be, thought Liz. 'Be on your guard, and if you do speak to him, don't let on that anything's changed, okay? Just act as you always have.'

Liz thought Carole the perfect person to be in charge of Paddy Sherriff's care. She was cool, intuitive and definitely no walkover. Paddy was in good hands.

When they were back in the car, David asked, 'That phone, can the police trace it?'

'If it's a smartphone it'll be easy, if it's a burner phone, not so much. They're essentially off the grid, which is why criminals use them. They have no internet connection, but they do have to go through a systems operator. It's only in the movies that they can't be traced. They can, and we can get an approximate location, the call log and so on, but it takes a lot longer and we need to know where it was purchased. So it's tricky.'

'And if he suspects anything, he ditches it and buys another?'

'Yup, it's one of a drug dealer's tools of the trade.'

Before they left, Liz rang in everything they had discovered to Bryn. He thanked her, saying he was especially interested in the vehicle, and would get someone over to Ravenswood immediately.

'Where to now?' asked David.

'Amblekirk, I guess. See if we missed something on our first trip to Lamplight Larry's old stomping ground.' She didn't think they had, but as Charley had said, it had to be significant for Alex and Toby to conceal the photo so carefully. 'Maybe we'll try and talk to a few neighbours other than Mr Woodhall.'

'Good idea,' said David, fastening his seatbelt. 'That was a great photograph, wasn't it, Liz, perfectly composed with the light just right. Though for some reason I got the feeling he hadn't planned it, you know, just saw that scene and clicked off some shots. Maybe he saved that one because it was the clearest, or because there was something particular in it. I'm still not certain what that shadow is.'

'Charley Anders was going to have their IT guys work on it and see if they could make it any clearer. I'll ring Bryn later and see if they've had any luck.'

Liz was just pulling into the road out of town when Matt called. 'Find out anything exciting from old man Boon?' she asked.

Matt's voice filled the car. 'That depends on how you feel about finding the mysterious Anna and then losing her again in the space of a few minutes.'

'Don't talk in riddles, Matt Ballard. Explain, please.'

She and David listened to his story in amazement. 'Then who was—?'

'Look, I'm not sure what your plans are, but I'm on my way home. Why not head back to Tanners Fen, then we'll grab some lunch and talk about it?'

'Sure,' said Liz. 'We're through at the nursing home, and were about to go to Amblekirk, but we can do that after lunch. In fact, you could come with us. Maybe we missed something last time.'

Liz turned off the road again and headed for Cannon Farm.

* * *

Matt was making sandwiches when Liz and David arrived home. He'd been going over in his head what Edward Boon had said but was no further forward.

They gathered around the kitchen table.

Liz handed out mugs of tea. 'So, this woman arrives at the solicitor's, with ID and a good knowledge of the Garnett family background. She tells them she's Anna Garnett and demands to see the property she might be about to inherit. Am I right so far?'

'That's right. Then, after she's been given a whistle-stop tour of the merchant's house, she says it's a pile of rubbish and she's not sure if she even wants it.' Matt frowned. 'She was pretty blunt about it too, apparently. She then marches out, telling them to verify her claim and she'll be in touch.'

'But she never did?'

'Nope.' Matt sat back. 'The thing is, old Boon told me that on closer inspection, it turned out that the birth certificate and most of the other documents were copies, not that that was unusual given her age. Lots of people don't have their original certificates, things get lost over time and if they need them, they download copies. Nevertheless, he said she knew enough about the Garnett family to convince him that she was the real deal. It was only when they checked in more depth that they found a death certificate.'

Liz nibbled on her sandwich. 'This raises all manner of questions, doesn't it, and not only about who the devil she was.'

'I wish we'd met this Jessie Wright, Anna's best buddy. I feel like I've been thrown into the middle of a TV drama and I don't know who half the characters are,' Matt said through a mouthful of food.

'I've had an idea,' said Liz suddenly. She pulled out her phone and a few moments later was talking animatedly to PC Debbie Hume.

'Sorted! In half an hour — so long as she gets the okay from Charley Anders — Debbie and Swifty will be here with the missing boy's sister, Kellie. She knows more about Jessie and her friend Anna than anyone.'

'Smart thinking, Liz. Let's get some questions together for her, shall we?' Matt went to find a jotter and a pen.

'According to Debbie, Kellie believes that Anna is behind it all,' Liz said. 'She told Debbie and Swifty that her late mother advised her not to trust that woman.'

'Curiouser and curiouser,' murmured Matt. 'So, what on earth is Anna's game?'

'Can I butt in?' said David. 'Who do we really think has kidnapped the boy? Anna — whoever she really is — or Jude?'

Neither Liz nor Matt answered. Finally, Matt said, 'Sorry, lad, but I have no idea. One minute I feel certain it was Jude Sherriff, the next Anna.'

'Me too,' said Liz. 'But if I had to make a choice, I'd go with Anna. After all, if someone as ruthless as Jude had found the boy and suspected he might have seen what they were up to, why not just kill him in situ? Kidnapping him could lead to all manner of problems, including having the police on his tail, hunting for the missing kid. Why attract unwanted attention when his main focus is the drugs operation?'

'Yeah, killing a little boy would mean little to Jude from what we've heard of him,' Matt said.

While they were still making notes of questions to ask Kellie Burton, they heard the crunch of tyres on the gravel drive.

Liz opened the door to admit Jack Fleet, Debbie Hume, and young Kellie Burton. They accepted Liz's offer of drinks and sat down at the kitchen table.

Knowing that she was only fifteen, Matt had expected Kellie to be shy and awkward but she had a confident air and a serious, intelligent face. Having heard from Debbie how, when Kellie thought her brother needed help, she'd gone to him, totally on her own initiative, he admired her already.

Once they were all settled, he thanked her for coming to see them.

'I'm glad you asked, Mr Ballard. I was going crazy doing nothing. I just want to help.'

'It's Anna we're really interested in, Kellie. Debbie said you don't trust her,' he said.

'No, I don't,' she said forthrightly. 'She bullies my aunt, I know she does. I know everyone thinks my auntie is just a nutcase, but she was so much fun when I was younger. She was kind of zany, Mum called her eccentric, but we had some great holidays with her. She was, like, artistic and sensitive. "Otherworldly" is the word for it, I think.'

How true, Matt thought. It was often the sensitive ones that were manipulated and bullied. Maybe this panic attack of hers wasn't so unreasonable after all, if she'd been coerced into doing something she didn't want to.

'I hated seeing her so confused in the hospital,' said Kellie sadly. 'She looked like a pathetic old lady, and she really isn't that old at all. And now they've taken her to a psychiatric unit and I'm not even allowed to see her. I'm certain it was Anna's fault she got like that.'

'It seems very strange to me that you never met Anna. In fact none of you did, did you?' Matt said.

Kellie shrugged. 'That was because Mum didn't like her, so when we went to stay with Auntie, she made sure Anna stayed away.'

'Had they argued?' asked Liz. 'There's usually a good reason why you dislike someone that much.'

'Well, Auntie Jessie was older than Mum, but Mum was the sensible one. Jessie and Anna had been friends since they were kids. I guess my mum saw a different side to her. Not long before she died, she said to me, "Don't trust Anna. I know you will spend time with Auntie Jessie, and that's wonderful, she loves you both to distraction, but don't believe all she tells you about what Anna says or does. I don't think she's good for your aunt." That's exactly what she said. I remember every word. Oh, and once, Mum was looking through a box of old photos of her and Auntie Jessie when they were young, and she started to tear some up. I asked what they were, and she said they were pictures of Jessie and Anna playing together. She looked really angry, which wasn't like Mum at all, and she wouldn't show me them. I looked in the bin later, and they were just old pictures of two little girls.' She shrugged. 'I didn't understand what was so awful about them.'

'And I guess you never knew where Anna lived,' Liz said.

'Well, it must have been close by, because she was always dropping in at Auntie's.'

'But you never saw her,' mused Matt.

'Never,' said Kellie. 'I did speak to her once on the phone. I rang Auntie, and Anna answered. She said Auntie wasn't well and she was looking after her.'

'Really!' exclaimed Debbie. 'What did she sound like?'

'Fierce! Kind of, like, real bossy. She reminded me of my history teacher, and she's a dragon.'

Matt recalled old man Boon saying how commanding, how headmistressy the woman had been.

All at once, Kellie burst into tears. 'If she's hurt Simon, I'll . . . I'll kill her!'

Debbie jumped up and went to her. 'Oh, Kellie, I'm so sorry. This is all too much for you, isn't it?'

Kellie sniffed. 'No! It's not, honest. I'm just so angry! He's a little boy! He's not strong either. It's just so unfair to do this to him. If he had a really bad asthma attack he could die! I know what to do if he has an attack, but I bet she doesn't! He could go down, then he won't be able to breathe, and if she doesn't get him sitting up, he could suffocate.'

Matt's heart went out to the girl. She had taken on the role of mother to the little boy, and this had happened. She was quite right, it wasn't fair.

Kellie blew her nose and apologised for being such a wimp. David said no, he thought she was a hero, especially for trying so hard to get information from her aunt when she was so anxious herself.

Matt had to smile at the blush that flooded Kellie's cheeks. She seemed to see David for the first time and was clearly impressed.

Kindly Liz jumped in to save Kellie any further embarrassment. 'Well, from what Kellie has told us, it certainly sounds as if it was the woman who turned up at the solicitor's and claimed to be the heiress. I have a hunch that during her trip around the merchant's house, or while she was in the solicitor's office, she stole a key to the place.'

'The key we found in Jessie's handbag,' mused Debbie.

'Which does sound like she put Jessie up there, but I have no idea why.'

There could be only one reason. Although he had no idea why, Anna wanted to take Simon and make it look like it was all down to flaky Auntie Jessie. Matt wasn't about to share this with Kellie, and anyway, it was a very shaky hypothesis. As they had said before, Anna could have taken him straight from Jessie's house, so why this elaborate subterfuge? He drank some tea to give him a moment to think.

'I've just thought of something,' said Kellie suddenly. 'Though I don't know if it's possible.'

They all looked at her.

'There's a letter. It was left with my father's solicitor. Even he didn't know about it until I told him the other day. It's from my mother, and it's not supposed to be given to me until my eighteenth birthday. Mum said it's about her family, and about Auntie Jessie. It might have nothing to do with Anna, but maybe if the police asked for it — well, it could be important, couldn't it?'

Family secrets. Matt knew a lot about those, and the trouble they caused.

Jack Fleet frowned. 'We can do that, can't we, boss? If there's a lawful reason for requesting its release.'

Matt nodded. 'I don't know if the law has been amended since I retired, but I believe that if we require access to personal data of this nature to assist with the investigation and detection of a crime, we can apply for it. I think it's an important factor, and if we're all agreed, I'll throw it straight at DCI Charley Anders to see what she thinks about it. It'll be down to her to put the request.'

All nodded, so Matt made the call. He waited for Charley to answer with a feeling of trepidation. Family secrets were rarely good news.

CHAPTER TWENTY-SIX

Niamh Conran was working on an article for the paper when she had a call telling her that the infamous Henry had been found dead in a deserted house in Cutler's Alley. The shock hit her like a runaway truck. Henry dead. It was inconceivable. She thanked the caller and immediately rang a friend of hers in the local constabulary.

'Can you confirm that you're investigating the murder of Theodore Henry Arbuthnot?' she asked without preamble.

'There'll be an announcement later, Niamh. The DCI is giving a press statement in front of the station at six. It'll be pretty succinct, I'm sure.'

Niamh thanked them and looked at her watch. It was only two, but the news had killed all desire to work, so she walked home. Her mind was in a daze. She'd known Henry quite well. They hadn't been close but she couldn't imagine the world without him.

Indoors, she kicked off her shoes, let her dog Monty out into the garden and threw herself down on the couch. Monty soon clambered up to join her, and she lay for a long time hugging the shaggy beast, feeling uncharacteristically tearful.

She extricated her phone from beneath the dog and read Henry's last message to her, a text that must have been sent not long before he died. Her uniformed friend had said the body had been found that morning. He was thought to have died the evening before.

She read it again. He had given her a name and then he'd been killed. Was it connected? The name still meant nothing to her, and she had been too busy to check it out at the time.

Suddenly she felt very tired. Life was a struggle these days. Gone were the days when she worked for the nationals and was a force to be reckoned with. She loved her town and enjoyed running the local rag but it wasn't the same. For a start, she had been fighting to keep it afloat. She was perfectly aware that the days of the printed newspaper were drawing to a close. Part of her wanted to fight on to the bitter end, but it was a losing battle. It would be nice to have more time with her partner and her dog, time to relax.

She stared at the name Henry had given her: Palmer. Had Henry given it to anyone else? For some reason she thought not. She had a strong suspicion that Henry wanted out of the life he'd been living, even if just for a while. By now he was rich as Croesus, and had recently made another packet, probably out of someone like Eddie Race or Raymond Leonard. And he'd found Ava. He was planning a new venture, and he wouldn't be alone. Niamh sighed.

She sat up, dislodging the dog. Ava! Oh my God, did Ava know what had happened? Perhaps she should ring her. She had her number. She had a lot of numbers. Contacts were the tools of her trade.

She lowered the phone. Being privy to that name meant she could be in possession of dangerous information. What if Henry's killer had taken his phone? They would see his text to her, see the name of the man he believed to be behind the biggest crime ever committed in Fenfleet.

Niamh jumped up, and to Monty's surprise, ran into the kitchen and grabbed his lead.

On the way to her car, she rang her partner.

'Fliss, darling. Listen, and don't argue, okay? Do *not* come home after work! I mean it. Go to your mother's and stay there. Don't call by to collect clothes or anything else, just make do until I contact you.'

'But . . . but why?' Fliss stuttered.

'I may have something valuable in my possession that a dangerous character wants to get hold of, and he might harm you in order to get it. I have Monty with me, so don't fret about him.'

'Are you in danger? Oh my God, Niamh, who's this person that's after you?'

'I have no answer to either of those questions, angel. I could be overreacting but I can't take any chances. I have to talk to a couple of people, then I'll call you again. Just promise me you'll go to your mother's. Leave work earlier than usual, go by a different route, and ring me when you get there.'

In a shaky voice, Fliss said she would.

That taken care of, Niamh drove to a tiny car park at the back of the town, tucked her small car in between two 4x4s and made her calls.

Albie Grant answered immediately. ''Ello, gorgeous. Got any sleazy stories to tell me?'

'No time for that, Albie. I need a name, and fast.'

'You in trouble, girl?'

'Maybe.' Niamh knew Albie well and liked him. They had been scratching each other's backs in a mutually beneficial relationship for more years than she could count.

'Go on then, tell me.'

She told him.

Albie let out a soft whistle. 'That's bad. You did the right thing buggering off out of your house. Palmer's not local, but he's got quite a reputation and it's not good.'

'Who do I give this to, Albie? The authorities, or the local underworld? I can't just go to the police. If I do, I'll burn all my bridges and I'll never get another good story. But Henry was killed. He deserves some justice, don't you think?'

Albie said nothing for a few moments. 'Okay. Where are you? I think I've got a kind of compromise for you. We'll take my car.'

A few minutes later, Albie's old Nissan chuntered into the car park and pulled up a short distance from hers. After a quick glance around to make sure no one was watching, she got Monty out of the back of the car and hurried across to where Albie was waiting.

'Sorry about the dog, but I was afraid to leave him.'

Albie snorted. 'It's me should be apologising to 'im. You haven't seen the state of this car. Come on, jump in.'

Niamh asked where they were going. Albie laughed. 'To see that compromise I was telling you about. He lives in this place called Tanners Fen, wherever that is.'

* * *

It was a busy day at Cannon Farm. Jack, Debbie and Kellie had just left when their next visitors arrived. Matt recognised Niamh Conran immediately. He watched her extricate herself from the old Nissan, wondering what had brought her here, chauffeured by Albie Grant of all people. Albie had called to say they were coming but not why. Whatever it was, it sounded urgent.

Niamh's giant mutt made a beeline for Liz. He jumped up, placed his front paws on her chest and gazed adoringly into her eyes.

'Oh, I'm so sorry,' gasped Niamh. 'He just loves women, and he's really taken to you. I hope he hasn't got mud all over your clothes.'

Liz laughed. 'Doesn't matter. He's adorable.'

Niamh called Monty to heel and explained her problem. 'I heard you'd retired, Matt, but it didn't dawn on me that you'd turned private detective. I guess it's hard to just switch off and leave it all behind, eh?'

'Something like that. But the name you've just given us has got me pretty worried.' And indeed, his anxious thoughts were snapping like firecrackers in his head. He knew of Palmer's reputation but had never come face to face with him. He was one of those shadowy figures, a faceless puppet-eer pulling strings from the back of the stage.

'And Henry said he suspected Palmer of being behind this massive drugs ring?' asked Liz.

Niamh took out her phone and showed her Henry's last message, looking sorrowfully at it. She missed Henry, as did many other people — including Liz and Matt. Henry had the gift of always making whoever he was talking to feel special, even though that person was perfectly aware of what a rogue he was.

'Fenfleet won't be the same without Henry, will it?' Matt said. 'And right to the end, he managed to keep one step ahead of us.'

'He certainly was smart,' said Niamh. 'He intended to live to a ripe old age, free to the last. I just hope the police catch whoever killed him. I know he was a criminal, but still . . .'

'It's small consolation,' said Matt, 'but even the DCI is pissed off about his murder.'

This made Niamh smile. 'He'd like that.' The smile faded. 'But what should I do with this information? I can't go to the police, it'd cost me my job.'

'I suggest you leave it with me. I'll make sure your name doesn't come up. Believe me, Niamh, we do not want that man in this neck of the woods; even the other criminals think he's vermin. Now we have the problem of what you and your partner should do. You obviously realise that Henry's message is a danger to you. Not only you but this Ava he seemed so enamoured with.'

'I was thinking of calling her but I wasn't sure if I should.'

'Do you have her number?' said Liz, getting her notebook out.

'And her place of work, though not where she lives.' Niamh gave Liz the details.

'Leave her to us,' Liz suggested. 'Better you keep at a distance from anything to do with Henry. Is there somewhere you could go and stay for a few days, Niamh? You and your partner, and this lovely chap,' she indicated Monty, 'would be safer elsewhere at present.'

Niamh frowned. 'I suppose I could, although I hate to leave the paper. It's a tricky time in the newspaper industry right now. But Fliss and Monty come first, so yes, I have somewhere to go. It's out of the area, and no one knows us there.'

'Can you go there now? Without going home? I mean, we could go with you, but I wouldn't recommend it,' Matt said.

'Well, the place is a bolthole we go to when we can. We leave a few clothes and toiletries there, so we can manage.'

'Good,' Matt said. 'Now, I'm going to make a suggestion.' He glanced at David. 'No one around here knows David, so what if Albie drops him wherever you left your car, then he can drive it back here to you?'

'If it's not too much of an imposition,' Niamh said.

'No problem. I'm happy to,' said David.

'Where's Fliss?' Liz asked.

'At work,' said Niamh. 'I asked her to leave early and go to her mother's place. She lives in one of the villages outside town. When I'm ready to leave, I'll ring her, pick her up and we'll ride off into the sunset.'

'Then let's get moving,' Matt said. 'You okay with that, Albie?'

'Ready and willing, Mr Ballard.' He turned to Niamh. 'See? Smart move coming here, wasn't it?'

She reached across and squeezed his arm. 'Thank you, Albie. I really do owe you one this time.' She looked from Matt to Liz. 'And I owe you too. I won't forget this, and please, do warn Ava. I'm as worried about her safety as I am about mine.'

Assuring her that they would, they left Niamh in the kitchen, on the phone to the paper.

Matt clapped a hand on David's shoulder. 'Go carefully, son, and before Albie leaves you, make sure there's no one hanging around her car. If there is—'

'I know the ropes, Mr Ballard, sir,' interrupted a grinning Albie. 'We leg it as fast as my old banger will go.'

'Well, lad, you're in good hands. This old reprobate will look after you. Just be vigilant.'

Matt was just about to go over their next move with Liz when Charley rang.

'Charley! You've just saved us a call. We have something else for you we reckon could be pretty big.' Matt put the phone on loudspeaker so Liz could hear.

'Fire away. I was only wondering if you'd had a chance to check out Amblekirk yet. Bryn and I reckon that photograph has to be connected to what got those two boys killed, but the gang never caught on.'

'Not yet. We'll be going out there in an hour or so. Meanwhile, we've not been slouching. We've been following up a lead from an old snout and the name Palmer came up. Seems he could be the head honcho of the drugs ring.'

Matt held the phone away from his ear as Charley let out a string of oaths. 'Where the hell did that come from?' she said after a while.

'A very reliable source, believe me. I think our Jude has teamed up with Palmer for this particular operation, Palmer being the brains. That's why it was running like clockwork until Mad Jessie decided the middle of their distribution centre would be a good place to keep her nephew for a bit. It would also explain the efficient clean-up job — both Jude and Palmer hate loose ends.'

Matt well knew that this was not the kind of news any DCI would want to hear. 'This could be a double-edged sword, Matt. Catching him will be like trying to knit with Fenland fog. But if we do get him, it'll be the best collar we've had in years. Having said that, I could have done without it now, what with the poor little kid still missing. With every hour that passes, his chances of survival are getting slimmer.'

'And is he being held by a psychotic killer or a long-dead woman?' Matt added. 'Take your pick.'

Charley groaned. 'Look, if you can, get out to that graveyard for me. Right now I've got every man jack on the force out looking for little Simon Burton.'

'We're on it, Charley. I'll contact you later.' He ended the call, then added, 'After we visit a certain lady called Ava.'

269

CHAPTER TWENTY-SEVEN

Jude hated feeling that events were slipping out of his control. He'd placated Palmer and won himself some time to sort the issues that were bothering him, but with police crawling over every inch of Fenfleet, he was far from being his usual cool self. For a start, he couldn't visit his father — the last time he'd tried, the police had been there. He was sure this had to do with Minty Agutter. This enraged him. Nothing got in the way of those daily visits, nothing! He had lost his temper twice recently, both times saying things he hadn't meant to.

Jude sat in his car and tried to calm the rage that even now threatened to boil over. At least his money had come through, the single positive in this whole mess. It had been good, too, Palmer hadn't lied about that. Going over the figure in his head, he came to a decision. He'd do one more, see one more shipment in and safely out again and then he'd bid Palmer, along with this godforsaken hellhole, a last farewell, and beat it out of the country. His mood darkened. First, however, he had some matters of his own to sort, starting with a certain lady.

He watched Ava get out of her car and make her way to her front door. As she turned the key in the lock, he was right behind her. She started.

'You got my message, then,' he whispered in her ear. 'Good. It's been a trying few days. I could do with some of your relaxation techniques.'

She immediately regained her composure, invited him in and offered him a drink. But he sensed the change in her. She was going through the motions. He was no longer her favourite client. He wasn't particularly surprised — after all, it had always been that way for him. Even in his childhood, his father had preferred the useless Fion, even though he, Jude, had been the one with the brains and the daring. Same with this trollop. How could she favour that pretty boy Henry? He smiled to himself. Well, she'd be getting no more visits from him.

All his pent-up rage found expression and he took her hard, in silence. When it was over, he accepted that drink.

She hated him now. Her hand shook as she sipped her drink. Without attempting to restrain him, she watched him reach across the bed and pick up the phone lying beside it. He found Henry's last message and showed it to her.

Ava set her glass down carefully. 'This isn't your phone, then.'

'No, it's not. You know very well whose it is.'

She remained silent.

'Come on, Ava. I thought you were supposed to be running away with him. Poor old Henry. Poor dead Henry.'

Still she said nothing, but she failed to mask the shock and desolation that took over her features.

Finally, she managed to croak, 'You killed him?'

'At this stage it doesn't matter much who killed him. The end product is the same.'

Suddenly galvanised, she fell on him, beating him with her fists, screaming that she hated him, until she had no energy left and she subsided on the bed, sobbing.

Jude started to laugh. He laughed until he couldn't see the joke anymore. Then he started to hit her back.

Only Jude didn't stop.

* * *

'Hi, Matt.' Charley's voice reverberated through the speaker in his car. 'I forgot to mention something. We have a hit on that partial registration number from the car in the photo, the one in Cutler's Alley. And it ties in a treat with what you've just told us about Palmer. The car, an Audi, is currently being used by a Dutchman, someone we and Interpol have been keeping an eye on. Ostensibly a high-flying business-man, he has some very influential international connections. But beneath this impeccable facade lurks the manufacturer of some of the most sought-after designer drugs in the world.'

'The stuff that Palmer is distributing,' said Matt.

'The same. It's no wonder that photograph had to dis-appear, and the photographers with it,' Charley said. 'Palmer knew that if the Dutchman found out he'd been caught on camera outside the store the latest shipment was headed for, he'd have pulled the plug on their imports and most likely have had both him and Jude terminated. Please convey our thanks to your young sleuth. That photo and what he saw in it are gold dust. Tell him he ought to consider joining the force.'

Matt winced. 'Touchy subject that, Charley. For one thing he's here with us in the car, and as a matter of fact, join-ing the force was exactly what he wanted to do but he failed the Bleep Test. As you can imagine, he's far from happy about it.'

'Really? Well, when all this is over, I'd like a chat with you, young man,' said Charley. 'There's more than one way to serve, you know. Maybe you just need a guiding hand from a virago with pips on her shoulder.'

'Can't hurt, can it?' said Matt. 'Thanks, Charley, we'll hold you to that.'

Call ended, Matt speeded up, now extremely concerned about this Ava woman. As soon as David had returned with Niamh's car, they had headed for Amblekirk, via the address they'd obtained from the health club where Ava worked.

It was a detached house in a sleepy avenue that led out into the Fen lanes. Matt's hackles rose as they drew up in front of it. There were no visible signs of anything being wrong, but alarms were sounding in his head. 'Stay here, David. You too, Liz. I'd like to take a look around first.'

Liz made to protest, but stopped when she realised he didn't want David left on his own.

Matt approached the front door, the alarms clanging louder with every step he took. The door stood ajar. He pushed it wider and called Ava's name, saying he was with the police and not to be frightened.

No answer came. He stepped inside, calling out to reassure her. The silence was palpable. Matt had lost nothing of his old policeman's intuition. Something was terribly wrong.

He found her in the bedroom. Without even pausing to check for any sign of life, he dialled 999 and called for the police and an ambulance.

To his surprise, he detected a faint pulse. Could she make it? He couldn't imagine how she could possibly have lived through such a brutal attack. Driving home the seriousness of her injuries, he told the operator that blue lights and sirens were the only thing between this woman and certain death. Then he raced downstairs to tell Liz and David to watch out for the ambulance and flag it down. 'Don't come in, guys. Crime scene. I can't leave that poor woman alone.'

He raced back upstairs two at a time and knelt down close to the bed. 'Ava. I'm Matt Ballard. Help is on its way. Just hold on, please.'

She breathed, a slight murmur.

'Shh, don't try to talk. The ambulance will be here soon.'

Watching closely, he realised she was trying to tell him something. He brought his ear close to her lips. 'You're telling me it's Jude who hurt you?'

She whispered a faint yes.

The ambulance seemed to be taking forever. While he waited, Matt rang Charley Anders. 'He has to have been here within the last hour. Get the SOCOs here, and an OIC. This is attempted murder, and if the damned paramedics don't get here soon, you can leave the "attempted" part out altogether.'

Charley said she had already been notified by uniform, and that some officers, including Bryn Owen, were on their way. 'Keep talking to her, don't let her think she's alone. Ring me later with an update.'

Time was not on Ava's side. God knew what injuries that madman had inflicted on her. It must have been an all-out frenzied attack, and as far as Matt could make out, he'd used nothing but his bare hands. Such rage was hard to comprehend.

Just as he was beginning to think help would never arrive, he heard the welcome sound of two tones coming ever closer. Then he heard something else. Ava was again trying to speak.

Initially he tried to stop her, then, when she began to get agitated, he stopped protesting and listened. But her tongue had probably been bitten, she had broken teeth and split lips. He strained to make sense of the words but her speech was slurred.

The door swung open. Two medics burst in and ran to her.

Matt was left trying to make sense of the odd words he had been able to understand, like a game of Chinese whispers. It wasn't until he was back in the car and waiting for Bryn that he realised she had been trying to tell him an address. It could only belong to the man who'd attacked her. She was trying to tell him where Jude lived.

The administrator at the nursing home had told them she thought Jude lived in the Ravenswood gated community. But that didn't tie in with any of the words Ava had uttered. He scribbled them down in his notebook: "*swan, black, tree*". *Drive*. They meant nothing to Liz either.

'Shall we give up on our trip to Amblekirk?' she asked.

Matt looked at his watch. 'We're halfway there. Let's check in with Bryn and then get Amblekirk over with. I don't think we'll see anything more than what you found last time.'

'Which was nothing,' sighed Liz. 'Still, Charley wants it done, so, yes, you're right, we'll do it and then go home.'

'Via the fish and chip shop,' added Matt to cheer them all up. 'It's been a sod of a day, so it's cod and chips and mushy peas tonight, and a couple of lagers, hey, David?'

'Perfect,' he said.

'I second that,' said Liz, 'and here's Bryn's car. We can tell him what we know and get ourselves over to Lamplight Larry's graveyard.'

Matt was beginning to worry about Niamh and her partner, Fliss. If Jude had Henry's phone, he would have certainly read the message he'd sent her. After all, that was how Jude knew about Ava and Henry preparing to go away together, and the reason for his attack on her. The fact that Henry had given Niamh Palmer's name left her very vulnerable. Matt wondered just how secret their bolthole was. He didn't want to scare her further, or bombard her with calls, but as soon as they had finished speaking to Bryn, he would ring her and tell her to go to some random hotel in the middle of nowhere, and to use an assumed name. They should ignore all incoming calls except Matt's, and should Jude make contact, they were to disbelieve everything he said and report it immediately to Matt.

On the drive to Amblekirk, his fears for Niamh's safety intensified. 'Liz. Listen. Ava told me it was Jude who hurt her. That's a fact. Jude had Henry's mobile phone, also a fact. So, he was in that merchant's house when Henry was murdered. But did he kill Henry? I initially believed not, because it's not his style at all, but seeing what he did to Ava, I'm not so sure. What do you think?'

Liz thought for a while. 'I think he did kill Henry.'

'Why?'

'I think the stress he's under is causing him to unravel. Think about it. His father is off limits to him, and he needs to see Daddy, maybe from guilt or a wish to control him, or for some other reason we don't even know about. They have lost what I believe was their best facility for storing and distributing the drugs. Plus — and this is speculation — suppose he was in a relationship with Ava, and found out she was about to ditch him and run off with Handsome Henry. It's all about rejection, Matt. We know his father rejected him; now "his" woman has done the same.'

Matt nodded. 'Yes, that's feasible. He's ruthless but he's always been controlled. Now he seems to be falling apart. You're right, sweetheart, he did kill Henry, in a fit of rage, and because he's never acted that way before, no one believes it was him. Certainly not Palmer, or anyone else he was working with.'

'One question remains,' said David from the back seat. 'What about the little boy? Did Jude kill him too? Or had someone already taken him?'

Matt had no answer to that. Neither, apparently, had Liz. They drove on to Amblekirk in silence.

CHAPTER TWENTY-EIGHT

'We've found the car! That Kia Picanto you're looking for!' Debbie's sergeant's voice rang out through the office. 'Get yourselves over to the hospital. It's in the visitors' car park.'

Debbie Hume and Jack Swift took one look at each other and raced out to their vehicle. 'I thought we checked the hospitals,' said Jack, unlocking the door.

'We did, but only admissions to A&E, as in accidents. And who's to say Belle Rackham hasn't parked it there and gone off somewhere else?'

In reception, they were told that an Arabella Rackham had been admitted to Ward Eleven, second floor.

They found her sitting in a chair next to her bed, looking pale and tired. When she saw the two police officers approach, she asked anxiously, 'What's happened? Is it Jessie? Her nephew?'

One look at Belle's face told Debbie that this woman had not abducted Simon. Her concern was obviously completely genuine.

'Can we sit with you for a while?' said Debbie gently. 'We've been concerned about you. You dashed off so suddenly, leaving your garage wide open. What happened, Belle? Were you taken ill?'

Belle pointed to the bed. 'Please do sit, and, yes, I have a blood disorder. Sometimes stress, or other factors, sends it into freefall. Luckily, I know the warning signs, and I can get myself straight here. I called for a taxi but they were all busy, so I drove over. I'm all right to drive in the early stages.' She looked up at them. 'But this visit isn't about my welfare, is it?'

'We still haven't found Simon, Belle,' Jack said. 'And, well, you see, we thought you might be the mysterious Anna, whom we suspect might have something to do with his disappearance.'

Belle gave a weak laugh. 'Me? Oh dear. That was what young Kellie thought, wasn't it? She's a bright one, that kid. I knew straight away that she'd picked up on my hesitation when she asked if I knew Anna.'

'And do you know her?' asked Debbie.

'First, can you tell me if Jessie has been found? I realise the boy hasn't, but you didn't mention her.'

'She's in Greenborough Hospital, Belle,' said Debbie. 'In the psychiatric unit. She's not well at all.'

'Best place under the circumstances. I'm sure they'll be able to help her.' Belle sounded relieved.

'So what do you know about Anna?' Jack asked.

Belle sighed. 'Nothing, really. I couldn't give you a description, because I've never seen her. All I can tell you is that Jessie can hardly take a breath without consulting Anna first.' She sighed. 'I spoke to Anna on the phone once, and didn't like the sound of her at all. One day I went to see Jessie about something connected with the village flower festival — I think the vicar wondered if she might play the piano on one of the open days, or something like that. Anyway, when I went up to the door I heard the most terrible argument. I recognised Anna's voice and decided to tiptoe away and return later. Actually, I waited for a while to see if Anna would come out — I was dying to get a look at her — but she didn't, so I went home.'

Debbie frowned. 'But why did you tell Kellie you didn't know her?'

'I don't know, really.' Belle hesitated. 'I suppose I just liked her, and I felt so sorry for her. She'd come all that way alone to make sure her little brother was okay, then found him gone. I hated the thought of her getting mixed up with her auntie's awful friend. Silly, I know, but that relationship is toxic, Officer! Poor Jessie is such a gentle soul, I hate to think of her being bullied so.'

Bullied. The same word Kellie had used. This Anna really was a piece of work, and she seemed hell-bent on putting Jessie Wright down. 'I wonder if it's jealousy,' Debbie mused, almost to herself.

'As in, Jessie is talented, artistic, creative and lovable,' said Belle. 'And Anna has none of those qualities.'

'That's about it,' said Debbie.

'Maybe she doesn't want other people to see her with Jessie because they might compare the two,' added Jack.

'Not only that, the real Anna Garnett died donkey's years ago, and this person is an imposter,' Debbie said. 'It's all very confusing.'

'What?' Belle said. 'You mean Anna isn't who she says she is? I don't understand.'

'Neither do we, unfortunately,' said Jack rather sardonically. 'What we do know is that Anna told Jessie she could use "her" house to hide in with young Simon. The house in question is empty, waiting for the solicitors to find the rightful heir to the property. Which turns out to be Anna Garnett.' He rolled his eyes. 'However, the woman who turned up to claim her legacy was not Anna Garnett because they found her death certificate, dated over fifty years ago.'

'So, who . . . ?'

'Don't ask, Belle,' Debbie said.

'And you thought I was her. That's upsetting.'

'In our defence, we knew nothing about you. And we know even less about this person who has been trying to destroy Jessie's sanity — or why, for that matter.' Jack sighed again. 'But at least she can't get at her in the psych unit. Jessie's safe there.'

'How do you know that? Is someone watching her twenty-four seven?' Belle said.

Jack looked at Debbie, eyebrows raised. No one was watching her, other than the medical staff. Every available officer was out looking for Simon.

'I see,' said Belle flatly. 'Well, far be it for me to advise the police, but maybe it's not just Simon who is in danger from this supposed Anna Garnett.'

* * *

Palmer had the jitters, which usually meant that something bad was about to happen.

He had no idea why. After all, he'd received regular updates from Jude, Deezer and Dassault. The cogs were all well-oiled, everything proceeding smoothly. Now that Cutler's Alley had been decommissioned, they had shifted the venue for their consignments to a second site and had a third ready to take any additional deliveries. The next shipment was on course, and everything was ready for them to take charge of it. Initially, Palmer had balked at continuing their activities while the town and the surrounding villages were alive with police on the hunt for the missing kid everyone was talking about. He relented when he calculated the profit to be made. It was worth the risk.

It had taken a while for Palmer to understand that the cause of his discomfort was Jude. He was acting strangely, with a kind of manic intensity about him. For the first time since he'd been working with Jude, Palmer had doubts about his judgement.

He sat at his desk and stared into space. It had all begun with their disagreement over Minty Agutter and what should be done with him. Since then, Jude had become secretive, especially about what was going on in that merchant's house. Following the call explaining his absence — in which his tone had been almost threatening — Palmer hadn't seen Jude at all. He communicated by phone, saying only that he was dealing with certain unforeseen problems and Palmer should leave him alone.

Palmer sensed he had lost the old Jude — the ruthless, calculating fixer he had come to rely on so heavily.

Jude's tone now verged on insubordination. Palmer's position as head of the organisation was inviolable, and Jude had just crossed a line. He could see this next shipment through, after which Palmer would terminate their association. All that remained was to decide how.

* * *

It was getting on for evening and the shadows had lengthened, stretching across the old graveyard. Liz glanced around involuntarily, half expecting to see Lamplight Larry on the path, still searching for his lost daughter. She could never come to Amblekirk without wondering what had happened to Larry's child. Liz hated unsolved cases, and having to retire from the force without knowing what had happened to young Adele was particularly galling.

This evening the church looked brooding and sinister. Gone was the echo of voices raised in song. A ground haze drifted low across the fields, tendrils reaching like fingers to brush the tombstones.

'Bugger this,' muttered Matt. 'It's not the best evening for a pleasant stroll, is it? Remind me what we're looking for, so we can piss off home.'

'A reason to take a photograph, and then realise it's so important you need to hide it,' said David.

'Right, our Davey. You're the ace when it comes to spotting things, so take a good look at that photo and describe what you see,' Matt said.

David extracted it from his pocket and moved to a spot where the last rays of the fading sun cast shafts of hazy light across the scene. 'It was taken from this path here and shows the place where the paths all meet below the lamp post. There are headstones scattered around, and a dark shape that may or may not be a person just at the edge of the treeline. The church is outside the frame, all we see are the paths and the lamp. There's nothing lying on the ground that I can see, and apart from a small gap in the trees on the boundary of the churchyard, it's exactly as it is now.'

Liz frowned. 'Can I take a look?'

She squinted at the photo. She hadn't noticed that gap in the trees before, but the photo had been taken at night and much of it was in deep shadow.

Now it was light, she saw the gap David had referred to. It gave a narrow view out across the fields. She moved over to the exact point from where the picture had been taken. Glancing back at it, she saw that there were several tiny glimmers of light out on the Fen.

Liz went to the gap and stared in the direction of those points of light. She realised that she was looking across the lane, directly at Barngate Farm.

'Okay, Ms Holmes. You can stop looking as if you've deduced something that Dr Watson hasn't,' said Matt. 'What are you seeing?'

'I think . . .' She continued to stare across the fields towards the old farmhouse. 'I think Alex saw lights on at Barngate Farm, and for some reason thought it significant.'

'But why would seeing lights on after dark bother him?' asked Matt.

'I have no idea, but for some reason I think it's important.' She recalled what Mr Woodhall had told them about the unfriendly new occupants and the huge renovations they were doing to what had been a rather lovely old farmhouse. 'Let's take a drive past. There's nothing more here for us to see, so we'll have a peek at the work going on there.'

They piled back in the car. Liz pulled up a short way from the entrance and they all cast their eyes over what was almost a building site. Fortunately for them, the setting sun emerged from the clouds for a moment, and the mist lifted.

'Much the same as before,' David muttered. 'Organised chaos.'

'*Exactly* the same as before,' whispered Liz. 'Nothing's moved, has it? The cement mixers, the JCB, the trucks, the vans, everything is where it was when we came here the other day.'

'Maybe they're doing the work themselves and have to fit it in with their day jobs,' offered Matt. His expression changed. 'That's odd.'

'What?' Liz said.

'Could be nothing, but I don't recognise a single local name on any of the works vehicles parked there. Er, Liz. Drive on, but slowly. I thought so. Someone is eyeballing us. Give him a friendly wave.'

Waving at the man glaring at them from the side of the main house, Liz moved off at a fairly normal pace for a Fen lane.

'Hopefully, he'll think we're just locals wondering what their neighbour is having done to their house.' Matt took out his notebook and scribbled down several names. 'David. Get on that smartphone of yours, lad. Look up these two names for a start — "Iron-Sea Property Care" and "JT Beer and Sons, Plumbing and Heating Engineers".'

David did as asked. 'Nothing at all, Matt.'

'How about "Brite Nite Electricals"?' He spelled the names aloud for David to search.

They knew what the answer would be.

'None of them are listed anywhere,' David said. 'These days every business, no matter how small, has either a website or a trade listing. They don't exist, do they?'

Out of sight of Barngate Farm, Liz speeded up, and soon they were passing through Ferndyke Village and on their way home. 'Well,' she said, 'my best guess is that our photography student couldn't pass up the opportunity to take an evocative night-time shot in that graveyard, then saw what he thought was a figure in the undergrowth.' She frowned. 'He took the shot hoping to capture the person — if it was one — on camera. Maybe he didn't even notice the gap in the trees and the lights on at Barngate Farm. Then, when he printed it off, he *did* see them and they bothered him for some reason.'

'Possible, but still all conjecture, sweetheart. But okay, let's just suppose that something they saw in Cutler's Alley brought them to that graveyard. It would mean they suspected foul play of some sort and were looking for clues. If that was a man watching them from the undergrowth, he was heading in the direction of the lane to Ferndyke Village — and Barngate Farm.' Matt looked over his shoulder at David. 'Was there a time on the photograph?'

David answered immediately. 'Two forty a.m. I remember it distinctly.'

'So, lights on at almost three in the morning would have been unusual,' mused Liz. 'I suppose there was no mention of this in that journal of Alex's, was there?'

'Not that I saw,' David said, 'but it might be worth going through it again. He might have hidden this episode in a different folder.' He grinned. 'Looks like another late night for me.'

'We'll make it worth your while in fish and chips,' Liz said.

'And don't forget the lager,' added Matt.

'What more could I ask for?' said David. 'Sleep, perhaps?'

CHAPTER TWENTY-NINE

Jude bundled all his bloodied clothes into refuse bags and took them to the big hopper that served the residents of Ravenswood. No one in that exclusive community would think of poking about in those foul stinking waste bins, and anyway, they were due to be collected the following day.

The madness had subsided, and he now felt oddly numb. But it wasn't his habitual icy calm. This was a different feeling altogether, and very unpleasant.

Never before had he lost control. It had been his main attribute, bringing him huge rewards for any work he did, and earning the respect of his collaborators. Nothing fazed him, and in the rare cases when things did go wrong, he always had a plan B ready. He never showed the slightest emotion, and he was proud of it.

Jude poured himself a drink, going over in his mind what had led to his despicable behaviour. The wheels had started to come off the moment he saw that idiot student taking photos in Cutler's Alley on the very night their supplier had chosen to inspect their set-up and had parked his car outside the merchant's house. One click of his shutter had sealed the student's fate, along with that of his friend. It had been the perfect double murder. A faulty gas water heater, who could

285

question that? But from that moment on, things had started to go wrong. Although he got the shipments through safely and made a small fortune doing so, he realised how much he hated working with Palmer. Then his father, calling out Minty's name. That unsolved mystery had eaten its way into his very bones. He could still hear his father, speaking after all those years, but calling out that bastard's name instead of his. It had cut him to the quick.

He flung himself down onto a leather recliner. Then, if that wasn't enough, Henry had turned up, posing a threat to his and Palmer's operation, along with all the money that drugs brought in. There'd been no time for a plan. He'd killed him, left him there, and flatly denied any involvement.

But what had completely derailed him was finding Henry's phone. Why had he read those messages? Why hadn't he just got rid of it? The cause of Ava's coolness being Henry, of all people, was mortifying. It had to be rectified.

Well, he'd rectified it all right. Whether she lived or died, Ava would never work again.

His thoughts caused the rage to boil up in him again. This wouldn't do. He had certain things to take care of tonight, and he couldn't do so feeling like this. He drank more vodka. Briefly, he regretted destroying Ava. She had always been able to relax him.

First, he had an important visit to make which couldn't be postponed. His second task could probably wait until tomorrow.

He stood up. And what then? Move on, what else? He had plenty of money, though he'd be throwing away thousands by leaving before the next shipment was due in. But he no longer trusted Palmer, and right now he no longer trusted himself. He would go far away and regroup. Later, he'd come back stronger than ever, strong enough never to need Palmer again.

* * *

By ten thirty that evening, David had located the hidden file that told of Alex and Toby's visit to Amblekirk, and why they had gone there.

The three of them read it through. It turned out that Liz had been right. As they were leaving Cutler's Alley on their last recce of the merchant's house, the boys had noticed a small white van drive away from the old property. They had decided to follow it and tailed it as far as Amblekirk where they lost it close to the church car park. For a while they wandered around the old church, then Alex decided to get a shot of the graveyard. He heard a noise and became convinced that they were being watched. The bushes stirred and he heard running footsteps. He took his shot and they got away from the place. It wasn't until he uploaded it that he saw the lights through the trees coming from Barngate Farm. Since they had traced the van from Cutler's Alley to there, they deduced that the people who had imprisoned the woman in the window were using those barns, probably for people smuggling.

'They got that wrong,' said Matt, 'but little else. Like us, they were fooled by the face at the window.' He pulled his phone from his pocket. 'Time to ring this in. I know it's late, but Charley needs to know. After all, if we add what young Alex wrote in his journal to what we saw for ourselves, I reckon we have another drug distribution centre.'

'The building work on the farmhouse is all a sham,' Liz said. 'Those vehicles aren't builders' vans at all, but are used to shift the drugs. You're as likely to see a plumber or an electrician at that farm as you are a fish climbing a tree.'

Matt made the call. 'Charley's well happy. She's going to set up round-the-clock observation on the place and wait for the next shipment to come in. They could get the lot — the drugs and all the people involved, including Dassault and Jude. I do believe this is all coming together at last.'

'Except for one lost little boy,' Liz reminded him. 'I know it's nothing to do with our case, apart from finding the room he'd been kept in, but I can't help worrying about him.'

'What are his chances, Auntie Liz?' asked David. 'I mean realistically.'

'They're getting slimmer with every hour that passes, David. We always say the first seventy-two hours are crucial, but this boy isn't just missing. He didn't run away, someone's taken him, and his safety, even his life, depends on how that person treats him — and why they took him in the first place.'

'So, it's in the lap of the gods,' David said, and sighed.

'No, son,' said Matt. 'Not divine intervention but good policing. Every man and woman in the division is moving heaven and earth to find him.'

'True,' said Liz, 'but a few well directed prayers wouldn't go amiss either.'

* * *

The small hotel that Kellie and her father had been moved to was very comfortable indeed, and at last Kellie was able to sleep. Even so, she woke early. While she was getting dressed, she heard the phone ring in the adjoining room where her father slept. She ran in, hoping it was news about Simon.

When the call ended, her dad said, 'They want us to go to Greenborough Hospital. There's been what they called a "development" with Jessie and they want to speak to us urgently.' He frowned, looking puzzled. 'The police too.'

Kellie went cold. 'Has something happened to Auntie? Please don't tell me that Anna woman has managed to get in and hurt her!'

'No, lass, I think it's something quite different, but they didn't want to discuss it over the phone. I had a bit of a job persuading them to let you come too.'

'Thanks, Dad. I can't be left out, not if it's anything to do with Simon.'

'You won't, love, I promise. Now, I'd better get dressed. Debbie and Jack are going with us. Oh, and Debbie thinks the DCI has managed to get your mum's letter released from the solicitor. It'll be available around lunchtime. Hopefully then we'll get some answers.'

* * *

Debbie Hume and Jack Fleet arrived at the hotel at just after nine. Not wishing to draw attention to Kellie and her father, both were dressed in plain clothes.

'Do you have any idea what this is about?' asked Donald. 'The hospital wouldn't say, but it sounded pretty serious.'

Debbie knew no more than him, except that Jessie Wright had had an "episode" in the night and both the family and the authorities needed to be made aware of it.

'I'm pleased the DCI was able to get your letter released from the solicitor's,' said Debbie on their way to the unmarked police car. 'She had to fight her way through the data protection regulations, but the seriousness of Simon's situation clinched it in the end.'

'I'm dead nervous about it,' said Kellie. 'I keep imagining that all sorts of terrible things are going to come out. When Mum told me about it, she looked really, well, serious. You know, like it was some dark secret, or something really bad.'

Debbie, too, had a vivid imagination and thought the kid was probably on the right track. You didn't leave letters disclosing family secrets with solicitors just for the fun of it. Oh well, no good speculating. Hopefully they'd know soon enough.

The half-hour drive to the hospital seemed to take an age. None of them spoke much. Jessie had been in a bad way when she was transferred to Greenborough, and the little they'd been told made it sound as if she had deteriorated further. Normally, it wouldn't have been appropriate to have a girl as young as Kellie accompany them, and Debbie silently applauded her father for insisting that she be involved.

Nervously, they trooped into the consultant psychiatrist's office. His expression did nothing to allay their fears.

He introduced himself as Dr Lane-Fitch, in charge of assessing Miss Wright's condition.

'I must say her condition has given us considerable cause for concern, and we cannot understand why she hasn't been receiving treatment for it. If it had been addressed much earlier, there would likely have been no need to have her brought here.' He looked at Donald.

'I'm sorry, but Jessie has been living alone for years. We live nearly two hundred miles away. Since my wife died, all my energy has gone into holding my family together. Though we're fond of her, Jessie has never made it easy for us to keep in touch. For a start, she's always hated using the telephone. She was a bit, er, eccentric, you see. My late wife, who was much younger than Jessie and who adored her, called her an enigma. Jessie is very artistic and quite talented, so we just put her . . . idiosyncrasies down to her imaginative nature.'

Kellie added, 'You can't blame Dad, Doctor. He's always busy, working hard to keep us in school and put proper meals on the table. My brother and me used to stay with Auntie Jessie in the holidays, and she was fun. She was a bit batty, but she was sweet and kind.'

The doctor nodded, looking faintly amused at Kellie's defence of her father.

'I see. Well, mental health issues are often cleverly con-cealed by the sufferers, and if you weren't close it's hardly your fault that her condition went untreated.' He lowered his gaze to the patient's records in front of him. 'Well, we know now that Jessie is suffering from a complex psychiatric condition and, at least for a while, will require specialist care and treatment — in hospital.'

Debbie wondered what he meant by "complex".

'What exactly is wrong with her, doctor?' asked Donald.

'We suspect a form of dissociative disorder, Mr Burton. In explanation, I would like to ask you a few questions and then show you a short video, if that's all right with you. It might be a little distressing but it will help you understand what we are dealing with here. I'll leave it up to you to decide if the film is suitable for your daughter.'

Kellie shot the doctor a poisonous glance.

'We'll start with Anna,' the doctor said, not missing a beat. 'What can you tell me about her?'

After a few moments' silence, Donald said, 'Anna has been Jessie's best friend since they were children. They were inseparable, apparently. Jessie was timid, delicate, other-worldly. Anna, slightly older, was the leader of the two — strong, independent. Jessie looked to her for everything.'

'She bullied my aunt, and she still does,' Kellie snapped.

'There's a bit of confusion regarding Anna, doctor,' Jack Fleet said. 'A search of the records showed that the woman we believed her to be had died over fifty years ago. Someone calling herself Anna has been playing the part of Miss Wright's friend ever since. We don't understand who this imposter can be because Jessie herself insists that this woman is her dear childhood friend. Yet the documentation says otherwise.'

'We're hoping that a letter the late Mrs Burţon left with her solicitor might throw some light on the mystery, sir,' added Debbie. 'We'll have it later today.'

The consultant nodded. 'I think I have an explanation for this, even without your letter. But first, the video. It will make everything crystal clear, but as I say, it's distressing.' He looked at Kellie.

'My brother is missing, doctor,' she cried, 'and unless you've been in this situation, you can't possibly know how much it hurts. If Anna has got my brother, I have to know every single thing about her, and if watching a video about my aunt's illness will help, then I have to see it! Please!'

Donald nodded at the consultant, who gave a slight shrug.

'This film was taken last night after Jessie went into a kind of fugue state following a panic attack. She suddenly became very calm, sat up in bed and began to talk. If you are ready?' He pressed play.

On the screen, Jessie became suddenly animated and started to address the empty chair next to her bed.

'I still don't understand why I'm here, dear. After all, it was just a bit of a panic that came on when I saw all those people in that restaurant. You know I hate crowds, and you, naughty Anna, didn't come to meet me like you said you would. I just felt out of my depth, that's all. It's quite simple and all very understandable, but now I'm in hospital. It's not fair!'

'Shut up and listen to yourself, Jessie! Come on, you're mad as a hatter, and you know it. Heaven knows, I've tried hard enough to help you, now it's time you admitted it. You are quite beyond help. You are, aren't you?'

Debbie felt her blood go cold. She wished they'd listened to the doctor and kept Kellie from having to see this. This voice did not belong to Jessie. It had a hard, commanding edge. It was deeper, harsher, and seemed to issue from a completely different throat.

No one spoke. The atmosphere in the office hummed with tension.

Jessie Wright began to march around the room, the strong voice reprimanding, chastising. Then, suddenly, she'd be sitting on the edge of the bed, hunched, simpering apologies and trying to placate her angry "friend". She even looked different in the role of Anna — she had a straight back and a haughty air that gave her more height. This was the "headmistressy" woman solicitor Boon had met.

The consultant stopped the video. 'It's called dissociative identity disorder, or DID, formerly referred to as multiple personality disorder or split personality. It's often caused by a childhood trauma. The sufferer assumes two or more distinct identities. You will now have realised that Jessie and Anna are the same person.'

It was hard for Debbie herself to take in. What it must be like for Kellie, she couldn't begin to guess.

'I spoke to Anna on the phone,' said Kellie in a small voice. 'That was what she sounded like. So, it was Auntie

Jessie all the time? She was Anna as well?' She looked at the doctor.

He nodded kindly. 'Yes, Kellie. She is a very unwell lady, but now we know what's wrong, we can help her. There are a number of therapies we can try.' He turned to Debbie. 'You mentioned a letter. If I could be made privy to its content, it would be of enormous assistance to us when we come to make our assessment of Jessie, especially if it says anything about the trauma that probably gave rise to her illness.'

Donald was nodding. 'The doctor has to have that information, Debbie — can you okay it?'

'I'll make the situation clear to the solicitor and to the DCI, never fear,' she said.

The doctor went on to tell them they feared that the stronger more dominant persona was beginning to take over and swamp the passive one. Then he glanced at Kellie and suggested they take her home.

Outside, Jack took himself out of Kellie's hearing and rang the DCI. It had occurred to both him and Debbie that since "Anna" had been in hospital when Simon had been taken from the room, the boy had to have been taken by Jude — or someone else no one knew about.

His call over, they headed back to the hotel. Debbie drove, her mind replaying again and again the terrible one-act tragedy they had just been witness to.

CHAPTER THIRTY

After Liz had spent a fruitless morning at the computer, David spent a further couple of hours trying to extract the name of a road, building or feature of the landscape from the words Ava had whispered. But he had no more luck than Liz. Matt decided she had been rambling and what he'd thought was Jude's address was no more than disconnected words.

'I wish Swifty would ring,' said Matt, starting on his third mug of tea. 'I hate being out of the loop like this.'

'Oh, I forgot to mention,' said David. 'I heard from Peter earlier. Minty hasn't turned up, but neither have there been any reports of anyone found injured or dead, and no strangers discovered in a local detective's potting shed as far as he knows. Peter reckons our bird just took fright for some reason and flew the nest.'

Liz nodded. 'Exactly what Isla McGowan said. I guess we'll just have to take her advice and hope for the best where Minty's concerned.'

Matt's phone rang. He grabbed it, sloshing tea over the table. Not Swifty, but Charley Anders.

'Several things, Matt, but I'll keep it brief.' Her tone was clipped; she was obviously busy. 'If you could go to the hospital as soon as possible, the officer on duty outside Ava

Kaminski's room has said she is conscious but will only talk to you. Can you do that for me?'

He assured her he'd go immediately.

'Good, and ring me straight after, please. Things are rather full on here, as you can imagine. Where Simon is concerned, it seems that the mysterious Anna is out of the running completely, and our fears have increased further, as we are left with Jude Sherriff as the main suspect in his abduction, which you can imagine is giving us serious cause for concern. Don't ask about Anna right now — Jack Swift will ring you shortly and explain. Sorry, Matt, but it's manic here and I'm due to give a press conference in ten minutes.'

'Is there anything else we can help you with, Charley?' he asked.

'After you've seen Ava, could you get over to the nursing home and see if Paddy Sherriff's son has been to visit? I doubt he'll try, but his father does seem very important to him, so maybe he'll risk it. Oh, and finally, some officers went to his posh apartment in Ravenswood and he's not been there for days. Another resident told us he has more than one place of residence, but doesn't know where it — or they — are. Apparently, Jude had said one was a relaxing retreat, but never mentioned where . . . Oh my God, look at the time!' Charley swore and rang off.

Matt finished his tea. 'Right, you lot. We're off again. Tell you what, I'll go to the hospital while you two check out the nursing home. They know you there, and maybe they'll let you have another word with Paddy. Get his take on whether he thinks Jude really would abduct a child, and if so, where he would take him. It's just dawned on me that Paddy has probably learned a whole lot about Jude from listening to him babble while he lay there pretending he couldn't speak.'

Liz stood up. 'You're right. We'll see what we can find out. Keep in touch, won't you, darling, especially if Ava gives you an address for Jude.'

'Will do. See you both later.'

Matt hurried to his car feeling that all the different strands were about to come together. He just hoped the threads would lead them to one little boy.

* * *

'Wasn't that Isla McGowan in that black car?' said David. They were turning into the entrance to the Linden House nursing home.

'There's no mistaking that hair,' said Liz. 'Which is not good news for us. If she's just spent time with Paddy he'll be needing to rest, so I doubt Carole will let us visit him.'

'I bet she's the one with the diamonds,' said David with a grin. 'Who else would he trust that much? They're clearly pretty close.'

'Soulmates,' Liz said, echoing Isla's words.

'She knows Minty, too, and all about the big secret. Yeah, it has to be her.'

'Well, that's one secret we may never be privy to, Davey-boy. No one is going to cough to having a fortune in stolen gems under their bed, are they?'

'Hadn't thought of that. Probably not,' muttered David.

Carole was not in the office but another member of staff allowed them a few minutes with Paddy, so long as they didn't overexcite him.

'I thought you'd be back. But we've not heard hide nor hair of him.' The old man chuckled. 'One thing's for sure, stopping his visits will hurt him a lot more than me. It's been ever so relaxing without him whining away by my bedside every bloody day.'

'We saw Isla as we came in,' Liz mentioned casually.

'She brought me a few things I needed. Now that's someone who could stay all day and I'd be all the better for it. Pity the boss doesn't feel the same way. She puts a limit on our time together. Miserable old cow.'

'Would it tire you if we asked a few questions, Paddy?' Liz said.

'I'll soon be having a very long sleep, won't I, so ask away.'

'It appears that Jude is in the frame for abducting that little boy we told you about, Paddy. Do you think he's capable of abducting a child?' Liz asked.

'If it's to his advantage, Jude'd do anything, so the answer is yes to that one. Next question?'

Liz wasted no time, mindful that at any moment Carole could turn up with an eviction order on them. 'We've been told he has left his main residence in Ravenswood but that he has other addresses. Do you know what they might be?'

'Can't help you there, I'm afraid. He only ever told me about Ravenswood. He did say he had a place close to water somewhere — relaxing, he said — but he never gave an address. I've a feeling he may have another apartment too. Smaller, not as classy as Ravenswood, but still fairly upmarket. Jude doesn't do slumming it. Oh, and he never buys, just rents. Says it's easier to up sticks and move on sharpish. And he has more than one because it makes him harder to trace.'

Liz said, 'I suppose you've not heard from Minty? He seems to have done a runner. Well, we're hoping that's the case. He's not where we hid him.'

Paddy frowned. 'Knowing Minty, something scared him and he's legged it. He'll be back, though. He knows I haven't got long and he won't let me shuffle off me mortal coil without saying goodbye. He'll just wait until the coast is clear. I'm telling you, my friends, Minty is a diamond.'

Liz noticed he was looking rather pale and decided he'd had enough. They stood up to leave.

'Hang on a minute,' Paddy said. 'Jude will come back here, you know. He has to, he has no choice. It could even be today. Can I ask a favour?'

Liz nodded.

'Your officers *have* to let him in. I've got to talk to him one last time. It's to do with our family. Can you make sure that happens? It's my one wish before I go.'

'I'll make sure everyone knows it's your wish, Paddy. I promise.'

He lifted his hand, and his eyes closed.

Carole still wasn't around, so they decided to leave. Back in the car, David said, 'It's not an act, is it? He really is close to dying.'

'Carole says so, and she'd know. Apart from the medical evidence, they get a sixth sense for impending death in places like this.'

'Then I hope Minty doesn't run into Jude when he comes to say his last goodbye.' David looked quite disturbed at the thought.

'All I can do is ring Bryn and give him Paddy's wishes in the hope he complies. Meanwhile, I'll get our scouts to watch out for Minty.' She glanced at David. 'I like old Minty too, Davey, and I don't want to see him in trouble with that shit, Jude.'

She decided to call Bryn immediately. He said that in any case it would probably be better if their officers took Jude on his way out of the home. That way they wouldn't disturb the patients. He also promised to watch out for Minty should he decide to visit at an inopportune moment.

* * *

Matt felt nervous about seeing Ava again. Her injuries had been so severe that even people she knew well wouldn't recognise her. He was surprised she had survived at all. He wondered what her life would be like from now on.

'Doc wants a word before you go in, Matt.'

Matt knew the constable on duty pretty well. He was an old-timer, retirement age or more. 'Sure, Alan.' He glanced towards the closed doors. 'How is she?'

'Touch and go, so they say. I've seen my share of beatings but this one takes the biscuit. They say you found her. That right?'

Matt nodded. 'Yeah, for my sins. And I agree with you about the attack. Brutal doesn't begin to describe it, does it?'

Alan pointed to a nurse's station a little further along the corridor. 'You want Doctor Malek. She should be down there now.'

Dr Zahra Malek looked relieved to see him. 'Mr Ballard? Good, good, and thank you for getting help for my patient. Any longer and she'd have choked on her own blood.' She ushered him into a small office and indicated a chair. 'She insists on seeing the man who helped her. She's terrified of every other man. The thing is, we're not sure if she'll pull through. She has internal injuries as well as severe facial trauma and head injuries, but we are monitoring them carefully in the hope that the internal bleeding will settle without surgical intervention. Our main problem was that her facial fractures were too severe for safe placement of an endotracheal tube, so we needed to take an emergency option. By this morning, though, things had improved and we were able to wake her up. As soon as she was stable, she began to ask for you.'

'I think I know why, doctor. She was trying desperately to tell me something when I found her. It's to do with the man who hurt her.'

Zahra Malek nodded slowly. 'Ah, yes, we did wonder. Now, before you go in, Mr Ballard, you need to know that she can barely speak, and we have to keep her as calm as possible. If she manages to tell you what's worrying her, just reassure her and then go.' She looked apologetic. 'I'm sorry, but we are far from happy with her condition. If it wasn't for the fact that it would be more upsetting for her not to see you, I wouldn't allow you to visit either.'

Matt said he understood. He made his way to the critical care unit slowly, reluctantly. He hadn't told the doctor that he wouldn't be able to bear staying with Ava any longer than was absolutely necessary.

His fears were realised. Matt hoped he would never again have to undergo such a shocking, saddening few minutes. He left the critical care unit sick to his stomach, so angry that he feared for his blood pressure.

Somehow, Ava told him what she needed to say. He thanked her and whispered that he'd move heaven and earth to bring Jude to justice. He meant it. Leaving her room, he ran to the gents' toilet and threw up. As he washed his hands and doused his face with cold water, he knew that should he ever meet Jude Sherriff, he would very likely kill him for what he had done to Ava Kaminski.

* * *

Simon heard the key turn in the lock. 'Have you arrested them, Inspector Sherriff?'

'It's imminent, Simon. That's what I came to tell you. My officers are getting ready for the raid right now, I just wanted to make sure you were okay first. Will you be all right for a bit longer? Our men are outside so you have no need to fear. Can you stay put and be brave for me, it'll just be a few more hours? Then we'll move you out of this safe house.' He tousled Simon's hair. 'You're not frightened, are you?'

'Not with you around, Inspector.'

'Good boy. Tell you what. How about you finish off that picture of the owl — the one we started yesterday? There's food in the fridge and plenty of soft drinks. I'll be back as soon as this is over, then we'll celebrate, yeah? Just you and me.'

Simon gave him a broad grin. 'Yeah!' His smile faded a little. 'Inspector Sherriff? Be careful, won't you. I'd hate the bad men to hurt you.'

'They won't hurt me, son. I'm the biggest, baddest man in town, believe you me! Now, I have to go. I'll lock the door and give the key to the officer watching outside. So keep your head down, no looking out of the windows, stay in this room and wait. That's your orders until this op is over. I'll be back as soon as we've slapped those handcuffs on the bad guys, okay? Now, remember. No one comes in except me. Got that?'

'Got it, Inspector Sherriff.' But Simon felt anxious. He recalled being told that very thing once before, and being left alone for ages.

300

'Hey, buddy! I'm not your batty aunt, okay? It won't be like before, I promise.' The inspector eyed him thoughtfully, flopped down on the leather couch and patted the seat next to him. 'Come here and sit with me. I'll tell you a story . . .'

Simon sat, and felt the man's strong reassuring arm around his shoulder.

'I know what it's like to be alone, sport. When I was a kid, I was lonely. I was ill too, just like you. No one loved or even liked me, and I had to learn to be brave and stand on my own two feet. Men like you and me don't need other people, kid, they always let you down. Think about it. Your dad sent you away even though you were poorly. And take your auntie — she said she loved you, but where is she now? See, she let you down too.' The detective drew him closer. 'Yes, I have to go out too, but I'm different — I'm going to catch those bad men you told me about, and when that's done, I'll be back. So, just be happy to be alone. It makes you stronger, Simon. I know, because it made me what I am today.' He stood up. 'Time for action! High five, pardner!'

The key turned in the lock, and Simon swallowed hard. He had no doubt that the inspector was a brave man and strong, but Simon couldn't help thinking he'd got it a bit wrong. Kellie loved him, and Dad. Even dotty Auntie Jessie did. Still, he was in trouble, and it was Inspector Sherriff who'd come to his rescue, so perhaps the detective was right.

He was certainly right about the bad men, though. Simon was sure of that. The inspector had told him that these men were clever. If they discovered where Simon was, they would pretend to be from the police. They might even say they'd brought his dad or his sister with them, a trick to get him to open the door. Inspector Sherriff said that wasn't likely, but they had to be prepared, just in case.

Simon got himself a drink, sorted out his paints and sat down at the table. *Just think, you could be on your way home later today.* Gosh, he'd have so much to tell Kellie. He couldn't wait to tell her about being saved by a real detective, just like in the films. When he grew up, he was going to be a detective too, a hero just like Inspector Sherriff.

CHAPTER THIRTY-ONE

Finally, the call he had been dreading. It came from the prearranged number, so it was genuine. Her voice had been solemn. His father had deteriorated suddenly and was indicating that he wanted something urgently. She could only think it was to see his son for the last time. He said he would come, but it would take him a couple of hours because he was working out of the area. That should buy him some time.

It was risky, but, foreseeing that this might happen, he had long ago worked out how to get in without attracting attention.

He left his car some distance away and approached the place by way of the grounds at the rear. He could see a marked patrol car parked close to the main entrance. They were waiting for him. He had expected this and had stayed away, but now he had no choice. He had to see his father one last time.

He would just have to avoid everyone, especially Carole and the other staff. It might be difficult if his father was in the act of breathing his last — they'd hardly leave him alone then, would they? Still, all he needed was a few minutes.

The fates were with him, it seemed. The two nurses who had been with his father left together and there was no one around. He slipped inside.

'Dad. It's me, Jude. They said you're not so good.'

His father looked pale, his nose sharp and narrow, corpselike. Jude stood looking down, shot through with fear and anger. Then Paddy's eyelids flickered.

He took his father's hand in his. 'Just you and me, Dad, father and son, like it always should have been. We'd have made such a partnership, the best team ever.' He sighed. 'Even after I got rid of everyone who stood in our way, you never accepted me. Why, Dad?'

Did he feel a slight pressure from the hand in his?

'Jude.'

He gasped. 'Dad! Yes, it's me, Dad! Jude, your one true son.'

His father struggled to say something else.

Jude couldn't catch it, so he leaned closer. His father made a sudden movement. At first, Jude hardly felt the long blade enter his body. He looked down at his father's benign face.

Paddy's voice was clear when he said, 'It's the kindest thing I could do for you, son. And I hope you rot in hell!'

Jude heard no more.

* * *

Matt was about to ring the station and let them know the address Ava had given him when he received Liz's call. She said she and David were on their way back to the nursing home and Matt should get there as fast as he could. She'd explain later, but the bottom line was that Jude was dead.

Matt arrived some fifteen minutes later to find Liz and David waiting for him in the car park.

'As soon as I heard he was dead, it all made sense,' Liz began. 'We saw Isla leaving here earlier. She seemed preoccupied and didn't see us. When I mentioned it to Paddy, he said she had brought him some "essentials". I should have twigged then. What essentials would Paddy need in that place? Jesus, Matt, she must have brought him a bloody great knife!'

'*Paddy* killed Jude?' It shouldn't have been a surprise, not after what he'd said, but somehow it was.

'Paddy told me that he might be able to lure his son to the home, then the police could catch him on the way out.' Liz exhaled. 'He used me, fool that I am, to make sure that the officers on obo let Jude in so they could have a supposed final few words. Have I got "mug" tattooed on my forehead?'

Before Matt could answer, a nurse hurried towards them across the gravel drive. 'Liz Haynes? Paddy wants to see you. Can you come, please?'

They all trooped after her, only to be stopped at the entrance. 'Crime scene, sir. Sorry, but it's rather unusual circumstances. I'm afraid it's only the sarge who can go in, and only after you've suited up.'

The PC handed Liz a coverall and boot-covers, while Matt stood at the door and gazed on the strangest tableau he had ever seen.

Paddy lay back in his bed, which was awash with blood, his arms around the body of his son. The old man looked almost happy.

He looked up when Liz approached him. 'Ah, my accomplice. I owe you an apology, I know, but it had to be done. It was the perfect solution.'

Matt was almost inclined to agree with him.

'I don't like being used, Paddy,' said Liz, almost tempted to smile.

'Smarts, don't it?' The old villain grinned at her. 'But you know what they say about breaking eggs to make an omelette. Anyway. The fact is, it's over. I suppose no one should set himself up as judge, jury and executioner but in this case, it was my right. After all, I brought the abomination into this world.'

As Liz turned to leave, Paddy murmured, 'Thank you, Liz, ex-Detective Sergeant Haynes. I still wonder if you didn't know all along, but anyway, I appreciate your help.'

Liz left the room without looking back.

Matt followed, trying to read the expression on her face. It remained inscrutable, but he could guess what she was thinking. Had she really not put two and two together?

Outside in the car park they breathed in the fresh air.

'I think he forgot one important thing in his "perfect solution,"' said David.

Matt looked at him.

'Simon. If Jude was holding him and Jude's dead, how do we find the boy?'

* * *

Matt thought he had the answer to David's question. The address Ava had given him was that of a riverside chalet that Jude used when he wanted to relax. There was a small cruiser there too, called the *Black Swan*. The words all tied in with what Ava had tried to tell him when he found her. The name of the chalet was Rowan Trees and it was approached from Marsh Drive.

But when the police got to the place, it was empty, with no indication that a little boy had ever stayed there; immaculate, as if waiting to be photographed for an interior design magazine. Jude's main apartment had been searched too, drawing another blank.

'We've come full bloody circle, haven't we?' cursed Charley Anders. 'First his crazy aunt turns into a fruit loop and forgets where she left him, now a psycho killer gets topped by his dad and we have no way of knowing where he's being held! Wonderful! Fucking wonderful!'

'Paddy says he has another apartment somewhere. How many can there be in a small town like this?' asked Liz.

'Too many! People call a flat an apartment, and there are big old houses all around the villages that are now split into, you got it, apartments.' Charley looked ready to blow. 'I'm giving yet another press conference followed by an urgent plea on TV for people to please check flats and rooms in shared accommodation.'

'It won't be anywhere rough, Charley,' Liz said. 'Paddy assured me Jude didn't do slumming it. It will be pretty high end, whatever it is. And judging by his other homes, he definitely liked luxury.'

'That helps,' said Charley, calming down somewhat. 'And we are checking with every rental and letting agent in the area in the hopes that he used his own name. That, however, is doubtful. His main residence was listed under a company name, and the bills were paid from an account abroad. He didn't want to be found easily.'

'If it's all right with you, I'd like to go back and see if I can jog Paddy's memory,' said Liz. 'Maybe he can come up with something that might give us a lead. He's been lying there for two years listening to his son deliver regular monologues. He has to have heard something in all that time. And the old bastard owes me, it's the least he can do.'

'Be my guest. He's under a hospital restriction order due to his failing health. He's going nowhere, other than a one-way trip in a box. Ring me direct if you get anything.'

'And maybe another chat with Isla McGowan?' Matt said.

'She's here, Matt, being interviewed about that knife.'

'Then maybe get whoever is doing the interview to ask her if she has any idea where Jude's third address might be. There's a chance she knows a bit about Jude Sherriff from his dad.' Matt would have dearly loved to have conducted that interview himself, but that wasn't going to happen.

'Sure, I'll send someone down straightaway. Now, forgive me, I have to prepare for this TV appeal. Keep in touch, okay?'

'Before we go,' Matt said, 'are you still raiding Barngate Farm?'

'Tonight. At nightfall. Why wait? Now Jude is out of the equation we suspect the whole thing will fold. I can't see them bringing in another shipment without him, and with the area alive with police, they definitely won't take the risk. We might as well go in and close it down.' She looked irritated. 'We'll miss getting our hands on Dassault, which is a bit of a bummer, but better we arrest whoever is there and hound the rest out of our area for someone else to worry about.'

'And Palmer?' asked Matt.

Charley shrugged, grabbed her bag and made for the door. 'He's the businessman, the man behind it all. He wouldn't dirty the soles of his designer shoes by actually showing up where the action is, so we wouldn't have nabbed him anyway. We have other people tracking him, and they're using some pretty sophisticated tools, so watch this space. But right now, all my thoughts are with that little boy, left alone again. Hell, what a world we live in!'

* * *

PC Debbie Hume had rarely felt so utterly helpless. It was her sworn duty to protect and save life and here she was, having to deliver the news to his father and sister that they still had no idea where young Simon was. Not only that, but they suspected he had been secreted somewhere by a man who had since been murdered. As far as she was concerned, they had failed this family.

She and Jack Fleet watched the DCI's emotive request for the public to join the search for this vulnerable little boy. A picture of Simon loomed large on the screen along with a helpline number.

A team of civilians had been drafted in to cope with the influx of calls, and volunteers travelled the streets of Fenfleet and the surrounding villages calling attention to his plight. Neighbours popped in on neighbours to let them know. Others checked empty properties and notified the police of any likely places.

It was hard to keep Kellie and Donald's spirits up when you felt so despondent yourself, and as the evening drew in, Debbie decided that if she didn't do something positive she'd start climbing the walls. Leaving Jack at the hotel with the Burtons, she drove back to the station and went into the control room. As she had hoped, one of the officers on duty was a guy called Rees. Debbie was well aware that he fancied her. She wasn't interested, but he never gave up hope. At least he wasn't a nuisance about it, and over time it had turned into a bit of a standing joke between them.

'Okay, Rees. I have an unofficial request. Will you help me?'

His face lit up. 'For you, Debs, anything.'

She gave him a quick hug. 'Then if any of the crews ring in with something really viable — and I mean really — will you keep me in the loop? I feel particularly responsible for that little lad and his family, and I want in on any possible locations where he might be being held. Can you do that for me?'

Rees's smile stretched from ear to ear. 'We'll discuss payment later, sweetie. But sure, anything I think worth following up I'll hand over to you.'

Even before she got back to the hotel, an unofficial heads-up was passing from crew to crew: 'All units. After official procedures are followed, alert our Debs if you have anything of interest. Could mean free doughnuts for a week.'

Debbie drove back to the hotel in a more positive frame of mind. It wasn't much, but at least if anything happened, she'd know about it immediately. Until then, all they could do was wait.

* * *

The SOCOs were still finishing up at the crime scene, Jude's body had been taken to the mortuary and Paddy had been moved to another room. Liz went in and found him looking exhausted. She guessed that now the adrenalin had worn off, he was beginning to grasp the reality of what he had just done. She was surprised the effort hadn't killed him, but when she entered, he gave her a tired smile.

'I know why you're here, but I really don't think I know any more than what I've already told you.'

'Come on, Paddy.' Liz pulled up a chair close to his bed. 'Jude sat here, talking, day after day. He must have said something about where he lived.' She looked at him, willing him to make an effort. 'We've got a loving father and a distraught sister going mad with worry over that little boy, who, to make it worse, is asthmatic. Help us out here.'

'I'm tired, Liz Haynes. It's been rather an eventful day, in case you hadn't noticed.' He closed his eyes.

'Then wake yourself up, you old bastard! You told me earlier that you'll soon have plenty of time to sleep, so make your last waking hours worthwhile. Help me find that child!'

He chuckled. 'I bet you were a force to be reckoned with in your day.'

'You haven't seen anything yet, Paddy Sherriff. And by the way, the boss isn't here tonight, so I'm free to get the thumbscrews out if I have to.' She fixed him with an unblinking stare.

'I'm beginning to wish I'd picked someone else to run that little errand for me.' He sighed. 'Okay, what kind of thing do you want me to remember?'

'Anything, no matter how unimportant it seems, about where he was living or staying. We know he had a chalet on the river, and we know about Ravenswood, it's the other place we think he's hidden little Simon in.'

Paddy shifted a little in the bed. 'I'm sure he never mentioned where it was. He only said that he felt easier knowing there was more than one place where he could hide if he needed to.'

'Did he ever say if it was far from his main home, or close by, or in a village, maybe? Or perhaps that there was something like a pub or a shop, or a church nearby?' Liz tried to think of anything Jude might have mentioned in passing. 'How about things he liked to do? Did he play sport, or do exercise?'

'He did go to a gym. He was a member of one, he said. He would work out, and then swim for a while. I thought that was funny because he hated water when he was a boy, and he was scared of the swimming pool.' He paused. 'Did you say this boy is asthmatic?'

'That's right. Why?'

'Then I can't see Jude hurting him. Jude understood about asthma. He was asthmatic as a child but he grew out of it. In fact, we wondered if it wasn't actually allergies caused his breathlessness. The thing is, it frightened him and he never, even as an adult, went anywhere without an inhaler in his pocket. He swore that if he always had one with him, he'd never get short of breath. He was a bit superstitious at times.'

That did interest Liz. It had been assumed that because they'd found an inhaler on his aunt the boy had been left without one. If Jude had taken him and did as his father had said, Simon had a better chance of surviving. She'd need to ring that in. But first, she had another question for Paddy. 'So where was this gym?'

'I don't know, but he said it had the best pool in the area, if that helps.'

She knew immediately which one he meant. Liz gave Paddy a break while she rang Matt. 'If I throw a few things at you, can you pass them on for me? Then I can press on here.' Matt naturally said he would. 'Right. Kingsmere Sports Club. I think Jude was a member. Check if he registered with them using a different address to the Ravenswood one. And, Matt, tell Debbie that Jude had an inhaler with him. Paddy doesn't think he'd hurt the boy, so there's a greater chance he's still alive. I'll pass on anything else as it arises.'

Paddy seemed to have drifted off to sleep. Liz watched him for a while, though she didn't intend to let him off that easily — she had more questions yet.

She went out into the hallway and had a few words with the officer assigned to watch Paddy. Infirm he might be, but he had just murdered his son and was therefore under arrest. She went to find an orderly and asked for tea for Paddy and herself. She was told that Paddy usually had a small malt whisky in the evenings, from a bottle his friend Isla brought for him, and since he was dying, no one saw fit to deny him this small pleasure.

'I'd make it a large one if I were you — he's had a bit of a day, what with one thing and another.'

She went back to Paddy's room and woke him up.

'Oh. You again. I was hoping you'd have gone by now. I'm thinking of asking to be taken in and put in a nice quiet cell where I can die in peace.'

'No such luck, chum. And anyway, you wouldn't get your evening Glenfiddich in the slammer, would you?' With a grin, she handed him his whisky. 'Cheers.'

Liz hated being so hard on the old man and wouldn't have but for the fact that Simon's plight was so desperate.

'I wasn't really asleep,' Paddy said. 'I was trying to remember something that might help you to find that kid. Like you said, I've lain here listening to hours of Jude going on about his life. Some of it made me sick to my stomach. He would tell me things he thought would make me proud of him but I wasn't, I was horrified.' He tilted his head to one side a little and said, 'Look, Liz, I've been bad, I admit, but I've never killed before today.'

'I know. You made plenty of noise but to my knowledge, you never actually harmed anyone. You were a bloody good jewel thief, though.'

'I bet you think I'm a monster for what I did. I mean, a father who deliberately kills his son; plans it, even. It would take a big heart to forgive that.'

'What you did was against the law, but he broke your youngest son's back and most likely caused your wife's death. I'd call that extreme provocation. You're not a monster, Paddy, and I'll never think of you that way.'

'Well, he did say something once. It was around a month ago, after that big wind that caused so much damage.'

'I remember. It blew some of the tiles off our roof.'

'Jude said he'd been asleep and was woken up by this huge crash. A massive old horse chestnut tree in the grounds had been uprooted and had come down across three of the cars in the car park. There are no old trees on the Ravenswood estate.'

Paddy was right. Ravenswood was one of those places with manicured lawns and walkways and flowerbeds, but there were no old trees. She recalled photos of the damage caused right across the county, including some showing trees lying across crushed cars. This was something they could check out.

'Thank you. You're a gem! That's the very thing we needed to help us find that poor frightened little boy.'

'I just hope I'm right about Jude not hurting him. Don't forget, my son was insane, so don't get your hopes up too much.'

'Enjoy your whisky and try to sleep, Paddy. And thank you again. I'm sorry I pushed you like that, I won't bother you again.' Liz suddenly felt sad, sorry that this would be their last meeting. How could she feel this way? The man was a criminal, a murderer. She'd have to think about that, but not now. She had calls to make.

CHAPTER THIRTY-TWO

'I know it,' Matt said. 'Abbey Meadows. It's a small luxury estate in the grounds of the old Cistercian monastery on the outskirts of Ferndyke. I remember that picture of the old tree and the three cars it wiped out. I even remember what they were — two Mercs and a BMW.'

'Then ring Charley immediately, Matt,' Liz said. 'And do me a favour and ring Debbie Hume as well. The constable outside Paddy's room says she's asked for a heads-up.'

'I'm on it. You on your way home?' He was already on his feet.

'No way. I'm off to Abbey Meadows,' said Liz. 'We might not be police anymore, but this case is partly ours. I'm not missing out on this.'

'We'll meet you there.' Matt ended the call and spoke to a very edgy Charley Anders, telling her what Liz had said.

'Yesss! We just need the actual address. I'll get some officers onto the residents' association there. It's a small community and I seem to recall they have a manager on site, but we'll knock on doors if necessary. I've got a unit ready to roll as we have no idea what we might find. Also, a couple of special victim officers are on alert to deal with the boy, plus we'll need an ambulance standing by. Thank Liz for me, would you? Actually, knowing you two, I'll do it myself. I'm guessing you're on your way there?'

'Well, you know how it is, Charley. Old habits and all that.'

'Just hold back until I have the units and personnel in place, okay?'

'Yes, ma'am. See you there.'

* * *

Debbie pulled her jacket tighter around her, but the cold she felt had nothing to do with the temperature. It was all due to her anxiety about what they might find in Abbey Meadows.

She was grateful to Matt Ballard for calling. She had told Donald and Kellie that they must be prepared for all eventualities. For a start, no one knew what Jude's state of mind had been when he abducted Simon from the merchant's house. Simon might not even be there. He could be hidden in any of the hundreds of deserted barns and outbuildings scattered across the county. He could be anywhere. It was also possible that Jude hadn't taken the boy at all, and Simon was in the hands of a complete stranger.

Sitting in the layby outside Abbey Meadows, Debbie went over all these possibilities in her mind. Her heart, however, told her that Jude Sherriff had brought Simon Burton here. Now Jude was dead and Simon alone.

Kellie had been silent the whole way. Now she said, 'He's here. I know he is.'

'Don't get your hopes up, darling,' cautioned Donald. 'This is only a possibility, so don't be disappointed if it's a false alarm.'

'He's here,' she said adamantly. Donald shrugged and stared out of the window.

After what seemed like forever, Jack, who had gone ahead to get a situation report, came hurrying back to the car and dropped into the passenger seat. 'They've located the address. It's not an apartment as Paddy seemed to think,

314

it's a single-storey detached residence, a bit like a posh log cabin. The DI has sent a drone to fly over the place and check for heat sources inside — indicating a human or animal presence. They've spoken to the warden, who said that Jude moved into the cabin six months ago. Makes life easier for our guys.'

Debbie's pulse rate increased. Not long now.

'They hoped the warden would hold spare keys, but apparently the policy is to respect the residents' privacy. So, the DI asked forensics to let her know if there were any keys on Jude's body and there were. They've been released to her so she can see if they fit the locks on the cabin. They're on their way now.'

Debbie looked over her shoulder at Kellie in the back seat. 'Not long to go. As soon as that drone confirms that there's someone inside, they'll be able to get him out.'

'He's in there,' Kellie said.

* * *

Matt watched the drone go up, frustrated that they could only sit and observe. He wondered if he'd ever get used to not being part of the action.

Jack Fleet was busy running between the active units, he and Debbie Hume keeping them all updated on the state of play.

David sat quietly, taking everything in, thrilled to find himself involved in a major incident like this.

At least the press hadn't got wind of it yet, although it wouldn't be long before news of a major operation taking place spread through the grapevine.

Jack approached their car. 'One hotspot on the infrared camera, boss, and it's not big enough to be an adult. The guv'nor is cautiously optimistic.' He stuck a thumb up and hurried off to take the news to his crewmate and the Burtons. Matt could only imagine the father and sister's reaction to this piece of news.

'Let's move forward on foot, Matt,' said Liz. 'Then we can get closer without getting in anyone's way.'

The three of them got out of the car and went to join the throng of people on hand in case the need arose. It was exasperating for Matt to be so powerless. Liz touched his hand and smiled at him in understanding. He glanced behind him. At the very back of the crowd, well away from the action, stood Debbie and Jack with Donald and Kellie Burton. Father and daughter were both white as ghosts.

Matt told himself not to be so selfish. The frustration he felt was petty compared to what that poor man and his daughter were going through right now.

The waiting crowd fell silent. You could have heard a leaf fall as two figures slowly approached the front door of the luxury cabin.

* * *

Charley Anders stared at the closed front door as if she might see through it. She and the child victim support officer knew exactly how to play a situation like this, but you never quite knew how the victim would react. He would be traumatised, that was for sure. They had no way of knowing what the boy had suffered in the time since his aunt had left him and had to work on the worst-case scenario. Everything depended on their ability to convey to the child that the danger had passed, and they were here to ensure his safety. Somehow, they had to win his trust.

Charley stood close to the door, speaking just loudly enough to be heard inside. 'Simon, it's the police. I'm DCI Charley Anders and we are here to help. Please don't be afraid. We have come to take you home. You're safe now, Simon.'

Silence. This was going to take some time.

* * *

His back to the wall, Simon sat on the floor, wedged between the end of the sofa and a long, low coffee table. As time had passed and DI Sherriff had not returned, he had begun to fear the worst, and now it had happened.

He heard a woman's voice, telling him they had come to take him home. His detective had said that the bad men would be clever, and using a woman was very clever indeed.

He remembered Inspector Sherriff telling him to hold out for as long as he could, because he would come for him. Simon would hang on.

More lies tumbled through the door, things the detective had warned him they would say. Well, he was cleverer than those bad men. He knew what they wanted. They thought they could hold him to ransom. And when they found out that his father had no money, they would kill him.

'I must hold on. I must hold on. He will come,' Simon muttered.

As his fear increased, it became harder to breathe. He pulled the detective's inhaler from his pocket and took two puffs. He closed his eyes and tried to concentrate on breathing. Yes, now there were two voices, both trying to trick him into believing them.

'I must hold on. I must hold on.' He stopped. Inspector Sherriff had been right. People did let you down. His father had sent him away. His auntie had deserted him. His mother had gone away for ever. And if everyone let him down, that meant Inspector Sherriff would too. He wasn't coming back.

'Simon, listen. I am going to unlock the door and come in. You mustn't be frightened. We'll wait just inside, okay? When you're ready, you can ask us in, or come towards us. You're perfectly safe. No one is going to hurt you again. We are here to help.'

He heard the scrape of the key sliding into the lock and screamed, 'No! No! Don't come in!' He took two more puffs from the inhaler, but couldn't seem to get any of the medication into his airway. Memories of how his sister had helped him whenever he had an attack rose into his mind. He remembered the pack of stamped postcards she had given him. Kellie loved him. Kellie wouldn't leave him. 'Kellie!' he cried. 'I want Kellie!'

He fought to breathe, hearing voices shouting outside the door. He managed to stand up and stagger out from his hiding place, then everything seemed to go into slow motion. He slid to the floor, gasping for breath.

* * *

Debbie heard the call go up and grabbed Kellie's arm. 'Quick! Your brother needs you.'

The girl and Debbie pushed through the throng of people. As soon as she saw them approach, the DI turned the key and they went in.

Debbie looked around for the boy, but Kellie was already beside him. She got behind her brother and hauled him up into a sitting position, propped up against her legs. She took her emergency reliever inhaler from her pocket and, timing the puffs, administered one every thirty seconds. All the while she talked, calming the little boy and, to Debbie's relief, he started to respond.

Two paramedics stood in the doorway about to go to him, but Charley held them back, asking them to wait until the boy realised he was safe. 'His sister is the only person he trusts right now,' she whispered. 'Let's not crowd him. And Kellie really does know what she's doing.'

Watching Kellie assist her brother, the medics nodded. 'Someone should suggest she takes up a career in the ambulance service,' murmured one of them.

While Debbie watched, Kellie sat on the floor beside her brother with her arm around him. She had stopped using the inhaler.

'Mum?' he whispered.

'No, darling, it's me, Kellie,' she said.

'I know it's you, but Mum — where has she gone?'

Kellie sighed. 'She's not here, Simon. She went away.'

'But she was! She was with me! She told me to call you. She said you'd come to help me.' He looked around almost accusingly. Then, seeing that his mother wasn't in the crowd of people by the door, he gave his sister a big, warm smile. 'She hasn't really left us, sis. Maybe we can't always see her, but she's with us when we need her. How cool is that?'

Debbie could barely see for the tears in her eyes. Brushing them away, she slowly approached the child.

'This is my friend, Debbie,' said Kellie, sniffing. 'She's been really worried about you. Everyone has.'

Debbie crouched down and smiled at Simon. 'Your sister is not kidding. We've had every policeman in the county out looking for you.'

Simon looked around him in wonderment. There were emergency services vehicles everywhere, their blue lights illuminating the room. He shrank back against his sister.

Charley ordered everyone to stay back until only Debbie, Jeanette — the Victim Care Officer — and she remained.

The three of them waited while Kellie spoke soothingly to her brother. All these people had come to help him, she said, make sure he was safe.

'Is the detective dead?' he asked.

Debbie narrowed her eyes. 'What detective, Simon?'

'The man who saved me — Detective Inspector Sherriff.' He turned to look at her. 'One of the bad men killed him, didn't they?'

You'll never know how close to the truth you were, my son, thought Debbie grimly. For indeed, one of the bad men had killed him.

'We'll talk about all that later,' said Jeanette, the VCO. 'Right now, we need to get you away from here.'

Frightened again, Simon began to breathe faster.

'It's all right, Simon, in your own time. Kellie will come with you. She won't leave you, will you, Kellie?'

Kellie said wild horses wouldn't drag her away from her brother now they had found him. 'And Dad's here too. He's been worried sick about you. Would you like to see him?'

Hesitantly, the boy shook his head.

'No rush,' said Jeanette. 'But he's missed you terribly. Whenever you're ready, he'll be really pleased to see you're okay. He loves you very much.'

319

It took a while for the little boy to feel confident enough to leave the house. Then he and Kellie were taken to a special trauma centre where he would be assessed.

Debbie found Donald Burton talking to the DCI and Jack Fleet.

'I can't believe my son didn't want to see me,' he said, his voice unsteady.

She squeezed his arm gently. 'Simon just needs a bit of time, Donald. We've no idea what lies he's been fed. We'll take you to the centre so you can be near him. The people there will tell you how he's doing. I'm certain he'll bounce back really quickly when he learns the truth about what happened.'

Charley nodded. 'That's exactly what I just said. And, thankfully, he doesn't appear to have been, er, harmed.'

Debbie was pretty sure he hadn't. She had seen victims of sexual abuse too many times in the past, and Simon didn't have that terrible haunted look they all wore.

'I'm just so grateful to have him back. From now on, I'm going to make sure he knows that he is loved and always will be. Things in our house are going to be different.'

'Well, you have a remarkable daughter, Mr Burton,' said Charley. 'And from now on I'm sure you'll support her in whatever she wants to do.'

'I think it'll probably be her supporting me.' He managed to smile. 'She has a much better head on her shoulders.'

Debbie smiled. 'Sensible man! First, let's get you all reunited.'

CHAPTER THIRTY-THREE

One month later

David stayed another week after Simon Burton was found, helping Matt and Liz tie up loose ends and prepare their reports to Charley Anders. David was a different man to the one who'd turned up at Cannon Farm having lost all hope of leading the life he wanted. He was with them when they gave Georgia and Terry Hallam the full story of what had happened to their son and his friend Toby and left the house determined to make more time for his own parents, separated or not. The deaths of Alex and Toby had made him realise that life was too short to waste in petty disagreements.

To Liz's surprise, he contacted Richard Lake, the boys' tutor. He told him of the incredible photographs the students had produced and asked Richard if, when they were released by the police, he would consider mounting an exhibition at the university in memory of his two talented students. Richard thought this an excellent idea and said he would contact the boys' parents and get their permission. He then suggested putting them online, and possibly holding a public exhibition. David was thrilled.

The icing on the cake had been a visit to Fenfleet police station to see DCI Charley Anders. She made time to take David on a tour of all the various departments, showing him numerous different roles he might consider. Becoming a detective wasn't the be-all and end-all of police work, she explained, and advised him to look for something he would really enjoy doing. Maybe he should consider going to university: a degree would give him even more options.

David left, full of gratitude to Matt and Liz. They had turned his life around, he said. The last few weeks had been the most thought-provoking, scary and rewarding of his life. 'If all my plans go tits-up, I'll be coming to ask for a job in your detective agency.'

They reminded him that there was a big world out there. Would he really want to spend years on the Fens? Nothing ever happened here. This made him laugh.

Having said their goodbyes to David, they paid a visit to Charley Anders, and were surprised to find that they no longer felt like outsiders. People acknowledged them now, like friends and colleagues. Matt realised that his old office no longer felt as if it belonged to him. It was Charley's and that was fine. Maybe he had moved on at last.

Charley was smiling at them both. 'I thought we needed a catch-up. We've had so many things occur in the last couple of weeks that I reckon it's time to dot the i's and cross the t's.'

'We were thinking the same, Charley,' said Matt. 'We have a few things to tell you too.'

The door opened and Charley's office manager came in with a large tray of teas and a selection of sandwiches.

'Not exactly the Ritz, but it's better than old custard creams, so dig in. I've told everyone I'm incommunicado for the next hour.'

While they helped themselves, Matt said how grateful they were for the interest she had taken in young David. 'He's well chuffed at your offer of a reference. He really appreciated the time you took to talk to him.'

'He's a very bright young man,' said Charley. 'It's such a pity when a health issue comes between someone and their hopes for the future. I'm just glad it lifted his spirits a bit.'

'Oh, it did that all right. He went home a completely different person to the one who arrived. His relaxing break in the Fens wasn't quite what he expected,' Liz laughed, 'but it certainly gave him a change of perspective — and of priorities.'

'Did you hear about Minty Agutter?' Matt said.

Charley nodded. 'Not the whole story, just that he was back.'

Liz placed her mug on the desk. 'He turned up exactly a day after Jude died. It was as if he had second sight. He went directly to see Paddy Sherriff and managed to talk his way into having fifteen minutes with his old friend. And later that very day, Paddy passed away.'

'Minty came to give us the news,' Matt said. 'He was well cut up. He said he suddenly had this strong feeling that if he was ever to see Paddy again, he had to go now, so he jumped on a train and went to Linden House.'

'Where on earth had he been?' asked Charley.

'He said he really liked it at the vicarage and wanted to stay, but one day he went into the village post office and saw a tall man stopping people and showing them a photograph. He didn't wait to find out what it was all about. He was certain this man had been sent by Jude to find him. He went back, grabbed his things and legged it.' Matt sipped his tea. 'He said he made his way to Norwich, hitching lifts, and got a bed in a shelter. He wanted to contact us but didn't dare. He stayed there until he got that weird feeling about needing to see Paddy.' Minty had told Matt a little more than that, but it was something not meant for official ears.

'Talking about Paddy,' Liz said, 'has Isla McGowan been charged with anything, Charley?'

The detective gave them a wry smile. 'Er, no. The staff at the nursing home swear she only called in to drop off a bottle of whisky for Paddy. He, in his turn, was adamant that the killing had nothing to do with Isla, and that someone else, who he refused to name, brought him the knife. Isla, too, denied it emphatically. So, without evidence, and following Paddy's death, we've decided not to proceed.'

'Mmm,' said Liz. 'Interesting.'

Neither Matt nor Liz believed a word of this, but Matt thought that in Charley's place, he would probably have done the same. 'So,' he said, dropping the subject, 'what do you have for us?'

'Ah, the big story!' Charley grinned broadly. 'Did you by any chance notice a general air of satisfaction in the place when you came in?'

They nodded.

'Well, it was down to "Operation Obscure," as we called it. The night you told me about it, we hit Barngate Farm hard and fast. You guys would have loved it! They obviously hadn't expected us to know about the second location, so had transferred everything there from Cutler's Alley.'

'Everything being what?' asked Matt.

'The designer drug. It was manufactured in an underground laboratory in Holland, a synthetic hallucinogen in the form of a crystal powder. Some was already packaged and labelled "Bullet Six," but we also found large bulk packs which they were busy emptying into sachets.' Charley took a couple of small tangerine-coloured foil sachets from her drawer and tossed them onto her desk. 'Meet Roolet, Second Generation.' She smiled smugly. 'We copped the lot — scales, measures, packaging, the heat-sealing machines, everything. Although Cutler's Alley was basically a storehouse where the shipments were held only briefly before being moved out, they still had a small packing plant in operation for special customers who preferred Roolet over Bullet Six, and that too had been shifted to Barngate Farm.'

Matt picked up a sachet and stared at it. 'Hard to think that this tiny pack can fry brains. Was the farm well set up?'

'Incredible, Matt. From the outside, it looked like an old house that was undergoing major renovation, but the outhouses and the barn cleverly concealed a mini factory. And of course, the vans with the bogus trade names that you guys clocked for us were delivery and collection vehicles.'

Liz eyed Charley speculatively. 'Okay, tell us the rest. Impressive as it is, you're far too upbeat for just that, so what haven't you told us?'

'Observant as ever, Liz Haynes. The raid on the house produced a laptop. Luckily, we got hold of it before they could delete anything. It contained lists of suppliers, dealers and middlemen, names and contact details. Their whole marketing network was there in black and white. Incontrovertible.' Charley tapped one of the sachets. 'And the funniest thing was that the laptop didn't belong to Palmer but someone else in his organisation, a villain with either exceptional skills as a hacker or connections to a professional IT baddy. Whoever it was, they had cloned Palmer's virtual little black book. How tasty is that?'

'And?' Liz said.

'And . . . wait for it — along with most of their gang, we got Andre Dassault! Arrested and charged, and well and truly up to his eyes in deep shit. Oh, how I love being a copper sometimes.'

Matt had never seen Charley look so delighted. After all the stress of the past months, she deserved it.

'The only negative is that we didn't get Palmer, but we are basking in the knowledge that his whole empire is wrecked beyond redemption. He'll probably regroup somewhere else one day, but this will have hurt, really hurt. The suppliers will be very wary of working with him again once this fiasco hits the grapevine.'

'And he'll find it hard to recruit another second in command with the same deadly skills as Jude Sherriff,' added Matt.

'And hopefully it will be far from here, praise be.' Charley drained her mug of tea and set it down with a flourish. 'This should be champagne. We would never have had a result like this without you two and your insistence that something was going on in the merchant's house.'

'The main thing was that you listened to us, Charley, and went out on a limb to get that warrant.'

'I wouldn't dare not listen to the inimitable Matt Ballard,' she said with a grin.

They sat eating for a while, going over the events of the past few weeks in their heads.

'How is little Simon? Is he doing okay?' asked Liz.

'What a resilient kid he turned out to be. He's home and happy, something else to be grateful for. With Kellie's help, he described a very different side to Jude Sherriff. The psychologists believe that Jude must have seen something of himself in Simon, especially when he found him alone and frightened in that old house. Simon told us he had an asthma attack when he was discovered, and Jude produced an inhaler and helped him over it. He honestly believed that Jude was a detective sent to save him.' Charley frowned. 'There is a grey area here. Henry must have walked in on them at some point. Simon said Jude bundled him out of the room and when he returned, he had blood on him. Jude told him it had been a bad guy, but he'd sorted him out. Simon never saw him again. So, we suspect that Jude killed Henry and hid him in the bathroom so that Simon wouldn't see the body when he got him out of the house.'

'Sounds about right,' said Matt.

'Simon said that while he was in the "safe house," Jude brought him a McDonald's meal one evening, and drew him a picture of a big tawny owl. The lad said he was brilliant at drawing, which was confirmed when we searched Jude's home and found artists' materials and some very professional sketches. Jude sketched the owl so that Simon could paint it, as he'd left his own painting book in the merchant's house. Apparently, he then read him a story and stayed with him until he went to sleep. Simon said that when DI Sherriff had been a little boy no one had loved him, and Simon felt sorry for him.'

'Does he know Jude's dead?' asked Liz.

Charley nodded. 'He's only been told as much as a child his age can understand, but Kellie is helping him work through it. She told Debbie, who keeps in touch with her, that the best thing of all is that Simon now talks about their mum. He even looked in a memory box his mother had left him, and asked Kellie to explain about all the mementoes and what they meant. He's going to be fine, I'm sure.'

'And Jessie?' asked Liz. 'I keep thinking about that poor soul and wondering what on earth happened to make her the way she is.'

'Ah, yes. Well, the letter that her mother left for Kellie to read when she came of age did explain it.' Charley sighed. 'It seems some of the girls in Kellie's mother's family had a tendency to become oversensitive to certain things. Girls who inherited this trait didn't cope well with situations that gave rise to stress or anxiety. Luckily, Kellie's mother wasn't affected, but her older sister Jessie was. Unfortunately, she had a friend called Anna, a very bossy girl who ordered poor Jessie around like a sheepdog herding a bewildered lamb. Anna was always trying to make the timid Jessie do things that terrified her. Even so, Jessie adored her and came to rely on her far too much. The letter said that one day when Jessie was about eight, they were playing in the farmyard where the family lived, and Anna tried to get Jessie to walk along the top of a high wall like a tightrope walker. Jessie refused, and Anna said it was easy, she'd go first to show Jessie how simple it was and how silly she was being. The wall was unsafe, and Anna fell. She impaled herself on the tines of a piece of rusty farm equipment that was leaning against the base of the wall. She bled to death in front of Jessie.'

'Oh, dear Lord, what a thing to happen,' breathed Liz, aghast.

'Indeed,' agreed Charley. 'Slowly, over the years, Jessie built up an image of her childhood friend in her mind, recreating her until she became real. Kellie's mother considered Kellie too young to understand, so told her not to believe what her aunt told her about Anna.' Charlie paused. 'I don't know why she never confided this with her husband, although she mentioned it was a subject not talked about in the family.

Maybe she believed that, as it thankfully had missed Kellie, she had no need to. Anyway, for the most part, Jessie remained the sweet, creative, artistic musician and artist that she always had been, but gradually, and especially recently, the persona of Anna began to take over.' Charley shrugged. 'She's been admitted to a psychiatric hospital long-term. No one knows how she'll respond to therapy. They can only hope.'

Matt felt terribly sad for her. If someone had understood her condition at the time, Jessie's life could have turned out quite differently. He sat back in his chair. 'There's one thing that still bothers me. The merchant's house. Was Anna really a Garnett?'

Charley said that she was. 'As a child, she had subjected Jessie to repeated stories of how she was an heiress to a fortune that her family wanted nothing to do with. She kept telling Jessie that when she got older, she'd fight for what was hers. She filled Jessie's head with stories of rich merchants and sailing ships and shipments of rare spices and beautiful silks. She repeated the names that she'd overheard her parents mention, and at some point, as the alternative personality began to grow, Jessie started researching Anna's family history. Old man Boon can only think that she saw one of the advertisements they had placed in *The Times* and the *Telegraph* in their search for the missing heirs and, finally, when the disorder really took hold, she visited them in the persona of Anna Garnett.'

Matt groaned. 'And now all the heirs are dead, and poor Edward Boon's lifelong quest has come to nothing. What a bummer.'

'Not quite, Matt. Last time I saw him he told me that they'd tracked down the last Garnett, who'd sadly committed suicide. But the man had a son! Boon has finally found the legitimate heir to the merchant's house, and believe it or not, the new owner is planning to renovate it. That sad old house might just rise from the ashes again.'

Matt let out a low whistle. 'And old man Boon can finally retire.'

'As soon as the dust settles, he tells me he's off to India, to visit the pomegranate-growing region where the Garnetts first started their business. He said it would bring his long, long journey to a perfect conclusion.' Charley grinned broadly. 'And good luck to him!'

'Hear hear!' said Matt, 'Well, we too are off on holiday in a day or so, to the Peak District, a less exotic destination but with plenty of beef and ale pie, good beer and long walks.'

'Sounds idyllic,' sighed Charley. 'When do you come back?'

'I guess that will depend on who rings the detective agency next,' said Liz. 'I just hope it's an easier case than the last one, and less traumatic!'

'Amen to that!' echoed Matt. 'Lost pets are looking more and more attractive by the minute.'

'Cobblers!' exclaimed Charley Anders. 'When it comes to investigations, the stranger they are, the better you like them. Now bugger off and pack your cases. I have proper work to do.'

With his hand on the door, Matt said, 'Oh, by the way, if you get stuck again and need a hand, you know where to find us. Shall I leave you our card?'

* * *

Back in their car, Liz nudged Matt. 'You left something out of that story about Minty, didn't you? And you didn't even tell me. Spill the beans, Matt Ballard!'

Matt chuckled. 'Well, between you and me, our Minty felt pretty bad about ditching the Reverend Peter, and lying to us about Paddy not speaking, so he decided to make amends. He's told me about the diamond necklace. In fact, he drove me to where he took it, and told me the story behind it.'

'You sly old fox! You never told me! Where was it, then?' asked Liz.

'A small home that cares for the disabled. It's where Paddy's other son, Fion, lives. Isla has been keeping in touch with him over the years, and has looked out for him. He's in a wheelchair and paralysed from the waist down, but he can talk. Minty says he's a kind and gentle man.'

'The complete opposite to Jude,' mused Liz.

'Absolutely. Along with the diamond necklace, Paddy left a name, that of a trusted associate of his from the bad old days who promised to fence it to a buyer who had been after it for years. Now Paddy's dead the deal will go through, courtesy of Isla and the bent accountant. The money they get from it will pay for disabled living accommodation for Fion, close to where Isla lives.'

'And you, a retired detective chief inspector, are not telling the authorities about this highly illegal offence?' Liz asked in her best outraged schoolmarm voice.

'Nope.'

'Good. That's sorted, then. Now, can we go home and pack?'

THE END

ALSO BY JOY ELLIS

THE BESTSELLING NIKKI GALENA SERIES
Book 1: CRIME ON THE FENS
Book 2: SHADOW OVER THE FENS
Book 3: HUNTED ON THE FENS
Book 4: KILLER ON THE FENS
Book 5: STALKER ON THE FENS
Book 6: CAPTIVE ON THE FENS
Book 7: BURIED ON THE FENS
Book 8: THIEVES ON THE FENS
Book 9: FIRE ON THE FENS
Book 10: DARKNESS ON THE FENS
Book 11: HIDDEN ON THE FENS
Book 12: SECRETS ON THE FENS
Book 13: FEAR ON THE FENS

JACKMAN & EVANS
Book 1: THE MURDERER'S SON
Book 2: THEIR LOST DAUGHTERS
Book 3: THE FOURTH FRIEND
Book 4: THE GUILTY ONES
Book 5: THE STOLEN BOYS
Book 6: THE PATIENT MAN
Book 7: THEY DISAPPEARED
Book 8: THE NIGHT THIEF

DETECTIVE MATT BALLARD
Book 1: BEWARE THE PAST
Book 2: FIVE BLOODY HEARTS
Book 3: THE DYING LIGHT
Book 4: MARSHLIGHT
Book 5: TRICK OF THE NIGHT

STANDALONES
GUIDE STAR

Thank you for reading this book.

If you enjoyed it please leave feedback on Amazon or Goodreads, and if there is anything we missed or you have a question about, then please get in touch. We appreciate you choosing our book.

Founded in 2014 in Shoreditch, London, we at Joffe Books pride ourselves on our history of innovative publishing. We were thrilled to be shortlisted for Independent Publisher of the Year at the British Book Awards.

www.joffebooks.com

We're very grateful to eagle-eyed readers who take the time to contact us. Please send any errors you find to corrections@joffebooks.com. We'll get them fixed ASAP.

Made in United States
Orlando, FL
16 June 2022

18860950R00202